THE WORLD RAVEN

A. J. Smith has been devising the worlds, histories and characters of the Long War chronicles for more than a decade. He was born in Birmingham and works in secondary education.

CHRONICLES OF
THE LONG WAR

THE
WORLD
RAVEN

A.J. SMITH

First published in the UK in 2016 by Head of Zeus Ltd

9 7 5 3 1 2 4 6 8

A CIP catalogue record for this book is available from the British Library.

ISBN (eBook) 9781784080891
ISBN (HB) 9781784080907
ISBN (XTPB) 9781784080914

Printed in the UK by CPI Group (UK) Ltd, Croydon, CR0 4YY

Head of Zeus Ltd
Clerkenwell House
45–47 Clerkenwell Green
London EC1R 0HT

WWW.HEADOFZEUS.COM

For Kathleen

FOURTH CHRONICLE OF THE LONG WAR

MAPS

THE LANDS OF
RANEN

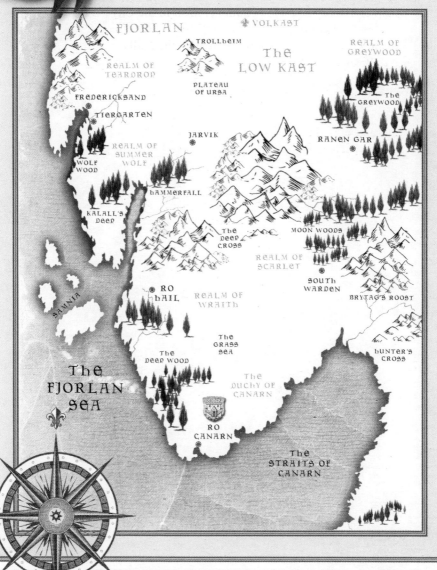

THE LANDS OF
RO

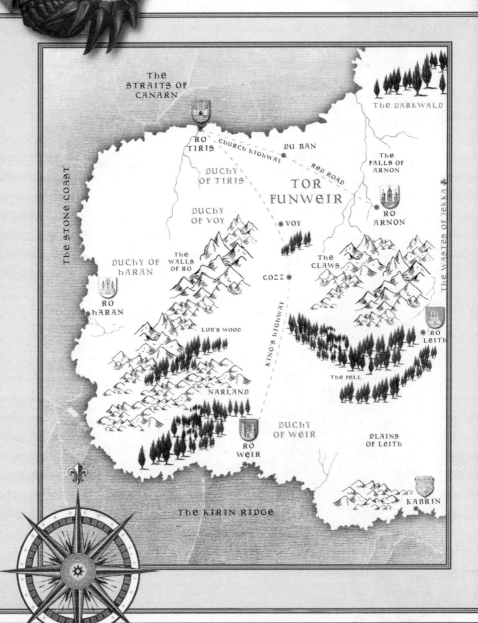

THE LANDS OF
KARESIA

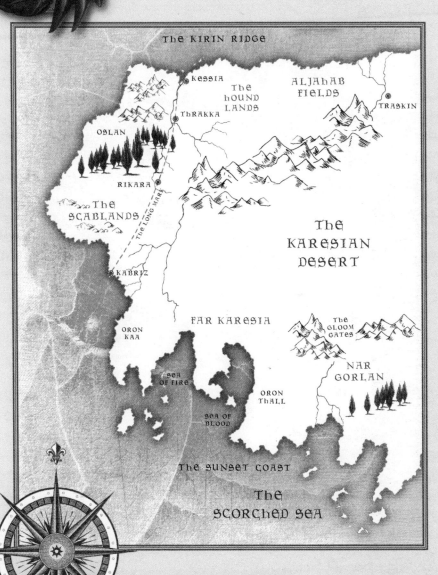

The KIRIN RIDGE

KESSIA

The HOUND LANDS

ALJAHAB FIELDS

TRASKIN

ThRAKKA

OSLAN

RIKARA

The LONG MARK

The SCABLANDS

The KARESIAN DESERT

KABRIZ

ORON KAA

FAR KARESIA

The GLOOM GATES

NAR GORLAN

SEA OF FIRE

ORON ThALL

SEA OF BLOOD

The SUNSET COAST

The SCORCHED SEA

THE CITY OF
RO TIRIS

STRAITS OF CANARN

SEA WALL

NORTH WIND
BAY

DASHELL'S
BAY

KING'S
DOCK

XIII

The
STONE
CLOISTER

X

STONE TOWN

V

I

XII

GUILD
SQUARE

XV

ChURCh hIGhWAY

VII

III

II

VI

VIII

IX

VI

IV

XIV   XI

KING'S
hIGhWAY

The KASBAh

LEGEND

I	KNIGHT MARSHALL'S BARRACK'S	VIII	RED BARRACKS
II	HOUSE OF TIRIS	IX	BLACK CATHEDRAL
III	SPIRE OF THE KING	X	PURPLE CATHEDRAL
IV	BLUE LIBRARY	XI	WHITE CATHEDRAL
V	BROWN CHURCH	XII	MERCENARY BARRACKS
VI	WATCH BARRACKS	XIII	SHIP GUARDS
VII	GUILD ASSEMBLY	XIV	THE TOR
		XVIII	BLACKSMITH'S ASSEMBLY

THE CITY OF
RO WEIR

LEITH
GATE

KING'S
HIGHWAY

WARDER'S
GATE

III

VII

KING'S
FOLLY

VI

GRAND
MARKET

HAWKWOOD
GATE

V

X

I

OLD TOWN

II

PORT SIDE

VIII

IV

The
DUKE'S
HARBOUR

KIRIN
TOR

EASTERN
HARBOUR

IX

LEGEND

I DUKE'S RESIDENCE
II KNIGHT MARSHALL'S
OFFICE
III WATCH BARRACKS
IV PURPLE CHURCH
V BLACK CHURCH
VI BROWN CHURCH

VII MERCENARY
BARRACKS
VIII HARBOUR MASTER
IX RAINBOW POINT
X MERCHANT'S GUILD

PART ONE

The Tale of the Shade Folk

WHEN THE LANDS of men were formed of nations without names or borders, death was not always the end. There were no priests or clerics, just those favoured by the Giants. Piety delivered survival beyond mortal death and the Shade Folk walked the lands in secret.

With one foot in the beyond and the other on the earth, they were the first true servants of the gods of men, taking their power and wisdom from the Giants themselves.

As ages passed and men named their realms and warred with their neighbours, the Shade Folk were both priests and generals, directing the Giants' armies, but never fighting themselves, for the shades had no form that could wield a sword or carry a shield.

They could not be killed or manipulated, and would not seek power or recognition. They lived and plotted in the shadows, appearing only to those of righteous intent. They gave their gods immense power and enabled their own defeat.

Churches, cathedrals and other monuments of stone were built to the gods, and fewer and fewer people were reborn as shades. The One was the first to raise a mortal man of god, the first to realize that the shades had served their purpose. He called his servants *clerics* and they had form *and* power.

The Shade Folk retreated in silence from the world they'd helped to build.

PROLOGUE

T HE FOOTHILLS QUICKLY gave way to vertical walls of jagged stone. The pilgrimage had been attempted by thousands of young Ranen, but no guide ropes had ever been added. If they died, they died. If they turned back, they were not worthy of the World Raven's blessing.

aThe wind was the greatest hazard. The Roost was exposed on all sides, lashed with gales and capped with thick snow. Dexterity and stamina would get you so far, but luck was a climber's greatest asset. Luck and wisdom provided the only recipe for success when you were dangling from rock, hundreds of feet above the ground. Having a sense of humour was also important: the ability to laugh at the stupidity of climbing a mountain unaided in the middle of a snowstorm.

Nice view, though, thought Fynius Black Claw. Well, it was a nice view when the sheets of cloud and snow allowed it to be. That is to say it was a shitty view most of the time. White, tinges of blue, the occasional glimpse of something green, but mostly just white. Clouds, snow, mist, fog – all of it white and all of it bloody annoying.

He'd made the climb before, twice before he was eighteen and three times since then. If he'd lived closer, it would have been a yearly journey. As it was, the captain of Twilight Company was rarely able to visit the World Raven in his own nest. His men were in South Warden, waiting for his return and their march to the ruins of Hail.

The lands of men were changing. Fynius didn't really care, but Brytag did. . . so Fynius did. The Ro were on a knife-edge, ready to be cut in two. The Karesians had fallen. The Ranen were battered and bruised, reeling from blood and conflict, but they were still fighting, still following Rowanoco. The twisted tree had not yet won.

'Let's see what we can do to help.'

He pulled himself over the last overhang and was battered by a fresh gust of freezing air. He screwed up his face and snarled at the weather. The snow didn't appear scared. The way ahead was flat. At least, it didn't require climbing.

Brytag's Roost was a single peak, rising above a ring of jagged foothills. At the top, in a deep indent, partially sheltered from the weather, was a dense, snowy forest. It was hard to reach. It was very, very hard to reach.

'I'm here!' he shouted. 'Do I have to walk to the middle? It's really fucking cold.'

He didn't get an answer. Brytag was very talkative when he wanted to be, but since the shade had appeared, Fynius's head had been curiously quiet. It was odd. The shade was miserable and had no sense of humour. He preferred it when he had to listen to random wants and desires.

'Stop thinking so much,' said Bromvy's shade, appearing in the snowy air.

'Go away, you're no fun,' replied Fynius.

'Is that what you need? Fun?'

'Right now I need a thicker coat. . . maybe a mug of mead.'

'Later,' said the shade. 'Now you walk.'

Fynius kicked his feet through the snow and stomped off towards the highland forest. His path dropped downwards, the swirling snow kept at bay by high walls of rock. It wasn't any warmer, but at least the wind was minimal. Brom floated across the snow next to him, his ethereal legs ghosting forward as if he was walking on thin air.

'Smug bastard,' grumbled Fynius.

'Focus, exemplar,' said Brom. 'You have work to do.'

'I liked the voice of Brytag; it was comforting to never be alone. Now I've got you. It's not the same.'

The shade ghosted in front of him, hovering at walking pace and blocking his view. Lord Bromvy had died young, maybe twenty-five or -six. He was tall and solid, though his eyes were sad. His hair was black and his hands rough. He looked like a Ro, but had the pale skin and light eyes common to those of Canarn.

The wind had dropped and the forest loomed ahead of him. Fynius mused as he entered the trees, wondering what the shade could offer that Brytag could not. If indeed that was the intention. Maybe he offered something different, rather than better. Or maybe he offered nothing and thinking about it was pointless.

'Anything to contribute?' he asked Brom, now gliding between thick tree-trunks and thorn bushes.

'Your mind is unfocused. It inhibits your intelligence.'

Fynius nodded. 'Good contribution.'

Brytag's Roost was the most sacred place for followers of the World Raven. Crows, magpies, rooks and blackbirds lined every branch. Tiny black dots cawed at him, huge glossy birds flared their wings. Every one pointed its yellow beak in his direction.

'What?' he asked. 'I'm expected.'

They carried on cawing and flapping, but didn't peck him or leave their branches. He strolled casually into the central clearing, staring in awe at the ring of huge trees. In the middle, small shrubs with bright green leaves sprouted from the snow and lines of shimmering light cut the thin mountain air.

Fynius approached the glistening leaves. He was a lone figure in the centre of a huge, white emptiness, looking at shifting patterns in the snow. The wind made swirls in the grainy surface underfoot, showing him the Long War. He saw the tapestry of move and counter-move, the ripples felt by exemplars and Shades as they walked their paths and fought their battles. There was power, but little focus, as if the Giants flailed from their halls in search of victory. The One, Rowanoco, Jaa: each was too removed from the world to be effective. They functioned in pockets of resistance, not seeing the whole.

He also saw lost pasts and possible futures. It was hard to put everything into order, hard to see what was real and what was potential. When all possibilities are mashed together, nothing seems truly real. But the last image he saw made him sad. He saw the possible future of the lands of men; he saw the Tyranny of the Twisted Tree.

'Brytag requires a council,' said Brom. 'The shades need to meet. The exemplars need to focus. We will send ravens to help where we can, but this battle will not end with small acts of kindness. The great Giants waited too long. . . their power enters the twilight of this world.'

Fynius let his eyes fall to the snow. He saw the exemplar of the One straight away. Fallon of Leith was taller and stronger than he knew, and stood out as a vessel of huge untapped potential. He had good counsel, but the Purple Shade, following in his wake, was fading from view, unable to teach Fallon of his true power. Things were little better in Fjorlan. Alahan Teardrop, the exemplar of Rowanoco, was a conflicted young man, wrestling with his name and his inheritance. The shade of his uncle was barely present, little more than a ghost, clinging to the world of men with a fingernail. But things were at their darkest in Karesia. The exemplar of Jaa was little more than a vagabond with no armies or devotion. He had never received instruction from his god, and the shade of Dalian Thief Taker was lost in the beyond, lacking sufficient power to reach the exemplar.

Fynius glared at Brom. 'How are *you* still here? Shouldn't you be fading like the others?'

The Shade pulsed with a pale blue light, and a hint of humour edged across its face. 'The World Raven is not currently engaged in hostilities. No armies tear down his altars or march on Ranen Gar.'

'Why would they listen to us?'

'Because without our help they will all die. You've seen the world that will emerge if Shub-Nillurath wins.'

Fynius stretched out with his mind and looked for the shades. He pushed into the shadows of the world, trying to contact those that dwell beyond the sight of mortal men. He found nothing at first, just lost spirits of once pious men. Then, refocusing on the Giants' anger, he found a handful of shades, scattered across the lands of men. From the Roost, he could look down and give each of them a nudge. One was far older than the others, and one was lost in the void, but all felt his polite invitation.

'I am Fynius Black Claw, exemplar of Brytag. I offer a parlay and a chance to turn the tide. We have power; you are each in need of power. You will come when the raven caws.'

CHAPTER ONE

RANDALL OF DARKWALD
IN THE CITY OF THRAKKA

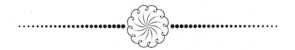

THE EARTHQUAKE SOUNDED throughout the night. Deep and rumbling with a tell-tale shake of the ground. It started as a tremor and rose to make the room vibrate. With each tremor he wondered if the building would collapse. The walls creaked, but the stone didn't crack. Dust fell from the rafters, but each tremor ended and he breathed easier. Until the next tremor.

He was tired and his head felt heavy. He'd survived the enchantment of one of the Seven Sisters. His mind was free, but it would never be the same. Ruth had caressed his soul and left a mark, strengthening him. He knew that the Seven Sisters' magic could no longer touch him.

'We are not leaving until you are ready,' said Ruth.

'Please leave me to think. It's the only thing I've got left.'

She was standing on a box, looking out of a square window into the dusty shards of morning sunlight. The room they stayed in was at the base of a vizier tower. It was bare, dirty and hot, but it was secret. They'd not been found and Randall had been able to rest after his encounter with Saara the Mistress of Pain, with the Gorlan mother watching over him.

'Patience,' she replied. 'We will find the Shadow just when he needs us to find him. Rushing your recovery will not change that.'

Another tremor made the walls shake.

'You never said Karesia had so many earthquakes,' he said, tensing as the rumbling got louder.

'This is exceptional,' she replied. 'The viziers will soon begin to panic.'

He coughed, feeling a dry scratch at the back of his throat.

'Their magic towers aren't immune to earthquakes?'

Dust now fell from the ceiling and the far wall cracked ever so slightly. It was just a slight break, but it made him scramble upwards. 'Is this building going to collapse?' he asked.

'Possibly. . . but the towers will collapse first. We should gather our belongings and relocate.'

'Err. . . if this isn't normal, do you want to tell me what's happening?'

'Their magic is failing,' she replied. 'Something is draining the power from Thrakka.'

'Something? Like what?'

She narrowed her eyes. 'Uncertain. They always believed the Jekkan magic was limitless. It appears they were wrong.' She paused, gazing off into space. 'I think Voon has taken Utha into a dangerous world.'

He snorted, gathering up their sparse belongings and packing them into his rucksack. 'How are Utha and Voon causing earthquakes?'

'Uncertain,' she repeated.

She knew something. A lot more than he did, certainly, but as long as they were leaving, he didn't really care. Utha would tell him about his new earthquake ability when they caught up. If they caught up.

Chunks of masonry now fell to the floor and the room shook. He hoped the towers would remain standing while they made their exit from the city. He didn't fancy dodging death at every intersection. The dust was bad enough; the viziers and warriors looking for them were worse. Rocks hitting them on the head just seemed unfair.

They left quickly. Randall was sore, as if his body weighed more than before he had been enchanted. Little things hurt. Whenever he raised a leg to walk or breathed in. Small movements were

12

effort. His old, canvas rucksack bit into his bare shoulders, and his skin itched.

'Perhaps you shouldn't look up,' said Ruth, making Randall look up.

The vizier towers of Thrakka, wondrous structures of equal parts magic and vanity, were crumbling. The walkways connecting them were empty, and citizens rushed from any structure above ten storeys. Chunks of rock and marble crashed into the dusty streets as awesome spires and garish minuets were felled.

'Do they know what's happening?' he asked, unable to look away from the towers. 'I mean, how many people are going to die?'

'I should think a great many,' she replied. 'And, no, they haven't got a clue what is happening to their city.'

At every street corner, at every intersection, hundreds of Karesians flooded from the buildings. Family units, clutching their belongings; men and women clustered together in carts and on horseback, trying to pick their way through the crowds and leave the city.

He balked at a pair of legs, poking messily out from under a huge boulder. A few streets away, a pile of broken body parts was scattered among some rubble.

Ruth walked brazenly in the middle of the streets, ignoring the press of running people all around her. He thought about leaving her and joining the screaming masses, fleeing Thrakka. Instead, he grimaced and forced himself to walk alongside his companion. He hated trusting her, but she'd saved his life – and his mind – once already.

He muttered pathetically to himself, trailing along behind her like a distressed puppy. Nothing hit them. No stone, debris or body parts. He didn't care whether it was luck or sorcery, as long as they weren't smashed into a mushy death on the streets of Thrakka.

He tried to stop looking up. The impact of falling bricks and mortar sounded all around him, each thud making him jump, but none struck them.

'Bloody hell!' he exclaimed, as a man was smashed into oblivion by a plummeting marble doorframe.

Moving away from the scene, they weaved down streets, through roiling dust and panicking Karesians. Ruth was unmoved by the chaos, flashing disdainful glances at the men and women rushing around her. Randall walked in her wake, scuttling out of the city with his eyes fixed on the street.

The destruction didn't abate. By the time they reached the Long Mark and left the city, the towers behind them were toppling. Dust boiled from the streets, rising in a black cloud and eclipsing the magical city. From every road out of Thrakka, streams of people flooded into the desert. Thousands of people, leaving thousands behind.

* * *

The next bit was a blur. They joined a broken line of travellers, all fleeing Thrakka. Clumps of people, spread out either side of the Long Mark; some crying, others shouting, all in a chaotic whirl. Horses and carts were in short supply and fights broke out over ownership. Rich men and viziers glided through the populace, protected by armed guards, taking what they wanted.

Most of those fleeing were heading north from the ruined city towards the capital, Kessia. Only the poor took the southern road.

It was dark and they'd camped well away from the Long Mark, amidst thinly spaced trees. Other campfires encircled them at a distance and the sound of crying still filled his ears.

'The next city is Rikara, an eldritch place of low darkness, but our road lies elsewhere,' Ruth murmured. 'West, through Oslan.'

'But Utha is south.'

She smiled. 'Perhaps you should stop thinking and kiss me. It has been a long day and coupling would relieve some tension.'

Randall's eyes widened. 'Please, Ruth, I'm really not up to it. And I smell.'

She closed her eyes and breathed in deeply. 'I like your scent. It is deep and manly.'

'Okay, just tell me where we're going. . . what's in Oslan?'

'The sea. Voon and I disagreed about the way south. He favoured the Jekkan causeway, I favoured the sea. If we are to follow Utha, we must be swift.'

'Which is quicker?' he asked, trying to focus on finding his master.

'The causeway, but not by much. It's not worth it. Utha will live, but Voon will likely be killed. . . you would be dead before we crossed the anchorhead.'

He slumped backwards, staring up, past the treetops to the starry sky above. She curled up next to him, her arm across his chest and her head nestled against his neck.

'Stop worrying so much,' she said.

He focused on the stars, letting his chest rise and fall as he tried to calm his mind. 'How do you know all this? You've lived in a forest for. . . I don't know how long.'

'You imagine I have been asleep? No, my kind were once common in these woods. We were gods and protectors to the Kirin people, before our might dwindled. But I have had many children and I have heard many things. I am well-prepared for travel.'

'Children? Why does that concept disturb me so much?' Randall squirmed and curled up on his bedroll.

'You are a young man of a young race. . . and true perception will always elude you. Do you know what has happened to your mind?'

He shook his head.

'I broke off a piece of my power and gave it to you. When the witch grasped your mind, I had to match her with equal power. My people have ever used this to invest our progeny with might. In time, you will understand the Gorlan more than you want to, for I cannot take back what I gave you. I am diminished by a fraction and you are now more than a mortal man.'

The gentle fingertip she'd stroked across his mind was like a film of warmth, keeping him safe and giving him clarity. When he spoke it was in a whisper. 'So what am I?'

'You're still Randall of Darkwald, but your life-force is now linked to mine. As I endure, so will you. It will make sense in time.'

He was silent for a moment. 'You saved my life. . . and my mind. I suppose I'll wait until it makes sense.' For a second, he just wanted to be back with Sir Leon in a dirty tavern, somewhere in Ro Tiris.

'Nostalgia is a curiously human trait.'

'Just shut up,' he mumbled. 'I'm going to sleep.'

* * *

It got hotter and hotter. As the fresh morning turned to burning afternoon, his skin became blistered and sore. The black robes sourced from a travelling family deflected the worst, but his skin just wasn't used to the sun.

They'd broken from the column of refugees and entered the woods of Oslan, but the thinly spaced trees did nothing to alleviate the heat. He trailed along behind Ruth, trusting in her sense of direction. They had been alone for days. None of the other refugees from Thrakka had taken their road, and a few had shouted warnings at them. Apparently, they were going the wrong way.

They were now deep in the forest, with blazing sunlight slicing through the open canopy. The ground was dusty and dotted with sharp stones and rocky river-beds, making the going slow and uncomfortable. The land was unspoilt; the trees huge and the dense shrubs wild, with no recognizable paths. Bumpy ground rose and fell in strange, jagged ways, making their path chaotic.

'Do the Kirin have towns?' he asked.

'Some villages, a few farms. No real civilization. . . not that you would recognize.'

Ruth stopped walking and studied a broad tree-trunk in her path. She stood on a grassy rise, nestled between rugged hills.

'What is it?' he asked.

'An arrow. I believe it's a territory marking.'

Randall joined her. The arrow was buried in the bark, with

nothing of the steel arrow-head visible. The haft was fletched in red with rings of blue around the wood.

'There is an old saying, young Randall. Well, old in the timescale of men. That the Kirin woods remain free only as long as their longbows remain the best and their arrows fly true. These lands are dangerous for outsiders.'

She took a slow look around the uneven, wooded ground. 'Let's keep walking,' she said.

'What. . . hang on!' he spluttered, as Ruth hopped from the grassy rise and walked off.

Randall followed, scuttling into a shallow valley between rocky hills.

'I've been shot before, you know. I got a crossbow bolt in the stomach. Here, have a look.' He pulled up his tunic to reveal the circular scar. She didn't look. 'It was in Cozz. It really hurt.'

The valley wended its way through a dry river-bed of sharp stones and soft mud. On either side, crumbling walls of earth and moss sloped away from them. The wind dropped and, for the first time in days, he didn't need to shield his eyes from the sun.

The valley turned and the ground fell away, a shallow gradient covered in grey stone and slowly trickling water. At the end of the gully, in the shadow of a huge, gnarly tree, was a wooden stockade. It was solid and dug deeply into the muddy bank.

'Randall, come stand by me,' said Ruth, stopping well away from the wall.

He didn't argue, hurrying over the rocks to join her.

'Can't see anyone,' he observed.

Ruth slowly looked upwards, away from the stockade and into the branches of the tree. Randall followed her gaze and gulped at four drawn longbows held by well-camouflaged Kirin men. They wore dark green cloaks, with thick hoods obscuring their faces.

'Nice day for a walk in the woods,' said a gruff voice from the tree.

Ruth didn't respond.

'Which one is the slave and which is the master?' asked the

Kirin. 'The Ro is only a boy, too young to own a woman like that.'

'Where's she from?' asked a second Kirin. 'She's not Karesian.'

'Or Ro,' offered a third man.

'How much are they worth, do you think?' asked the first man. 'The woman should fetch a nice price. Not sure about the lad, he's a bit scrawny.'

'Err, can you relax the bows?' spluttered Randall.

One of the Kirin slung his longbow and swung from his branch. He dropped to the high ground next to the stockade and strolled along the wooden structure to stand before them. He was swarthy, but his features were sharp and delicate.

'This is not a place where travellers wander lightly,' said the Kirin. 'We are far from roads, towns. . . no-one strolls into these woods.'

'We really should just kill them,' said another Kirin.

'Please, just shut up!' said Randall, louder than he intended. 'We're only passing through. We're not an army of Purple clerics.'

There was silence. Ruth raised an eyebrow at him, the Kirin man pursed his lips and the longbows remained drawn.

'Hmm,' said the Kirin man, elongating the sound. 'My name is Arjav.' He drew his bow and placed the arrow carefully, not taking his eyes from Ruth, and looking at her down the wooden shaft. 'Why are you here?'

'Passing through. We are bound for the coast.'

He hadn't lowered his bow. 'That's no easy journey,' he replied. 'You'll be shot at a lot. And how are you with spiders?'

Randall barely contained a laugh.

'You've not put down your weapon,' observed Ruth. 'You may regret that. And I am well-acquainted with spiders.'

Her lip curled into the thinnest of smiles and her eyes darted across the stockade to the forested brush nearby. Randall, standing behind her shoulder, followed her gaze and gasped as the bushes began to shake. From the forest floor, scuttling en masse, came Gorlan, lots and lots of Gorlan. Some were the size of large dogs, others as small as a fist. They appeared from bushes, grass and, most alarmingly, from the high branches of the Kirins' tree. The archers, utterly surprised by the flood of arachnids, turned their bows towards the larger creatures and shouted alarm at Arjav.

The Kirin leader spun round and loosed an arrow at a large spider, then ran for the tree to assist his fellows. They were frantically trying to fire and reload before they were overwhelmed by web and fang. The larger beasts dropped vertically on lines of thick silk and attacked ferociously, biting and enveloping the three Kirin men quicker than Randall's eyes could follow.

'Arjav!' gurgled one of the men as a huge Gorlan began to wrap him in silk.

The creatures stayed back from the leader, allowing him a small circle in which to move without being bitten. He twitched manically, flexing his bowstring in shaking hands as his friends disappeared in a whirlwind of legs, fangs and web.

'Drop. Your. Weapon,' ordered the Gorlan mother.

He dropped the bow and held up his hands. 'Where in the halls beyond did they come from?'

'We picked them up travelling through your woods,' she replied. 'My companion is a little skittish, so I commanded them to scout ahead. They found you before we did.'

Randall frowned, before accepting that he was indeed skittish.

'Thanks for keeping them away,' he said quietly.

'My pleasure,' she replied out of the corner of her mouth.

Arjav moved back to the stockade, keeping his haunted eyes on the larger spiders.

'Who are you? *What* are you?' he spluttered.

'I am called Ryuthula. I am marked by Atlach-Nacha. I am a herald of silence and a child of deep time.'

Realization slowly dawned on the Kirin's face. Legend said that the greatest Gorlan lived in these woods. The man would live, day-to-day, with huge spiders. Randall didn't know whether he'd ever have met one as old as Ruth.

'You're a Gorlan mother!' said Arjav, his eyes wide and bloodshot. He dropped to his knees and averted his stare. 'Forgive me, great mother. Forgive my people.'

The swarming spiders moved back, many disappearing as quickly as they'd appeared. There was no sound other than the low clicking of their legs. A handful of dog-sized creatures remained, hanging from the branches of the large tree.

'You are forgiven,' replied Ruth. 'If you do as I ask.'

'Anything, great mother,' said Arjav.

She smiled, appearing like nothing more than a woman rather pleased with herself. For all her enormity and power, she still had a girlish side that Randall found unnaturally attractive.

Arjav, clearly more afraid than impressed, was still kneeling. His delicate features were pinched into an expression of extreme fear, his hands shook and his mouth quivered.

'You will escort us through this forest and assist us in reaching the coast. We are bound for the south.'

* * *

The Kirin man had stayed ahead of them, glancing back only to make sure they were following. He led them through winding, wooded passageways between rocks, trees, gullies and other primeval landscape. They passed occasional structures and lone settlements, well-hidden in the forest, whose inhabitants timidly kept behind walls and glanced through narrow shutters. There were numerous bowmen, positioned in high trees, but they were waved away by Arjav.

Ahead of them, a wide valley stretched away into the wilds of Oslan with a flowing river at its centre. Farms and homesteads lined the riverbanks, with cattle pens and windmills at the edges. Small, wooden jetties and riverboats lined Randall's field of vision and the smell of fish hit his nostrils. From the crystal blue of the water, across the vibrant green of the valley, to the deep grey of the mountains, it was a beautiful scene.

'It's almost a town,' observed Randall. 'At a distance.'

'So it's not just a rumour,' said Arjav, turning back to them. 'The arrogance of the Ro.'

'Sorry,' replied Randall.

'Great mother, he is a strange choice of pet,' he said.

'He is my lover, not my pet,' she replied.

Arjav was stunned, glancing in disbelief at the young squire. Randall smiled, nodding awkwardly. He wanted to make some show of manly virility, but he knew he just looked like a boy, hopelessly out of his depth.

'Perhaps he has qualities I'm unable to see,' replied Arjav with a straight face.

'He has qualities *he* is unable to see,' she said.

The Kirin's face creased with confusion, but he let the matter drop. 'These people are common folk,' he said, 'they have seen few outsiders who didn't mean them harm. Please respect that, great mother.'

'We are not interested in you or your people,' replied Ruth.

They continued walking. The valley twisted and turned away from them, each new turn revealing more homesteads and more Kirin. They went about mundane tasks, barely registering the two travellers. Children played in the grass, fishermen hauled in their catch and daily tasks were completed. It was a fishing village, hidden deep in the forests of Oslan, with none of the criminality Randall associated with the Kirin people.

'They can be at peace here,' said Ruth. 'The Kirin are a godless race. No Giant or Old One gives them sanctuary, so they skulk at the edges of the world, making do with scraps. Scraps of lands, food, prosperity.'

'The only Kirin I'd met was an assassin called Rham Jas who killed my old master.'

Randall hadn't thought about either man for some time. Rham Jas would hopefully be well on the way to eradicating the Seven Sisters, and Torian would be at peace in the stone halls beyond the world.

At the far end of the valley was another huge, wooden stockade with an open sluice, allowing the river to flow loudly over jagged rocks and tumble away from the farmsteads. The structure was old, but solid, and well-maintained. It was built from one sheer

21

cliff face to another and had numerous platforms and walkways from which bowmen could keep watch. Arjav led them to a large farmhouse, built partly atop a huge boulder. A plume of smoke rose from an irregular chimney and a plump woman of middle years sat on a stool outside. She puffed happily on a long, wooden pipe, surveying the valley.

'You've found some new friends, my boy,' said the woman.

Arjav ran to her side and whispered in her ear. Her eyes flickered and became wide as she listened and looked at Ruth. She stood suddenly, knocking her stool to the wooden porch. 'Great mother!'

Ruth gave her a shallow nod. 'We require food and rest.'

'Of course. My home is yours.'

Arjav stood to the side and bowed his head. 'This is Lylla Vekerian, protector of the Creeping Downs.'

The woman smiled, revealing dimples and small, sparkling eyes. 'A terrible name, I know, but it serves to scare interested men with swords. Please, come inside. Arjav, bring food.'

'At once.'

The Kirin man turned quickly, glad to be leaving Ruth's presence, and they followed Lylla Vekerian into her home. Randall felt his body relax, as if his every muscle untensed at once. Within, he faced a wide sitting room of thick, red carpet and low, mahogany armchairs. There was a lot of clutter, piled in corners and upon tables. Discarded crockery, broken arrows and dusty books. The fireplace was empty and an ornate katana was displayed above.

'Who are you, young man?' asked Lylla, tapping out her pipe on the side of a chair. 'You are a man of Ro, unless my eyes are deceived.'

He shook his head. 'I am just a man of Ro, but I need your help as much as my companion. And my name's Randall.'

Lylla made a sweeping motion with her arm, indicating the chairs, and then sat down herself. Ruth maintained her poise, keeping a straight back and not sinking into the padded armchair, while Randall let out a grunt of pleasure and slumped into the thick cushions.

'I hope my house is comfortable for you,' said the Kirin, averting her eyes as she spoke to Ruth. 'We have few luxuries here, but such a mighty guest can have all she wishes.'

'Randall needs to eat and sleep,' she replied, 'and we require assistance in finding a ship to take us south. We are on a hunt of sorts and our quarry has a good start.'

'Well, food will be here presently. Rest can be had at your leisure. We welcome your presence for as long as you wish, great mother.'

'And a ship bound for the south?' asked Randall. 'We need to get to a place called Oron Kaa.'

Lylla Vekerian jolted backwards and gulped. The city at the edge of the earth held some special fear for this woman and she took a deep breath before opening her mouth to reply. Her words were halted by running feet as Arjav and a young girl hurried into the farmhouse with a basket of bread and fish. They noted the haunted expression on Lylla's face, but didn't comment as they silently laid out a platter of food for their guests. The young girl, an eager Kirin child of no more than ten years, looked at Ruth with fearful reverence, as if she'd asked to come just to get a glimpse of the Gorlan.

'Thank you,' muttered Lylla, trying to smile at Arjav. 'Will you eat, great mother?'

Ruth looked at the child, narrowing her eyes in curiosity, until Arjav ushered the girl back out into the valley.

'I will,' said Randall, grabbing a hunk of buttery bread. The fish was smoked to a golden colour and gave off a rich, savoury smell. His belly thanked him with a contented gurgle as he chomped on mouthfuls of dense bread.

'Oron Kaa,' said Ruth. 'The name disturbs you. Why?'

Lylla refilled her pipe. 'My son is afraid of it too. Why in the halls beyond does your road lead to such a place? You would be welcome to stay here as friend and guardian.'

'I am no longer looking for worship,' replied Ruth, making Randall stare at her. 'Perhaps a century ago I would have taken your offer, but I find that I am in a hurry.'

'A shame,' said the Kirin. 'Our land is in need of some protection. It appears the Twisted Tree likes us no more than the Purple clerics of Ro.'

'It's happening everywhere,' said Randall, spitting crumbs on the floor as he spoke. 'I don't think the Twisted Tree likes anyone. I suppose we're. . . fighting against it. That's why we need to get to Oron Kaa.'

'I have four sons,' said Lylla. 'One was executed in Kessia for speaking against the Twisted Tree; one was inched in a Thrakkan dungeon for the same crime; and the remaining two are ship captains. . . perhaps the only people who will still be free in ten years. My eldest son, Raz Mon, will be able to help you.'

Randall finished his mouthful and smiled at the woman. 'You might be the friendliest person I've met since I left Tor Funweir. I don't really know how to say thank you any more.'

'You need not say anything, young man,' replied Lylla. 'If your road leads to Oron Kaa, I can assist, but I would bless the earth and the stone if the fates would gift me with a Gorlan mother to protect my land.'

'I am sorry,' said Ruth, her eyes strangely sad and wistful. 'We are few. Our days guarding the deep woods are ended.'

* * *

He slept well in a large bed, under warm blankets. The room was a box, with just the bed, a window and a standing basin of clean water, but to Randall it was better than the finest tavern. The Kirin farmstead was quiet and smelled of fresh bread and freshly cut grass. From his first-floor window, when he woke, Randall could see a bright morning sun, spreading as a golden line across the valley. He hadn't found Utha, but he'd found a degree of peace, if only for a single night of good sleep in a welcoming Kirin village, deep in the woods of Oslan.

Ruth had said that he was now more than a mortal man. He didn't feel any different, certainly no less mortal. He felt refreshed and strong, but that could just be a good night's rest. Perhaps there was something else, a gradual lessening of worry and fear, as if his mind no longer needed to concern itself with things that used to terrify the young squire. Unfortunately, the only way to test his new might was to stare down another of the Seven Sisters. . . and this was both unlikely and unwise. Greater than a mortal maybe, but still not a fool.

There was a knock on the door. Just a gentle sound, but enough to get him out of bed. 'I'm just getting dressed,' he said.

There was no reply. He dressed slowly in freshly cleaned clothes that hugged his tired limbs, and left the small room. Standing in the corridor, arms crossed, was a tall Kirin man, wearing only laced-up leather trousers and a matching waistcoat. The black clothing was stained and ripped at the joints, revealing scarred flesh and large muscles.

'Hello,' said Randall. 'Are you a friend of Lylla's?'

The tall man assessed him, then strode away, back down the stairs. 'Come, boy. Ten hours is enough rest.'

The young squire belted on the sword of Great Claw and followed. Back in Lylla's sitting room, he found a half-eaten breakfast of fruit and bread and three leather-clad Kirin men. Their katanas and bows were stacked in the corner and they stopped eating to cast wary eyes at Randall. Without Ruth or Lylla there, he felt naked and alone under their hard glares.

'Sit, boy, eat,' said the tall man.

Randall did as he was told, perching on the only free armchair. He munched on a shiny, green apple. 'Do you four live here?' he asked politely.

The three seated Kirin frowned at him. The tall man, now standing over his shoulder, grunted, as if he'd completed his assessment of the young man.

'We do not,' he replied. 'We arrived early this morning, and we have heard a strange tale of strange visitors.'

Lylla Vekerian emerged from the kitchen, wearing a white apron and carrying a smoking platter of fried fish. 'Ah, young man, good that you're awake. Hungry?'

He nodded and took another bite of his apple. 'Where's Ruth?'

Lylla smiled at him. 'She's been standing on the western palisade for hours, just staring into the woods.'

'If she likes it so much, why doesn't she stay?' mused the tall Kirin man. 'We could accommodate this one if she needs to keep him around.'

'Manners,' snapped Lylla. 'Young Randall is a guest in my house. Sorry, young man, my son has been travelling through the night and his mood appears dark.'

'Your son?' enquired Randall, looking up at the man. 'One of the sailors?'

'Raz Mon Vekerian,' said the man, 'captain of the *Black Wave*.'

'He can take you south of Skeleton Bay,' said Lylla, 'to the edge of the world.'

Her son gritted his teeth. 'Maybe,' he said. 'But my crew will not be happy. Certain destinations can lead to mutiny. Especially when there is money to be made ferrying refugees from an imploding Karesia.'

Randall finished his apple and flaked a fillet of fish across a thick slab of bread. 'Where can they go? Tor Funweir is no better.'

Raz Mon Vekerian didn't display emotion. His face was still and ice cold, though his three shipmates grinned at Randall's naivety.

'There are other places, boy,' said one of them. 'Most are bound for the twin cities, some even for the Freelands or to chance their luck in Fjorlan. Anywhere that doesn't revere this Twisted fucking Tree.'

'We seek to oppose that tree,' replied Randall. 'I make no claims to being a mighty warrior or shrewd tactician, but I have a close friend who is both. . . and he's bound for Oron Kaa, with a good head start.'

Again, the Kirin balked at the name. One of the seated men bit his thumb and looked up, as if to ward against evil spirits.

'Why does it scare you?' asked Randall.

'We don't talk of it here,' said Raz Mon Vekerian. 'It causes an ill wind to discuss such places while ashore. At sea a man can be free to talk of whatever he wishes. He can be free to worship any gods or none. There is no blasphemy at sea.'

Lylla sat next to him and filled her pipe. 'The settlement you wish to reach is known to our family.'

'Mother, please. Not here. The winds will listen and punish us.'

Randall finished his slice of bread and fish, and took an offered mug of sweet tea. 'So, once we're at sea, you'll tell us all you know of. . . the settlement?'

'Once I've killed any of my crew that refuse the journey, yes.'

CHAPTER TWO

GWENDOLYN OF HUNTER'S CROSS IN THE RUINS OF COZZ

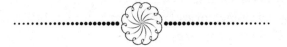

THE SOUTHERN GATEHOUSE was just a pile of blackened wood and steel, with motionless and twitching limbs poking out from between planks. The black armour of the Hounds had been turned into mangled metal by the fire, looking like a garden of jagged points. It made searching difficult. Alexander Tiris, the Red Prince of Haran, had not been found in the open, so, as morning rose, they searched through the debris. Under the ruined gatehouse, Tyr Sigurd had seen the tip of a large sword and Gwen commanded the remaining troops to clear the smouldering pile of rubble.

The Merchant Enclave of Cozz was no more. No buildings stood and no citizens remained. It was no more than a monument to brutal warfare and suicidal madness. She didn't know how many people had lived in Cozz, but it was several thousand certainly. Some would have escaped, others would be languishing as slaves, but most were dead. Even before the Hawks arrived and the world went black, the enclave had been smashed and smashed again. Her warrior's mind imagined how any rebuilt settlement would be stronger, with artillery and a dedicated force of guardsmen, as its strategic importance demanded. But for now it appeared almost dreamlike, with wisps of memory and death floating in the ash-filled air.

'My lady,' said Sergeant Ashwyn, pulling the tarnished blade from the rubble.

Gwen and ten Hawks of Ro stared at the blade. It was Peacekeeper, Xander's bastard sword.

'Clear the rubble. . . clear it quickly!' she snapped, dropping to the floor to heft planks of wood out of the way. 'If he's under there, we must find him.'

Sergeant Ashwyn shouted orders and men and Dokkalfar set about the large pile of rubble, frantically clearing wood, metal and body parts, cutting themselves on jagged steel.

Images and memories flooded her mind, making her light-headed. Flickering paintings of moments she'd shared with Xander, but might never share again. They'd met in conflict, and each day since they'd fought one battle or another; against tradition, prejudice, blades – but they'd never lost. Had the bluntness of the Hounds truly defeated them?

She could hear him saying '*stay alive*', as he had done every time they'd ridden into battle. She wanted to say it to him, whisper in his ear that he must live. . . for her, for the Hawks and for Tor Funweir. He would be the king now, as the only living man of the house of Tiris still in the lands of Ro. A man who had attacked and liberated his own capital city and killed his own cousin, all to free Tor Funweir from the tentacles of the Twisted Tree.

They'd come south from Ro Tiris with two thousand hawks and two Lords of Ro. One lord, Bromvy Black Guard of Canarn, was certainly dead and the other was missing. As for the warriors of Haran and Canarn, few had survived. She was in command of a broken force. Only the surviving Dokkalfar remained stoic. Tyr Sigurd and his forest-dwellers were quietly following orders and tending to the wounded men, while the rest tried to lighten their mood with hopeful talk of finding their general alive. Now, for the first time since the enclave had detonated, they all worked together to clear the rubble of the southern gatehouse.

'There, at the bottom,' she grunted. 'That's Brom.'

Sergeant Symon, her self-appointed aide, moved to her shoulder and, bending his back, hefted a large plank out of the way. On the other side, when they heard their lord's name,

Tyr Sigurd and the Dokkalfar of Canarn doubled their efforts. They'd found his severed arm the previous night, but his body had so far eluded them.

When the final plank was removed and a section of ground cleared, they saw two bodies and everyone froze, standing in a circle. Brom, his body half-burned, was splayed across another form, lying motionless beneath him, a form he had shielded from the explosion. Sigurd was the first to move, retrieving Brom's raven-hilted sword and rolling him to the side.

'General!' gasped Ashwyn.

Xander wasn't moving. He was on his back and, thanks to Brom, largely untouched by the fire, but blood covered his legs and chest. Gwen didn't need to order her men to help him. Everyone close enough moved in, with Ash and Symon positioning themselves to lift the general.

'Be careful,' she whispered. 'Is he breathing?'

'Unknown,' grunted Ash, getting a good grip under Xander's armpits. 'Let's get him out of here.'

They moved his limp body from its blackened wooden shell and placed him on the dusty ground of the southern courtyard. Brom was lifted by Sigurd and laid out next to Xander. The lord of Canarn's face was visible, but the rest of his body was broken.

Gwen dropped to her knees next to her husband. His arms and legs were intact, his breastplate unbroken and his sword still in one piece, but he wasn't moving. 'Sigurd, can you help?'

The forest dweller left Brom's corpse and crouched down with Gwen. His grey face twisted in concern as he inspected the Red Prince. 'His back is broken. His head has been struck repeatedly. His left leg is cut to the bone in three places. But he lives.'

'He lives,' she repeated, leaning over to kiss him on his blood-stained lips. 'You live.'

* * *

Her eyes hadn't left his face. As they carried him, from the bloodied square to the relative security of the forward gatehouse, Gwen had looked at nothing else. The thirty surviving Hawks and seven Dokkalfar trailed behind them, their excitement tinged with worry. The general lived, but he was badly wounded. As afternoon wore on and Tyr Sigurd tended to Xander, the mood became more and more tense.

'We need a White cleric,' said Ashwyn. 'Maybe Brother Daganay could do something.'

'He'll be with Major Brennan,' she replied. 'They'll be here before nightfall. An army of Ro from Canarn, Haran, Tiris and Arnon. They'll be looking for their general. . . perhaps their king. I hope there is still a man for them to find.'

Ashwyn put his hand on her shoulder. 'These forest-dwellers are clever bastards. Since we left Canarn I've seen Sigurd work wonders with a few roots and some berries. He says it's not magic, but it looks like it to me.'

'The Dokkalfar don't think of magic as we do,' she replied. 'Half of what they know and do is magical to us. To them it's just craft. Ancient and powerful, but craft nonetheless.'

'Well, with their craft and Brom's courage, he'll wake up, my lady. You listen to me now, Alexander Tiris is the toughest man I've ever known.'

She tried to smile. 'Thank you, Ash. But I just keep thinking about a king who may never be crowned.'

'And a queen?'

She blushed suddenly, averting her eyes.

'Never thought I'd see Gwendolyn of Hunter's Cross turn into a bashful young girl.' He winked at her. 'Don't worry, my lady, when your husband wakes up I won't tell him.'

They'd remained at Xander's side for the first few hours, but had now retreated to the ruined forward battlements, giving Sigurd room to practise his craft. Gwen had used a damp cloth to wipe blood from Xander's face, until he looked like her husband again, and she'd left only when his face was imprinted behind her eyes. His pulse was weak and his chest barely moved, but she could not help him. Of the remaining soldiers, only the Dokkalfar had such skill. She had no choice but to return to the men and once more be a warrior, awaiting reinforcements. Ashwyn remained with her, while Symon kept a watch over the southern plains, mindful of the surviving Hounds mustering again for an attack.

The shadows lengthened and the sky darkened until, barely an hour before dusk, sounds started to travel from the northern horizon, breaking the tense atmosphere. At first a dull thud, then a clank of metal, then the neighing of horses. Armoured men appeared on the high ground. A few at first, mounted and flying the banner of Ro Haran, then more, from every angle she could see, until the horizon had filled with an army of Ro.

Twenty cohorts, tightly organized into columns with banners flying overhead. The red hawk of Haran, the black raven of Canarn, the gold eagle of Tiris, and others she didn't recognize. The men of Haran were in the vanguard with ranks of watchmen and mercenaries behind.

'Look yonder,' said Ashwyn, pointing to a separate force riding over the hill. 'That's Markos of Rayne.'

A line of white rode slowly under a silvery banner showing a dove. Lances were held high and each horse wore a skirt of metal, making their approach slow but loud.

'Men of peace, clad in death,' she murmured, sharing Daganay's wariness of the White Knights.

Lord Markos rode before his men, now clad in glittering silver armour. His greatsword was visible across his back, and he held the reins in one gauntleted hand. He led five thousand Knights of the Dawn – the entire order of paladins.

'Nineteen thousand warriors, the best we have without the Red Knights,' stated Ash.

The army deployed slowly, coming to a stop on the fields north of the ruined enclave. Major Brennan, Brother Daganay and Lord Markos met at the front of the force and, with disbelief on their faces, rode towards the ruin. Gwen jumped from the skeletal battlements and ran to meet them, as the other survivors poked weary heads out from their places of rest to greet their brothers.

'Gwen!' shouted Daganay. 'What in the halls beyond happened to Cozz? And where's the general?'

She reached them and, as the Blue cleric dismounted, she grabbed him in a tight hug. 'Xander's barely alive. Brom's dead. Come quickly.'

He held her tightly, briefly, nodded and started to run back towards the ruin. Lord Markos and Brennan followed, passing orders to their men to set camp. Despite his paunch, Daganay easily kept up with her, and they met Tyr Sigurd at the gatehouse. The forest dweller wiped blood from his hands, and the smell of his ointments and salves hung in the air.

'Just in time, Daganay of the Blue,' said the tall Dokkalfar, showing no emotion about his grisly work. 'Your general fades.'

They quickly entered the gatehouse, one of the few buildings that still had a roof, and clustered round a wooden table, upon which lay Alexander Tiris. He was wrapped in makeshift bandages, and pungent herbal poultices covered his leg and forehead.

'His back is broken,' said Sigurd. 'And his head bleeds internally.'

'Markos,' said Daganay, 'you're of the White, only you can. . .'

Lord Markos of Rayne set aside his sword and knelt next to the stricken king. He assessed the dying man, his eyes seeing and showing how grievous were the wounds. 'My general, my king. Word has reached us from the Freelands. Your brother, Sebastian, is dead. The light of the One fades, from you *and* this world. I would see you stand once more. I would see you as king of Tor Funweir and protector of the Ro.' His eyes were closed and the words formed a prayer.

Xander's face twitched, as if he had heard that his brother was dead, and knew that he was now the only man of Tiris left alive. Then Markos removed his gauntlets and placed his hands on the general's chest. 'You, risen man, remove your herbs.'

Sigurd didn't argue but did as he was told, lifting off the poultices to expose the deep gashes in Xander's leg and forehead. Gashes that began to shine with a dull light.

'Whatever power is left to me,' whispered Markos. 'As a paladin of the White and a servant of the One God, I ask that it be given to him. My lord, if you have one shred of power left in your land, use it now.'

The shine lengthened and rose across Xander's body, flowing from the paladin's outstretched hands and obscuring the wounds. Gwen had seen a thousand White clerics heal a thousand wounds, but never with such reverence, as if the power was now being squeezed from an empty reservoir. But, slowly, the One answered the prayer and gave back Xander's life.

At the edge of her vision she saw a Purple cleric passing through the tent, ghosting through fabric and wood like a dream. He looked down at the Red Prince and nodded. No-one else gave any sign of seeing the apparition, but all simply knelt before Xander.

'My general, my king,' said Brennan, breathing heavily as the general's eyes snapped open.

'My general, my king,' agreed Markos, removing his hands as the light faded, revealing clean flesh where before there had been blood and bone. The king shifted his weight, flexing his newly repaired back.

Gwen just fell against him, ignoring the ghostly figure and wrapping her arms a round her husband's neck. When she looked up, the faded Purple cleric was gone.

'Easy,' he breathed. 'Easy. . . easy.'

'Stay alive, my love,' she whispered, crying against his face.

Daganay gave them a moment before inspecting Xander's wounds and nodding at Markos. 'A worthy prayer, my lord. And I thank you for it. The One hasn't totally abandoned us.'

'He gives me strength,' replied the paladin. 'As long as I have strength, so the One God endures.'

'Did we. . . did we take Cozz?' slurred Xander, blinking his eyes and coughing.

'We did,' she replied, kissing him softly. 'And you are to be king of Tor Funweir.'

* * *

'We don't have time for this,' she said, running a comb through her tangled hair.

'We're making time,' replied Daganay. 'Everyone knows Sebastian is dead. Everyone knows Xander is next in line. But such things need to be formalized, so the Lords of Ro don't argue when he tells them to bring every man they've got.'

She glared at him. 'Formalize? With a bloody Brown cardinal? So, we stage a coup, seize Tiris, crown our general king, and use a bloody Brown cleric to formalize it?'

Daganay shrugged and poked his head out of the large tent. 'Cerro was closest,' he replied. 'And he *is* a cardinal. Severen and Mobius are both dead; the Gold bastard, Animustus, is hiding in Arnon. Maliki Frith is in Ranen. Who else would you pick?'

'What does it look like out there?' she asked, binding her hair back into a topknot.

'Like a military exhibition of some kind. Brennan has everyone assembled in ranks. You should probably go and make sure your husband is ready.'

'He nearly died yesterday. Maybe we could put a crown on his head when he's rested for a few days.'

'I've had enough rest,' said Xander, emerging from an adjacent section of the tent. He had washed and his armour had been repaired, but there were deep bags under his eyes. His strength had not fully returned, and there was a vulnerability about him. 'I assume Cerro bought the crown with him.'

'Aye, my lord,' said Daganay, 'everything is ready. We just await our new king and queen.'

The Red Prince took a deep breath and tried to smile at her. 'Queen Gwendolyn Tiris, how does it sound?'

'It's okay when *you* say it,' she replied. 'I'm just not sure I want everybody saying it.'

He stroked a stray hair from her forehead. 'A long time ago, I met a woman in Hunter's Cross. She was the most dangerous,

35

most fierce creature I'd ever met. . . and I fell in love with her. I made her my wife and she became the Lady of Ro Haran. I never thought she'd become my queen, but I can think of no more worthy soul.'

He held her hands and they kissed slowly, before turning and exiting the tent. Daganay held open the tent flaps and they emerged between a line of Hawks, each man saluting with shortsword and shield. Banners of red and gold flew overhead and the press of warriors flowed over the hills, up to the ruined northern gates of Cozz. Tents and pavilions dotted the landscape, and the crisp morning breeze caught each banner. Thousands of warriors: mercenaries and watchmen from Tiris, guardsmen and Dokkalfar from Canarn, Hawks from Haran and White Knights from Arnon. Beyond the warriors, at the end of the line, was Cardinal Cerro of Darkwald, the most senior Brown cleric. He stood on a raised wooden platform, with Major Brennan and Lord Markos.

'Look upon this man,' announced Cerro, so all could hear. 'He is the descendant of High King Dashell Tiris. By blood and law he is our king.'

'Look upon this woman,' he continued. 'By love and law she is our queen.'

They walked slowly, taking in the silent respect, their hands locked together. When they reached the platform, under thousands of eyes, Daganay took the lead and preceded them up a hastily erected staircase. Neither Xander nor Gwen was used to the formality, nor the theatrics involved in crowning a new monarch, but they kept their chins high and their backs straight, looking down across a sea of people. They turned on the platform, presented to the soldiers of Ro like the unveiling of a new cathedral or some wondrous painting.

Again, she saw the Purple cleric. He hovered in the air, above the closest ranks of soldiers, and bowed his head to the king and queen. Xander gasped and looked at her, making her realize that the apparition appeared to only the two of them. A sense of duty and order came from the ghostly figure, and a sense that it

36

approved of their coronation. The shade held no fear for either of them and, as it faded from view, they shared a smile.

'I'd say stay alive,' whispered Gwen, 'but I don't think we're in any danger.'

He tried to hide his smile as Cerro addressed the throng. 'On this day, under this sun, on this earth, I proclaim to every man and woman of Ro that your new king is Alexander of the house of Tiris.' He held aloft a crown of bronze and gold, decorated with jewels of a dozen colours. The crown of High King Dashell Tiris, the first man to unite Tor Funweir under a single ruler, was placed slowly on Xander's head. 'Look upon him and his lady, Gwendolyn Tiris, hereafter your queen.'

Bugles were blown, horns sounded, flags were waved high and the armies of Tor Funweir roared their approval, each man and woman saluting their new king and queen.

The Brown cardinal turned his fatherly gaze towards them and spoke quietly. 'Your grace, perhaps a few words of encouragement.'

Xander gulped, his eyes twitching as he looked at the sea of cheering people camped on the northern fields of Cozz. Gwen imagined that his arms must be bristling with goose bumps, as hers were, and that they'd both need time to process their new station.

He raised his arms, gradually silencing the crowd. Neither of them were dressed for a coronation, both wearing battered leather and steel armour, but the masses didn't care. They stared at their new king, proud to have been present when he was given his crown.

Xander puffed out his chest and lifted his voice to the crowd. 'My father was crowned in the Purple cathedral in Ro Arnon. My brother was crowned in the Gold cathedral in Ro Tiris. Around them both stood a hundred clerics and a thousand lords and ladies of Ro.

'I am *proud* to have been crowned on the fields of Tor Funweir, standing with an army of my countrymen.'

Cheers erupted again, more raucous now, flowing across ranks of Hawks, lines of guardsmen and mercenaries, and reaching the mounted Knights of the Dawn in the distance.

'Our country has been invaded,' continued the king. 'Even now, thousands upon thousands of Karesians camp round Ro Weir. And in their minds sits an enchantress, a witch of the Twisted Tree. I will rouse every fighting man of Ro and I will march south.'

Gwen put a hand on his shoulder and stepped next to him. 'We pulled down the banner of the Twisted Tree in Tiris,' she shouted. 'We pulled it down in Cozz. . . we will pull it down in Weir!'

The cheering rose and extended, becoming a glorious cacophony of guttural shouts. Somewhere, deep within the cacophony, Gwen could hear their names being chanted. King Alexander and Queen Gwendolyn. They'd thrust themselves into power. In times of peace their actions would be considered little better than a coup. But with the Twisted Tree consuming Tor Funweir, and Sebastian's death, the usual rules did not apply.

The cheers appeared to last forever; she certainly wanted them to, for as long as they cheered, they were happy. But reality intruded and formalities needed to be observed.

Cerro raised his arms for silence. 'Riders will be sent to every free corner of Tor Funweir, announcing our new king and queen. They will receive oaths of fidelity from every lord and lady of Ro. . . and we will once again be united.'

* * *

Their first night as king and queen of Tor Funweir was spent under canvas on the northern fields of Cozz. A fire burned outside and took the edge off the night breeze, allowing them both to remove their armour and sleep in comfort under a thick, woollen blanket. They'd retreated early from the celebrations, but allowed everyone to drink and feast with no restrictions. Their coronation aside, this might be their last chance to enjoy the simple pleasures. They were riding to war and, when the sun rose, that would once again be all that mattered. Brennan had organized the army into cohorts and companies, while Ashwyn and Symon drew up plans for supply lines and ways of keeping the army fed and healthy as they marched to war.

But that felt far away, too weak to pierce their armour at that moment.

They'd not spoken of the ghostly cleric. No words were necessary, just an understanding that the One God was paying attention on the day they became the king and queen of Tor Funweir. Neither of them were pious. A former Red Knight and a woman of Hunter's Cross. But it was nice to know their way was finally the right way.

He kissed her and pulled her against him, to rest her head against his chest. She stroked her fingers along the faded scars where Markos had pulled him back from death and almost thought to offer a prayer of thanks.

'We should probably have a child,' he said suddenly.

She sat up and looked at him. 'I think I missed the conversation that led to that decision.'

'We always said we would one day. Just seems more urgent now.' His eyes were sad, as if he felt obligated to provide an heir.

She kissed him again. 'That's the wrong reason to have a child. I'm not saying the idea isn't pleasant, but a warm sitting room in Ro Haran is a far better place to raise a child than a military camp. If you can tell me we won't be at war for longer than nine months. . .'

He wrapped his arms loosely around her neck and their bodies entwined into a tight embrace. 'I don't want you to die,' he whispered. 'And I don't want to die. I want something of us to remain.'

'You should probably try to keep me alive then. I'm the one who carries the child. You're expendable.'

They kissed passionately, between shared laughter. Gwen kept hold of the blanket, making sure their naked shoulders were covered, and the laughter slowly turned into moans of pleasure. Somewhere in the corners of her mind, they were in that warm sitting room in Ro Haran. Or maybe now it was Ro Tiris. Somewhere, a child played across red carpets, and happy folk enjoyed the summer warmth of a world at peace.

CHAPTER THREE

INGRID TEARDROP IN THE CITY OF FREDERICKSAND

THE SPRING MONTHS had always been a time of fun in Fredericksand. She used to love the rivers of snowmelt that dribbled their way from the mountains, through city streets, to the low fjords. She made bridges and small model boats, racing them down the fast-flowing streams of crystal-clear water. Her father told her stories of the first thains and how they built their city around sluices and wide sewers, enabling the yearly flood of water to drain off. When she was thainess, Ingrid would have a yearly festival, letting children race boats down the sluices, with prizes for the winners.

'Girl! Come away from there, you'll fall in.'

The speaker was Beirand Rock Heart. He was really tall and his chest bulged through his bear-skin robe. He was her babysitter. He said he was her protector, but they both knew he was her babysitter. She was fifteen and didn't need a babysitter or a protector, but the men of Ursa who held Fredericksand were worried she'd sneak off. She probably would.

'I've never fallen in. I'm not fat like you.'

She was small for her age, but her arms and legs were solid and she had limitless energy. Alahan used to say that she'd never wield a battleaxe, but would be a nightmare with a knife.

She smoothed back her long, brown hair and smiled at the man of Ursa.

Beirand grumbled over his matted black beard. He had hit

her several times until Rulag Ursa told him not to. Now she tormented him at every turn, confident she'd not lose any more teeth.

'I'm gonna slice you up the moment we don't need you any more.'

Ingrid glanced at her feet and pouted. 'Did I say something wrong? I was just saying that you're fat. . . you *are* very fat.'

She smiled and darted away from him, sprinting along the sluices. She hopped from stone wall to cobbled path, nimbly heading into the centre of Fredericksand. Beirand swore and wheezed as he tried to keep up with her.

The city of Teardrop was spread out from the harbour, across the fjords, to the low cliffs. Most of the buildings were stout, built partially below ground to protect against the cold. Stone domes and thatched roofs were plonked chaotically in a huge, sloping semi-circle against the Fjorlan Sea. It was her home. It was her father's and her brother's home. But it was different now. The crying dragon had been replaced by a red bear claw. Her father was dead and Alahan was. . . somewhere.

She ran into a man leaning on the sluice. He wore chain mail that cut her face, and his rough hands grabbed her neck.

'You going somewhere, Little Wolf?'

It was Harrod. He was a priest. At least, everyone called him Father and he appeared to be a priest. To Ingrid, no true priest would be as horrible as Harrod. Her Uncle Magnus had hated him, and her father had exiled him from Fredericksand. He'd come back with Rulag.

'Just helping Beirand get some exercise,' she replied, rubbing a cut on her chin. 'He'll be here in a second, ask him.'

Harrod smiled. His teeth were brown and his face had boils. She didn't like looking at him. His hair was thin and greasy, and his fingers were too long.

Beirand appeared from a side street. He was panting and his face was red.

'Father! Sorry, the little bitch was giving me the run-around.'

Harrod kept hold of Ingrid's neck, roughly pulling her to stand upright. His hands were sweaty and she hated the feel of his skin. All of Rulag's men smelled bad. It appeared to be a curse of Jarvik.

'You need to keep an eye on this one,' said the priest. 'She's a slippery one. Never does what she's told.'

'I *do*, just depends on who's doing the telling.'

Ingrid smiled again. 'My dad said I was rebellious by nature.'

Beirand caught his breath and spat on the snowy ground. 'Your father's wisdom served him well. . . before we cut him up.'

They were only words, and she'd heard similar a hundred times or more, but they still hurt. He'd always just been there. Algenon Teardrop had taught her right from wrong, chided her when she misbehaved and hugged her when she was good. He was the strongest, wisest, funniest man she'd ever known. And now he was dead.

'Manners, Beirand,' said Father Harrod. 'She's been through a lot.' His smile was gloating and unpleasant. The teeth just made it worse.

'My brother's going to kill you,' she said, her eyes wet and her throat dry.

They laughed, glowering down at her with ignorant, sneering eyes.

'And Wulfrick, he's going to kill you too.'

'Let's get this little bitch back to the hall before we get killed,' said Harrod. 'The Lord Bear Tamer is almost ready to leave.'

A glimmer of hope appeared in the vaults of her mind. If he was leaving, she'd be free of him. Left with only Beirand as a guardian, she'd be free in no time.

'Stop smiling, little wolf,' said Harrod. 'You'll be coming with us.'

* * *

Her father's hall had changed. It was still huge and wooden, but the warmth had left. The trophy skulls of trolls and ice spiders had been taken down, as had the ancestral weapons. All trace of the house of Teardrop had been removed. Even their home, sitting unobtrusively at the back of the hall, had been gutted and turned into Rulag's inner sanctum.

It was horrible, as if Rulag was afraid of Algenon's memory. He'd been afraid of his axe; now he cowered in front of his legacy. This was her armour. Ingrid was a Teardrop – she had strong blood and a stronger brother. Too strong for Rulag to sweep aside.

She was led into the hall, guarded by Beirand and four men of Jarvik. All the men in the hall had strange weapons. Glaives, she knew they were called. Long hafts of wood and a saw-toothed axe-blade. Further into the hall sat dozens more swarthy men. Rulag's captains were almost as bad as him; they stubbornly shouted about their superiority, spitting at the other cities of Fjorlan and pledging their warriors to the house of Ursa. He'd offered them power and influence in the 'new Fjorlan'. They'd be thains and axe-masters, enforcing Rulag's law. Just as he enforced the law of the Karesian witch. They talked about her all the time, as if she was their secret weapon. Half a world away, but her influence was felt in the hall of Teardrop.

'How far is Tiergarten?' she asked Beirand, looking up into his bearded face. 'I mean, how long will it take an army to get there?'

'Shut up,' he replied. 'Just be silent and I won't have to slap you.'

She turned to look up into a different bearded face.

'How far is Tiergarten?' she asked another man. 'Beirand won't tell me. I just like knowing things. It's okay if you don't want to tell me. I'll find out.'

She was led past cold fire-pits and empty feast tables, to the raised chair at the far end. Red banners with the bear claw of Jarvik hung from the rafters. It was a dirty red, stained and faded. Patches of it were mottled and the black woven claws were frayed and split. She preferred the crying dragon of Teardrop. It was dark blue and made her smile. When she was small she had had the image on her blanket. Her father said the dragon was sad because men still killed each other, and it was a creature of peace.

Raucous laughter cut the cold air. From the rooms beyond the chair – Ingrid's former home – Rulag Ursa swilled greedily from a brass tankard and guffawed at some joke or other. The men with him sat round a circular table and joined in the laughter. They didn't see Ingrid approach. A Karesian man was also sitting at the table. He wasn't laughing or drinking and was slim and delicate compared to the Ranen warriors.

'My lord Bear Tamer,' said Beirand.

The lord of Jarvik stopped laughing. His piercing green eyes turned to them. His shoulders were huge and his matted brown hair fell in tangles down his back. Frothy beer ran through his beard and he spat on the floor as they approached him.

They all looked at Ingrid. Six men of Jarvik, bulky from bear-skin and chain mail, were silent.

'How far is Tiergarten?' she blurted out.

Still silent, their dark eyes narrowed. Some chewed on meat or swallowed their mouthfuls of beer. Under their meal was a canvas map of Fjorlan with Tiergarten marked in red. It didn't look to be far from Fredericksand.

The Karesian man studied her. She didn't recognize him and didn't know why he was here.

'No-one will tell me,' she said nervously. 'I don't see what harm it could do.'

Rulag stood and looked down at her. 'You've not learned to keep your mouth shut, I see. Perhaps I should have told Beirand to keep hitting you. Knock out a few teeth and mess up your face.'

She raised her eyebrows at him and imagined stamping on his foot and kneeing him in the face. 'You killed my father,' she murmured.

'What? Speak up, ya little shit,' barked the betrayer.

'You killed my father, you fat bastard,' she shouted.

Rulag struck her, the back of his hand connecting with her jaw. The other men laughed. The Karesian rose from his seat, as if to help her, but was waved away by Rulag.

Hate and embarrassment filled her thoughts. She wished she

was taller and stronger. She wished she had an axe and the skill to swing it. She wished that Alahan would burst through the door with Wulfrick and a hundred men. She cried, 'Alahan is going to kill you. He's tougher than you, cleverer than you. . . thinner than you.'

'Pick her up, Beirand,' said Rulag.

The axe-man grabbed her arms and hefted her upwards.

'Your brother is not going to kill me. He's going to die.'

He towered above her, massive and wide, his eyes showing waves of hatred. He hated her family, her brother, her father, her legacy. He hated everything about her, especially her name.

'My lord, she is only a child,' said the Karesian, still standing. 'She is no threat to your cause. And women should not be treated so.'

Rulag guffawed, turning away from Ingrid. 'You men of the sun don't know how to treat women. Fjorlan is a man's world.'

'Fjorlan is a primitive world,' the Karesian corrected him. 'The Mistress of Pain would not like you mistreating this girl.'

The foreigner didn't flinch as Rulag's captains glared at him. He was smaller than all of them, and dressed in a thick, black cloak, though he wore two nasty-looking blades in his belt.

'Saara didn't send you to be a fucking adviser, she sent you to deliver the trees,' replied Rulag, showing his back to Ingrid.

If only she had a knife or something sharp. She knew there was a target in the thigh. Alahan had told her to aim for the groin and twist the blade. But she didn't have a blade, just a sore face, wet with tears.

The Karesian strolled round the feast table, stepping past Rulag and approaching Ingrid. He produced a small, red handkerchief and extended it towards her.

'Dry your face, girl. If you do, one day, see your brother die, you should greet it with fortitude, not tears.'

She took the handkerchief. 'Who are you?'

'My name is Kal Varaz. I am a wind claw of Karesia and I was sent by my mistress to help kill your brother and overwhelm Tiergarten. But I do not raise my hands to women.'

'What?' She threw the handkerchief back at him and stepped away.

Kal Varaz slowly bent down and retrieved the square of red fabric. He was maddeningly calm and his eyes showed no emotion. Al Hasim was the only other Karesian she'd ever met, and he'd been funny, friendly and frequently drunk. Kal Varaz was, so far, the complete opposite.

'My lord Rulag, can we proceed, now that you have exerted your dominance over this girl?'

'We'll go when I'm good and ready,' replied Rulag. 'I haven't told young Ingrid the happy news. I planned for you to marry my son when this was over, girl. Consume your name like a mouthful of meat. But he was too weak. So, you will have the honour of marrying me.'

* * *

Ingrid was given an hour to gather some belongings. She had been staying in a small room, well away from the main hall, where Rulag didn't have to look at his future bride. She was allowed some clothes and a few pairs of shoes, but little else. An old bracelet, a thick winter coat and a pouch of pretty stones. The stones had been found along the fjords and were a collection from when she was small. They made her smile and reminded her of peace and happiness.

She'd already packed her rucksack and was using the extra time to sit and look out of a window. The sky was pale blue, and the mountains cut across her field of vision as a zigzag line. The world seemed bigger. All of a sudden, everything was huge and complicated, when before it had been small and simple. Or maybe she'd just been a silly child and now she'd grown up.

Birds fluttered past the window, beating their wings in shallow sweeps and soaring towards the sea. They sang and played in the air, unconcerned by the problems of men and girls. It would be nice to be a bird. She remembered stories her father used to tell her about Brytag, the god of luck and wisdom. She hadn't really understood about gods and had preferred the stories about Corvus the Crow, a mischievous character from a book she loved. He was always getting into trouble and wriggling his way free. She had empathized with his adventures, even going so far as to pretend to be a crow when she was alone. But that was long ago.

She went to the window and crossed her arms on the sill, gazing into the pale blue of the sky.

Caw

'Go and fly,' she said to the large, black bird. 'I'd fly if I could. I wouldn't be sitting on a girl's window sill. The sky is massive and endless. It doesn't have walls or doors. You can never be a prisoner in the sky.'

Caw

'You're a really big bird.' It looked at her, its yellow beak bobbing from side to side. 'And you're very friendly.' She didn't know much about birds, but it was inches from her face, and that didn't seem normal.

Caw

'Okay, okay, stop squawking at me.' She took a step away, thinking the beak looked rather sharp and pointy. Though strangely she knew the bird wouldn't peck her.

The bird hopped forward and landed on her shoulder. It was heavier than it looked but she was too stunned to move. The wings flapped gently next to her head, the feathers soft against her skin. The jewels of black that were its eyes were deeper and more textured when viewed from close up and they peered at her, while the yellow beak continued bobbing up and down.

'Hello,' she said through quivering lips. 'I'm Ingrid. . . Ingrid Teardrop. . . Do you have a name?' She knew it was a stupid question, but she asked it anyway. 'We can be friends if you like. . . lots of my friends are dead. I wish I could fly like you, though.'

She raised a shaking hand and encouraged the bird from her shoulder. It paused and flapped on to her forearm, nearly taking an ungainly tumble to the stone floor.

'Corvus,' she said. 'You can be called Corvus. Do you want

47

to come to Tiergarten with me? Otherwise I may die from the stench of hairy old men. You don't smell. . . and you're not fat.'

Caw

Her smile widened as she stroked under his hooked yellow beak. He juddered in enjoyment, fluffing his wings and giving an endearing chirp. Used to the weight now, she sat back down on her bed, inspecting the friendly bird. His grip was soft and his movements gentle, as if he didn't want to hurt her. His talons were large and looked cruel, but they merely padded tenderly on her forearm.

'You can't travel with me though. . . I fear they'd hurt you.' Her smile became broader. 'But you can fly.'

He flared his wings, appearing to double in size. Ingrid gasped, but didn't stop smiling. She liked Corvus, and was glad to have a friend again.

A sharp bang on the door. 'Wolf bitch – hurry the fuck up,' said Beirand, coughing between words. 'It's not getting any warmer outside.'

She puffed out her cheeks and lost her smile. Corvus pecked gently at her cheek, making a low murmur, but her smile wasn't coming back.

'I need to go,' she whispered to the raven. 'But I'll see you soon. We'll have to camp. I could sneak out and we could go and cause mischief.'

'You there?' grunted Beirand.

'Unfortunately,' she replied. 'No-one's come to rescue me yet.'

'You're funny,' he replied. 'Hurry up.'

As she left the room, hoping that she'd find a way to escape her captors, Ingrid thought of Alahan. She loved her brother and, as long as he was alive, she knew he'd never stop fighting. She hoped he was alive. *Please be alive*, she thought.

* * *

Leaving the city took no time at all. The warriors of Ursa flowed out of Fredericksand like a snake of steel, spreading out along the north–south road, with the Fjorlan coast on their right side. Sled-loads of planking and equipment followed, to be assembled into engines of war when they drew closer to Tiergarten, accompanied by the yelp of huskies marking their passage. Ingrid was kept in the middle of the army, far from anything she could break or steal. She thought about tripping up a few battle brothers, but Beirand never took his eyes from her.

She was teased about her upcoming wedding. Much of it was crude and made her feel sick. Luckily, Rulag would not wed her until Alahan was dead, and Ingrid still had faith in her brother. By the time they stopped for the first night, she'd taken to picturing his face as armour against their nasty comments.

'I feel helpless, Corvus,' she said once, when she was finally alone in a small tent, feeding worms to her new friend. 'I'm not as strong as Halla Summer Wolf. Maybe I will be one day, but what can I do now? I'm just a little girl.'

Caw

She smiled and sat up on her bedroll. She knew he wasn't just a raven and he made her feel confident, as if nothing could touch her with him as a companion.

'Are you Brytag?'

He tilted his beak and gave his long wings a gentle flutter.

'If you are, can you help me kill Rulag?'

She didn't really want an answer. She just wanted a friend.

Suddenly he leapt from her side and flew through the tent flaps. She gasped as a dozen men swore at the huge, black bird, but none of them could throw an axe quickly enough to hit him. The flaps billowed in the raven's wake and Ingrid glimpsed a handful of men, roused from round a campfire. None of them looked at her and on an impulse she took a deep breath, stood up and went out into the open. She stood outside the tent for a moment, looking carefully at her captors. The men obviously couldn't see her; they simply carried on drinking.

Caw

The raven circled in the crisp night sky, his cheerful squawk marking his flight. He had obscured Ingrid from those who would cage her and she grinned broadly, feeling free for the first time since her father died. With a spring in her step, she strolled away from her tent and moved forward, along the rugged coast, through the ranks of Rulag's army. No-one looked at her, but she still had to stay alert to keep from bumping into drunken men. They rolled around the camp, between fires and tents and smithies, spinning tales of the new Fjorlan and the new era of strength. They didn't speak of Rowanoco, as if he was no longer in their hearts. This made Ingrid cross. It made Corvus cross as well. The Ice Giant stood for strength, honour and freedom, but these men disagreed.

At the southern edge of the camp, protected from the wind and the ocean spray by the gullies of the Crystal Fork River, she found the biggest tents. They were made of thick canvas and secured by black metal spikes, with the red bear claw of Ursa prominent on every piece of fabric. Still no-one looked at her. She didn't feel invisible, just. . . difficult to see, as if she walked in the shadows of the world, just out of sight. As long as her footsteps were light and her movements slow, she could remain obscured from normal eyes.

The largest tent smelled of meat and ale. It was well-guarded by men with glaives and Corvus had settled upon its high frame. She walked round the tent, looking for a good vantage point, and found a small gap in the fabric through which she could squeeze. Ingrid found herself amidst barrels of ale and sides of salted meat in the outer section of the tent. Deeper inside she could hear men talking.

'And the Green Men? They've been hiding in Tiergarten for months.' The speaker was Harrod. 'Halfdan has a few hundred men hidden.'

'They can keep hiding,' replied Rulag. 'If old man Green wants to be thain of Tiergarten when all this is over he'll do what he's bloody told. That means killing Alahan when I say so and not before.'

Ingrid bit her lip, trying not to gasp in alarm and reveal her hiding place.

'He's had his instructions,' continued Rulag. 'When we're close enough that he can see the fires, he gets those loathsome children of his to cut up young Teardrop. Preferably in his sleep. It's what the Karesian witch wants and I'm happy to oblige.'

She skulked down at the base of the fabric, getting as close to the speakers as she could.

'Will they fight once he's dead?' asked another man.

'Probably. The Mistress of Pain assures me that her Dark Young will stifle any attempt at a long campaign. She says to birth them, unleash them, and watch the walls of Tiergarten melt away. Kal Varaz has already sent three of them ahead. I saw the bloody things. From a distance, but that was bad enough.'

'You trust the enchantress?' asked Harrod.

'No, but I trust that she wants Teardrop dead as much as we do. It serves our purposes to ally with her for now. Just don't tell Kal Varaz anything about our plans. We can't be sure he doesn't have a way of talking to his mistress. If the trees prove less than promised, I'll kill the Karesian bastard myself.'

'And her god?' queried another man. 'I don't fancy worshipping a tree.'

'We don't need to,' said Harrod dismissively. 'Once Fjorlan is under heel, we'll make a peace with her Twisted Tree. She can have Tor Funweir and Karesia, we'll have the Freelands and Fjorlan. We don't need her god *or* Rowanoco.'

Rulag let out a deep belly laugh. 'We'll prune the weak and slice up the lands of men. In time, I'll be high thain of all Ranen. Then the Ice Giant will pay attention. Honour and freedom be damned – strength is all that will be left. We will remake this land and remake our god.'

'So, Alahan Teardrop gets his throat cut,' said Harrod gleefully, 'then the trees breach the walls, then *we* attack. There might not be much left, but we won't waste any of our men.'

'And One Eye the axe-woman?' asked Rulag. 'What word of her?'

'No word,' was the quiet reply. 'Grammah Black Eyes has been silent for weeks. Either he's lost his cloud-stone or Halla's got more men than we think. If she took the Bear's Mouth—'

'She'll be on her way to Tiergarten,' interrupted Rulag. 'No matter, the Green Men will welcome her home properly.'

Ingrid smiled. Halla was still alive. She was almost as strong as Alahan. With the two of them defending the city, nothing could defeat them. Her smile turned to a frown as she realized she was being a silly girl. It still pleased her to imagine that her brother and Halla were unbeatable, and a few years ago she might even have believed it, but she now knew how fragile life was. How a blade in the dark or a well-planned attack could fell the mightiest warrior.

She backed out of the tent, muttering to herself. 'What can I do to help? What do they need? Maybe time? How can I give them time?'

Corvus left the command tent and glided away, over her head. He was silent, drawing no eyes upwards but hers, and made his way to the edge of the army. She followed his flight, feeling tears dampen her cheeks. She still had her friend and she still couldn't be seen, but hearing the bastard of Ursa speak had made everything worse.

Beyond the command tents was the vanguard of the army, a closely packed group of tents, housing the best and soberest fighters. They were the ones who protected the sleds and gathered the gangs of dogs. Hundreds of grey and white huskies, tethered to metal stakes, slept in the low ground where the breaking waves of the Fjorlan Sea could not reach. They yawned and stretched, emitting yelps and barks. They were essential to the swift movement of Rulag's army, pulling his tents, supplies, weapons and siege equipment.

Ingrid left the tents and crouched next to the closest dog. He was thick-bodied with a long muzzle and dense, white fur, but his face was happy and his eyes sparkled. Brytag's illusion didn't appear to affect the dogs; the husky looked her in the eye and then licked her hand enthusiastically. Those dogs nearby looked up, as if happy to have someone pay them attention that didn't involve a whip or a boot. The men in the vanguard ignored the activity and Ingrid moved silently among the dogs, stroking and patting each animal. When she reached the middle of the mass of sled dogs, she began to loosen their tethers. They were just simple metal clasps attached to a leather strap, and it was easy to unclip each restraint.

'You should be free,' she whispered, nuzzling into the beautiful furry face of a huge husky.

It took less time than she had imagined to unclasp every restraint. The dogs remained still, but each mouth was open and panting, and each tail wagged excitedly. Corvus sat nearby, on the high glacial wall of an inland gully. He was quiet, with his beak tilted to one side as if concentrating and, with a sharp twist of their necks, every dog turned to look at him.

'Something's spooking the dogs,' said a man of Ursa, rising from his fire.

More men joined him and they warily approached the clustered huskies.

Ingrid moved to the gully to stand beneath Corvus's wall, and looked at a hundred pairs of sparkling eyes and a forest of wagging tails.

'What's the matter with them? Why are they being so quiet?'

Caw

As one, the massed dogs leapt to their feet and ran into the gully. Ingrid ran with them, excitedly petting each dog that passed, until the whole white and grey wave of fur had sped inland, followed up the gullies by the echoing cries of their handlers. When they'd outpaced her, she stopped with a broad grin on her face. Corvus would make sure the sled dogs kept their freedom and Rulag would have to send men back to Fredericksand to get more dogs. Two or three days at least. Ingrid would return to her tent and play the part of a good little prisoner. . . until her next opportunity to cause mischief.

CHAPTER FOUR

HALLA SUMMER WOLF IN THE CITY OF TIERGARTEN

'Twenty men, I think,' said Falling Cloud. 'Scouts. Men of Ursa. They didn't spy me.'

'Did you see it?' asked Halla. 'The city?'

He smiled. 'I did. It's still there.'

She smoothed back her hair and took a deep breath. They stood in a crevice, ahead of her main company, looking down on to the plains of Tiergarten. They were on the high plateau, east of the city. The crisp sea air was the same. The wind, the pine trees lining the ridge. Even the black sea, rolling away from them. It was all the same. The Crystal Fork River marked the north–south road and its frozen surface added texture to the vast, open plain.

'You're almost home,' said Wulfrick, nodding at her. 'You've got that faraway look in your eye.'

For a moment she softened and allowed herself a smile. 'Don't pretend you aren't itching to see your young thain.'

His wide, bearded face split into a toothy grin. 'Wasn't trying to. Alahan Teardrop is down there and I want to see him as much as you want to see Tiergarten.'

Falling Cloud waved his hand, breaking their eye-contact.

'Twenty men,' he repeated. 'I think they're scouts, watching the city.'

Behind her, practically vibrating with anticipation, were a hundred of her battle brothers. These men were all survivors of the dragon fleet, warriors who had travelled thousands of miles and killed hundreds of men to get where they were. Many were from Summer Wolf or Teardrop and had not seen this land for almost a year.

'There are twenty men to kill,' she whispered behind her. 'We move forward and kill them. Then we knock on the gates of Tiergarten. . . and go home.'

'Aye!'

She unslung her axe and strode along the crevice. Wulfrick and Falling Cloud followed, leading the rest of the men. Their boots formed a rhythmic stomp on the ice. A dull thud, barely announcing their presence.

She was in the lead, two strides ahead of Wulfrick. He could outpace her easily, but he was letting her get first look at the city. Round the corner, over a thin gap in the crevice, in the shadow of an icy overhang of Giant's Gift, she saw Tiergarten. It appeared in increments, a glimpse of cold, grey stone, then a tower and a ballista. Finally, as the cliffs sloped downwards, she saw Kalall's Steps and knew she was home.

'Halla, to the left,' said Wulfrick, nudging her with his axe.

She looked across, to a snowy ledge out of the wind. Skulking behind a rock wall were a few shoulders and a shield or two. Only three men were visible, but the rest would be further round the ledge, spying on Tiergarten. She couldn't tell if they'd seen Halla's men.

Then an arrow thudded into the ice next to her head. Ten men of Ursa stood from the rock wall and drew short bows.

'Cover,' she commanded as the scouts launched a volley at them.

Her men halted in the crevice, hunkering down. She pointed to Falling Cloud's throwing-axes and motioned for ten men to step forward.

As one, they rose from cover and threw their blades, end over end, towards the enemy archers. Four died instantly and three more were wounded. The rest – twenty men, disorganized in a mob – dived for cover.

'Up and over,' said Halla, waving her company forward.

'Bloody axes, boys,' roared Wulfrick, carrying her command to everyone within earshot.

They rushed the men of Ursa, forming into lines and vaulting over the rock wall. Halla's axe struck first, thudding into a man's shoulder and splitting his flesh to the bone. The other men, startled by the number of attackers, tried to run. They were far from their allies and knew they couldn't win.

Wulfrick and Falling Cloud led her company in two waves, cutting down the smaller force. Necks were sliced, limbs were severed, chests were caved in. It was quick, clinical and brutal. The men of Ursa had little fight in them.

'Enough,' she shouted when only cleaved bodies remained. 'Falling Cloud, check for signal fires. They must have had a way of reporting back.'

'Aye.'

He sheathed his axes and moved along the ledge. After a few moments, he shook his head. 'A few embers. Looks like a cook-fire. If they're reporting back, they've already done it.'

Halla kicked a twitching body off the ledge, sending it tumbling to the plains below. 'The main army must be close,' she replied. 'Let's get everyone behind big, stone walls. We'll worry about Rulag's dubious tactics later.'

Falling Cloud vaulted over boulders and hefted himself up out of the ledge. On the plateau above, illuminated by the winter sun, he waved an axe behind them.

'Up!' he roared.

From every visible angle, stretching east from the city, Halla's full company emerged. A thousand warriors rose from concealment. Rudolf Ten Bears and Heinrich Blood led the survivors of the dragon fleet. Rorg and his Low Kasters stayed back, with Unrahgahr and the trolls well away from the main company. Moniac Dawn Cloud led the ranks of cloud-men, and it looked more like an army than ever before.

'That's a tough bunch o' bastards,' observed Wulfrick. 'Even with the trolls.'

She looked at him. 'Don't forget the youngsters and the old men. Not every axe you see is held by a tough bastard.'

He shrugged. 'Enough. Enough are.'

* * *

The route down to the plains of Tiergarten was steep. Men stumbled, axes clattered, curses were made, but they arrived at the city gates intact and in boisterous good humour. Bugles sounded from the walls and hundreds of men appeared on high battlements. The city ballistae were turned and short bows were aimed, but they appeared more confused than aggressive. Where did this bunch of laughing warriors come from?

She stood within an axe-throw of the huge city gates. Beyond, in stepped sections of grey stone, the ancient city rose away from her. At the base, it was level with the rolling sea and the Crystal Fork River; at the top, behind the Hall of Summer Wolf, was the high plateau and a ridge of spiky pine trees.

'Point arrows somewhere else,' shouted Wulfrick. 'Do we look like men of fucking Ursa?'

More laughter, now flowing across her entire company.

'Rexel, shut them up,' she said, trying to stifle a smile.

Falling Cloud, a broad grin on his thin face, turned and let his voice boom up to its highest volume. 'The lady wants quiet. You. . . will. . . be. . . quiet.'

They stopped laughing in gradual waves, taking note of Falling Cloud's smile. After a few minutes, giving the city defenders ample time to get a good look, the army was quiet.

Halla took a deep breath, feeling goose bumps on her arms and neck. Stepping forward of her company, she pointed her voice at the gatehouse, where stood a red-haired axe-man with a huge, bushy beard. She recognized him as Tricken Ice Fang, her father's chain-master.

'I am Halla Summer Wolf,' she announced. 'I stand in the realm that bears my name and I ask entrance to the city where I was born.'

A clank of axes started on the battlements, rising in volume as each man of Tiergarten saluted her. Then cheering from behind them. Shouts of welcome and howls of fidelity to her and her house.

'Open the gate!' commanded Tricken. 'And welcome our lady home.'

A deep creak of old, old oak and the foot-thick gates slowly parted. Kalall's Steps appeared again and a tear appeared in Halla's eye. She was home.

* * *

All Halla could think about was her father and Algenon Teardrop's axe. Her people had welcomed her home with gusto, fighting to shake her hand and praise her house, but she could no longer enjoy it. As soon as the gates opened, Wulfrick was no longer her man, and all that mattered was his young thain. A brief moment of elation had been cut clean through by thoughts of all that still needed to be done. And thoughts of a thrown axe embedded in Aleph Summer Wolf's chest.

'Wulfrick, slow down, you'll give yourself a heart attack.'

He'd almost run up the last few landings of the steps.

'Was Kalall a fucking sadist? Why did he build so many steps?'

'He was a good man,' she replied. 'The first priest of the Order of the Hammer. My great, great, great. . . grandfather. Maybe a few more greats. He planted the first crops, built the first ballistae.'

'And caused me to get fucking backache,' replied Wulfrick.

They were in front of the Halls of Summer Wolf at the top of the endless steps. She glanced behind and saw the entire population of Tiergarten welcoming her company. She could see Scarlet's Edge, where she was born; the Nook, where she'd won her first fight. It was eerily empty. So many men had left with Aleph and so many men had died with the dragon fleet. She'd seen glimpses of the toll, travelling through Hammerfall, but the true cost of Rulag's treachery was suddenly visible. Tiergarten had barely a garrison to defend her.

'My lady,' said Tricken with a polite cough. 'Things are not well here. Since Alahan killed Kalag, we've been functioning on adrenaline – and the odd angry speech from Old Crowe. Your men are not the worst thing we've seen this year.'

'Is that a thank you?' she asked.

'Well, it's nice to have a Summer Wolf here again. I'm sick of being a chain-master to this Teardrop cunt. I suppose he's all right, but he ain't you or your father.'

Luckily, Wulfrick was several steps ahead and hadn't heard him.

She put a hand on Tricken's shoulder. 'Is it still my city? Or does Alahan Teardrop command?'

'He's a tough cunt. Can swing the axe, shout the words. Crowe gives him shit and he shrugs it off. The people are pretty taken with him. The young high thain and all that. He killed Rulag's son and everyone saw. They've even named his axe – Ice Razor.'

'Well, I need to speak to him,' she replied, gritting her teeth.

Halla and her captains reached the top of Kalall's Steps. Most had never seen Tiergarten and stood in awe of the stone spectacle. The Hall of Summer Wolf was immense and carved out of the mountain. The cliff face was called Giant's Gift and had provided every brick within view. There was thatch and wood too, but the city was made of more stone than any other in Fjorlan. It was older than Fredericksand and Ranen Gar. Old Father Crowe said it was the oldest city of men.

'Where's my thain?' roared Wulfrick, bent over and out of breath.

'Can we see the men tended to first?' she replied. 'There must be empty houses, we can use them. Food, clothing, fresh weaponry. The city has a garrison now, let's settle in.'

'I'll see to it,' said Tricken. 'These your captains?'

She nodded. 'Rexel Falling Cloud, Heinrich Blood, Anya Cold Bane, Rorg the Defiler. You know Wulfrick. Everyone, this is Tricken Ice Fang, my chain-master.'

He smiled at her. 'That I am, my lady. Go remind *him* of that.'

From the stone archway and the oak door, two men approached. Tricken saluted and left with Falling Cloud and Heinrich to see to the men. Wulfrick ran forward to greet his high thain.

Alahan Teardrop was a young man, bearded and tall. He looked like his father, with black hair and wide shoulders. His eyes were blue and sad, pinched slightly into a look that approached guilt. He looked more thoughtful than Halla had expected. Next to him was the old man of Tiergarten, Brindon Crowe. Even taller than Alahan, but much thinner, clad in leather and furs, with grey hair hanging from his head and face. His expression was scornful, and exactly as she remembered.

'Halla, welcome home,' said Father Crowe. 'I am your servant, as I was your father's.'

Wulfrick ignored formality and grabbed his young thain in a rough bear-hug, lifting him off the ground and roaring, 'You do not leave my side, young Teardrop!'

'It's fucking good to see you,' replied Alahan, genuine affection in his eyes.

Wulfrick lowered his thain to the cold stone and took a knee.

'Alahan Teardrop Algeson, I pledge my life and my axe to you and your house. I pledged both to your father and I had to watch him die. I will *not* let that happen again.'

'Stand up,' replied Alahan. 'I need a friend, not an axe-master. And I don't plan to die. Not just yet.'

He noticed her for the first time. His eyes narrowed again and he patted Wulfrick on the shoulders, stepping past him to approach Halla.

'Welcome home, my lady.'

'I don't know how to address you,' she replied. 'My lord? My thain?'

'Call him Alahan,' said Brindon Crowe. 'He's no thain, not yet.'

'Am I still a Teardrop?' snapped the young man.

'Apparently,' replied the priest.

'Easy,' interrupted Wulfrick, rising to stand behind Alahan. 'The day is good, let us drink and keep it that way. Men are home, other men see a bed for the first time in a year. I see my thain, she sees her home. Arguments can wait.'

From the great hall, running like a troll, came a huge man. He wore leather and furs, but his chest was bare and covered in blue tattoos. His head was bulbous and wrapped tightly in old leather, but the strapping didn't stop flashes of grotesque skull poking through. He was a Low Kaster, but much more deformed than any of Rorg's men.

'You are the Daughter of the Wolf,' he intoned, kneeling before her.

His head pulsed like an insects' nest, pressing against the leather, but his eyes were deep and sincere.

'I am,' she replied, looking at Brindon Crowe.

'This is Timon the Butcher,' said the priest. 'He's pledged his fate to your family.'

'He's my friend,' offered Alahan.

She didn't know how to react. The berserker, the young thain, her homecoming. She wasn't ready, but she couldn't admit it. Months upon months of travelling, fighting, shouting, commanding. Now she was home. Now she was the Lady of Tiergarten.

'Halla, you've got that faraway look again,' said Wulfrick. 'We're all still here.'

'I might need a drink,' she replied. 'And I definitely need to sit down.'

'It's your hall,' offered Old Father Crowe. 'Lead the way.'

She walked slowly, not trusting her coordination. The arched stone doorway cast a shadow across her face and a gust of warm air emerged from the great hall. Her last visit to this hall had been to tell her father she planned to accompany him to Fredericksand. He'd died in the assembly; she'd gone with the dragon fleet and seen Algenon Teardrop die. The world had changed since then.

Within, a long, stone space emerged, punctured by roaring fire-pits. The Hall of Summer Wolf. Along the left wall, a dozen huge mead barrels; on the right, twenty wooden tables. It was warm, in temperature *and* atmosphere. Even empty, the hall spoke of hearth and hospitality. Though she *had* been away for a year, and may have been biased.

'Forgotten how to sit down?' asked Crowe. He looked her up and down. 'You look different, young Halla.'

'You look the same. Maybe your beard is a bit longer.'

'Well, I'm going to drink, whether you are or not.'

The Order of the Hammer priest retrieved a well-used mug and poured himself a frothy draught of mead.

'It's his seventh since this morning,' said Alahan, smiling at her.

'Are we that close?' she replied, with no smile. 'You can make jokes like we're old friends?'

'Easy,' repeated Wulfrick. 'We have warmth and we have booze. Fighting can wait.'

They sat down round the closest table. Halla, Wulfrick, Crowe and Alahan Teardrop. The berserker, Timon, perched on the next table. Standing with a grin at the main door was Earem Spider Killer, a friend of her father's.

Wulfrick got a drink for Halla and himself, and they sat in silence, the noisy slurping of Crowe the only sound. Before the nervous eye-contact between Halla and Alahan had turned into actual words, the priest had returned to the barrel for a second mug.

'Honey and water,' said Crowe, returning to his seat. 'The purest gifts the Ice Father gives us. Gloriously combined into a liquid solution to any problem. . . or we could just sit here in silence, lamenting the loss of our fathers.'

She wanted to speak some wise words, perhaps find some way of making her presence felt. For a year she'd asked questions with her axe and answered them with shouting. Commanding her battle brothers was easier than being face-to-face with the son of Algenon Teardrop. She'd assault the Bear's Mouth a second time before choosing this meeting.

'Where do we stand?' asked Alahan. 'And don't give me any troll shit.'

Wulfrick chuckled. 'We got plenty of that. A gang of berserkers and a family of trolls.'

'Yeah, Timon heard the Ice Men coming. They really don't eat men?'

Halla took a swig of mead and wiped the froth from her chin, letting the small talk flow. Wulfrick and Alahan discussed troops and the incredulity they shared over Unrahgahr and his family, and the logistics involved in keeping them away from the city. She remained quiet, sharing loaded glances with Old Father Crowe.

They had a thousand warriors, enough to give the walls of Tiergarten some strength, and the surprise of Rorg's berserkers and the trolls to make things more interesting. They talked of it in detail, but Halla didn't contribute.

'We could do with a scouting party,' said Alahan. 'We know they're close. Somewhere along the Crystal Fork. Something's delayed them and given us time.'

'We'll sort that tomorrow,' replied Wulfrick. 'Everyone needs some rest in a bed and some food wasn't salted.'

Halla stood up and walked to the barrels for a refill. They stopped talking and both looked to her. Crowe carried on drinking, noisily draining his mug.

'Are you two reacquainted?' asked the priest. 'Caught up on current events? Can my lady now get a word in?'

'It's okay, Brindon,' said Halla. 'I'm framing my sentences carefully.'

Alahan looked guilty again until a reassuring hand on the shoulder from his axe-master made him smile.

'Halla, please,' said Wulfrick. 'We all want the same thing.'

She drew the mug of mead slowly, not looking at them. Crowe did the same, leaning down next to her.

'Your hall, your city, your land,' whispered the priest.

She returned to her seat and looked at Alahan. He returned the look, but his eyes were narrow and uncertain.

'This is my hall, my city, my land. We can fight side by side and defend Tiergarten, but you're thain of Fredericksand, not Fjorlan – not yet.'

'Halla,' implored Wulfrick.

'We both want Rulag dead and Fjorlan free,' she said, not turning from Alahan. 'But I don't know this man and I won't pledge the realm of Summer Wolf for him until I do.'

* * *

It was a bed. A genuine feather bed. The pillows were plump and soft, the mattress enveloped her like an old friend. She fell into a peaceful and dreamless sleep and enjoyed every second of it. By the time she awoke, the cold breeze didn't chill her but just reminded her she was home. The draughty doors and ancient stone were a world of memories, feeling much further away than a humble year. Nostalgia and extreme fatigue were a soporific combination. She barely thought of the young thain. . . barely.

She'd have slept for a day and a night if the world let her. She'd have forgotten Fjorlan and drifted back to the warmth of her bed and the peace of oblivion. But the world *wouldn't* let her. It didn't bang on her door, or rouse her from sleep. It just scratched at the corners of her mind, reminding her that she still commanded men. Even more so, she commanded a city. Did that make her a thain?

Awake at an early hour, with cold wind and miserable thoughts for company, was a poor way to begin the day. At least the sleep had been good – while it lasted.

She paused before dressing, inspecting herself. She had many new aches and pains. A wide gash on the shoulder from the Bear's Mouth, an ugly scar on the forearm from Ro Hail, and other nicks and cuts from endless fighting and travelling. Her hands were hard and calloused, with dead skin at the tip of each finger. Two puncture marks in her chest, from ice spider fangs, had only recently healed, and Halla's body was now a painting of war and struggle where before it had been smooth and innocent. She'd never been a prize, never paid much attention to her appearance, and now her body matched her mind: scarred and tough. Her long red hair had been tied back for so long that it looked strange flowing to her shoulders, and stranger still being clean.

She dressed in fresh linen clothes and warm furs. Her armour was being repaired and her axe sharpened. For now, she looked almost like a woman. The thought made her smile. *Almost, but not entirely, like a woman.*

The corridor outside her room welcomed her with a sudden hit of freezing air. The passages and staircases of her hall were older than any in the lands of men, but they were in dire need of maintenance.

She walked quickly, hurrying towards the great hall and the ever-burning fire-pits. The warmth carried, but only to the closest chambers. The bedrooms were not close to the hall and had to make do with fireplaces. She jogged the last few steps, gathering up her fur cloak.

'Halla!' said Tricken Ice Fang, with surprise.

He sat alone in the middle of the hall, his battleaxe on the table in front of him.

'Up early or late?' she asked, standing by the nearest fire-pit and letting the fire warm her shivering limbs.

He rubbed his eyes and appeared to compose himself. 'Early, my lady. . . lots to do. I've got a lot of bastards to see to. Bastards from all over wanting food, shelter, every other fucking thing.'

She stood rubbing her hands. Morning light streamed in through the high windows, casting shadows across the mead barrels.

'They'll be settled in a day or two,' she replied. 'If Rulag is good enough to give us the time.'

He stood and puffed out his chest, his shock of bright red hair making him appear almost comical. 'It's no bother, my lady.' He averted his eyes. 'I was sorry to hear of Aleph's death. I liked him. We all did.'

It was nice to hear. Tricken had been a chain-master to her father and knew him better than most. She nodded her head in thanks and stepped closer to him.

He didn't look at her. 'Everything's changed, Halla. I feel like we're on the edge of something. . . death or something worse.'

'We are,' she replied. 'But it's still in our power. We can win – freedom, victory, a new life. Look at me, Tricken.'

He tilted his face upwards, revealing red eyes.

'We need to inspect the defences this morning. Would you do me a kindness and rouse Wulfrick and Falling Cloud?'

'Aye, my lady,' he replied, with a tentative smile.

Faces appeared from antechambers as servants heard her voice. They whispered happily to each other that their mistress had returned, but they were too nervous to enter the hall. Young men and women, their faces obscured by doors and shadows, darted across openings, asking each other if they should go about their morning duties.

'You may enter,' she shouted. 'These fires need stoking. And breakfast would be pleasant.'

She sat at the end of the hall in an old chair her father used to sit in. She mused upon the future, wanting an adviser or a spark of inspiration to appear. Her destination had always been Tiergarten, since Rulag used the krakens to sink the dragon fleet, but she'd given little thought to what happened next.

She stayed in the chair, leaning her elbows on her knees, as the Hall of Summer Wolf slowly awoke. The fires leapt, displacing the cold night air, and a hearty breakfast was laid out. Within minutes, her captains and the commanders of the city had assembled. They ate quietly, with little mingling between the groups. She stayed in the centre, eating sparingly and watching the seated battle brothers and sisters share an awkward breakfast. Some, like the Low Kasters Rorg and Timon, had enough in common to bridge the gap, but only Wulfrick and Alahan actually sat together.

When the food was done and the dishes cleared away, the defenders of Tiergarten ran out of excuses to keep to themselves and Halla took a deep breath. She stood from her father's chair and walked down the middle of the hall.

'Rulag the Betrayer will attack any day now,' she said. 'If luck is with us, we may have a week to put everything in place. We have men and trolls to marshal as effectively as possible.

Even at the most optimistic estimate, we will be outnumbered ten to one. But we have our walls.' She frowned and nodded her head. 'Tricken, Rexel, let us leave the warmth of my hall and take a look over the city. Wulfrick, you and your lord Teardrop may come too.'

She turned and flung open the huge, wooden doors, letting flecks of snow and whirls of wind break their warm repose. Most of the warriors remained seated, waiting for their instructions, while a handful lingered in her shadow, eager to have their say in the defence of Tiergarten. Halla walked across the High Hold to the edge of Kalall's Steps. The city of Summer Wolf was grey stone, built into the mountains by the ancient men of Fjorlan. In a thousand years it had never fallen to attack. But it had never had so few defenders.

She stopped by the railing, letting the sharp wind pull her hair out of her face. Tricken and Falling Cloud stood either side of her, but waited for her to speak first.

'How many warriors do we have?' she asked.

'We *had* six hundred that can fight,' replied Tricken. 'Another four or five hundred who aren't trained, but want to fight. And a load of old folks that are half-blind or can barely stand. You bring a further thousand.'

'And a dozen trolls,' added Falling Cloud. 'And we can include Rorg and his Low Kasters in that number. They're almost as unmanageable.'

'Where did you put the trolls?'

Tricken and Rexel looked at each other. They had only met the previous day, but had bonded over a shared responsibility for organizing Halla's army.

'Where are they?' she repeated.

'They buried themselves outside the city,' replied Tricken. 'Never seen anything like it. They dug massive holes with those claws of theirs and covered themselves with snow. You wouldn't even know they were there. Rorg and his men helped cover them over.'

She noticed that Timon the Butcher, Alahan's strange companion, had come out of the hall and was standing next to Wulfrick.

'You, Timon, come here,' she said, making the huge man lope over to the railing. 'You know of trolls?'

'Yes, Daughter of the Wolf,' replied the Low Kaster, his leatherbound head pulsing as he spoke. 'I saw the Ice Men go to sleep.'

'Sleep?'

He nodded, looking like an eager child delivering good news. 'They sleep in the ice, awaiting their time. They will act as they see fit. I don't think they should form part of your plans. They will have their own.'

'And you?' she asked. 'How do you fit into our plans?'

'I will do whatever you ask, Daughter of the Wolf. I no longer want to make my own decisions. I have pledged my fate to you.'

'He doesn't fight,' offered Alahan, moving to join them.

Timon nodded. 'When I gave up my fate, I gave up violence. I am a fearsome warrior and did not want to fight until told to by a more worthy spirit than my own. If I am not directed, I am too dangerous.'

'You *will* fight,' said Halla. 'You will fight to defend the freedom of Tiergarten and her people.'

The monstrous man stared at her, processing the command. Then his face split into a gummy grin. 'It is nice to have permission,' he said. 'Though I will need an axe.'

'Tricken, get someone to find him an axe,' she said, narrowing her eyes at the strange Low Kaster.

'Aye, Halla.'

Timon the Butcher scuttled away with the man summoned to take him to the armoury. Alahan didn't back away but stayed next to her, making sure he was close enough to contribute. Wulfrick was always over his shoulder, never more than a few feet from his young thain. Halla no longer knew how to talk to Wulfrick. He had been her friend and her battle brother through many dangers, but they'd returned to civilization and the rules they'd lived by for almost a year didn't apply any more.

'Let us walk,' she said, heading for Kalall's Steps.

Brindon Crowe appeared from the hall and joined them, motioning for Alahan and Wulfrick to remain behind. If they took offence, they didn't show it, but Halla knew she'd need to talk to the young thain before many more days had passed.

The highest landings were filled with people, some moving their provisions as far away from the walls as possible, while others boarded up windows and secured doors. Rulag would likely bombard the city, and those who would not be fighting were preparing their homes. Old men wore antique axes, and many children had struggled into armour far too big for them. If the streets erupted with combat, these citizens of Tiergarten would not give their lives or their possessions easily. Many of the old men had to be told not to join the defenders. They had a stubborn resilience that had no time for creaking limbs or old bones.

From their high vantage point, Falling Cloud pointed out the ballistae on the forward walls, each one freshly oiled, with crews at the ready. Tricken showed her the ranks of cloud-men stationed in Ulric's Yard, readied for any attack on the gates. Halla would be on the walls when the attack came, leading her best battle brothers, but she knew their greatest enemies would be fatigue and their small number. Rulag could leave men in reserve and send fresh waves of attack, whereas the defenders of Tiergarten would have to snatch rest while at their posts.

Out of the corner of her eye, Halla saw the glint of a blade. She turned just in time to see a young man lunging at her from out of the press of people. The blade was aimed low and her slight movement caused the knife to catch in her cloak. The attacker pulled back the blade as Falling Cloud and Tricken rushed to tackle him. She raised her hand to defend her face as the man lunged again, and the thin knife skewered her palm.

She cried out in pain and fell backwards. The man fell on top of her. A moment later, as he tried to pull his blade from her hand, the assassin was wrestled to the floor by Tricken and kicked in the stomach by Falling Cloud.

She pulled the blade free and blood pooled on the wide steps. She sat back, gritting her teeth. The man was restrained, but his angry eyes stared at her.

'Not the cleverest thing you've done, young man,' said Tricken.

Halla grasped the wound tightly, trying to stop the flow of blood. It hurt, but she'd had far worse. She stood, with the help of an offered hand from Falling Cloud, and looked down upon her would-be assassin. 'What's your name, boy? And how have I offended you so?'

'Kagan Green,' he replied. 'You are not fit to rule Tiergarten, One Eye. My father will be thain in the new era of strength.'

'Your father is Halfdan Green?' she asked. 'Where is he hiding?' His family were wealthy merchants, originally from Jarvik, and her father had hated them.

Kagan spat at her feet. Old Father Crowe assessed her hand. He frowned and pressed at the wound, almost making her yelp in pain.

'Lucky it was a small knife,' said the priest. 'You'll be fine. And as for this new era of strength, does your father no longer revere Rowanoco? Has Rulag's poison infected him so totally?'

'Rowanoco will be remade in our image,' replied Kagan Green. 'Freedom and honour have ever held us back. The Lord Bear Tamer brings only strength.'

'Not strength enough to kill me, it seems,' she said. 'If you tell me where your father and brothers are hiding, you will merely be imprisoned. I haven't got time to worry about a hostile family hiding in my city.'

He laughed, but it was tinged with fear and desperation. Around him stood half a dozen warriors, each of whom would kill him instantly at Halla's command. He closed his eyes and took a deep breath. 'Kill me, for I will tell you nothing.'

'Very well,' she replied. 'Tricken, take him to the chain-house. I'll deal with him when my hand has stopped bleeding.'

The man was roughly taken from her sight to be chained in a cell and await execution. Crowe and Falling Cloud flanked her as they made their way back to the High Hold.

'Halfdan Green has several hundred retainers,' said Crowe. 'He could cause a lot of problems. The caverns under this city are vast and we can't spare the men to do a search.'

'As long as he doesn't open the gate,' said Falling Cloud. 'Or send a better killer. We can't spare the men to guard everyone important either.'

'There'll be none of that,' said Halla. 'My life is my responsibility. If he tries again, and I'm on my own. . . well, I'll have to move faster.'

CHAPTER FIVE

TYR NANON IN THE FELL

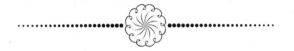

'So, I can't die?' asked Keisha.

'Not easily, no,' he replied. 'Your father survived all sorts of things that would have killed any other man.'

'I've always been quick,' she said, flexing her slender hands. 'And my eyes are sharp. Is that something to do with it too?'

He nodded. 'I imagine being a slave made it tricky to explore your talents.'

'Oh, no,' she replied with a smile. 'If anything, being a slave made them more acute. It's a world where you only have yourself. All a slave has is her body. No freedom, no possessions, just her arms, her legs and her mind.'

Nanon didn't understand slavery. Not the corporeal kind practised in Karesia. They employed flesh for labour, sex, war and general amusement, using people until their flesh gave up.

'I'm sorry,' he muttered. 'I can't imagine anything worse than the loss of freedom.'

Her smile faded and she turned her dark eyes towards him. Keisha's long, black hair was tied back and the dusky skin of her face fell into a frown. 'It'll never leave me,' she replied. 'Being a slave, I mean. But I've felt more alive in the last few days than. . . well, I don't think I've ever really felt alive. Can I be a soldier of the Long War, like you?'

'Would that make me your spiritual father?' he enquired.

She laughed, revealing girlish dimples. 'I suppose so. I never knew my real one.'

Nanon tilted his head at the girl. He had been distracted since they left Ro Weir and hadn't had the opportunity to study her. He had a basic understanding of her motivations, but her humour was a little elusive. She was Rham Jas's daughter, a dark-blood, and also a sarcastic young human girl. Clever, but irritating. Complex, but blunt.

'*I* did,' he replied. 'I know he'd be proud of you. And he'd come back and haunt me if I didn't look after you.'

'I don't believe in ghosts,' she stated. 'I don't believe in gods, monsters or magic. I just believe there are things I haven't yet seen. . . and things I can't yet explain.'

'We won't stay in the Fell for long,' he said. 'You and I have much work still to do. A dead god thinks to reassert his might. . . and a soldier of the Long War such as yourself should help me try to stop him.'

* * *

The Plains of Leith were colder than usual. The sky was muddy black and the clouds crackled, arcing flashes of lightning into the dark night. Nanon felt low, pensive, as if something was awaking or waiting to happen. The edges of the forest loomed ahead of them, beyond huge swathes of burnt tree-stumps: the result of the Hounds' bombardment.

'Where are the Karesians?' asked Keisha, running alongside him. 'You said there were loads of them – and those Dark Young.'

'Something's changed,' he replied.

'They burned a lot of trees,' she said. 'Big trees. Won't grow back for ages.'

'I know.'

'They could be further north. Are we going to run into them?'

'No, they've left,' he replied.

The young Kirin girl looked at him as they ran. 'You're being strange. Why are you being strange?'

Nanon stopped running. They were dots in the middle of an endless plain of wet grass and dark sky. 'I don't think I'm strange,' he said. 'Your father used to call me strange.'

74

She shrugged. 'This whole situation is strange – you're strange, I'm strange, that forest is strange. I get over the strangeness by asking questions. Your purpose is to answer those questions.'

'My purpose?' he asked incredulously.

'Yup. If you don't answer, I'll have to find someone else to be my spiritual father.'

He tilted his head at her. 'Don't do that.'

'And don't tilt your head at me, it means you're about to say something strange.'

'Strange is relative,' he replied.

She nodded. 'Point proven, I think. Now, do we just wander into the trees?'

'I know the way. I've been here a few times – well, many, many times.'

He resumed running, but more slowly. She followed as they picked their way through blackened tree-stumps and ash-covered ground. The earth smouldered and the smell caught the back of his throat. Hundreds upon hundreds of the trees were dead, burned to stumps. Nothing more than mounds of black, dotting the landscape. But the Hounds had left. They'd left because there were no more Dokkalfar in the Fell.

'It hurts,' he muttered.

'What does?'

'The Shadow Flame. Most have already walked in. Maybe a handful are left.'

'Explain?'

Speeding up, he entered the tree line. The forest was ghostly quiet.

'Hey! Didn't I tell you your job?' Keisha shouted after him. 'Your purpose is to answer my questions.'

'Just shut up and follow me,' he snapped, losing his patience with the human girl.

She sulked, but at least she sulked quietly.

Nanon couldn't feel his people. Only echoes and memories. The Fell Walkers had followed Vithar Loth into oblivion. Mass suicide was no way to fight the Long War, but they'd lost hope and that was a dangerous contagion. The Dokkalfar of the Fell had followed their Shadow Giant into the dust of the world. But maybe not all of them.

'Some are unsure,' he said to himself. 'They wait, trying to gain the courage to leave these lands and step into the beyond. We must reach them.'

Nanon ran into the trees, stretching his legs into a sprint. His humour had left. He had given up his feeble attempts at relating to humans. At that moment, he was an ancient Dokkalfar, a soldier of the Long War, with a purpose. He must save the few remaining forest-dwellers. If the Fell Walkers could lose hope so completely, then the world was a darker place than he thought. Was the Long War even worth fighting if he couldn't protect his own people?

'Hey, slow down,' shouted Keisha, trying to keep up.

He just ran, reaching out with his mind, trying to sense his people. Tendrils of pain and tiredness lashed through the forest, crawling up trees and weaving through the canopy. He could feel death. Death in its purest form. The loss of hope and the acceptance of oblivion. Something more maybe. . . but it was continually eclipsed by the pain.

Dokkalfar lived long lives. Some, those ancients who kept up with the passing ages and stayed sane, could live forever. Their lives were not trivial. They were not expendable. Births were rare and deaths were times of great sadness. For a whole settlement to kill themselves. . . it was unthinkable. It was the kind of pain that could kill a lesser Dokkalfar.

'I can't keep up with you, freak face!' shouted Keisha.

Nanon stopped running. He felt like he was moving through thick treacle and his head was heavy with emotion. Emotion not his own.

'I'm sorry,' he murmured. 'I'm. . . not at my best. I can feel things I can't control.'

'You look ill. Well, as ill as you *can* look. You look pretty strange anyway.'

He frowned, distracted for a moment. 'Stop calling me strange. I'm not strange, I'm just different.'

Keisha moved her eyes from Nanon to slowly gaze around the forest. She wrinkled her nose up and pouted. 'I don't like this place. The trees feel angry.'

He stood and faced her. 'You can feel that?'

She nodded.

'You shouldn't be able to. I don't think your father could.'

A shrug and a cheeky smile, and she strolled off in the direction Nanon had been running. She was frustrating and very human, but she had successfully distracted him from the pain of his people. Perhaps a human spiritual daughter wasn't really so bad.

'Keisha, wait for me. We'll walk the rest of the way.'

This seemed to please her. At least, she didn't complain.

'How far?' she asked.

'At walking pace. . . maybe an hour. If the feelings are so strong this far out, you may need to help me stand upright when we get closer.'

'My arse, you can keep yourself upright.'

She frowned, scratching at her head.

'What? Are the feelings too much?' he asked.

'Are they always so. . . well, spiky?'

'Spiky? They're not spiky.' He faced her. 'Tell me exactly what you can feel.'

Her nose wrinkled up. He could sense her confusion, the difficulty she was having putting the feelings into words. They were uncomfortable for her. But not in the way they were for Nanon. Could she feel something else?

'It's like they're. . . hidden. . . and sharp. I keep thinking they're going to cut me. Don't feel any pain really. Deception, chaos, weird stuff.'

This was worrying. Nanon couldn't feel anything of this kind.

'I don't think you're feeling the same things as me,' he replied. 'The only things I know that can cut you like that are— shit, I think I've been tricked.'

He spun round, frantically flashing his eyes through the encircling trees.

'Tricked? By who? Calm down, you're scaring me.'

'There are no survivors. I've been lured in. Lured in by something that likes to feed off Dokkalfar energy. And now there're no Dokkalfar to stop them.'

Keisha was not vulnerable to mental deception, it seemed. She'd cut through the illusion of anguished forest-dwellers and seen the Jekkan magic at its heart. The Fell Walkers were dead and something else had come to claim the energy of the Fell.

'Nanon, talk to me!' she barked at him. 'Your eyes have gone weird. And why have you drawn your sword?'

He hadn't noticed, but his katana had whistled free and he held it defensively. Paranoia and fear crept up on him. From out of nowhere he felt the chaos magic of the Jekkans.

'Good evening, knife ears,' said a sibilant voice from the darkness.

* * *

Nanon couldn't remember when he'd first encountered the Great Race of Jekka. They'd always been there, a constant, shadowy reminder of deep time. He remembered stories and he remembered fear. Long before he actually met a Jekkan, he was taught to be wary of them, to treat them as elders of the world, too powerful and chaotic to dismiss.

They'd had an empire once. Maybe 'empire' wasn't the right word; perhaps it was just a culture, a dominant civilization. They called it a caliphate. The forest-dwellers had fought them when they were already in decline. There were no tales of the heights to which they rose. Even the Dokkalfar weren't that long-lived. Maybe the Gorlan mothers knew more, but they were not given to casual conversation on the subject.

The shadows of the Great Race that remained in the world were barely a myth, forgotten lore from before the nations of men that the eldest Tyr were taught as part of their education. These shadows didn't understand order or compassion. They were creatures of instinct, of whim. Their rituals were sexual and violent. Their craft was twisted and chaotic. Their servitors were formless and alien. It took a lot to scare Nanon, but the Jekkans dug into his head in a way few other creatures – or anything – could.

It was their magic, their alien craft. They worshipped the Old Ones, creatures from before the Giants walked their paths of divinity. The Great Race had taken unknowable sorcery from these titans of deep time, and used it to build mighty cities, an infinite empire of chaos and domination. But still they had fallen. Their citadels had faded from memory, their armies defeated and their magic pushed back into the veins of the world, hiding and festering as only true power can.

But all knowledge of them was only a legend. Through such spans of deep time, truth was irrelevant. The reality was bad enough without speculation upon where they had truly come from. They had merely arrived from the void.

* * *

'This forest isn't for you,' he said, looking into darkness and shoving Keisha behind him.

There was no clearing, just endless tunnels of darkness leading between the trees. Nanon was holding both his swords, but he doubted their usefulness against Jekkans. Perhaps another form? Would a ravening lion or a monstrous griffin be more appropriate?

'Keisha!'

'Yes, Nanon?'

'I think we should run away.'

She hunkered down, narrowing her eyes and breathing quickly. 'What is it?'

'I'll tell you after we've run away,' he replied.

A deep rumbling sound rolled from the darkness, a repeating cry that cut into his brain. He recognized it as not speech or any natural sound, but the alien undulations of a primal creature too horrible to describe.

'Run!' shouted Nanon, terrified at the presence of a Jekkan servitor somewhere in the Fell.

Keisha didn't argue and they both turned and broke into a sprint, grabbing at and pulling the trees in their haste as the sound rose in volume.

'What the fuck *is* that sound?' barked Keisha.

'Just run,' he replied, leaping over a bramble bush. 'Get out of the forest and we can escape it. In here we're basically dinner.'

The darkness was total, seeming to Nanon to be some unnatural sorcery designed to disorient and confuse. There was a Jekkan here somewhere, perhaps watching them and directing its servitor.

'Which direction?' asked Keisha. 'It all looks the same.'

'Just run,' he replied, stretching his legs into even more frenetic motion.

The Kirin girl easily kept up with him, using her unnatural blood to match his pace, but they were no closer to the edge of the forest. Or maybe they were. Even with Nanon's advanced perception, the darkness meant he had no indicators of the correct direction. In fact, he feared they were lost. The vibrant life-force of the Fell was drained and his senses were dulled.

Keisha gasped, her eyes straying into the darkness all around them. 'What was that? I saw a face.' She stopped abruptly.

Nanon grabbed her arm and pulled her away. 'Whatever it was, you don't want to see it again.'

She was reluctant to move with him, staring instead into an ominous, black passage between the trees.

'Come on!' he virtually shouted, trying not to look into the gloom.

Then the creature appeared, rushing forward, displacing darkness, like an emerging sea monster breaking the water. It was taller than a horse, wider than a house, and comprised of black, iridescent bubbles, rippling into numerous eyes and tendrils. At the fore, merging into the sticky surface, was a face. A Dokkalfar appeared to have been subsumed into the mass, its face locked in an open-mouthed scream of terror. It was Tyr Dyus the Daylight

Sky, formerly a warrior of the Fell and Nanon's ally, now just a pained echo of his untimely death.

Keisha froze, blood beginning to trickle from her nostrils as the maddening beast approached. A dark-blood she may be, but her mind recoiled from the Jekkan servitor.

Nanon shoved her aside and faced the creature.

He had one chance to keep them both alive.

'I am Tyr Nanon the Shape Taker, warrior of the Heart and soldier of the Long War. Face me and die!'

He shrugged off centuries of appearing meek and unthreatening. He delved deep into his memory and grew in size, displaying his might as an ancient Dokkalfar Lord. Ten feet tall, hugely muscular with eyes of burning red. It was his natural form and a shape he hadn't taken for five hundred years.

The servitor stopped and began flapping at the air with fleshy tendrils. It was hesitant. Perhaps it had never felt raw, natural power of this magnitude.

'Back!' roared the old Tyr.

He knew he couldn't kill it, but maybe he could scare it off.

'Back!'

Keisha was on her knees, too shaken to run and too cowed to fight.

He took an enormous stride forward, fighting his fear to approach the servitor.

'I am not a mortal. You can't scare me with your chaos magic,' he bellowed. 'I am not a child or a man. Chain your pet and face me!'

It was a gamble, almost a bluff. He didn't know how far his power would stretch, whether he could withstand an assault of Jekkan magic. The servitor was mostly mindless. The creature behind it was far more dangerous.

'There is much here to consume,' said the sibilant voice, slicing the bark of a tree next to Nanon. 'Your people are dead, but their might lingers. It's intoxicating.'

He felt every single death. All of a sudden, wave upon wave

of hopeless suicides flooded over him. The Fell was a tomb, a monument. Nothing more.

'Back!' he repeated, shouting through a quivering mouth and black tears. 'Get the fuck away from me!' Now he was shrieking.

He discarded both his swords – now seeming like nothing more than large knifes – and strode forward again. He growled at the servitor, tears smearing his face and energy crackling across his fingertips.

The face of Tyr Dyus appeared again, screaming at him as the servitor reared up.

'Just die, knife ears. . . accept your fate and leave this Long War. You cannot defeat Shub-Nillurath.'

He considered it. For a moment, Nanon wanted to die. For a moment, he felt as if he had nothing left. He couldn't remember when he'd last cried. It might have been a hundred years ago. It might have been more. His head whirled as he began to lose control. His iron resolve, his mask of normality; it all cracked slightly, a fissure of doubt and anger running through his mind.

'Just die. . . fall into forever and join your lost people.'

The servitor could sense his rage. It was a primal, unintelligent creature. It couldn't reason out what it experienced; it could only feel the immense power before it. If Nanon's mind had been more focused, the beast would have killed him. As it was, his unchecked rage cowed the creature.

'You have always been afraid of your power,' said the voice. 'It makes me glad to see you like this. You should join us in the Tyranny of the Twisted Tree.'

'Stand before me,' roared Nanon. 'You are of the Great Race of Jekka, you are not an assassin who skulks in the darkness.'

The servitor retreated. Moving slowly, it rippled flat, the face disappearing, until it was nothing more than a patch of moving darkness, playing off the trees as eldritch tendrils of shadow. Was it afraid of him? Or had it been commanded away?

'Nanon,' murmured Keisha. 'I can't see you. I just see dark.'

'Stay still,' he replied. 'Stay down. Don't look.'

She moved shaking hands up to her face and covered her eyes, curling her body into a ball on the grass.

Sound disappeared from the woods. No tree rustled, no wind blew. Even Keisha's heavy breathing was silent, emerging from her mouth as nothing more than a fog of cold air. He braced himself, calming his mind but keeping the rage intact.

Then it appeared. A Jekkan, in the realms of men. Nanon had never seen one outside of their chaos-infused ruins. It looked the same – tall, slim, robed in black, with luxuriant whiskers and hooked claws. Around it, a nimbus of shimmering blue obscured any fine detail. It appeared to hover, rising several feet above the dark grass and swaying in a sensual dance. He couldn't approach it. The nimbus was woven from chaos magic and would unravel his mind if he touched it. But he could stand his ground.

'What do you want? Why did you come down from the Claws?' he asked, tensing his huge body, attempting to keep his power focused forward.

When it spoke, its words split the bark from trees and cut Nanon's arms. It took several words for the speech to settle into a form that didn't cause damage to the Fell.

'I have a new purpose,' replied the creature. 'I have been offered a place in the lands of the Twisted Tree. I will be the Tyrant of these lands. The energy of the Fell is a beautiful bonus. Enough energy to maintain my power for a thousand years. Each dead Dokkalfar leaves a wellspring of thoughts and craft. And the forest itself is majestic in its primeval power. Its energy now nourishes the new world, the Tyranny of the Twisted Tree. There will be other Tyrants, but I will be the first.'

Nanon could feel it. The Fell was like an empty glass, drained of all its rich liquid. Before him stood a bloated sack of raw energy, gorged on magic too old to truly comprehend. Like a stuffed leech, it strained at the seams, barely able to contain the power it had stolen. Power that would bring men to heel. It could not bring back its caliphate, but it could forge a realm of chaos under the branches of the Twisted Tree.

'I warned you,' said the Jekkan. 'I warned you to wait until this battle was done. I warned you that you couldn't win. Now you pay the price for your ignorant flesh.'

'I'm not ready to die.' He didn't shout or spit the words. He kept his focus and whispered them, talking to himself as much as the Jekkan.

'Death?' replied the Jekkan, making Keisha scream in pain. 'Death is insignificant. It is a process, not a result. Just a step on an infinite journey. Give yourself to me, knife ears. Become a slave to Shub-Nillurath. I will use you as a weapon against those who displease me.'

He shook his head, fighting confusion. The Jekkan didn't need to attack him; its very presence was distorting reality.

'Give yourself. . . give yourself.'

Nanon felt as if a weight pushed him down, or maybe his legs refused to keep him standing. The chaos magic of timeless aeons flowed over him, force that would annihilate a lesser being. He couldn't turn to see how his companion fared, though the Jekkan was not focused on her. Nanon didn't know what a dark-blood was capable of. Could Keisha withstand the force?

'That's it, knife ears. . . fall into a deep, deep sleep.'

Now his eyes dipped, the lids refusing to stay open. He was on his knees, his hands grasping at the dark grass. Then nothing but empty blackness and oblivion as chaos magic overwhelmed him.

* * *

Caw. Hello. Apparently my name's Corvus.

'What? I don't know. . .'

It's okay if you're confused, I think you're nearly dead. Something is consuming you.

'I can still hear, but I can't see. . . or feel.'

I'm here to help. Brytag sent me. Caw.

'The god of luck and wisdom, of the Ranen – I'm. . . not Ranen, not a man. I have no god. Not any more. . . where am I?'

Nowhere. . . not that you would understand. A moment and

a thought, a sliver of reality where death can't travel. I'm keeping
you from falling into forever.

'The Jekkan. . . it'll kill Keisha.'

It is frozen in the same instant as you. . . your friend is safe.
Friends are important. She's fallen asleep. Her mind and body are
strong. She'll be there when you return. . . if you return.

'I'm tired. I'm tired. . . I don't think I can carry on fighting.
Maybe the Jekkan's right. I've lost. . . it's not so bad, I've lived many
lives, I've seen many wondrous things. Many dark things too.'

Caw. You're a soldier of the Long War. Caw.

'Am I the only one? Cannot another warrior fight this battle?
The Jekkan said I couldn't win. Was it right?'

We don't know. The future is closed to us. But we are still
fighting nonetheless. As should you, Tyr Nanon. There are others,
fighting in their way. Hope is powerful, but not as powerful as
despair. Caw.

'I have much of one. . . and little of the other. Shub-Nillurath
almost has his Tyranny. I've lost. Just let me fall into forever.'

If you ask me a second time, I will do as you ask. Caw. But
think carefully.

'What am I fighting for? Just answer me that.'

* * *

Nanon awoke on a rocky beach with a warm breeze caressing
his face. He wore loose, grey robes of spun wool and soft leather
shoes. Above him, lancing across the blue sky, were sparkling
white pathways from horizon to horizon, through which lights
of a hundred colours flew. The sea beyond was calm, with a
gentle ripple of clear water splashing on to the rocks. It could
have been the Drow Deeps, beyond the Lands of Silence, if it
weren't for the sky.

'Is this forever?' he asked the crisp, clean air.

'Not yet,' replied a huge black raven, suddenly appearing in the
gently lapping waves. It hopped from rock to rock, splashing its
feet in the frothy water. 'But there are rules, old, old rules. I can

only pause your demise for so long – beyond that time, you must go. . . somewhere. I chose here.'

'It looks like the Drow Deeps.'

'By design, I have no doubt. A place you feel comfortable and at peace.'

'I *wish* to see the Drow Deeps?' exclaimed Nanon. 'That's interesting. I haven't thought about it for centuries.'

He took a deep lungful of soothing sea air and scanned his surroundings. Behind him, a far coastline plunged from gently rolling rocky shores to lush, green hills. There was no sign of man or Dokkalfar. No buildings, trees or civilization. Just the beach, the sea and the hills. And above, textured in constantly shifting colours, ran the white pathways.

'What are they?' he asked. 'I've never seen things of this kind.'

'Void paths,' replied Corvus, the words coming from a click of the beak and a flap of the wing, somehow forming recognizable words. 'Roads. . . of a kind. They ferry travellers from realm to realm and hall to hall. If you know the way, endless vistas of terror and wonder can be yours. But those paths are barred to you, Tyr Nanon.'

'These are the halls beyond the world,' Nanon said. *Caw*

The raven hopped next to him and he closed his eyes, drinking in the serenity of his surroundings.

'That name is misleading,' said the bird. 'The halls are merely realms of the beyond. Old and powerful. . . but still a part rather than the whole.'

'So where are we?'

'Leng,' replied Corvus. 'The very edges of Leng. It is a forgotten place where few beasts of the void deign to hunt. It's a chaotic realm, easily shaped and manipulated to be as the viewer wishes. We can be at peace here. . . for a time.'

'Why did you leave the Drow Deeps?' asked the raven, its beak twisting into a strange frown.

Nanon pulled himself into a cross-legged position and spun

round to look inland. 'I don't remember,' he replied. 'Age does not guarantee recall. Wait a moment. . . how can I even be here? I am not a creature of the void. Should my mind not unravel?'

'You underestimate your power,' replied Corvus. 'The oldest forest-dwellers are mighty in spirit and mind. . . and you are the oldest, though you do not remember. We have always liked your people.'

Nanon thought of Keisha and the frozen moment back in the Fell. The Jekkan was still there, as was the servitor. They waited in the dark forest for him to decide his own fate. But he decided their fates too. Certainly Keisha's. Much of him just wanted to rest, to give up and fall into forever, but he couldn't condemn Keisha so lightly. He may have been fighting the Long War for millennia, but the young Kirin girl had barely begun her journey. And he had made her a promise. A promise he didn't plan to break.

'Do you know how old I am?' he asked. 'I'm not sure any more. I think twelve hundred years. . . but much of that is from flashes and images that I've just pieced together. It's half-remembered.'

The raven flared its wings. 'You've forgotten many more years than you can remember.'

'And how old is Keisha? Yet to see her twentieth year.'

He looked up at the void paths as he spoke, imagining other beings in other realms, making their own life-or-death decisions for their own reasons. Absently he followed the trajectory of a single path. It began with bright sparkles of dancing red and gold, flickering from the horizon into the crisp sky. As it crossed other paths and the colours changed to blue and black, it began to fade. By the time it reached the other horizon, far out to sea, it was a grey shadow, stark against the blue water.

'Why do they fade?' he asked.

'*That* one fades because it leads to the fire halls. As belief in Jaa dies, the paths become harder to traverse. The same is true of the stone halls of the One. Belief is finding it harder and harder to reach its master.'

'So answer me this. Can this war be won?'

'There are shades of victory and defeat,' replied Corvus, appearing to realize how unhelpful he sounded.

Nanon tilted his head. 'I suddenly know how Keisha feels. Old things are invariably weird things. Straight answers are clearly a symptom of youth.'

'We cannot see the future. . . things would be a great deal easier if we could. We can only guess. We did not predict what would happen to your people in the Fell.'

Sudden sadness engulfed him. He'd been too occupied to think about his fallen brethren. He'd faced down a Jekkan servitor and travelled to the beyond, but now thought and remembrance flooded his head. A thousand Dokkalfar, maybe more. They had all walked willingly into the Shadow Flame and turned to ash. Whatever victories could be had would not bring them back.

'I think I know why I wanted to see the Drow Deeps. It's the only time I remember not being a soldier of the Long War. But I don't remember having any friends.'

'Friendships are important to you?' asked the raven.

Nanon smiled, a human expression that said a lot on the face of a forest-dweller. 'Friendships are why I stayed. . . why I wished I'd found the lands of men in my younger days. I wasted so much time in Imrya and the Nar Scopian Deeps. I spent a century at least in the Wicked Lands of Mordja. I made no friends until I came to Tor Funweir.'

'Many are dead,' observed Corvus, his beak dropping in a facsimile of anguish.

'Indeed,' answered Nanon, pushing his memory back over centuries of lost human friends. He wished he could remember each one. Some had died of old age, some at the edge of a blade or through the fog of illness and disease. Tyr Dyus, Dalian Thief Taker and Rham Jas Rami were merely the most recent additions to his memory. Perhaps Lord Bromvy and Kale Glenwood too. In fact, Nanon wasn't sure that he had any friends left in the lands of men.

Caw

Nanon stood and flexed his back. It wasn't sore, but he felt that it should be, that his encounter in the Fell should have tired him out.

His grey, woollen robes were unfamiliar. Clothing he'd not worn within memory. They were loose and allowed constant airflow, a stark change from the thick green and black fabrics he usually wore. When in the lands of men, it was wise to wear the garb of men, though he refused to forgo his segmented leather armour. Wearing it under a cloth tunic even gave him a bulk his familiar form lacked.

'Why do you hide yourself?' asked Corvus. 'Even here, where form and void are one and the same.'

'It's not conscious any more,' he replied. 'It was harder than I imagined to shrug it off in the Fell. But it's harder to make friends when your eyes are burning black and you're ten feet tall.'

'Let me show you something,' said Corvus, his beak rising in sudden excitement. 'It will help.'

'Will it bring my friends back or stop Vithar Loth leading the Fell Walkers into the Shadow Flame?'

'You know the answer to that,' replied the raven.

'Then there's nothing you could show me that would help.'

'At least one of your friends wouldn't want to be brought back. His journey continues in death.'

Nanon tilted his head. 'You mean Dalian.'

'The Karesian, yes. He has a special place in the Order of Jaa. We don't know if the Fire Giant is capable of emotion, but we think he likes the Thief Taker.'

'I am glad of this news,' said Nanon, with no smile. 'As I'm sure he is – well, as glad as the miserable old sod ever gets.'

'You speak like one friend talking of another,' said Corvus.

A slight smile. 'I always envied Rham Jas his gift of the cutting phrase. I only got the knack by mimicking him.'

'Look to the sky, Tyr Nanon. See that one of your friends endures.'

Depthless layers of light fell into his eyes as he looked. Multitudes of different realities stretched away as tightly packed bundles of wafer-thin parchment. He half-glimpsed towers, mountains, strange structures not made of stone, wood or metal, and every kind of life and death, playing out beyond the simplicity and natural laws of the physical realm.

'If I look too long, will I lose my mind?'

'You will not. Just look beyond the end of your nose and shift your perceptions.'

Nanon kept looking, allowing his ancient eyes to see further than they ever had, to let the patterns come and go without being drawn into every passing realm and hall. He felt as if he was using a new part of his brain. Maybe a new nerve in his eyes, awakened by Corvus and the World Raven.

Then his eyes paused, drifting away from the endless sky to fall upon a plateau of fire and smouldering rocks. The smell of sulphur and ash flooded his nostrils and the air was thick with powerful energy, crackling through the charged atmosphere. It was a realm, or perhaps a hall, that had drawn his eye.

'Where is this?' he asked, watching plumes of fire rise from the rocks and dance in the air.

'It is further away than the sun that warms your world,' replied Corvus, now just a voice in his head.

'Wait, I see something!' exclaimed Nanon, focusing on a jagged line of red-hot rocks. There was a break in the landscape. Just a narrow black crevice, pulsating with gouts of spewed flame.

'What is that?'

'It is a nostril,' replied Corvus, as the plateau surged into life.

The whole landscape shifted and cracked like rocky skin, turning and curving into the snout of an awesome creature. He couldn't see the rest. To look from the snout to the body would be to look through mist from one coastline to another. If its shape had recognizable form, its features were lost in the far distance of the void. Even the rest of its head was hidden behind ridges so big they'd be mountains in the physical realm.

'What is it?'

'*You* were drawn to it,' replied Corvus. 'That should tell you much.'

Nanon kept his eyes focused on the snout, processing its enormity. If he were able to step back and see its expression he imagined he'd see annoyance, as if the Giant had an itch it couldn't scratch, maybe a sadness that things were just out of reach. He felt empathy for it, though he didn't know why. The feeling just jumped into his head, suddenly there, letting him share the Giant's emotions. It was the Great Fire Giant. It was Jaa.

'Don't be sad, my friend,' he whispered. 'You have not yet lost. A being as mighty and timeless as you should not be sad. Your shade still endures.'

He could feel Dalian, taking small chunks of power from the immense creature, perhaps keeping himself alive as he searched for the exemplar. But it *was* Dalian. The Thief Taker's journey was not over, as Nanon had felt it was when he visited him in the hanging cells of Ro Weir. His god saw his worth, his great conviction and piety, and wanted to preserve it. In time, the shade would accomplish great things. As the world broke, the Shade of Dalian Thief Taker would remain to fight any battles that could still be fought. On an empty battlefield, with dead and dying men, Dalian would be there at the last, fighting against hope for his people and his god.

'Good to see you again, Karesian man. Though we'll never speak again, know that I will always be your friend.'

'It is time to leave,' said Corvus. 'If the great Fire Giant notices us, we will be subject to its will.'

'I don't want to be rude,' replied Nanon, feeling a tear well up in his eye. 'If only we were closer and could see the full majesty of the fire halls. I would slip gladly into forever with such a vista burned into my memory.'

He pulled back his perception and left the majestic fragment of Jaa to brood on his coming battles. He knew Dalian was at peace, and that knowledge gave him new steel, perhaps a reason to carry on. If the Karesian man could not be stopped by death, who was Nanon to give up at the mere sight of a Jekkan and the loss of the Fell Walkers?

CHAPTER SIX

FALLON THE GREY
IN RO CANARN

THERE WAS NO border between the realm of Wraith and the duchy of Canarn. The grass didn't change, the winds still blew and the Red Army still rode at a crawl. There was no texture to the landscape or points of interest to break the monotony.

He felt like a Red Knight again, swept up in a whirlwind of horses, canvas and cook-fires. Only the presence of Vladimir Corkoson and Al Hasim kept him centred. They found the organized rituals of the Red Knights to be amusing, and their wry humour – frequently accentuated by drink – made Fallon laugh in spite of his instincts.

Their journey, from South Warden to Ro Canarn, had been a crawl. Armies move as slowly as their slowest element, and the supply carts were like mobile taverns: they moved, but only reluctantly. Fallon had been in the vanguard, but retreated to the bulk of the army when he was tentatively asked to help with nightly watch. Word had spread about him, as it always did among knights, but nothing solid was known. They called him the Grey Knight and knew he was more than a swordsman.

'Set camp,' came the relay of shouts from each sergeant. The army was stopping within sight of the city. 'Get to your evening duties. No rest 'til we have stockade and guards on post.'

Groans and low-key insubordination. Knights of the Red could grumble like no other soldiers. It was instilled in them from their first day in armour. They never complained openly, just bickered among themselves, proclaiming all the things they'd do differently were they in charge. Fallon had been the same, until he was made captain, after which he'd realized how pointless it was to complain.

'I never thought I'd be part of a Red Army of ten thousand knights,' said Al Hasim, dismounting next to Fallon. 'Well, maybe as a prisoner.'

'Bronwyn got sick of you?' he asked.

The Karesian chuckled, stretching his back. 'My charms can't compete with a glimpse of Canarn. She's a duchess, remember.'

Fallon vaulted to the ground and groaned. Even at the back of the column, he was surrounded by armour, horses and carts. If General Frith wanted to take this army anywhere at speed, they'd need to ditch half the men, or risk starving.

Brother Lanry and Vladimir Corkoson approached from one of the wagons. They'd both complained sufficiently to not have to ride any more. The men of the Darkwald Yeomanry, languishing at the back of the army, didn't need their lord's word to follow in the wake of the Red Knights.

'My arse feels like a rutting stallion's gone at it,' said Vladimir.

'A pot of steaming tea would be pleasant,' said Brother Lanry.

Hasim and Vladimir looked at him with raised eyebrows.

'What?' exclaimed Lanry. 'We're not all interested in alcohol and. . . and women of disrepute.'

'I assure you,' said Hasim, 'my interest in women of disrepute is entirely honourable.'

Fallon began to unbuckle his saddle. 'I don't think there are many whores in Canarn,' he said. 'Not from what I remember.'

Lanry winced. 'Please, Sir Fallon, can we call them women of disrepute?'

'Rather than whores?' interjected Vladimir.

'What about beer?' asked Hasim. 'Can we still call that beer?'

Lanry flapped his hands at them, burbling something about the One.

'Don't concern yourself, Brother,' said Fallon. 'Our Karesian friend is deeply under the thrall of Duchess Bronwyn. I doubt she'll indulge his interest in whores. . . sorry, women of disrepute.'

'It's just not that kind of city,' mumbled Lanry, disappearing in the direction of the supply carts.

'I'll take tea, beer *or* a comfy bed,' said Vladimir. 'Just some warmth would be nice.'

'Don't make me laugh,' said Hasim. 'You couldn't last an hour without a bottle of wine.'

The Lord of Mud feigned offence. 'How dare you, sir! I am equally comfortable quaffing beer, ale, mead and spirits of all kinds.'

'Ever tried desert nectar?' asked the Karesian.

'Once. I believe I was robbed by a couple of young ladies shortly after my fourth glass.'

'Had you paid them?' asked Hasim.

'No,' replied Vladimir. 'One expects to be robbed in a brothel. This was just an unfortunate tavern incident. Somewhere in Weir, I think.'

'Let's try to re-create that incident in Canarn.'

'We won't be staying long,' Fallon told them. 'I don't think Canarn would welcome another Red Army.'

'I think *I* might stay,' said Hasim.

'You're welcome to ride with me, my friend,' offered the Grey Knight. 'There's a war brewing and those scimitars of yours could make a difference.'

The Karesian shook his head. 'One way or another, the Seven Sisters have claimed a lot of my friends. If I'm to keep fighting, I'd just as soon do it with my brain – and my brain is telling me to stay here. Gods never did much for me.'

'A luxury not all of us are afforded,' replied Fallon.

For a change he actually wanted to speak to Torian's shade. In fact, it was probably the first time ever. The apparition had been quiet, without so much as a terse declaration to remind Fallon he was more than just a swordsman. At this particular moment, he thought, he'd welcome some reassurance, or even basic guidance. But none came. What *did* come was darkness, and in the northern plains of Canarn it came remarkably quickly, creeping up the horizon until it was total, with barely five minutes of twilight. At least it wasn't raining.

* * *

Ro Canarn was bigger than he remembered. Compared to the ruins of Hail and the wooden stockades of South Warden, the city was huge. It had a solidity that was missing in the lands of the Free Companies. It wasn't just that it was constructed and walled in stone, or that its towers were rigid and tall, built as a direct extension of the high cliff face. No, it appeared solid because that's exactly what it was, an old stone fort built to defend an indefensible land. When it had fallen, it had fallen from the sea, an invading fleet exploiting its only real weakness. From the land, its towers and battlements were near-perfect defence – on high ground, overlooking acres of farmland. A few hundred crossbows and some artillery and it could hold indefinitely.

The city had weathered more than its share of trauma, but the tower of the World Raven still stood, defiantly watching over the lands of Canarn. William of Verellian called them a tough people who would only get tougher after the invasion. Certainly the approaching Red Army was not greeted with any joy. Only the presence of Lady Bronwyn caused the gates to open, and even then the gate guards allowed only ten riders to enter, under the sight of a dozen crossbows. The bulk of the army camped to the north, largely out of sight. The men and women of Canarn knew they were there, but weren't constantly faced with another army marching to their city under a banner of Red.

With the duchess rode Fallon, Sergeant Ohms, Al Hasim, Brother Lanry and Malaki Frith, along with four personal aides – seasoned Red Knights with peace-tied longswords. It was a varied group: some knights, some traitors, a cleric, a noblewoman and

a. . . whatever Al Hasim was. Whatever he was, he was as close to Bronwyn as their horses would allow.

Through the northern gate, they rode from thinly placed cobbles to a stone courtyard, with the inner keep rising high above them. The drawbridge, leading to the keep, brought back a hundred memories of dull weeks spent on itchy bedrolls complaining to Verellian. It had been many months since Fallon rode north from Canarn, and the city felt no more like Tor Funweir than it had then. The winding, narrow streets, leading towards the harbour, opened into courtyards and small gardens. It was more enclosed than Tiris, cleaner than Weir and far smaller than both. It had none of the enforced piety of Arnon. There were no banners of the One God, just the tower of the World Raven and a newly constructed monument of a longsword, a leaf-blade and an axe. The city appeared to be empty, or at least no-one was wandering the streets. Smoke snaked upwards from chimneys and smells of meat and fish filled his nostrils, but the population stayed indoors.

At least Bronwyn and Lanry were pleased to be home. The duchess practically leapt from her horse, while the cleric dismounted as quickly as his old bones would let him. The watchmen, men and risen men in light blue tabards, encircled them, reserving their most hostile glares for the Red general and his men.

'Thought it was a rumour,' muttered Ohms, turning his nose up at the risen men.

'Never seen them this close up,' replied Fallon.

'Are we okay with this?' asked the sergeant.

Frith clearly wasn't. He pointed at the non-humans, spluttering something about heresy. One of the watchmen, a man of rank with pale skin and wide shoulders, stepped forward and aimed his crossbow at the general.

'Got a problem, Red man?' demanded the man of Canarn. 'You're lucky we let you though the fucking gate.'

'Auker, this is Knight General Malaki Frith of the Red church,' said Brother Lanry. 'Should probably watch your manners.'

'Fuck him,' replied Auker. 'We don't answer to him. Not now – not ever.'

Frith's guards wheeled their horses threateningly, but the general kept his composure.

'Lady Bronwyn,' he said, 'your choice of watchmen aside, do we have permission to enter your city?'

She breathed in deeply, letting her eyes play over the rooftops of Canarn. Fallon imagined her mind as a whirl of emotions. The death of her brother, her return to the city. . . it must have been overwhelming.

'Auker, they are welcome,' she said softly. 'General Frith, you have no authority here and are my guest.'

Again, the knights glared and their hands clutched at their longswords. A shake of the head from Frith calmed them, but the atmosphere was tense.

'This *is* still a city of Ro,' said the general. 'I was not part of the attack on your city. That was Commander Rillion and Cardinal Mobius. Along with their enchantress. They are all dead. There is no-one left to blame.'

Bronwyn appeared to ignore him, and instead turned her back on the riders and addressed Auker. 'It's good to be home. I would like rooms prepared for these men and food provided. The army to the north will remain where they are. If they encroach, let them know they are not welcome.' She bowed her head, glancing at Lanry. 'Lord Bromvy is dead. We will have a memorial when I am settled.' She marched off, unaccompanied but for the watchmen and the Brown cleric. She reached the drawbridge and turned, locking eyes with Fallon. 'If you have a plan, Fallon of Leith, I'll be in the great hall in four hours, after I have washed and slept. And, General Frith, you and I need to establish a chain of command.'

* * *

News of Brom's death made the atmosphere even more hostile. As the sun descended and Fallon woke from two hours' sleep, he felt great empathy for the population of Canarn. He'd been pragmatic up to this point, trying to rationalize everything as a necessary consequence of humanity, but Bronwyn and her city didn't deserve the treatment they'd received.

His room – small, square and draughty – was off the great hall and he'd descended into sleep with difficulty and awoken tired, listening to crying servants and angry watchmen. The proud people of Canarn were in mourning for their duke. No-one could actually say how he'd died, only that Bronwyn knew, and they trusted her, just as she trusted the insane bird man, Fynius. This was no consolation to hundreds of grieving citizens, all wanting to know how Bromvy had died.

'He died quickly,' said Torian's shade, appearing as a ghost in the corner of the room. 'There was no pain, just peace. And his sacrifice was not in vain.'

Fallon groaned as a sharp pain enveloped his head. 'Where the fuck have you been?'

Torian bowed his head. The wall was clearly visible through him and there was little fine detail in his appearance: the cloak, the steel breastplate, the sheathed longsword. He looked like a Purple cleric, but without any texture or expression.

'Divine energy is becoming a finite resource,' said the shade. 'The One is losing his hold on the world. It takes much effort to appear to you. The barriers beyond are more solid than they have been for aeons.'

The words were scratchy and uncertain, as if heard through layers of cloth or a closed door. Fallon stood, feeling sadness flowing in waves from the shade. 'I need *something* from you. If the One God wants me for his exemplar, he *must* give me something – anything. I can't take men to war if I know we're all going to die.'

'There is a possible alliance,' replied Torian doubtfully. 'We have been contacted by the exemplar of Brytag. He wishes a council. The World Raven's power is not fading and he has offered help for the people of Ro. Perhaps power enough to train you properly, to turn you into the exemplar the One God needs.'

'Who's going to the council?' asked Fallon. 'There are other shades? Other exemplars?'

Torian looked down, as if remembering a mistake. 'Each Giant has an exemplar. Shades have not been needed for many centuries. Perhaps unwisely, they have only recently returned to the world. It appears the World Raven wishes us to coordinate to defeat the Dead God. The idea has some merit.'

Fallon smiled. 'Brytag helped free the king and South Warden, that buys him a fair bit of trust. And Fynius killed Mobius. That's a good start.'

'Perhaps,' murmured Torian, 'if the World Raven does not use all his might to empower Rowanoco, his friend. We will not accept help if we must crawl to the Ice Giant.'

'War has come to all the lands of men; perhaps old grudges should be laid aside. If there are other exemplars still fighting, they deserve that power as much as me.'

'We would sooner see the Dead God rise than act outside of our nature.'

'Well, that sounds fucking stupid,' said Fallon. 'Grovel, beg, plead, whatever you need to do to save Tor Funweir. If I might die and get men killed, the least you can do is show a little humility when offered help.'

Torian flared, momentarily becoming more visible, as if his power rose when he was angered. Fallon balked, thinking he'd gone too far and insulted his god. But, slowly, the flared anger dissipated and Torian smiled. 'We chose wisely,' said the shade. 'You will be a fine leader for the Knights of the Grey.'

'I'm to choose others?'

'You are to knight those you think worthy. An order of the Grey must be formed. Until I return, you must act without me. Muster what forces you can and ride south. Test your skills whenever you can, for when I return, the One God will have need of your sword arm. A shadow will fall on the battlefield and it must be met with divine strength.'

'Picking a fight won't end this.'

'Depends which fight you pick,' replied the shade. 'If that is too vague, a new king has been crowned and you must reach him.'

'Xander Tiris,' replied Fallon. 'A fine general, but a king? What do the Purple think of that?'

'He was crowned by a Brown cardinal; there are no living men of the Purple who outrank him. We have blessed the coronation.'

'Perhaps a former Red Knight, crowned by a cleric of poverty, is exactly what we need. Please hurry back – and accept any help the World Raven offers.'

* * *

A dozen men of Ro, a Karesian, a duchess, a lot of swords and a smell of dirt and sweat. Fallon was the last to enter the antechamber and it was packed practically to the wooden-vaulted ceiling with people. Lady Bronwyn, looking flushed, was seated at the head of the oblong table, flanked by guardsmen who were armed and on edge, with Brother Lanry and Hasim seated next to her. There was a gap the size of three chairs on either side of the table and the visitors clustered in the other half of the room, with General Frith, also looking flushed, facing Duchess Bronwyn.

'You've been arguing,' said Fallon, sitting down between the two groups.

'Just a disagreement,' replied Brother Lanry. 'My lady is concerned about welcoming another Red Army to Canarn. Given the way she was chased out of this very city.'

'No-one round this table was to blame, Lady Bronwyn,' said Fallon. 'Mobius, Rillion, the king. . . they're all dead. If you want to blame someone, blame the Karesian witches that started this.'

She kept her composure, but emotion hid behind her eyes. 'So much has changed,' she said. 'My family have been consumed by this war. I've been blaming the Red Knights since you and Verellian chased me to Hail.'

'I'm sorry for any part I played in your sadness,' replied Fallon. 'But you know the truth now – Canarn was sacked and the Freelands invaded by men enthralled to the Seven Sisters and their dead god. We're merely the lucky ones, we survived. But there is still a war to fight in Tor Funweir.'

'You have a plan, Sir Fallon?' asked General Frith. 'I have an army but no enemy to fight and no king to follow.'

'I'm riding for Weir, to meet King Alexander Tiris,' said Fallon, making everyone look at him. 'My lord Frith, you should follow. Send riders after me and the bulk of the army as fast as they can move. Muster in Tiris.'

'King Alexander?' grunted Frith. 'How did you come by this information?'

'I know the One God blessed the coronation,' said Fallon. 'And I know the armies of Tor Funweir need help.'

'We were months arriving,' said Frith. 'It'll take months to get everyone back to Ro Tiris. There aren't enough ships.'

'As fast as you can,' replied Fallon. 'If you can't ride to our aid, you can save what is left.'

'This is a lot to accept, even from you,' said the Red general.

Fallon *did* sympathize. The general was a solid, pragmatic man, steeped in ceremony and averse to change. He was a true servant of the One, a man who genuinely didn't think that Tor Funweir could fall.

'I don't know what power exists in my blood,' said the Grey Knight, 'but I know we might lose. Your men may have to take off their Red tabards and become protectors. Ten thousand Knights of the Red won't dent all the Hounds of Karesia, but they might save the people of Ro.'

Frith hung his head. 'I need time to think on this, Sir Fallon. It is difficult to realize that you have been made a fool of. We were led away so Tor Funweir could burn.'

Brother Lanry coughed politely. He leant forwards and smacked his wrinkled lips together into a smile. 'Sorry for the impertinence, but I believe I can adequately cross the battle lines.' He drew a bent finger across the middle of the table. 'The One God has given us an exemplar, Maliki, and we should support any action he decides.'

'Got *my* loyalty,' grunted Sergeant Ohms, wrinkling up his grizzled face.

'And mine,' said Vladimir Corkoson.

Fallon didn't mean to, but he leant back and his shoulders appeared to swell, a subtle mantle of white emanating from his head. It wasn't conscious. If he'd had the choice, he'd have preferred to appear like the rest of them. As it was, he was now apart, a creature of power among mortal men. It was Torian's parting gift to him, perhaps the last shred of his power, used to display might to any doubters in the small antechamber.

Lady Bronwyn and General Frith were stunned. The Red Knights, at their ease in the doorway, looked in awe, and Brother Lanry placed his hands together in prayer.

'General, please believe that I never wanted this. I was more surprised than you are now. And it is not a glamorous endeavour. . . to be exemplar. To serve a god that you don't understand.'

Lanry stopped praying and chuckled. 'I don't think understanding is a requirement.'

'Then, a luxury I am not afforded.'

'I will do as you ask,' spluttered Frith. 'As the One God bids me. I will remain Cardinal of the Red until I am no longer needed.'

The white light faded and Fallon tried to smile, as much for his own benefit as for those who were looking. 'Thank you, General Frith. We will leave Lady Bronwyn to her city, a city that must be kept strong, for if Tor Funweir falls, Canarn will be a bastion of refuge.'

* * *

The new gaoler of Canarn was a cheerful man with a chubby face and huge arms. He looked after twelve cells and one prisoner, and he did so while sipping from a cup of wine and telling bawdy jokes. Fallon liked him, but was getting sick of waiting.

'Sorry, milord, but the duke needs to okay every visitor.'

'Duchess,' corrected the Grey Knight. 'And I understand. I just wish she'd hurry up.'

'She's got a lot to ponder, that one,' replied the gaoler. 'Letting you visit the crippled red man ain't that important.'

'Crippled? He's lost fingers, not legs.'

He shrugged. 'I know a few game girls that would argue on that point – if ya know what I mean?' He grinned and his chin wrinkled up.

'I was a knight up until recently,' replied Fallon. 'My knowledge of *game girls* is minimal.'

'Truly? Strapping young lad like you?' His grin remained as he inspected the tall swordsman. Fallon frowned, feeling suddenly aware of his piecemeal armour and unwashed face. 'Actually, maybe not,' said the gaoler eventually. 'Ladies like a man with a sense of humour. You're just a grim slice of muscle.'

Fallon laughed. A grim slice of muscle indeed.

From the moss-covered stone steps leading to the keep, Auker appeared. The sullen guardsman was alone and noisily munching on a handful of grapes. 'Evening,' he grumbled, spitting out a pip. 'Lady Bronwyn has decided that she doesn't give a shit if you want to compare tales of woe with William of Verellian. She's busy resupplying the Red Army and mustering any ship she can beg, borrow or steal.'

The dungeons of the city were as modest as its crime rate. A small, coastal city with ample food and space for all. There was little need to steal. He imagined the cells spent much of their time empty, with only occasional Ranen priests or turncoat Red Knights in residence. As a result, the space was not comfortable or warm.

'You know I've been listening to you whinge at the gaoler for half an hour?' said a deep, gravelly voice. 'I've not lost my ears.'

'Should have said something,' Fallon replied, coming to a stop in front of a smiling mess of dirt and stained red clothing.

'You should have bought me some fucking food,' said William of Verellian, sitting up in his cell.

The old knight looked the same. He was dirty and thin, but his sharp face hadn't changed. He still looked like a bird of prey, even with a few months' growth of hair.

'Never seen you with hair,' said Fallon.

'Do you know, the good people of Canarn don't seem to care about my appearance.'

They both chuckled and Verellian rose, offering his crippled right hand through the cell bars. Fallon grasped it warmly and the two old friends shared a moment of laughter. It had been a long time and much had changed, but they would always be brothers.

'Still alive,' they said in unison. It was a simple declaration, but one they'd shared a hundred times since they packed their saddlebags and left the barracks at Ro Arnon. For a Red Knight it was the most to be hoped for.

'Lots to say,' said Fallon. 'Wish we had some wine.'

The old knight captain raised his eyebrows. 'Last we spoke you still wore Red. You hadn't yet uncorked – or turned your cloak.'

'Does information not reach the dungeons?' quipped the Grey Knight.

'I heard rumours. . . something about South Warden, but nothing clear. Fallon of Leith turned his back on the knights. . . may my eyes see the halls beyond before they see such a thing again.' He looked his old lieutenant up and down. 'Light armour, no helmet – where's *your* sword? That hunk of iron's a piece of shit, soldier.'

'Some Red Knight has it, I think,' replied Fallon. 'That pig-fucker Jakan took it. He's dead by the way.'

'You?' asked Verellian with a smile.

Fallon nodded. 'He was good. . . but arrogant.'

Verellian breathed in deeply, a look of quiet contentment on his sharp face. 'It's good to see you, Fallon.'

Catching up took time. The gaoler wouldn't open the cell, but he at least provided a chair. A bottle of cheap red wine lubricated their conversation and an hour came and went in jovial discourse. At least it was jovial until Fallon said he was the exemplar of the One and intended to ride for the south. Even Verellian, his oldest friend, thought him insane.

'You're mad,' said the old knight.

'I don't think so,' he replied. 'I think I'm important. I never wanted to be important, but someone in the halls beyond disagrees.'

'Do you want me to come with you?' asked Verellian. 'Even with three fingers I'm worth something in a fight.'

'But I'm mad.'

William smirked, looking like a young man for a second. 'You're my friend, and a madman needs friends. I was never as good as you,' he said, holding up his maimed hand. 'Now I'm not as good as an average knight. But I'm still better than any fucking Hound.'

'There's something more,' said Fallon. 'I'm to found a new order – the Knights of the Grey. I'd like you to join. We're to stand for honour and you're the most honourable man I know.'

'High praise, coming from you,' replied William. 'And will Knights of the Grey be able to drink? Or are we going to be humourless bastards like the Purple?'

Fallon wanted to make some kind of quip back, but he felt protective over his new order of knights and didn't want to begin in humour. 'I'll know more soon,' he replied, not divulging the existence of Torian's shade. 'But we will have to rebuild. The One God has put his faith in us. I don't think nobility, war, poverty, death or any of his aspects are what he wants any more. He's chosen to make honour his highest aspect, and he's chosen me to represent it. So, I don't care if you drink.'

'Fuck a pig, Fallon,' snapped Verellian. 'Why is this happening now? Why not twenty years from now when I'm warm and fat in my own keep? The world could end then and I'd raise a glass to its passing.'

'Don't you want to be Sir William of Verellian again? And follow honour rather than war?' He looked at the battered old soldier. 'Have you held a sword since Jakan beat the shit out of you?'

'Nope. And before that I hadn't held one since Captain Horrock beat the shit out of me in Hail.'

'You obviously need the practice,' said Fallon. 'There'll be plenty of Hounds to kill where we're going. Make a difference from killing Ranen.'

Verellian frowned. 'The blood always comes out the same colour.'

They looked at each other. The old knight tried to stare him down, his gaze conveying doubt and pride in equal measure. He was a clever man, and Fallon had no doubt that his head would be whirling with questions and speculation, though his hawk-like face was intense and still.

* * *

On the high battlements of Canarn, with a harsh sea breeze whipping across the cobbles, Fallon looked at the men who would be the first Knights of the Grey. They would be the first to set sail from the city and the first to strike at the enemy. They would be mounted on fresh horses, armed with sharpened blades and supplied with food and water. Two fast sloops would take them to Tiris and from there they would ride hard to catch up to King Alexander. Though an army would follow, they knew that much rested on their shoulders.

He had selected two hundred men, mostly Red Knights, with a scattering of yeomanry, but each chosen for his honourable reputation and skill with the blade. Frith had recommended many of them, insisting that Fallon take only his best knights.

William of Verellian and Ohms of the Bridge had been Fallon's own choice, but one he knew he wouldn't regret.

'We are the last of the old order and the first of the new,' he said reverentially. 'We are Knights of the Grey.'

Fallon drew his sword and dropped the blade on to William's armoured shoulders, knighting him for the second time. 'I name you Sir William of Verellian, Knight of the Grey and protector of Tor Funweir. You follow the aspect of honour.'

Verellian closed his eyes as the blade touched each of his shoulders. A sliver of glowing light left the blade and caressed his sharp features, flowing into his extremities and disappearing. He was the second Grey Knight and stood as if he knew what it meant, his hawk face locked into an expression of certainty. 'To the end,' he said, offering Fallon his hand.

They grasped forearms. The old knight was revitalized, much as he would have been when he first took the Red. The One God, through his exemplar, had blessed him with a new office, though his true power was dependent on Torian's shade returning.

Fallon repeated the ritual for Ohms and then Lucius of the Falls, a young knight captain, and then the rest of his company, letting the One God bless each of them with a new strength of purpose as a Knight of the Grey. There were only two hundred of them, making them the second smallest order of churchmen in Tor Funweir after the Black clerics, but they would one day be the largest. It was as if the kaleidoscope of colours before their god's eyes had parted and allowed honour to return.

CHAPTER SEVEN

UTHA THE GHOST IN ORON KAA

HE OPENED HIS eyes and saw blue sky and a burning orb of yellow. Was it real? Or some new part of his journey through the Jekkan causeway? It played tricks on him. Some strange battle of wits, designed to disorient and confuse. The ancient magic could not harm him directly, so it sought to lead him astray or cause him to become lost. None of it had worked. He'd followed the story across a hundred pillars and forced the chaotic magic to show him the way out.

He rubbed his eyes and looked again. The sky was still there, as was the blazing sun. Utha hadn't seen daylight for. . . he didn't know how long. Weeks certainly, perhaps longer. Was this still Karesia? Had he found Oron Kaa at the edge of the world? He didn't remember leaving the causeway or falling asleep.

Looking down, he reassured himself that he was still whole. Two arms, two legs, everything where it was supposed to be. His sword and mace were still in his belt, his boots were still tied and a cough confirmed he still had his voice. His fingertips crackled with sensitivity as he clenched his fists in the sand.

Still he felt the pull south. Something was drawing him there. The staircase, the labyrinth and the Guardian. Were they in Oron Kaa, or was it just another step on the road? Voon had told him that it was the last place from where a mortal ascended to the halls beyond. Even to Utha this was an impossible thing to comprehend. It was a riddle, a mystery, a tangle of eternity he could never unravel. He constantly tried. In quiet moments and hours of sleep, it was all his mind gave him. More questions

109

and no answers. Who was he? Why did the Shadow Giant still call to him? The god was dead, but he was still dreaming. *Am I just a part of his dream?*

First things first, get up and get moving.

There was no road, no signs of civilization, just the endless sky and the featureless desert. At the edge of his vision, shimmering on the southern horizon, mountains formed a jagged line. He imagined he was the only traveller within a thousand leagues.

He stood up. His breathing was steady and he wasn't tired. His head was clear and his limbs felt strong. The power he'd stolen from the Jekkans was still with him. It would take time to understand exactly how he had changed, but, for now, Utha took a deep breath and started to walk towards the mountains.

* * *

Hours sped past and he started to see things, emerging out of the distorted horizon. Figures moved across his vision, formed from rippling sand and swaying mountains. They danced left and right as wispy, rolling forms, disappearing before he could focus on them.

He stopped walking as a figure stopped moving. It formed like the others, flowing from sand and rock, but it didn't disappear. Stranger still, it slowly became red in colour. Not vibrant, but bright enough to stand out.

He rubbed his eyes again and focused. He was sure of what he was seeing. This was not the Jekkan causeway. This was the land of men and he was seeing a figure moving towards him. The figure was robed in dull red, flowing from head to toe. The wispy fabric was tattered and torn and the figure glided above the desert floor, a sprite of colour and texture amidst grey nothingness. A strange buzzing sound accompanied the creature and a spidery tingle travelled up his spine.

The figure stopped a distance away. There were no discernible features and its limbs were formed of opaque cloud.

'I am the Queen in Red.' The voice was in his head. It was a woman's voice, old and cracked. 'It is time to take off your mask.'

'I am Utha the Ghost, last Old Blood of the Shadow Giants. And I wear no mask.'

'Then I welcome you to Oron Kaa,' said the red figure. 'You will be treated with reverence. You will sample delights, both human and godly. You will forget your life through pleasure and pain. Join your friend, the exemplar.'

Voon! At least the Karesian had found his way out of the causeway.

He felt enchantment. It was subtle and strong, coming from an ancient wellspring of power that he didn't understand. But it didn't affect him.

'I don't think so,' he replied. 'Lead me to Oron Kaa; release Voon.'

The figure moved closer. Red rags cocooned it, wrapped tightly around the torso and face, and yet something maddening, more maddening than the buzzing, shone from behind the dull fabric. Utha was difficult to scare, especially so now, but he took an involuntary step backwards all the same.

'What are you?' he asked, looking for something tangible or human in the floating apparition.

'I am the beginning and the end. I am the Tyrant of Oron Kaa. I am the mother of insects and the daughter of Shub-Nillurath.'

'You're the matron mother,' he said. 'You're just an old woman.'

The red figure tried again to enchant him. It was like a war-hammer to the head, a huge thump of violent pressure pushing into his mind. He winced and pulled himself upright.

'Give yourself to me.'

'Didn't you hear me?' he growled. 'I'm Utha the Ghost, last Old Blood of the Shadow Giants.'

He pushed forward, a surge of energy emanating from his outstretched arms. It began in his mind – just a thought to make the creature disappear – but it left his body as a pulse of raw force, smashing into the Queen in Red and overwhelming her.

111

The enchantment stopped and the apparition recoiled, its red robes shrinking into a tight mass.

He kept his focus, pushing more and more force at the creature. It was as if he'd discovered a new sense, a new way of interacting with the world.

And then it was gone.

* * *

The minaret was visible over the line of saw-toothed mountain peaks. It bulged from a narrow tower and was topped with a needle-like spire, pointing upwards into the shimmering sky. Was it a town or just an old monument? Glinting sections of reflective glass blinded him every few steps, frustratingly close.

Utha was walking through foothills, imagining there would be a mountain pass somewhere. There was no sign of the sea or a road. No civilization at all beyond the strange minaret. It felt like the edge of the world. The mountains were now lower, but no less impassable. There were caves – some tiny, others twice as tall as him – but all appeared empty. Even the vegetation was minimal.

He trudged onwards. The mountains got lower and lower until the minaret was fully visible and maddeningly close. It was red and gold, and of a construction he'd never before seen. Different from the architecture of Kessia and a world away from the grey stone of Tor Funweir. Its surface was covered in shining squares of coloured glass, alternating red and gold. Twisted forms weaved round the windowless structure, seemingly narrow tubes connecting the levels.

Then a break in the mountains appeared and he stopped walking. Through a narrow fissure in the rock face, Utha spied low buildings and a craggy coastline. The pathway appeared to be a natural break in the landscape.

'There you are,' he muttered.

He slowly made his way through the dusty fissure. Walls of sheer stone rose either side of him, creating a dusky, twilight glow.

The buildings ahead were squat and domed, like smaller versions of the minaret, including more twisted tubes. As he moved along the fissure, the settlement took shape. It was larger than it had first appeared. The motionless sea claimed a small portion of the vista and an empty harbour was built on to the low rocks. He wouldn't call it a town; maybe a village or a large monastery. The smaller domes were arrayed round the minaret in a tight, organized circle. It looked like no town of men he'd seen. The streets were too narrow; most buildings had no entrances; only the thin tubes connected the structures. The place made his spine tingle.

He reached the end of the fissure and stood in awe. The mountainside had been carved into grotesque images. On either side of him, rising fifty feet or more, were Dark Young, hewn out of the rock face. They flanked the entrance to Oron Kaa and blocked out the rising moonlight. The branches were thick tendrils of chiselled stone, snaking into the air. The detail was maddeningly accurate. Each line and curve of the bark was skilfully etched out of rock. If they'd been painted black, they'd be near indistinguishable from the real thing.

Voon was in here somewhere, as was the matron mother. He'd worry about the staircase, the labyrinth and the Guardian after he'd rescued the exemplar.

With the looming statues behind him, Utha stepped on to a paved street. It was one of many, all narrow and leading directly to the minaret. Now that he was closer, the detail made him pause – strange symbols and eldritch patterns, weaving colour into each building and tube. Amber, glass, crystal, all intricately embedded into the surface of Oron Kaa.

There was something else. As he squeezed past domes and inched towards the minaret, Utha felt a sensation like pressure building. It began as a hum, getting louder as he moved forward. There was power here. Real power. Not the parlour tricks of the White clerics or the enchantment of the Seven Sisters. It was more, deeper, older.

Towards the centre of the settlement, where the spire thrust upwards, a shape darted across his vision. Utha froze, pressed against a domed building, and drew his sword. The blade felt somehow inadequate.

'Show yourself,' he snapped, stepping cautiously towards the central minaret.

It loomed over him now, rising from a narrow base to a bulging blob of coloured glass and amber with strangely angled tubes emerging like arteries. It was huge, but had no windows or identifiable entrance.

The figure moved again, slower this time, stopping in front of him. It was Voon.

The Karesian was pale and his eyes were hollow. He wore the same robes, with his spear, Zarzenfang, strapped across his back, but his hands shook. The humming noise accompanied him; dull and sonorous, it came from all directions at once.

'Voon? Are you unhurt?'

The exemplar was unfocused. He looked right through Utha, his face twitching as he opened his mouth to speak.

'You must come with me,' said Voon, his voice dry and croaky with a barely audible buzz behind his words.

Utha squeezed through the last narrow gap and entered the open space beneath the minaret.

'You must come with me,' repeated the Karesian.

Utha lowered his sword. The open space was large, but languished in the shadow of the building above. The moonlight barely penetrated, but still there was a strange red glow.

'What's happened to you?'

Voon didn't answer. There was no life in his eyes. When he spoke there had been no texture to his words.

Utha was surprised to see more figures appearing silently from between the buildings. A dozen or more figures, mostly Karesians but also two Kirin, all with the same dead eyes. They wore robes of black with red embroidery.

'You must come with us,' they said in unison.

He spun round, sizing up those encircling him. None were armed.

'You try and coerce me and I'll make a hell of a mess before you succeed. The threat of twelve men doesn't intimidate me like it used to.'

'Calm yourself,' replied a female voice.

Utha looked upward. From an opening, ten feet or more above the ground, stood an old woman. She wore red and she gestured to him with cracked and wrinkled fingers. The opening had not been there a moment before. It was halfway up the spire, just beneath the minaret.

The matron mother could have been a hundred years old. Her skin was tight and deeply veined.

'You have no respect,' rasped the old woman. 'You are a primitive piece of flesh, walking in the Footstep of the Forest Giant. You are ignorant of how powerless you are here.'

At her words, the blank-faced acolytes closed in. Utha raised his longsword and gritted his teeth, preparing to kill anyone who got too close.

'Is this the best you can do?' he asked the matron mother. 'You were the Queen in Red a few hours ago. Now you're just a frail old woman with empty people doing your bidding.'

The humming got louder. From every tube and every building, the sound echoed.

'This is no city of men,' said Utha in a whisper.

Each of the dozen figures now opened their mouths wide and a cacophony of buzzing filled the air. Utha winced as the sound became high-pitched and painful. Their jaws cracked slightly as something tried to squeeze its way out of each mouth. He looked at Voon, and saw two antennae snake their way out of the Karesian's mouth. Then two large eyes and a segmented body. Insects the size of large birds emerged from every mouth. They fluttered on three pairs of wings, wriggling their grotesque, furry bodies into the air. Each creature had a curved sting on its abdomen, mottled in shades of green and red. They surrounded him.

'Rejoice, Old Blood,' said the matron mother. 'Death is not the end. You are welcome in the Tyranny of the Twisted Tree.'

The torpid men remained still and lifeless as the insects left them, scratching at the air around him. Utha raised his sword with a guttural growl.

More of the creatures appeared from the domed buildings, buzzing out of openings and filling the air. The matron mother held her arms wide and laughed, a whip-crack cackle, edged with insanity.

'Rejoice! Rejoice!'

'I am Utha the Shadow!' he roared.

He tried to focus his mind, to push them away, but the buzzing of the swarm drove him to his knees. He could feel their hairy bodies against his skin and their fibrous wings beating against his face.

He screamed as the insects stung, their barbed abdomens piercing him in the chest, neck and legs. As his screaming trailed off, an insect began to force its way into his mouth.

* * *

Shub-Nillurath, the Dead God, the Forest Giant of pleasure and blood. Utha now understood what had driven Jaa, the One and Rowanoco to war against him. They had allied to stop him returning to the world of men. The Forest Giant was losing his ages-long war with Jaa and had tried to cheat. But once a creature has truly ascended, he can never go back. For a creature of such might to re-enter the world would mean the destruction of all. It would have ended the Long War. The other Giants could not allow it. The One found him, Rowanoco fought him and Jaa stole his power. But Jaa was greedy. The Fire Giant of Karesia used the divine energy he'd stolen to empower his followers and he let the echo of Shub-Nillurath fester at the corners of his land. He never cut down the darkwood trees, he never questioned the loyalty of the Seven Sisters and his eyes did not see the Builders of Oron Kaa. His hubris would rule the fate of all.

It was Utha's last thought.

* * *

'Awaken.'

He turned in his bed and looked at his mistress. She wore a red robe and fingered a grotesque token that lay around her wrinkled neck. It was a bulbous spider with a golden abdomen and spindly legs.

'Yes, matron mother,' he replied.

'You have slept long enough. The Builder is happy with the merging.'

'I am complete?' he asked.

The old woman flashed a euphoric smile, licking her cracked lips.

'You are a new being, part Old Blood, part Builder. You will be a revered servant of Shub-Nillurath. Perhaps even a Tyrant one day.'

She'd visited him every day since he was born. Each day they had spoken of eternity and the empire to come. The Tyranny of the Twisted Tree was already growing and he knew he had an honoured place in it. Many beings had already given their might to the new world, and many more would soon kneel at the altar of pleasure and blood.

'I am ready, matron mother. I no longer feel like two beings. I am one, though I have no name.'

'That will come later. For now, follow me.'

He was eager to learn more, to see the world he had heard so much about. One day, he would see the heretical men of Ro and Ranen, but for now Oron Kaa was his home. It was the city of insects, the footprint of the Forest Giant, and the holiest place on earth. The Builders of Oron Kaa had maintained it for their master, showing the patience of centuries as they feigned allegiance to Jaa.

The minaret was segmented into regular chambers, each the same size. The walls, mottled in dark crystals of blue and black, reflected no light. Orbs of yellow shone in each chamber, but the rest of the minaret was in perpetual twilight. It was impossible to determine the time of day until the Builders returned, when he'd know it was evening. He'd only seen the world, inside and out, in twilight.

'How are the girls?' he asked.

'Only two needed flaying today. The rest are progressing nicely,' replied the matron mother.

They walked through a curtain of darkness and into the girls' residence. Sitting round an oval table, wearing bloody rags, were ten identical young women.

'Where do they come from?' he asked, glaring at the potential enchantresses. They didn't look up from their soup. Each girl had been tortured into compliance and owed their life to the lord of pleasure and blood.

'We claim them from towns and cities. It has ever been the way that we can take whoever we wish. I cut and twist their faces, until they look as they should. They are flayed and healed and flayed again, helping them to reach a transcendent state and catch the notice of our lord. If he favours them, they are given the power of the Seven Sisters. For centuries it was thought that they caught the notice of Jaa – until I revealed the truth.'

'Your patience is admirable, matron mother. It must have sickened you to serve the Fire Giant.'

She glared at him. Her mouth was wide and her lips thin, slightly parted, revealing teeth that looked like gravestones. 'I did what was necessary. Shub-Nillurath needed much time to regain his strength. I told the Seven Sisters only what they needed to know. . . but when I told them the truth, they rejoiced. When they left Oron Kaa and forgot the Builders, they moved through the lands of men with a new purpose – to conquer the lands of men in the name of the Twisted Tree.'

Around the girls moved servants, each one a mindless shell for a Builder. They were taken from ships or kidnapped from trade caravans, and given the gift of compliance. They cared for the girls and served as necessary, giving their bodies until they could no longer serve. The Builders lived long lives and could merge with hundreds of different mortals before they themselves entered their death cycle, to be reborn from a black chrysalis.

His merging had been different. The Builders had fought to merge with the white-skinned creature, knowing that great power dwelt within. A demi-god with no power of belief, a titan cowed. A rare treat for the slaves of Shub-Nillurath. The creature was powerful enough to survive the joining with an intact mind. Mortal creatures could not keep their wits when merged with a Builder. The Old Blood was different. The creature he had become, the joining of Old Blood and Builder, was unique. In time, he would be the mightiest of beings. For now, he had much to learn.

'I wish to see the footprint, matron mother. I wish to feel the power of our lord.'

'Of course,' crackled the bent old woman, a rippling smirk flowing over her face.

They left the young girls and moved to the edge of the minaret. The dark glass walls were cold to the touch and cast dull, fractured reflections over his face. He didn't like his white skin or his pink eyes. Bright light made his face itch and his eyes sting. The Old Blood had been deformed. A hereditary defect.

An opening appeared in the mottled glass, and a platform rose to meet them. He stepped on to it with his mistress and saw the sun for the first time. It was hotter than he had expected, but his pale skin did not blister as it should have. The Old Blood had strength, such strength. The creature had barely begun to recognize who or what he truly was. Exploring his power would be wonderful.

'The mountains hide the true majesty of Oron Kaa,' said the matron mother. 'They are merely the ruins of an ancient altar. Flesh and strength turned long ago to stone.'

The platform took them to ground level and the old woman led him away from the minaret. The city of insects was empty. A hundred globed buildings in a circle round the minaret, but no inhabitants. Mountains ringed the settlement, giving only a small portion of land to the sea and a bare harbour. It was the edge of the world, a place the servants of the Twisted Tree could live in peace, away from the heresies of men.

They'd suffered much, been persecuted, hunted, killed – and ultimately forgotten. It was only the great wisdom of the matron mother and the loyalty of the Builders that had saved them from extinction. She'd known the truth, that Jaa had stripped power from the greatest of Giants. He'd gifted his faithful with stolen energy, energy they could now bask in, as the truth gave them might. She had rebuilt his altars, woken his Dark Young and decried the treacherous Fire Giant. Shub-Nillurath infused her being, seeping back into the world as a beautiful virus of pleasure and pain.

'Come with me,' she demanded, striding away despite her bent back and wrinkled frame. 'The caverns are a distance.'

* * *

The mountains had not always been mountains. They did not rise from the earth over the passage of millennia. They were formed from broken pieces of a form too colossal to imagine. Under the abbey, through layers of black rock, they walked deep into the earth, down tunnels hewn by the Builders of Oron Kaa. Few creatures ventured to the Footstep of the Forest Giant. Few creatures could remain sane when viewing a spectre of true divinity. He was different. He could feel the power calling to him, dragging him further from the lands of men, and deeper into his destiny. Only the matron mother was strong enough to accompany him, to join him as the divine power began to wash over them.

'It is close now,' he said, striding down rough-hewn rocky steps, lit only by torch-light. 'It calls to me. I feel it flow into the world. Tell me the story, my mistress.'

'The cowardly Giants did their work well,' grunted the old woman. 'While Rowanoco fought our lord, the One touched its mind to a tentacle, turning a limb into broken stone and creating the mountains. We walk within the fossilized remains of that limb. It took the Builders centuries to unearth the tear, and centuries more to rebuild Oron Kaa, all the time fawning over the Fire Giant. The arrogant god accepted their prayers, until we revealed ourselves and severed his power. Every scrap of energy Jaa gave into the world came from Shub-Nillurath, so he was powerless to stop us.'

At the bottom of the stairs, a swarm of Builders clustered on the bare stone, crawling over each other, a vibrating mass of hair and legs. Beyond them, sending waves of green light across the buzzing insects, was a tear in reality, a hole to the halls beyond, bubbling with the seeping life-force of Shub-Nillurath. Over the centuries, the Builders had gnawed at the tear, widening it and allowing more and more power to return to the world. They had been the first slaves of the Forest Giant, created out of his malevolence and only partly corporeal. As long as they stayed close to the tear, they were all but invisible until they desired to be seen or wished to meld with another creature. Anyone that left Oron Kaa forgot about them within minutes and they had been easy for Jaa to overlook. They endured as slaves to the last tendrils of their master, forced to comply as strongly as if he had succeeded and returned to the mortal world.

He filled his lungs with the beautifully rotten air and approached the Footstep of the Forest Giant. 'If you would give me a place in your Tyranny, my lord, I would serve you with every ounce of my flesh. I desire to be your slave.' The Builders fluttered into the air, swarming around him like a mantle of fetid divinity. They joined him, basking in the light of their god, as a euphoric laugh erupted from his mouth.

CHAPTER EIGHT

SAARA THE MISTRESS OF PAIN IN THE CITY OF RO WEIR

I T WAS TIME for her to emerge from isolation. A week had passed, slowly and with little sleep, but she was still alive and she was still sane. The door had opened each day, nothing more than a crack and a sliver of light, for her to receive food and written notes. She'd eaten barely half the food and read none of the notes. She had matched strength with a Gorlan mother and lost. Her last reserves of energy were needed just to keep her ageless body from withering into that of an old woman. But her strength had now returned.

Maybe it's over, she thought. Maybe they'd already won. Maybe the Red Prince was dead and their enemies were defeated, torn to shreds along the King's Highway and on the muster fields of Weir. Maybe Fjorlan was secure, controlled by the fool Ursa. Maybe her Dark Young were planted in every corner of the Lands of the Twisted Tree.

No. This news would have reached her. Someone would have shouted through the door; yelled and banged on the wood, maybe even demanded she answer. The circumstances would have allowed it.

Her normally lustrous black hair was greasy and tangled. Her purple dress was stained and torn. The washbasin was replaced daily, but she used it only to remove the vile taste from her mouth. Soaps for her skin and oils for her hair had piled up, unused, in the corner. The only thing she waited for, the only thing she craved, was drugged oblivion. Each day a fresh supply of rainbow smoke was delivered and each day it was smoked in a few hours. Stronger and stronger drugs were becoming necessary to keep her focused during her battle with her own mind.

She had one sister left. Chained to the floor in a locked vault was Isabel the Seductress. Saara had used her mind to shoulder some of the burden, but she was now hopelessly insane, unable to deal with the flood of memories and desires from her deceased sisters or the crawling assault of the Gorlan. When her mind finally broke, she would free Saara from the torment of those she'd enchanted. Until then, they shared the burden.

But there was something else. Some reason that she should rise now, at this moment. Something had happened in Oron Kaa. A shadow and a buzz gnawed in her mind. An old power spoke to her across leagues of deserts, mountains, plains and seas. Geography and distance were no barrier to the Queen in Red; she spoke and the meaning carried. Some new power, or rejuvenation of an old one.

Awaken, girl.

'Matron mother. I . . . struggle to focus.'

You will do as you are bid. . . as the Twisted Tree wishes. Your focus is not relevant. Neither is your comfort.

Saara pushed back her greasy hair and closed her eyes. The bent and cracked old woman was a world away, but her words still cut like a kris blade to the heart. Each thought carried with it thousands upon thousands of hours of torture, perversion and cruelty. The Queen in Red spoke with a cacophony of screams behind her.

'I am awake,' muttered Saara. 'I am awake. I will wash and rise.'

You will listen to me! We have gained new power.

She grasped the sides of her head. Pain behind her eyes made her cry.

Do not whimper, girl.

'No, of course not. I am listening, matron mother.'

Listen well, for our cause is strengthened. A creature has risen; an enemy felled, and an ally gained. The Old Blood is now mine.

As we speak, he kneels at the Footstep of the Forest Giant. We have also removed the exemplar of Jaa. His mind is gone.

She couldn't smile, though the news was welcome. Behind the mother's words was a mocking comment on Saara's inability to stop Utha or kill Voon. She'd sent minions to chase them halfway across the world and gained nothing but dead minions and a dead sister. But Oron Kaa had now claimed them.

'I rejoice,' she muttered, blinking to remove soreness from her eyes.

And how fare you?

The Mistress of Pain took more deep breaths and clenched her fists, calming her mind as best she could. 'Tor Funweir is all but ours,' she said. 'The exemplar of the One has yet to reveal himself, but there is an army to be disposed of.'

And the Ice Giant?

'Rowanoco's exemplar lives,' she replied. 'But I have swayed Rulag Ursa from his god. He believes himself greater than the Ice Giant. He will stamp out childish notions of honour and freedom. In time, he will realize that Rowanoco no longer sings in his heart.'

It pleases me that you remain loyal, even after your failures. Our Lord may yet see fit to reward you. He has carved up the lands of men and gifted Tyrannies to those who will serve. A Jekkan has returned to the world and will be the first Tyrant of the Twisted Tree. Perhaps, one day, you will join him.

Saara's face twisted into a euphoric smile, even as waves of pain caused her skin to crackle. A power was returning to the world and in its wake was unimaginable pain and hatred. She felt, just for a moment, the eldritch caress of Shub-Nillurath. As faith died, so was faith reborn. All that was dead will rise, all that now lives will fall.

* * *

Elihas of Du Ban appeared surprised to see her. He sat behind Duke Lyam's desk like a commander, sending men to do his bidding with stern certitude. Wind claws, whip-masters, watchmen, merchants – they acted as they were told, giving everything to the Lands of the Twisted Tree. Purges had pruned those unwilling to serve and her empire was controlled through pain and pleasure. Men and women from as far away as Kessia and Leith were under their sway, some enchanted, others threatened, many willed to serve with promises of riches and influence.

When Saara arrived, flanked by wind claws, every man save the Black cleric left the room. They didn't look at her. Many had never seen her this close up, and she felt their fear as they remembered a hundred stories, each more terrible than the last.

'I would like a report,' she asked, when the last man had closed the door to the duke's office.

The pale man of Ro still wore his black armour. He wore it when he gave orders, when he was at rest and when he burned men alive. She imagined that he slept in it, his body not reacting to the cold metal.

'You have been absent for over a week.'

'I needed rest. I am now rested,' she replied, perching on the edge of the wide desk. 'My last remaining sister bears much of my burden.'

'Yes, she has been a most stimulating prisoner,' replied Elihas. 'As for a report, well, things have progressed in your absence.'

'The Red Prince?'

'Word from Cozz is that Alexander Tiris lives and has been proclaimed king of Tor Funweir.'

The world fought her every inch, making her earn her honoured place in the Lands of the Twisted Tree.

'But our advantage of numbers gives us control of the battlefield,' said the Black cleric. 'We will be able to outflank them. They advance south from Cozz.'

'A king can command more loyalty than a prince,' she replied. 'He is now a banner for the warriors of Ro to rally behind.' She smiled at him. 'But, sweet Elihas, your knowledge of military tactics is far superior to mine.'

'He'll be in the duchy of Weir within three weeks,' replied the cleric. 'Plenty of time to assemble packs behind them. Sixty thousand Hounds will cut them off from the rear. They have only barely twenty thousand warriors, plus whatever reinforcements answer the new king's call.'

'Will we need additional Hounds? Many more are on their way from Kessia.'

He shook his head. 'They've lost. All they have left is courage and a few swords. The nobles of Ro never know when they're beaten. They are arrogant enough to think they are. . . chosen. That somehow they'll prevail over any odds, no matter how overwhelming. They forget the teachings of the Black – that their duty to the One is to die for him.'

'And *your* duty to the One?' she asked.

He snarled at her, his pale face contorting. 'I feel the power leave me as my god dies. People have called me insane all my life, but I am infused with death and I will only be complete when all is dead. Killing the One is my purpose, it is all I exist to do.'

She wanted to grab him in a passionate embrace and angrily remind his flesh that it was not yet dead. But she resisted. She would find a less valuable thrall to consume.

Elihas grunted. 'Never question my faith again.'

'I wouldn't think of it,' she replied, biting her lip. 'But, tell me, who tends to the Young?'

'No-one tends to them. That section of the catacombs has been sealed for the duration of your absence. We do not need your monsters to control Weir.'

She expected the answer. Her wind claws and subordinates would lose their minds if they looked too long upon the Thousand Young of Shub-Nillurath. But it didn't matter; they would only have grown in the time she rested. They'd have grown and they'd have become strong. As for the aberration that had been Rham Jas. . . she didn't know. It could be her greatest asset or her worst liability. And it would need to feed.

'I wish the catacombs opened. I will tend to them myself.'

'As you say,' replied Elihas, his usual stoicism replacing his anger.

'I will be back when I have defiled a few men,' she said, moving towards the door. 'Ah, yes, that reminds me, would you be so kind as to deliver Kale Glenwood to the catacombs? I believe I have an appropriate end for him.'

She felt better. A sudden elevated mood made her smile and quicken her pace. A tingle of pained arousal travelled down her spine as she made her way to the catacombs. Her guards surrounded her, needing no instruction to clear the way. They'd not seen her for days and not seen her eyes sparkle for even longer.

Isabel's mind had finally imploded and she was now the perfect vault to store Saara's phantom thralls. It was a feeling of weightless freedom, as if her power was returning in waves of warm air. The future was no longer painful and the possibility of defeat no longer intruded upon her thoughts. She felt younger, and silently wished that Zeldantor or Keisha were present to massage her shoulders and tell her how beautiful she looked. Perhaps, when Kale Glenwood was dealt with, she would even attend to her flock and enjoy their adoration.

She strode, with her head high, through the levels of the knight marshal's office, passing rooms of plundered gold, to the lowest level where the whip-masters of her army organized the campaign. Everyone nodded their head in silence as they saw her. Some rich merchants of Karesia, being divested of their wealth, fell to the floor in reverence, trying to reach her feet. She sneered in delight as the men were beaten by her guards. There was a time to have your feet kissed, and there was a time to enjoy the pain of others.

* * *

When the forger from Leith was thrown at her feet, he cut an unimpressive figure, pale and sweating, wearing stained finery clearly unwashed for weeks. He was still enchanted, and had been locked in a room during Saara's absence. He would have wondered

127

what he'd done to displease her. He'd pulled out chunks of his hair, and scratched deep lines across his face and arms.

'You've served your purpose, Kale,' said the enchantress. 'You've helped us kill your friend – your only friend. The pain this is causing you would make you a rebellious thrall, and I need an offering.'

'I don't feel any pain,' he whimpered. 'I am happy that the dark-blood is no longer an obstacle to our cause.'

She caressed his scratched face, smiling. 'Sweet Kale, you feel no pain because I have my hand round your heart. When I release it, you will hate me more than your own father.'

'But I want nothing more than to serve you,' he said, tears appearing in his eyes. 'Please.'

'But you now have no value to me, except as an offering.'

'But I would serve you gladly. . . I love you.'

She looked at him and touched his mind. She flowed over his thoughts, memories, desires. . . everything, every corner of who he was. From his childhood in Leith, his criminal enterprise in Tiris, his assassination tour with Rham Jas. She knew everything he'd ever done, everything he'd ever thought.

'Relax, my darling, this will cause you great pain.'

She pulled her mind back, removing every hook she'd buried in his consciousness. It was quick, brutal, and it caused him immense pain. One moment, he would have given himself to her – heart, body and soul; he would have killed or died for her and her cause. Then nothing. No love, no compulsion, just hate. He spluttered and his eyes shot back and forth.

'What the fuck have I done, bitch?' he roared, leaping at the Mistress of Pain. He stopped in mid-air, unable to attack her as waves of hatred and self-loathing washed over him. 'You killed Rham Jas – you made me help you.'

He fell to the dusty catacomb floor, inches away from impenetrable darkness. Behind him, the Dark Young swayed as rippling patterns in the blackness. Glenwood looked around and realized where he was. He tried to get to his feet, but she pressed against his mind and kept him cowed.

'You saw Rham Jas die on this stone,' she said, relishing the twisted pain in his stomach. 'It seems only fit that you will provide the first meal for the creature he has become.'

He looked at the scratch marks on his arms and felt for torn patches of hair. Then a savage growl sounded from the darkness, mere feet from where he sat. 'What the fuck is that?' He tried to move again, but was powerless to get past her.

Saara spread her arms wide and addressed the aberration that had been Rham Jas. She could feel its mind, and the malevolence that festered within. 'I make you this offering,' she whispered. 'That we might work together against the heresies of men.'

She pushed out with her mind, barrelling Glenwood into the darkness. He howled in fear and tried to claw his way back to the light, but something grabbed his leg and began to eat him. She saw only glimpses of muscular, black limbs and gnashing, glass-like teeth. Glenwood's face was locked in primal terror and he died as much of fear as of gruesome wounds. He was flung from one stone wall to another, always partly in darkness, as the creature tore his body apart and gulped the chunks into a shimmering black mass, always just out of sight.

Saara watched, feeling waves of pain and hatred pulse into her head. It was almost too much for her, as if the Forest Giant was showing her the power she could inherit if she remained loyal. She was used to the pain, but not the hatred. The Aberration was as pure a servant of Shub-Nillurath as existed and was comprised of both. Surges of spite and vengeance drove her to her knees, showing her the beautiful malice of her god. The Aberration would lead the Thousand Young into battle and its emergence would signal the age of the Twisted Tree.

She fell back against the stone, hearing the creature's desires in her head. It asked for more. It was hungry and wanted to feast. As Glenwood's head, now a frozen mask of terror, disappeared into darkness, Saara knew the creature was not sated. Getting to her feet, she clung to the wall, needing its help to stay upright, as she backed away from the darkness. It roared again, more savage this time, though tinged with a gurgle, as if the creature was busy swallowing Kale Glenwood. The Aberration needed strength and needed to consume others to get it. It was a primal reflection of Saara's own needs.

'I will get you more,' she whispered. 'You will eat your fill.'

She turned and edged her way along the wall, creeping towards the stone entrance to the catacombs. The distance stretched and the Aberration growled, showing her flashes of pain and torment with each sound, but she reached the doors and stood unaided. A firm knock and her wind claws opened it from the other side.

'My lady, you are unwell?'

She stopped the doors from opening fully and squeezed through the gap, almost falling into the arms of the waiting man. Her guards closed the door and surrounded her, but she refused their aid and stood on her own. She needed more offerings and these men were closest.

'My lady. . .'

She composed herself and locked eyes with the first of the five wind claws. She was surprised at her own strength as her mind assaulted the man. It was the first time she'd enchanted a man in over a week, and his mind opened before her like a beautiful flower. She didn't care about his history or his name; she only cared about his flesh. In turn, she enthralled the minds of each of her guards, commanding them to enter the catacombs and be food for the Aberration.

'At once, my lady,' said the first wind claw. 'I will offer myself to our lord's most fearsome servant.'

With wide eyes and blissful smiles, they opened the door and went swiftly to their deaths. When the door was again closed, Saara fell back against the wall and listened to the thrashing gurgle of the Aberration feasting. Each man was swept up and consumed, their flesh nourishing the creature. Yet still it was hungry and still it called to her.

'I will get you more,' she said, pulling herself away from the catacombs.

She couldn't feel its intentions, only its hunger. It may have shouted to the world, desperate for sustenance, or it may have seen her as an ally who would provide food. Either way, she needed to find more offerings. If she fed it enough, perhaps it would talk to her and convey its feelings and desires. It had been starved in her absence, and she had now awoken a terrible hunger. A hunger that must be filled.

She walked alone up bare stone steps, back to the lower levels of the knight marshal's barracks. She shut out the intrusive babble of those above and entered the cloistered ground level. Before her, a hundred pairs of eyes showed fear at her emergence, pausing in their conversations and bowing their heads. She knew none of their names and cared nothing for their adoration. In that moment, she just needed their flesh.

She glided across the marble floor, from one line of pillars to another, keeping every man's attention focused on her. At the end of the cavernous room, huge double doors led out into Ro Weir, and hundreds more men were stationed outside. Each wind claw commanded a company of Ro guardsmen, and used the hall to direct their men to any that needed imprisonment or immolation. Of the Hounds, only the whip-masters and mistresses were permitted into the city, while the balance of her enormous army slept on hard ground on the muster fields of Weir.

She assessed those before her, looking for food that she wouldn't miss. The dungeons and the hanging cells were filled with dissidents, but Saara wanted a fresh feast for the Aberration, not the rotten limbs of imprisoned, starving men.

'Listen to me,' she said quietly, her words carrying to each of the hundred people in the hall. 'Close the doors and all of you step forward.'

They obeyed without question and a mixed group of warriors, administrators and guardsmen clustered in front of her. She reached out and touched the first mind, an older man of Karesia in a colourful robe of red and purple. His name was Al-Tassin, a rich slave trader from Kessia. 'Not you,' she whispered in his mind. 'Return to your offices and forget this.'

The merchant nodded and left the hall, a euphoric look on his face. He was too valuable to be food. She assessed the next man, and then the next, releasing a handful of valuable wind claws or influential merchants, but keeping the majority. She enchanted them effortlessly, which reminded her of how easily her power used to flow and how easily it would flow again. She'd not felt so strong in almost a year, nor had she enchanted so many at once since long before she battled the Gorlan mother.

She walked among them, slicing off any pieces of rebellion or individuality that remained until they stood in ranks, seventy or eighty men, with slack-jawed compliance and floppy limbs.

'You few have been chosen,' she purred. 'You no longer need your flesh, but Shub-Nillurath needs it. I ask you to give it gladly and know that your energy will nourish the roots of the Twisted Tree.'

They didn't show any expression. She had dulled their emotions and, though inside they were screaming, on the surface they were as still as a millpond. She closed her eyes and breathed in the exquisite pain. It was a first course to the meal of torment she would receive as the Aberration feasted, but *this* nourishment she did not need to share.

She weaved her hand in the air and, like a snake charmer, pulled every set of eyes to the sensuous swaying of her wrist. She backed away towards the catacomb entrance, coaxing the thralls to follow in a dull procession. Down the dark stairs they followed, able to walk only two abreast, until she pulled open the doors and once again felt the ravening hunger of the Aberration. The creature was still eating, though *what* it ate was uncertain. Glenwood and the wind claws were gone before she left.

'Wait here,' she commanded the thralls.

Within the chamber, the sheet of darkness still obscured the creature, but she could see bloody pieces of flesh sprayed across the floor and walls and broken black armour wedged in the flagstones.

At the edge of the darkness, the thick tentacle of a Dark Young was thrashing wildly, mixing its black ichor with the human blood. The Aberration was eating one of its brothers, squeezing the trunk into an unseen mouth. Hate and pain assaulted her again. She only hoped her seventy new thralls would be enough to sate the creature and prevent it from consuming more of its kin.

The Aberration gulped down the last of the Dark Young and bellowed at her. It was so very hungry. With a wave of her hand, she summoned the waiting men, bringing them into the catacombs in groups of four. Blindly, her new thralls walked into the darkness and to their death. It was a gruesome procession. Each group was torn to pieces by the frenzied creature, always staying just out of sight. All she saw were its teeth, glass-like and gnashing; and its skin, black and muscular. The Aberration gorged itself on the blood, with tendrils of shadow gathering up the chunks of fresh meat and shovelling them into the gnashing mouth. Saara stood in the midst of the carnage as more and more hapless men marched to their deaths. Arms, legs and heads were severed and flung across the stone, spraying blood across her dress. But still it was hungry.

She took a step forward, wanting to enter the darkness and see the creature, but it hissed at her, a ferocious warning that she was not welcome. The creature considered the catacombs to be its personal domain, where no-one could enter, with the darkness marking the line beyond which even Saara could not intrude. All it allowed her to see were cat-like flashes of movement and its teeth, shimmering and opaque, coated in blood.

The pain was intoxicating. It flowed and grew as the Aberration feasted, gaining renewed strength from each chunk of flesh. Its hunger was a bottomless pit, and she wondered if it would ever be full or if she'd need to keep feeding it. If its great hunger was not sated, she feared that the Thousand Young of Shub-Nillurath would sustain it. At least until it was unleashed on the unsuspecting lands of Ro. On that day the creature could eat all it wanted, sustaining its hateful form with dead warriors of Tor Funweir.

Perhaps even the new king would be food for the Aberration.

'Rejoice,' she muttered, feeling drunk on sensation. 'Rejoice, for the Twisted Tree can no longer be defeated. Rejoice, for we will remake this world in pleasure and pain.'

The creature halted in its meal, leaving the last few men to stand on the blood-soaked flagstones. She could feel its disagreement. To the Aberration, pleasure was an alien concept. All it felt was pain and hatred.

CHAPTER NINE

RANDALL OF DARKWALD
IN OSLAN

A DOZEN OR SO Kirin lay unconscious or dead at the mouth of the cave, but still they attacked. Ruth stayed within the arc of shadow, rising high on to her back legs to pluck arrows from the air and slap aside any katana-wielders who got too close. She hissed and her feelers clicked in front of her bared fangs.

Vekerian's crew had been far less friendly than Randall had hoped. When Lylla's son had announced his intention to sail south of Skeleton Bay, fully a third of them roared with defiant anger, as if their captain was breaking a rule of the sea. When he deferred to the great mother, standing demurely behind him, the defiant third had screamed foul sorcery, accusing Ruth of bewitching Raz Mon. They'd attacked a moment later, ferociously pushing Ruth to the mouth of a wide cave. Vekerian and his loyal men stood back, allowing the Gorlan mother to exert her dominance.

A squelchy sound echoed from the cave entrance as Ruth plunged her fangs into a man's chest. She lifted him up, spraying blood across the rock, and flung his limp body to the side. The Kirin ricocheted and landed a few feet from Randall. He was young, maybe eighteen, and his chest was open. Ruth's fangs had sheared through leather armour, flesh and bone, allowing Randall to see the rocky floor through his chest.

'I wonder what your name was,' mused Randall.

The dead man was dark-haired and tufts of greasy hair sprouted from his chin. But he had two holes in his chest and was unlikely to be a potential friend.

Ruth smashed two men's heads together and flung them aside. She had arrows in her legs and abdomen, but showed no signs of pain, or even fatigue. The huge spider hunkered down, ready for the next attack. Randall moved from the wall as the attack didn't come. For now, they appeared to have stopped throwing their lives away. It had taken them about twenty minutes.

He moved a little closer to the cave mouth, keeping a good distance from Ruth, and shouted, 'Captain Vekerian, are they finished attacking us?'

He rose on to his toes to see over Ruth's abdomen. There were a few black-clad men, holding position in the far trees, and the smell of salt water hung around the cave entrance, only partially eclipsed by the smell of blood and death.

One of Vekerian's loyal men, bow drawn, stepped towards the cave. He moved tentatively, keeping his bowstring loose and his eyes on the Gorlan mother. The other Kirin stayed in the loosely packed trees, and Randall could hear more men on the gravelly beach beyond.

'I believe so,' replied the Kirin captain.

Ruth responded by gathering up her huge legs and moving to the side of the entrance, allowing Randall to walk past her. He sheathed his sword and tried to adopt a smile.

A few dozen arrows were aimed vaguely in his direction and plenty more were still in quivers. The beach was identifiable only by the tops of wooden structures built along its length, and the cove was ringed by jagged cliffs.

Raz Mon Vekerian strode to the cave and, standing amidst dead mutineers, addressed the multitudes of Kirin sailors who were skulking in the trees or hiding, just out of sight, on the beach below. 'Does anyone else wish to express their discontent at our destination?'

There was silence. Twenty men or more were dead and the

remaining mutineers had decided that their discontent was not worth dying over. The rest of the crew, awed by the spectacle of a Gorlan mother, remained loyal to their captain and began to round up anyone who had spoken against her. Most averted their eyes or bowed in fearful respect. A few even flung themselves to the dusty grass and cried in reverence.

Great mother, forgive us! Great mother, forgive us!

When they'd finished worshipping Ruth, many looked at Randall. He imagined they were asking themselves the same questions he was. Who was this young man of Ro and what was he doing here? How did he arrive with his travelling companion? Was he irreversibly insane? Their eyes betrayed no emotion, just the cold, thousand-league-stare of professional men. At least the bows weren't pointed at him.

Vekerian, just as reverent as his men, turned to face the huge Gorlan. 'Would you deign to take your lesser form, great mother? My men will work quicker with less distraction.'

She clicked her feelers, rubbing them together against her huge fangs, and backed away into the darkness of the cave.

'Takes a few minutes for her to change shape,' said Randall.

The cold-eyed Kirin just nodded. 'That will give me time to muster my men. With no more distractions, we should make sail in an hour or two.'

'And then you'll tell us about. . . that place we're going to?'

'I will,' he replied. 'When we reach the open sea.'

Randall left Ruth to change form, and Vekerian to shout orders at his crew. He strolled to the grassy bank and got his first look at the Oslan coast. Beneath, a lattice of wooden platforms snaked from the rocky beach and out beyond the flanking cliffs. Three ships were in the cove, seagoing galleons with tall sails. Vekerian's ship, the *Black Wave*, was the largest. It had three masts and black sails, with catapults forward and aft. It was still at anchor, while the other two ships slowly bobbed out to sea. Both decks were full of people and the ships rode low in the water, struggling to make way. As Vekerian had said, people were leaving these lands, fleeing the Seven Sisters and their Twisted Tree, heading to strange and far-off destinations in the hope of finding peace.

Down a dirt track below, men were relaying Vekerian's orders and loading barrels on to the deck of the *Black Wave*, while others coiled ropes and scuttled up the rigging. The ship was an elegant sight, rolling gently in the water; it had a carved figurehead, depicting a woman with a longbow. The sailors whispered to each other, spinning tales of the great mothers and bemoaning their lack of payment.

'These men will soon turn to piracy,' said Ruth, silently appearing next to him. 'Legal trade will dry up in a few short months and they will have little choice but to plunder the Kirin Ridge. The Twisted Tree will eventually consume even the woods of Oslan. But Lylla Vekerian was right – at least the sailors will remain free.'

'Will *we*? Will Utha?'

'I cannot speak for Utha, but your fate is now bound to mine. As I survive, so will you.'

* * *

No-one questioned him. Most of the Kirin sailors didn't even look at him. To them, he was just another of the great mother's peculiarities. But they were skilled, and confined themselves to their work, making sure the *Black Wave* was ready to leave as their captain bid. The dead mutineers were piled in the cave and everyone watched with astonishment as Ruth placed a hand to the rock and caused a huge cave-in, entombing the dead. Even Randall didn't know how she'd done it, only that the rock seemed simply to obey the Gorlan mother.

The first mate, Jez Ran, who Randall had first met in Lylla's sitting room, was a nightmare to the crew. He swore more than any man Randall had ever met, but appeared to know what he was doing.

'If those fucking crates aren't below by the time I've finished scratching my arse, some cunt is going to die,' shouted Jez Ran, his voice turning hoarse.

The other sailors began to sweat, but thankfully, the first mate took his time relieving his itch, and the crates were safely stowed below as the topsails dropped and filled with wind.

'Keep 'em trimmed. Nice and slow 'til we pass the cliffs.'

Randall stood on the forecastle, leaning against a wooden rail, with Ruth and Captain Vekerian standing in front of him. The sea breeze cut a line down the centre of the ship and sparkling sunlight made the black, wooden deck shine. They were going south, past Skeleton Bay, to the edge of the world. He didn't know exactly why the destination terrified them, or why it terrified him, although he had no doubt that Ruth was the only reason they had complied. But Vekerian knew something more. Randall had high hopes that, once the *Black Wave* left the bay and turned down the Oslan coast, he'd tell them what he knew.

The ship gained speed and the looming cliffs, bristling with palm trees and moss, rose above the sails to eclipse the sunlight. Jez Ran continued swearing and the sailors hurried about their duties. It was only the second ship Randall had been on, and it was far bigger than Captain Makad's vessel that had taken them to Kessia. The difference was intimidating. There was more of everything, from the ropes to the sails and, most especially, the crew. Ruth had killed a chunk of them, but there remained almost a hundred sailors, mostly men, with a few women in the rigging. The remaining Kirin did what they were told, glancing up at the limp bodies of the remaining mutineers, hanging from a low beam and dripping blood on the railings. Jez Ran had killed them as soon as they'd been dragged away from the cave and disarmed. Kirin ships had rules, and punishments were brutal. As long as Raz Mon Vekerian was the captain, they were bound to do as he commanded.

'A pleasant day for another voyage, no?' said Ruth, dropping back to join him against the rail.

'As pleasant a day as I've seen for a while certainly. It's nice to be with allies – or at least people who aren't enemies.' He smiled at her. 'So, you're a god to them?'

'Not really,' she replied. 'These people never had a god, so they revered power whenever they found it. As much for their own protection as genuine reverence. Many Gorlan mothers lived in Oslan, long before the Kirin arrived, and they were powerful indeed. There was a time when a hundred villages worshipped a hundred great mothers, and the Kirin's enemies were unable to intrude. Those days are long gone. The followers of the Twisted Tree can no longer be repelled by the might of my kind.'

'What happened to them?' he asked. 'I only know legends, and they're vague at best.'

'I may be one of the last Gorlan mothers,' she replied, without emotion. 'The power that sustains us is gone. In time, we will fade entirely from this world. Perhaps we will enter the next world, or perhaps we will enter the dirt.'

'Are you godless too? Like the Kirin? I suppose I never thought about it.'

She looked around, making sure the Kirin sailors were occupied and unlikely to hear their conversation. 'You have a piece of me in your head, young Randall. I think you deserve to know a little about my kind. If only so you can tell future generations, once we are gone.'

'That's a very morbid thought,' he replied. 'You're not dead yet. I've not seen anything that can actually harm you.'

'You cannot always fight death,' she said, directing her eyes at the black wood beneath their feet.

'So, tell me,' he said. 'Are the Gorlan just spiders that grew?'

She smiled suddenly, allowing his flippancy to cut her dark mood. 'No, I'm afraid not. Spiders are a separate species. They were our first servants, our first worshippers. Insects and arachnids have existed since the dawn of time. When Rowanoco first rose to his hall beyond, there were ants, flies and spiders, clustered around his feet.'

'That's unnerving,' replied Randall. 'You've been here all along.'

'There was a Giant,' she said, the sea breeze flinging her dark hair over her shoulders. 'A Void Giant, the first Giant, and she created many things. The earth we stand on, the mountains we look up at, the sea that laps at our homes, and the creatures that crawl at our feet. When she created the Old Ones, to fight for her pleasure, ages before Rowanoco rose, they claimed servants. Atlach-Nacha, the Spider Mother, chose those who crawl as her servants, and she created the Gorlan to rule them.'

He took a moment, looking at her deep violet eyes. He'd never asked how old she was, never let it affect his feelings towards her. He was a lad of nineteen years, and struggled to think about the deeper mysteries of time. 'So, the One, Jaa, Rowanoco, they came later?' he asked, surprised at how quickly his mind processed the information.

'The gods of men were the strongest survivors of the Long War, the war started by the Void Giant. She was called the First Aggressor, but she fell asleep long before Rowanoco first broke her rules and ascended to the halls beyond. He was born in her world and evolved naturally. He was the first god born to a mortal. He changed the rules. The others followed him.'

'And the Gorlan?'

'We never ascended, for Atlach-Nacha was never defeated. She was the only Old One to survive the Long War, and we survived with her, crawling at the feet of the Giants. We lived and we endured. Enemies came and went, but none threatened us. When the Jekkans arrived from the void and built their caliphate, we hid in the forests and the deep mountains. When men came down from their trees, they worshipped us. And now. . . long ages spell our doom, for Atlach-Nacha no longer weaves her web.'

'What happened to her?' he asked.

She touched his cheek and a tear tumbled from her eye. 'A story for another time, young Randall. For now, let us enjoy the sea air and hope for a swift voyage south. Utha the Shadow needs us and we should not disappoint him.'

141

* * *

On the second day, while waiting for the captain to finish his breakfast, Randall saw convoys of ships beginning to leave Karesia. Across the northern horizon, cutting through the morning sun, were dozens of sails. They came from Oslan, Kessia and all along the coast, leaving a land that was changing. The Kirin sailors were miserable, thinking with longing of the money they could be making, shipping refugees from the Lands of the Twisted Tree. They wouldn't mutiny, but their displeasure was clear, giving Jez Ran ample opportunity to swear and kick people.

Randall had remained on deck, gazing at the waves as they broke against the hull of the *Black Wave*. Without Utha, he had no-one to tell how scared he was. Not of swords any longer, nor of crossbows, monsters or enchantment, but of Ruth and what she now meant to him. She'd retreated below deck early on the first day, and he'd not sought her out. The cabin they'd been given was the second largest on the ship, after the captain's quarters, and was usually reserved for rich passengers. Randall had used it only to sleep, and had stayed on deck in silent thought since daybreak. He waited for Vekerian to invite them into his cabin and he looked south.

'You, boy, come with me.' The speaker was a one-armed sailor, a wild-eyed man Randall had seen at the wheel of the *Black Wave*. 'The captain wants a word.'

'Are we far enough away from land?' asked Randall. 'I don't want to make him anger the sea.'

'Was that a joke?' said the sailor.

'Actually, no. Your captain has been good to us, and it seems to mean a lot to him.'

'It does. It does to us all. The fates of men are capricious; they lead us this way and that. Why anger the sea as well?'

Randall followed the one-armed man below deck. The *Black Wave* had four decks, though he'd only seen two of them, and was a warren of latticed wood and cabins. Every corner of every room was cluttered with ropes, tools and supplies, and every wooden ladder creaked as the Kirin went about their work. The bowels of the ship were as dark as the deck was bright, with few open portholes, and swaying lanterns providing most of the light.

'Through there,' said the one-armed Kirin, pointing to a staircase at the rear of the ship.

Ruth emerged from their cabin, gliding over the wood to stand at his side. 'Is the captain ready?' she asked.

'I am,' announced Raz Mon Vekerian, appearing from the downward stairs. 'Come with me.'

He strode down to a single wooden door, with a blood-red flag hanging above. Inside, at the back of the *Black Wave*, was a wide state room, with secured wooden furniture. It was dark brown and musty, with dust rising from piles of parchment and old leather satchels. Maps were rolled out across tables, showing strange seas and far-off places. Randall wanted to linger, to ask questions about the bizarre coastlines, but Ruth hurried him up.

'Don't stare, young Randall,' she said, pointing towards a side room and Vekerian's cabin. 'Kirin sailors guard their maps jealously.'

'Indeed,' said the captain, taking a seat behind a mahogany table. 'Those maps are worth a fortune to any sailing man. No map-maker of Ro or Karesia knows of half those places.'

Randall pulled himself from the table and joined Ruth in the small side cabin. It was still musty, but the windows were open and the smell of the sea gave the captain's cabin a hint of freshness.

'Sit down, great mother,' said the captain. 'I trust my crew have been polite.'

'They have,' replied Ruth, demurely perching on a chair. 'They have shown adequate respect.'

'Agreed,' said Randall. 'So, Oron Kaa?'

'Yes, Oron Kaa.' It was the first time the Kirin had used the name.

Randall sat down next to Ruth, with the sparkling blue ocean over the Kirin's shoulder. Raz Mon Vekerian leant back in his chair. There was intelligence in his eyes and a twitchy curiosity levelled at his two guests.

'There are stories,' said the captain. 'Stories you only hear at sea. When ships pass we share what we've seen. Sometimes a story scares you and you try to forget it – until you pass another ship and you tell them, and they're scared too.'

Randall suddenly imagined they were sitting round a midnight campfire, telling ghost stories over a bottle of wine. Vekerian was a hard man, but his eyes became moist and unfocused as he spoke of Oron Kaa.

'People go missing,' said the Kirin. 'Sailors who get too close, travellers from the Long Mark. Sometimes you see them again, but they're not the same. They serve. . . something else, something old. That's all you'll find there, blank-faced men and women serving an old power.'

The ship surged and the cabin appeared to tip towards the crystal-blue ocean. Somewhere above, the wind had picked up and the *Black Wave* was now gliding quickly south.

'Your mind whirls,' said Ruth 'Tell me why?'

Vekerian grunted and rose from his seat. He was unaffected by the movement of his ship and strode on sure feet to a drinks cabinet.

'Karesian desert nectar. Even a Gorlan mother should appreciate liquor of this quality.' He resumed his seat, holding a gilded bottle of thick liquid. 'Unfortunately, no glasses.' He uncorked the bottle and took a small swig. He then offered the liquor to Randall.

'I think her question is a fair one,' said the squire, taking the bottle.

He drank a little, finding it overly sweet and wanting to spit it out when the thick liquid began to coat his tongue. Ruth ignored the offered drink and kept her gaze on the Kirin.

'My brother,' said the captain. 'My only living brother. He was taken.' The Kirin was unemotional. 'He took his ship too close to Oron Kaa and didn't come back.'

'What happened to him?' asked Randall.

The Kirin pursed his lips and grunted. 'We found his ship, splintered, south of Skeleton Bay. Two crew still alive. . . all they'd say was that they could hear buzzing. They said it for two days until one stuck a knife in his own ear and the other jumped ship and swam at a shark. We looked for Kel Mon – we looked until the only place along the coast we *hadn't* looked was Oron Kaa.'

'You went there, didn't you?' said Ruth, leaning in across the table, her hand demurely cupping her chin.

Vekerian nodded. 'Had to kill half a dozen of my men to make the rest sail there. We lost a dozen more when we went ashore.'

'That was foolhardy,' replied the Gorlan mother.

The pirate captain glared at her across the bottle of desert nectar. 'I know. But my mother would have never forgiven me.'

'You must have known he was dead,' she said, showing no tact or compassion.

If Vekerian was offended, he didn't show it. He didn't show anything. 'If he was dead I wanted his body. He should be returned to the Kirin Ridge. I still want his body – or his bones.'

'Why the Kirin Ridge?' asked Randall.

'It's what you gave us – the Ro. No land, no crops, just the fucking ocean. It means something to us and we sink our dead in its deepest trench.'

Randall bowed his head. 'Sorry. I'm from the Darkwald, I didn't grow up learning much history. I'd only met one Kirin before we came to Karesia and I hated him.'

Ruth patted him on the leg, a patronizing gesture that made him stop talking.

'You see something when you look at me,' she said to Vekerian. 'Tell me what it is.'

The Kirin didn't change expression. 'I see an opportunity,' he replied. 'Strength such as you possess is rare in this world. If you won't stay in the Creeping Downs, I ask that you help me find my brother. I will take you to Oron Kaa and follow you ashore.'

She leant in. 'What did you face when you went there? What killed your crew?'

'As I said, blank-faced men and women. But hundreds of them. They made a buzzing sound that I could still hear days later. We're not soldiers – when we're afraid, we run away. And we were very afraid. I keep thinking there was something more, but it might just have been a nightmare.'

'I do not believe these blank-faced individuals will impede me. I suspect I know what they are and who they serve.'

A bell rang from up on deck and the captain frowned.

'What does that mean?' asked Randall.

'It means ship ahoy,' replied Vekerian. 'If you'll excuse me, great mother.'

'We will accompany you,' said Ruth.

The Kirin just nodded and left his state room. They followed, hearing the insistent ringing rise in volume as they moved up the stairs and on to the rear deck. The one-armed man stopped ringing the bell when he saw his captain, and gestured ahead of the ship.

'Trouble,' said the helmsman.

Vekerian hopped down from the forecastle and moved forward, along the high railings of his ship to where other sailors were clustered, pointing at something further south. Randall stayed on the forecastle and rose on to his tiptoes to see what they were looking at. It was another ship. No, two ships. One was a tub, headed towards them and loaded down with people. The other, flying the banner of the Twisted Tree, was more sleek and warlike and was launching flaming rocks at the fleeing ship.

'They're just trying to leave,' said Randall. 'They're not even allowed the luxury of starting a life elsewhere.'

The ship was aflame and people dived into the sea. Men, women and children of Karesia, trying to flee from the new order, were either burned to death or picked off from afar with short bows. The warship had a serrated battering ram, two masts and was filled with Hounds. The fleeing tub began to list as its sails caught fire and its crew dived overboard. The Hounds did not allow a single person to flee; nor did they let up their bombardment until the ship was engulfed in flame.

The *Black Wave* had slowed and the dancing fire was all that obscured it from the Karesian warship. Slowly, the Hound vessel turned from the burning wreck and pointed north.

'Hard to starboard!' shouted Vekerian, running back to the fore-castle. 'Lay on some canvas, pull out to sea. We can outrun them.'

Two young women, already high in the rigging, tugged on coiled ropes and released the billowing topsails. The one-armed man flung the wheel to the right and relayed orders to those around him. Jez Ran stayed at the front of the ship, shouting for sailors to climb the rigging and release as much sail as possible. The wind was low, but the ship did lurch away from the coast with sudden speed.

'Great mother, if you would care to hold on to the railing,' said Vekerian, taking over at the wheel.

The wind caught the sails and the *Black Wave* tilted sharply to the right, sending barrels and katanas skittering from one side to the other. Randall nearly lost his footing, but clamped his hands firmly to the wooden railing just in time. The sound of dying men and women faded quickly, and he dug his nails into the wood. The warship pursued them, framed by fire, it sails unfurled.

'Why would they just kill them?' he asked Ruth. 'They could have captured them, let them go home.'

'You have a gentle heart,' she replied. 'The Twisted Tree does not. It will kill and keep killing, until its perverse appetite is sated.'

'But. . .'

He had nothing really to say. He'd seen so much and had so much more to see, but he'd never got used to seeing death. He'd killed men and seen Utha kill dozens, but none of it had been indiscriminate. The Seven Sisters and their Twisted Tree killed for no reason. They annihilated families and destroyed towns, and he'd seen too much of it first-hand.

'Can we outrun them?' Ruth asked Vekerian.

The captain looked over his shoulder, then up at the sails. 'Maybe. They're heavier and built for war, not speed. I hate to say it, but hopefully there are more loaded ships leaving Kabriz.

Hound warships go for easy targets. We may prove to be too much effort.'

The Kirin moved quickly, responding to orders and steadily increasing the speed of their ship. Vekerian spoke quietly to Jez Ran and to the helmsman, who roared his commands to the crew. As Randall looked back, he saw distance gradually appearing between the *Black Wave* and the Hound warship.

'Ship off the port bow,' screeched the lookout.

Everyone looked to the left, but the new ship was just a dot on the horizon. Vekerian gave the wheel to the one-armed helmsman and produced a looking glass.

'Fuck!' exclaimed the captain. 'Hounds hunt in packs, even at sea.' He looked up at the sails and judged the wind. 'We're in trouble.'

Randall didn't understand the ships' movements, but he could see enough distressed faces to know that their ship was being herded. The wind was taking the *Black Wave* along the coast, making her tack as she tried to lurch out to sea, whereas the second warship was sailing *with* the wind, moving faster than the Kirin galley. They would be cut off from the south.

'What does this mean?' Ruth asked the captain, though she did not appear concerned.

Vekerian exchanged words with Raz Mon, and the sails were trimmed, making the ship slow but increasing her manoeuvrability. 'Uncertain, great mother,' he replied. 'They have the wind, they have the numbers.'

'What do we have?' asked Randall.

'A Gorlan mother,' offered Ruth.

'Yes,' agreed Vekerian. 'It would seem you are our only advantage.'

For a change, Randall did not have confidence in his companion. Killing Kirin sailors on land was a world away from defeating a laden warship at sea. He didn't even know if she could swim.

'Did you expect this?' he asked Vekerian.

The Kirin looked at him, showing that he had, but he said nothing. He shouted forward, getting more men to climb the rigging and others to secure the deck and prepare for combat. Barrels of katanas and longbow arrows were placed against each railing and the sailors readied themselves.

The warship ahead of them had two masts and black sails, billowing with wind. The ship's lines were low and jagged, with metal spikes fore and aft, creating the image of a predatory fish. The ship was filled with Hounds, though these had no helmets and wielded short bows. It was the first time Randall had seen their faces and, somehow, this made them less intimidating. The catapult crews didn't even wear the ubiquitous black plate armour; the only sign they were Hounds at all were the tattoos covering their heads. It appeared that the rules of the armies of Karesia were less strict at sea, the better to manoeuvre their vessels and use their weapons.

He looked at Ruth, trying to detect some glimmer of confidence to help him feel less afraid. What he saw was her usual expression of untroubled grace. The warship ahead would cut them off shortly, and the one behind would catch them just after, but she didn't appear to be afraid.

'Are you going to do something?' he asked.

'Not yet,' she replied. 'I cannot swim. I need to wait until they're closer.'

He smiled at her manner, though it was gallows humour. Her confidence was even more unshakeable than Utha's. He began thinking about the ways a huge spider could win a sea battle. The image of her climbing the rigging on dense layers of web filled his thoughts, but he doubted she had anything so simple in mind. The catapults and bows would find her an easy target and even Ruth was vulnerable to repeated wounding.

'Captain Vekerian,' she said. 'Get alongside that ship.'

'What?' he exclaimed.

'If you stay on your present course, they will begin to launch flaming boulders at you.'

Randall looked across the water and saw tightly wound wooden limbs being winched into place. The captain saw the same thing and reluctantly nodded agreement at Ruth.

'Heave to,' he shouted. 'Jez Ran, get us alongside that ship.'

'Captain?' queried the sailor.

'Just fucking do it, we have no chance in open water.'

'Aye, captain.'

Half the sailors drew katanas or longbows and half looked at Ruth expectantly, presumably hoping that she would save them from an overwhelming force. Randall couldn't see how many Hounds were loaded aboard the warships, but he could see how few Kirin were aboard the *Black Wave*. The galley listed to port and bore down on the southern warship. The one in pursuit had trimmed its sails and moved to cut off any avenue of escape. Everything was happening so fast, with the gap of crystal-clear water between the ships rapidly disappearing.

'Should I be afraid?' he asked Ruth.

'If you think it would help,' she replied.

He rolled his eyes. 'Just once it would be nice to get some reassurance.'

Before he could complain any further, she left the forecastle and glided towards the port-side railing, facing the approaching ship. The sailors stayed out of her way, looking to their captain for the same kind of reassurance that Randall wanted from Ruth. They received no more from Vekerian than he had from the Gorlan mother.

'What does she plan to do?' the captain asked him.

'I wish I had an answer for you,' he replied. 'I'd advise your men to take some cover. They're about to start shooting at us.'

Almost before he'd finished speaking, the Hounds launched a narrow sheet of arrows. The *Black Wave* was now too close for the catapults, but dozens of arrows blanketed the galley.

'Cover!' roared Vekerian, ducking down behind the wheel as an arrow thudded into the deck nearby.

Randall joined him and heard the sudden wails of men struck by wooden shafts. He could no longer see Ruth, but he knew a couple of arrows wouldn't bother her.

Two sailors fell from the rigging and two more were barrelled overboard with arrows in their chests, but most of the Kirin had found cover behind railings or barrels. A few men emerged with longbows and returned fire, but most stayed out of sight.

'Captain, we're going to hit the cunts,' shouted Jez Ran.

Randall chanced a look past the wheel and saw Ruth casually removing an arrow from her shoulder. The warship was now right on them and the two vessels headed together.

'Brace!' shouted Vekerian, swinging the wheel hard to starboard as the ships struck.

Water flew across both decks and everyone lost their footing, before the ships settled side by side. The *Black Wave* was taller, but the sailors could now look down upon multitudes of Hounds, throwing grappling hooks and securing ladders, ready to board the Kirin vessel.

Randall drew the sword of Great Claw and edged along the railing towards Ruth, who stood in the open, surveying the Hounds beneath her. The black-armoured Karesians were unaware of why this strange woman didn't appear afraid, but it didn't slow them. Commands were relayed and the Hounds lined up to flood aboard the *Black Wave*, while the Kirin stayed behind cover, waiting with longbows drawn. The sailors were outnumbered at least five to one and the panicked looks they threw at their captain showed little confidence in Ruth's ability to save them.

He kept his head down and reached his companion. 'Are we close enough yet?' he asked.

'Yes, I believe so,' she replied. 'Ready yourself to kill any that get past me.'

He made a grunting sound, questioning his ability to do what she wanted, but she ignored him and took a large step upwards, on to the narrow railing that separated the two ships. Randall turned to look across at Vekerian, who had drawn his own bow and sat ready, with twenty or so bowmen in a line ready to repulse boarders. The rest held katanas and waited for either their captain's orders or a display of strength from Ruth. What they got was a booming announcement from the Gorlan mother.

'You do not own the sea,' she stated. 'Your Twisted Tree does not grow here and you will enslave none of these people.' She spread her arms wide as three arrows thudded into her chest. Instead of falling backwards or crying in pain, she appeared to break apart, her body actually growing in mass, seeming to become a huge carpet of fist-sized spiders. The creatures flooded over the side of the *Black Wave* and engulfed the first rank of Hounds. There were hundreds of them, each acting independently as they crawled inside armour and dug their fangs into any exposed flesh. Randall had seen her change form many times, but never like this. The Hounds screamed and stamped on any spider they could isolate, but there were too many of them, acting together to swarm the Karesians.

'Help her!' shouted Randall, standing and waving his sword at Vekerian.

The Kirin were almost as afraid as the Karesians, but survival instinct took over and they moved to the port railing, hesitantly aware that the Hounds were too busy to return fire. They knocked arrows and picked off any men that Ruth had not swarmed. A few Hounds scrambled up ladders towards the *Black Wave*, but were cut down by katanas. Randall killed two, chopping downwards into their exposed heads, but the Kirin did most of the work, showing controlled skill with their razor-sharp blades.

'Hold fire!' shouted Vekerian as the Hounds melted away. Some jumped overboard, but most now twitched on the deck of their warship with pulpy spider bites covering their faces or longbow arrows embedded in their chests.

Jez Ran moved along the railing, cutting their ship free of a dozen grappling hooks. Other men tipped the ladders backwards and sailors were quickly ordered back to the rigging. Behind them, slowed to a crawl, the second warship approached warily, unsure of what had transpired.

'Let's get the fuck out of here,' roared Jez Ran, 'before they recover their senses!'

A slender hand appeared in front of Randall. 'A little assistance,' murmured Ruth, her voice a dull croak.

The spiders were gone, though many were dead, scattered across the deck of the warship. The Gorlan mother looked ill, with drawn skin and sallow eyes. Her hand as Randall grasped it was wrinkled and skeletal and he feared he would hurt her. Vekerian ran to help and the panting woman was tenderly lifted back to the *Black Wave.*

'Our thanks, great mother,' said the captain.

Above them, sails were unfurled and the ship inched away from the stricken warship. Behind, the other vessel was now almost stationary, clearly not intending to pursue. Randall imagined they were confused about how a humble Kirin galley could best a company of Hounds so quickly. But Jez Ran was right – their confusion would not last forever.

'I need to rest,' whispered Ruth, as she lay in Randall's arms. 'That was most. . . stimulating.'

'Fuck the Twisted Tree,' stated Vekerian with a grateful smile. 'We would follow you a thousand times before we knelt before that dark altar.'

CHAPTER TEN

INGRID TEARDROP IN THE REALM OF SUMMER WOLF

S HE SMILED AS the worm wiggled in her fingertips. Corvus snapped at it, playfully clicking his beak at her hand and flaring his glossy black wings. He liked worms and Ingrid enjoyed finding them in the muddy ground. The snow was melting and small streams turned the earth mushy. She got her hands dirty and her cloak muddy. She preferred it to being clean. And Beirand hated it, so she liked it even more. The fat old troll-belly was floundering around the base of some rocks, looking for her. He'd been there, with a stupid expression on his face, for a few minutes, while she giggled from a rocky ledge above.

Corvus clicked his beak in an imitation of a chuckle, snapping up the worm and contentedly shrugging his wings. He was the perfect partner in crime, whimsical, stealthy and cunning. Ingrid didn't like admitting it, but the raven was her only friend.

'Don't worry, we'll be free soon.' She tickled under his beak. 'You'll like Tiergarten – it's taller than Fredericksand. My uncle said it was built by Giants as a gift for the first Ranen.'

'Get down here, bitch!' Apparently Beirand had spotted her.

'Are you talking to *me*?' she asked.

He pulled a small axe from his belt and backed away, getting a good foothold on the rocks and waving the blade above his head. 'I could hit you from here, ya know? Not kill you, just make you bleed and cry like the little bitch you are.'

154

Ingrid smiled and picked up a small rock. She took good aim and launched it at the fat man's head. He winced and tumbled backwards as the sharp stone struck his crown, causing blood and cursing. As he stumbled to regain his footing, he hurled his axe, but it went harmlessly upward, lodging in the rocks.

'Sorry, did my rock hit you?'

She skipped away from the ledge and crawled back towards the Crystal Fork River. She could hear him shouting and fumbling to follow, but she was too fast. She'd slow down in a while and let him catch her. It was the only way they wouldn't put a chain on her leg. Since she'd released the dogs, she'd sneaked out every night, under the mask provided by Corvus. She'd stolen screws and wooden pegs from sleds, making them break as they moved. She'd kicked over barrels of ale and tipped ten full sacks of grain into a crevice. No-one in the army knew why they were plagued by accidents; to all outward appearances, Ingrid spent most of her time sitting quietly in her tent. The previous night, she'd even managed to unbalance a cart of glaives and send it hurtling down the Crystal Fork River.

* * *

On the other side of the rocks, sheltered from the sea winds, Rulag's men were fighting. They'd assembled a ring from shields and were betting on duels. The main army was a mass of sweat and fur, camped in the low ground, with only the captains allowed to frolic in such a fashion.

She'd never seen so many men. The Fjorlan Sea was black, the realm of Summer Wolf was white, but the army was muddy brown, plonked like a pile of excrement in the snow. It had taken them a week and a half to get enough replacement sled dogs and move the swarm from Fredericksand. Many men of Ursa had found an excuse to leave the army, preferring the warmth of Fredericksand to the freezing tents of a stationary force. Some had returned with the sled dogs; some had not. Some had been executed trying to leave; others had sneaked away in the night. Many more had died through the nightly ritual of fighting and punishments that formed an integral part of Rulag's army. Ingrid didn't know how many men had left or died as a result of her delaying tactics, but it was a lot. She fouled their supplies whenever she could, realizing that a hungry army doesn't stay loyal for long. The remainder had now settled in, ready to move at last, north of the plains of Tiergarten, on the banks of the Crystal Fork River.

'Come on, wolf girl,' snapped Beirand, shoving her forwards. 'No more running away, or I'll leave you to the trolls next time.'

She smiled sweetly at him. 'Do they smell better than you?'

He moved to backhand her, but the blow was sluggish and she ducked underneath it easily.

'Come on, fat boy,' she said, jumping over rocks and away from the angry man.

She squeezed her way through the ranks of gawking spectators and moved round the edge of the fighting circle. A man was being beaten up in the middle, his head providing an unwilling anvil to another man's war-hammer.

Suddenly, she was swept up in a pair of strong arms. Her feet left the ground and her face was enveloped in flowing black robes. The Karesian man, Kal Varaz, held her firmly around the waist, cradling her head gently.

'Going for a walk, little wolf?' he asked.

'Just helping Beirand stay fit.'

The puffing fat man emerged through the sweaty spectators, growling at Ingrid as Kal Varaz lowered her back to her feet.

'Perhaps you need additional guardians,' said the Karesian. 'Or chains.'

Beirand snatched at Ingrid's arm, pulling her away from the foreigner.

'Don't need your help, man of the sun. Fuck off and tend to your risen men.'

'My cages are well-tended. I have ample time to enjoy the hospitality of Fjorlan. If your dogs had not escaped, my Dark Young would have already taken the city.'

Ingrid shrugged off Beirand's grip and stepped to the side. Corvus was nowhere to be seen. He didn't like these men and she feared a random idiot would shoot an arrow at him.

'Can't we just be friends?' she asked, smiling at the two men.

Beirand slapped her. He'd learned his lesson and the blow came quickly, striking her sharply on the cheek. It really hurt. He went to hit her again, but Kal Varaz grabbed his forearm.

'Are you a man I can kill?' asked the Karesian.

'What? Let go of my fuckin' arm.'

'Can I kill you, or does Rulag need you?'

Beirand shoved Varaz backwards. The other man stumbled, but didn't fall. He was graceful, moving quickly and taking the power out of Beirand's shove. The men around them parted. The fight in the middle had ended when the man's head could no longer be used as an anvil, and everyone now looked at Beirand and Kal Varaz.

'Should we be betting on this?' joked a battle brother of Ursa.

Ingrid rubbed her cheek and stood up, backing into the press of laughing men. They threw insults and jokes at the Karesian, mocking his slight build and wavy-bladed knives. The general consensus seemed to be that he needed a battleaxe in the head.

'Okay,' said Varaz. 'Make your peace, for you are about to die.'

The laughter rose in volume.

'Step into the circle and draw the knives,' challenged Beirand.

The Karesian barely paused. Ingrid was unsure who she hated more: the cold foreigner or the idiot fat man. Hopefully they'd kill each other.

The circle of shields was opened for them and the previous combatants – the dead man and his killer – cleared the ground, leaving only a smear of blood on the churned snow. Beirand hefted an axe and a circular shield, adopting a strong stance. Varaz drew his wavy-bladed knives and twirled them gracefully, stepping tentatively round the larger man. He was jeered and snowballs were thrown at his feet, but his dark eyes focused only on Beirand. Ingrid began to move away, but was stopped by several of Rulag's captains, insisting that she wasn't going to be permitted to sneak off. For now, she had to watch the men fight.

To his credit, Beirand was not afraid of the strange Karesian and levelled a series of ferocious attacks at the man's head. He swung the axe in arcs, keeping his shield across his chest. Varaz danced backwards, keeping the knives low. He didn't fight properly. His movements showed no strength, just fluidity and balance. The black robes whirled as he moved, making it difficult to see where the man ended and the fabric began.

'Smash his fuckin' head in,' bellowed a nearby warrior.

Despite Beirand's wobbling belly, he was a surprisingly effective fighter. Alahan would easily beat him, but she'd seen worse axemen. He still hadn't connected with Varaz in any meaningful way, but his form was good. His skill wasn't going to kill him; his fitness was. The Karesian was much faster and made no effort to attack. Their blades had not yet clashed and Beirand was starting to tire.

Then Varaz attacked, slicing Beirand across the cheek. A line of seeping blood ran from his nose to his hairline, but it wasn't deep, just insulting.

'Fuck you, man of the sun,' spat Beirand.

Varaz lunged, staying low and attacking under the fat man's axe. Both his blades struck home and he stepped forward, skewering the larger man in the sides.

'Enough!' shouted a voice from the crowd.

The jeering stopped and everyone turned to watch Rulag Ursa and Harrod approach the circle of shields. Beirand had dropped his axe and was gargling blood.

'Step back, Karesian,' said Rulag.

Kal Varaz withdrew his blades and let Beirand die in the snow. He then bowed. 'Of course, my lord Bear Tamer.'

Ingrid was grabbed by a couple of sweaty men and marched to stand before Rulag. She shrugged their hands off, but didn't try to run. A little piece of her was glad she'd caused Beirand's death.

'Causing problems again, little wolf?' asked Harrod, waving away the crowds.

'Go find some axes to sharpen, you gormless bastards,' ordered Rulag, dispersing his men and clearing the shield circle. 'We're moving at first light, before any more troll cunts run off.'

The dead body was pulled away and Kal Varaz sheathed his knives. The Karesian gave Beirand's corpse a hateful sneer and approached Rulag. His breathing was steady and he looked like a predatory cat.

'I don't think I told you to kill him,' said Rulag.

'He made me angry,' replied Kal Varaz. 'I do not like men who strike women.'

'I've lost enough men to cold, hunger and boredom,' grunted Rulag. 'I don't want to add impoliteness to that list.' The lord of Jarvik glared down at Ingrid. 'If we're to be married, young lady, I think you should start to learn your place.' He slapped her hard across the cheek and she fell to the floor. 'Does that anger you, man of the sun?'

'Yes,' replied Kal Varaz, 'but you are not someone I can kill. The Mistress of Pain considers you important. Especially as you are finally beginning your attack. Tell me, will you be fighting yourself? Now that your army has shrunk?'

Harrod spoke before Rulag could exert his dominance over the Karesian. 'Someone take the little wolf back to her tent and put a chain on her leg.'

Rulag's annoyance faded and he scowled at Kal Varaz. 'It's time to unleash your Dark Young. If they are not as promised, I'll shove my axe down your throat.'

'They will be ready at first light,' replied the Karesian.

* * *

Ingrid was bored sitting in the tent. Her wrist was chained to a huge iron ball that was far too heavy for her to move. She had about three feet of slack and a dirty black tent to explore. All those nightly excursions, and now here she was chained up because two men had fought over her. The army was moving in the morning. They were going to hold position on the Plains of Tiergarten and wait for something. Something to do with the risen men and the Karesian's cages.

Caw

Corvus nudged his way under the tent flap and hopped over to her. He flapped his wings at the chain, shaking the metal links.

'I don't have any worms for you, but I'm bored of this tent,' she said with a smile, pointing at the chain. The raven pecked at the links, shaking the steel. The chain clanked and began to distort, as if Corvus had unnatural strength in his beak. Gradually, with more shakes, the steel twisted out of shape and snapped. For some reason Ingrid wasn't surprised.

'We make a great team. Let's go and be nosey.'

She pulled on a heavy brown cloak and poked her head furtively out of the tent. It was freezing cold outside and the snow was drifting in huge, rolling clouds. Dotted across the dark riverbank, in globes of firelight, sat thousands of men of Ursa. They were fewer than a week ago, but still a huge army. Her tent was near the middle of the encampment, set back near Rulag's command tent and the smithy. All around her in the snow were blobs of brown and black. Men, axes, wagons and supplies. The army, stationary in the freezing cold for over a week, had turned into a makeshift town.

'Where are they keeping the risen men?'

Corvus flapped to her shoulder and pointed his beak to the south, over the rise, past a bend in the river. The realm of Summer Wolf was craggy and rough in the north, green and cultivated in the south. It was the most fertile land in Fjorlan, but from where she crouched, in the shadow of her tent, it was an undulating world of black and white.

With the cloak over her head she darted away, trusting that Corvus would obscure her. There were guards, but they were slumped round a fire. They glanced occasionally at her tent, paying lip service to their duty, but were otherwise unconcerned. She'd been chained in the tent for four or five hours; they had no reason to be alert.

Keeping to the shadows, she skipped from one tent to the next, passing drunken men, sleeping men, fighting men, swearing men. Rulag's tent was the largest and crested with multiple muddy banners. The red bear claw of Ursa annoyed her. It now stood for denial of Rowanoco and it didn't belong here. She moved along the rear of the command tent, a tiny speck in a sea of brown and black.

It took a while to reach the edge of the army, but it was fun to ghost along behind the smelly axe-men with Corvus on her shoulder. They spent every night drinking and fighting and it never bored them. Each new evening was a new opportunity to drink and fight. If they waited for a few months, Rulag wouldn't have an army.

She left the low ground and moved into the dark rocks, away from the river. The area was off-limits to the men of Ursa, judging by the guards and remote location. These men, who weren't drunk, protected an enclosed depression north of the Plains of Tiergarten. She had thought the area would be well-defended, as it lay between the army and its prize, but all she could see was a handful of guards and a few open cages; no stockade or defences.

Corvus flew from her shoulder, gliding upwards over the rocks. He circled the depression before landing near the guards. A loud caw from him and they all looked in his direction, allowing Ingrid to slip over the rocks and hop down into the guarded section.

Once she had reached a shallow ravine cloaked in darkness, she crouched as low as she could. There were shapes in the darkness, irregularly dotted across the snowy ground. Somewhere to the south, quite close, across rocky plateaus and the icy river, lay Tiergarten.

One of the shapes moved and she froze. She'd thought them trees or maybe twisted brambles, but they moved like creatures. Each one swayed and then, as she watched, its extremities shivered in the air. She saw no risen men, dead or otherwise, just these undulating shapes groping at the hard ground.

Corvus returned, but stayed well away from the shapes. They were strange in some way. Not natural maybe. She wasn't sure.

They made her feel funny, but she wanted a closer look.

No-one was watching the isolated circle of snow, and she could freely skulk from the ravine towards the shapes. She gulped as the lines and texture of the nearest shape became visible. She saw the pieces of a broken body, formed upwards into the shape of a tree. The arms and legs had twisted together into a wrinkled trunk of black flesh, and the face. . . the face howled in silence from within the trunk. It was a risen man, or at least it had been once. Now, a contorted column of black flesh, it burrowed into the ground.

She vomited. She'd barely eaten for a long time and her throat had to reach deep into her stomach to produce anything. It burned and made her lips tingle. Retch followed retch and she turned away and sank down, curling into a ball on the snow.

Corvus flapped above her, warning her of danger, but she couldn't stop vomiting. What were these things?

* * *

Her stomach was too twisted and her head was too sore. She couldn't fight, run or even think. She didn't resist as the guards picked her up and carried her back to the camp. Corvus had made her visible, so they would come to help her.

'Little bitch, how long you been there?'

'She's puked on my boots.'

'It's the trees, they've fucked her up. It happened to Ulf yesterday. We're not supposed to look at them.'

Ingrid held her head. Behind her eyes the risen men screamed. The image wouldn't leave her. It scratched and gnawed into her head. Unimaginable pain and sorrow, reaching further into eternity than she could comprehend. She cried. She vomited again. And then she cried more.

'Throw her on the bedroll,' said a distant voice. 'She'll be okay. Stupid bitch.'

'Beirand's dead. Who was watching her?' It sounded like Harrod.

'Marron and Ulf. They're pretty drunk.'

'Take a finger from each of them. And set them guarding the trees.'

The voices were distorted and weirdly pitched. She half-recognized some of them, but couldn't see any faces to match with the sounds.

'Are they as bad as they say? I mean, look at her. She's lost her fucking mind.'

'Three of the things have already scuttled off to the south. Scouting or some such. What if they come back? I'll go to the ice halls before I look at them.'

'If the man of the sun is true to his word, the beasts may end this fight before we swing an axe,' replied Harrod. 'Tiergarten's walls are high; I'd just as soon end this without a siege.'

'They've only got a few hundred men. Old men. . . kids, angry women.'

Ingrid vomited again. There may have been a man in the way. Certainly someone swore loudly and stood up. It was mostly bile, but it smelled really bad.

'Send the little fucker to the ice halls. She's puked on my axe.'

'So clean it and shut up.'

Harrod loomed in over her. 'Are you listening, you little shit? Or have you lost your mind?'

She groaned, trying to frame an insulting response. Dogged by the constant urge to vomit, though, nothing came to mind. The vision of the risen man was slowly fading from her eyes and her head no longer throbbed.

'I'm okay,' she mumbled.

She looked up and saw that she was in a tent. Maybe five men. Everything smelled of vomit. She sat up. She was back in her own, isolated tent, her arm chained to the same metal ball. She had a horrible taste in her mouth. Her throat was raw and her teeth felt sticky.

'Old metal links. You should get them replaced,' she said, pointing to the broken links.

'Nice trick,' replied the priest. 'Or good luck.'

'The world conspires to free me whenever I get trapped. It's a gift.'

Harrod crouched down next to her bedroll. He picked absently at a splodge of mud on her cloak.

'Do you know where I'm from, Little Wolf?' he asked.

'No. Just that my dad and my Uncle Magnus hated you.'

'Your father took my name,' he replied. 'Dishonour, he said. Old man Teardrop was not a thain with vision. Strength will always defeat honour.'

'According to you,' she replied. 'So, where? Where are you from?'

'Old Gar,' replied Harrod. 'I came to the fine realms of Fjorlan to seek strength. I found it in Jarvik, not Fredericksand.'

'My brother's stronger than Rulag.'

'Stronger than a blade in the dark? Your family are soft. They have ruled too long.' He sat on the floor, crossing his legs. 'This is what I want you to understand, girl – your brother is going to die. He's going to die and you are going to live. How easily you live is up to you. You'll be the bride of the high thain, in a new land.'

'I don't want Fjorlan to change,' she replied.

'Not your decision to make. We have decided to free ourselves from Rowanoco and force our will on this world.'

'I still don't want it to change.' She coughed, her throat scratchy and painful. 'Can I have a drink?'

Harrod put a hand against her forehead. 'You'll live. The things have a disquieting effect. Good thing too; Tiergarten might consider fighting otherwise.'

He grabbed a dirty canteen and removed the stopper, slowly pouring water for her to drink. It was cold and stung her tongue, but it soothed her throat. She took the canteen and swilled out her mouth, spitting into her washbasin. The taste of vomit didn't disappear.

'Now, I'm going to leave you,' said Harrod. 'There will be five guards outside. They will not be drinking. If you try to escape – or go on any more night-time adventures – I'll cut off your foot and Rulag can marry a cripple. I am *not* bluffing. Good evening, Little Wolf.'

He walked from the tent with his men, leaving her alone. He probably *wasn't* bluffing, but she was going to escape anyway. When they were close enough to the city, she'd make her grand exit. He could cut his own stupid foot off.

* * *

After a few hours of dreamless sleep, Ingrid opened one eye and looked out of the tent flaps. Snow fell thickly across the gap, masking those outside, but she could hear them. They grunted and cursed, complaining about the cold, the food, their hangovers. Men of Ursa appeared always to be miserable. They didn't laugh or tease each other. They just swore and bullied each other. She didn't like them. In fact she hated them.

Shielding her eyes from the snow, she took a peek outside. Everyone was moving. Most tents had already been broken down and packed on to sleds. The clank of arms and armour carried far across the snowy expanse and Ingrid had a sudden sinking feeling. Even more so when she saw the siege equipment, which had obviously been transported from Fredericksand in pieces and was now fully assembled. Six large wooden towers mounted on a wide base, pulled by teams of dogs, alongside thick tree-trunks swinging on chains from a wooden frame. Battering rams and siege towers. She'd never seen them before, but she knew what they were. Suddenly things seemed awfully real – and awfully serious.

'Hey, stop gawking,' grunted another fat axe-man. 'Go back inside and I'll unchain you when we're ready to move.'

'Are you attacking?' she asked. 'Today?'

He laughed, a gross gurgle that ended with a messy spit on to the snow. 'We're not that close, you little idiot. But we need to be ready to fight.'

'And the tree-things?' she asked, with a quiver to her lip.

He glared at her, no longer laughing. 'I don't know nothing about them things.' He marched off.

She frowned and went back into her tent. Her bag was in the corner, still fastened tightly shut. She'd not felt like opening it since they left Fredericksand, knowing that looking at her collection of stones would make her upset. The last thing she wanted was to be reminded of when she was happy. Ingrid didn't know how she would get out of her current predicament, but she was sure that she needed to be tough, not crying all the time. Her stubborn disobedience and her smile were the only things she had left, and no collection of pretty stones would change that.

She left the bedroll and her blanket in a haphazard pile, and pulled on her boots. Her toes tingled in the freezing air, but she quickly got warm under her thick, woollen cloak.

'Time's up, girl,' said a voice.

She took a moment, trying to breathe slowly and compose herself, then she slung her rucksack on and left the tent. Within a minute, two waiting men had struck her tent and stowed it. All around her the camp quickly disappeared, becoming a convoy again. Men who'd been permanently drunk as they waited were suddenly soldiers again, formed into columns, units and mobs. However rough and ready they appeared when at leisure, they had an air of professionalism when moving. But there were fewer of them now.

The endless gullies leading from the Crystal Fork were now full of men as Rulag squeezed his army towards the plains of Tiergarten. Orders were shouted and relayed by men now holding axes, glaives and shields, with their personal gear stowed on sleds. Last to leave the camp was the siege equipment, each protected by its own crew and followed by a heavily armed rearguard. Ingrid felt like a speck of dust on a huge canvas of brown and black.

'Things progress, young mistress,' said the Karesian, Kal Varaz, appearing silently on her left. He rarely made any sound.

'Don't sneak up on me,' she replied. 'I can't smell you coming like Beirand. . . or my grotesque future husband.'

He grunted. It may have been a stifled laugh. Or it may just have been a grunt. She glared at him. His dark face was pinched, with creases across his usually smooth cheeks.

'You saw my mistress's gift; I can see it in your eyes.'

She nodded, gulping down a wave of sudden fear. 'No-one would tell me what they were.'

'They are children of the Forest Giant. You should remember them, for they will be your priest and your altar.'

She gulped again, searching for, but not finding, a clever response. 'Will you tell me what they are? What they are *now*, I mean. I know they *were* forest-dwellers.'

'Some knowledge is dangerous,' he replied. 'Some dark corners of the world are not to be explored with freedom. . . and young minds are fragile minds.'

She was suddenly indignant, as if her fear had been displaced by the suggestion that she was in any way fragile.

'I saw them once,' she said, as if bragging. 'They were horrible, but my mind didn't unravel. I must have a strong mind.'

'Indeed!' he exclaimed. 'Perhaps you do.'

'So, tell me.' She was staring at him now.

'Hmm. . . let us just walk for now. Enjoy some of this beautiful scenery.'

She looked around. Beyond the solid line of marching warriors and laden sleds were endless plateaus of rock and ice, with a liberal sprinkling of dusty snow. Harsh, barren, featureless – certainly not beautiful.

'I'd never seen snow until I came to your delightful, barbarian nation. I find it strangely calming.'

'You don't have snow in Karesia?' she asked. 'What do you have instead?'

He smiled. It was still sinister, but she no longer felt as if he meant her harm. 'We have sand. . . and heat. . . and culture.' He suddenly laughed. It was restrained, but definitely laughter. 'Thank you, young mistress.'

'For what?'

He put a hand on her shoulder. 'For taking me out of reality for a moment. For engaging me in a mundane conversation – talk of the weather, the landscape.'

'I prefer conversation over fighting,' she replied. 'Maybe we can get all Rulag's men to stop and chat about the weather.'

'That would indeed be pleasant,' said Kal Varaz. 'Perhaps when the fighting is done, we can all just talk of the weather.'

Their conversation was interrupted by a deafening creak from a nearby siege tower. The six-storey wooden structure had stalled on a patch of jagged rocks and two of the four huge wheels were off the ground. Men whipped the sled dogs, shouting and swearing, trying to free the tower, but it was wedged securely and swaying dangerously overhead.

'Is that going to fall over?' she asked eagerly, excited at the prospect of a dozen men being crushed before they got a chance to kill any people of Tiergarten.

'Doubtful,' replied Kal Varaz. 'It is heavily weighted at the base. Though it may not make the remainder of the journey.'

'How do they work?" she asked.

'Well, I believe the idea is to get them to the walls of the city. Once they are in place, men will attack from the top levels. I imagine the defenders will manage to bring one or two of them down, but the remainder will form the vanguard of the attack. But they will not be needed. A lucky thing, for the loss of your future husband's men would make a frontal attack problematic. If he is to rule Ranen in our stead, he will need to inspire more loyalty, or command more fear.'

Ingrid walked alongside the Karesian, not talking or stepping into his eyeline. She wanted Corvus to swoop down and peck him in the face, but her friend stayed away during the daytime. She thought of the night to come and what mischief there was left to cause. She could tip out more ale or blunt more axes, or she could escape and hide, trusting Corvus to keep her hidden. Perhaps it was time to leave Rulag's army.

CHAPTER ELEVEN

HALLA SUMMER WOLF IN THE CITY OF TIERGARTEN

T HE ATTACK HAD still not come. Rulag had allowed them ample time to work on the defences, and Tiergarten was now well-prepared for a siege. Early each day Halla toured the walls, meeting defenders and commanders, making sure everyone knew their job and what was at stake. The time had allowed them to lay on extra supplies, which were portioned and protected on every level. Barricades had been erected on each landing, and supplies of throwing-axes and shields were stored at regular intervals. She had even devised one or two surprises for Rulag's army.

Greta Cloud Seer, the commander of the ballistae crews, was almost as tireless as Halla, snatching sleep as she could while keeping her eyes on the plains. The young axe-maiden was tall and slim, with a terse manner that made her an ideal commander.

'Anything to report?' asked Halla.

'Nothing,' replied Greta. 'Though Alahan Teardrop came here looking for you, my lady. About an hour before dawn.'

She had avoided him for over a week. Every time Wulfrick tried to get them to talk, she'd found an essential task to keep her away. Brindon Crowe and Tricken Ice Fang had tried to mediate an appropriate meeting, but she'd resisted. A bit of her hoped that Rulag would attack and she'd be able to avoid the conversation entirely. Unfortunately, the lord of Jarvik had not obliged her.

'He said that he'd be in the barracks if you wanted to talk to him,' said Greta. 'He looked tired, like he wasn't sleeping.'

'What would *you* do?' she asked the young commander. 'Would *you* talk to him?'

'I'll never be thain of Tiergarten,' replied Greta. 'But, if I was, I'd think that speaking to Alahan Teardrop was the only remaining thing I had to do before the city was truly ready for war. We've had two commanders since you arrived, my lady, and he's been the quieter of the two.'

She nodded, taking a final look across the Plains of Tiergarten. Then, with a deep breath, she left Greta to tend her ballistae crews and headed for Ulric's Yard and the barracks. The lower streets were clear, with only a few guards on watch. The city had been holding its breath for days, waiting for the attack. In the days of waiting, Halla had spoken to anyone and everyone she could – apart from Alahan Teardrop. She'd given words of encouragement to any warrior wielding an axe for Tiergarten, but she'd avoided the young thain of Fredericksand. Was there truly anything he could say to her that would make any difference? He couldn't strengthen their walls or provide more defenders. He couldn't even justify his father's actions.

She swung open the doors of the barracks, nodding her head to the dozens of defenders within. The axes were sharpened and the armour was ready; the men were concentrating now on preparing themselves with training and tactics. The walls must hold, and everything shouted by Falling Cloud or Tricken had instilled this in the defenders.

'He's in the storeroom, Halla,' said Rudolf Ten Bears. 'He said he had to think.'

She wanted a reason not to speak to him, and took the opportunity to stand with Rudolf as he wound flammable fabric around huge ballistae bolts. Greta and her crews would be responsible for bringing down any siege equipment that Rulag sent against the walls, and they'd had the leisure to prepare a fiery reception.

'Are you going to help me, talk to young Teardrop, or just stand there?' asked Rudolf. 'The world isn't going to get any easier while we wait.'

She padded her feet against the stone floor. 'If Rulag had attacked when we expected him to, I wouldn't *have* to talk to him.'

He gave her an amused look, raising an eyebrow.

'Okay, okay,' she conceded. 'That was a stupid thing to say.'

He smiled, but was nice enough not to agree.

She left him to his ballistae bolts and headed for the storeroom. Bushels of food and flagons of water filled the space, ready to be portioned out at any breaks in combat. Through a side door, sitting on a barrel, was Alahan. His feet kicked absently at wooden planks, left over from their barricade-building on the second level, and his eyes widened when he saw her. He was a few years younger than her, in his early twenties, and had a haunted look in his dark brown eyes. He was considered handsome by many, but Halla did not like his thick, black beard or the high cut of his cheekbones. He looked too much like his father.

'You have words for me?' she asked, standing just inside the door.

'Yes,' he spluttered. 'I. . .' The young thain looked at his feet and screwed up his face, as if he was surprised that Halla had finally decided to talk to him. 'I wanted us to reach an accord. I don't care if we're not friends or confidants, but we must be allies.'

'Must we be?' she replied drily. 'The defences are in place and we are not yet allies. Tiergarten is ready to fight Rulag Ursa with no accord struck between you and me.'

'You don't understand,' he murmured, still not looking at her.

'If those are all the words you have, I am needed elsewhere. We are going on patrol this morning.' She nodded and made to leave.

'Have you heard of Alguin Teardrop?' he asked, making her turn back round. 'The first thain of Fjorlan.'

'That's as much as I know about him,' she replied.

'He was my ancestor. He built Fredericksand and united the

clans of Ranen. My father thought that his bloodline was the oldest in the lands of men.'

'I've heard that,' she replied. 'It's impossible not to if you live in Fjorlan.'

'There's something you won't have heard,' said Alahan, hopping off the barrel. 'His bloodline – my bloodline – we have a responsibility to this land. We have ever been the exemplars of Rowanoco. His generals in his Long War.'

She was startled by this, but not so much as to lose her composure. 'And what does Rowanoco's general think about the defence of Tiergarten?'

The young thain laughed ironically. 'I have no fucking idea. My father never told me what I was supposed to do and neither did Magnus Fork Beard, Brindon Crowe, or any other Order of the Hammer priest. I *had* a friend, someone to tell me what Rowanoco wanted, but I've not seen him for weeks. I suppose I've been thinking about drinking in the ice halls when all this is over.'

She looked at him, assessing whether or not this was a ploy to curry her favour. In his eyes she saw, far removed from thoughts of a city preparing for war, a rippling well of divine might, locked out of sight. It was a jewel of ice, but it faded, falling further away with each beat of her heart. He *did* have power, but he doubted it. She thought that he doubted everything. 'I don't know what you want me to say. I have a lot of people relying on me, and this doesn't contribute to the defence of my city. Unless this power you have can crack the sky and summon the Ice Giant himself.'

Alahan kicked the barrel over and stood, gritting his teeth in anger. Grain spread across the stone floor and made Halla step back from the young thain. He clenched his fists and looked as though he wanted to punch something, but composed himself with a few deep breaths.

'At times I feel it,' he said, looking at his shaking hands. 'It's as if I can reach people's hearts. But then I doubt it and it scares me. And I have dreams about a twisted tree.' He glared at her with fear and envy. '*You* reach their hearts, not me. I was a poor choice for exemplar.'

She kicked a pile of grain out of the way and approached him. 'That seems to be the trouble with trusting such things to a bloodline, rather than to merit. The same is true of me, though my name is not as renowned as yours. Perhaps neither of us truly deserve our stations. Our fathers condemned us to our responsibilities, we didn't choose them.'

'Does it always come back to *them?*' he asked, meeting her gaze.

'They cast a shadow,' she replied coldly. 'It's hard to forget that your father's hand killed *my* father. And now I hear that he was Rowanoco's chosen when he threw his axe.'

Alahan averted his eyes. She felt that he was as uncomfortable speaking to her as she was to him. Especially so when Algenon Teardrop was mentioned.

'I ask that you don't blame the Ice Giant for what my father did,' implored Alahan. 'He needs your faith as much as I do.'

She narrowed her eyes and shook her head. 'Many of my friends drink with him in the ice halls. My faith in *him* is undimmed, but my faith in you. . .' They locked eyes, two children of dead men and two thains of Fjorlan. 'If you are his exemplar, you must prove it. Rowanoco must show me you're worthy of my faith.'

* * *

She'd ignored Wulfrick's prattling. From his rising, through breakfast, to their exit from Tiergarten, the axe-master had spoken of nothing but his young thain. He stopped just short of insulting her, rising to a height of calling her unreasonable but wisely not going any further.

'Wulfrick, give it a rest,' said Falling Cloud. 'We're scouts. Scouts should be quiet.'

There were ten of them, lightly armoured, moving through the foothills. They were some of her most trusted and loyal men, men who had been with her for a year. She hadn't needed to command anyone to accompany her; the best few were simply waiting outside the great hall, among them Rudolf Ten Bears, Lars Bull, Colm Tide Bound and Heinrich Blood.

The Crystal Fork River was ahead of them, flowing over rapids to the Fjorlan Sea, with endless icy gullies cutting through the rocky terrain. The mouth of the river was within sight of the city gates, with the north–south road the only practical way of moving an army. So far they'd seen nothing but empty trenches in the rock.

'What are we scouting for?' replied Wulfrick. 'There's nothing here.'

'They wouldn't camp within sight of the city, you idiot,' said Halla.

'Oh, you *can* talk. Good to know you were just ignoring me.'

'Seriously, give it a rest,' repeated Falling Cloud. 'They'll have scouts too.'

Wulfrick spat on the ice and meandered off on his own, grumbling something about loyalty. He turned a corner and disappeared down a nearby trench.

'He can fight and he can shout, but he's terrible at conversation,' observed Falling Cloud. 'You know what I mean – he doesn't express himself well. . . unless he's fighting or shouting.'

'Let's keep moving,' she replied. 'He'll catch up.'

They were now distant from the city, with only plumes of smoke telling them of Tiergarten's location. They'd stayed off the north–south road, keeping to the craggy trenches cut by the river. The snowy hills and the crisp, blue sky melted together into a vast canvas. An army – even a large one – could hide in any number of locations in the north of Summer Wolf.

'We need some high ground,' she said. 'They can hide the men, but armies make noise. They need fires, supplies.'

Falling Cloud nodded and scanned their surroundings. He pointed to a landslide that appeared to provide a way out of the trenches, and darted up it in a few long strides. Halla smiled. She couldn't have done that, at least not so fast and with such dexterity. Falling Cloud shielded his eyes from the glare and peered to the north.

'Anything?' she asked.

He shifted position, leaping on to a higher rock. He was not a tall man and had to stand on tiptoe to see further. 'Yeah, you should probably come up here.'

'Wonderful,' she replied, looking at Rexel's route upwards. Falling on her arse in the snow would not be a good way of showing leadership.

The young priest Heinrich Blood, bringing up the rear of the group, sensed her reluctance and lent a discreet hand. She may not have been as dextrous as Rexel, but she made up for it in brute strength, tensing her thigh muscles and powering her way upwards.

The glare was considerable. From her elevated position, the northern plains appeared endless. Summer Wolf flowed into Teardrop, then there was nothing but ice and snow until the northern realms of the Volk.

'Look west,' said Falling Cloud. 'The break in the river.'

Shielding her eyes, she saw at the edges of her vision muddy black plumes of smoke. They rose in irregular lines, bisecting the featureless white of the coast and the undulating black of the sea.

'That's a lot of fires, Halla. And lots of fires means lots of men. Hard to tell the number from this distance, but a few thousand at least.'

'We need to get closer.'

'Aye, my lady.'

There was a maze of deep trenches between them and the smoke. They couldn't risk the road, so would have to pick their way through zigzag fissures in the ice. Falling Cloud stayed on the high ground, leaping across the gaps, but she doubted any more of her men could manage such a thing. She knew *she* couldn't.

'Rexel, don't get too far ahead,' she ordered, as Heinrich helped her back down. 'Find us a way through.'

'Aye,' replied the cloud-man.

Her men – nine without Wulfrick – moved quickly along the trenches, with Falling Cloud giving directions from above, and

Heinrich and Colm bringing up the rear. They moved left, right, left again, straight on and over a ridge. Within half an hour they were next to a narrow spot of the Crystal Fork, and closer to the open plains. Wulfrick had been spotted, trudging reluctantly behind them, but hadn't rejoined the group.

'Halla, something ahead,' said Falling Cloud, emerging on a high ledge. 'Dead trees, looks like.'

The trench they were in was wide and got wider still as it met the river. On either side a vertical escarpment blocked their view, rising twenty feet or more in a jagged line. They were close to the army now, but the trench didn't allow even a glimpse of the smoke from their cook-fires.

'And past the trees?' she asked Rexel.

'The river. Then the plains open out. There're banners. . . a red splodge, looks like a bear claw. There's a shitload of men, Halla. Siege towers too.'

'Get down here, Rexel, they'll have scouts.'

He vaulted to the trench floor in a single leap.

'We're safe up to the trees,' he said. 'We can get a good enough look from there.'

Halla signalled for her men to draw weapons, and they edged quietly round a sharp corner.

'Rudolf, Bull, take the lead.'

The two men, both survivors of the dragon fleet, crouched and kept their footsteps light. Ahead, the trench sloped away from them, ending in an icy waterfall that flowed into the Crystal Fork. Beyond the three black trees, the smoke from cook-fires was now obvious. Hundreds of grey plumes mingled in the air, making a fog above the plains. Rulag Ursa's army, many thousands of men, was camped less than a day's march from Tiergarten.

'Seen enough?' said Wulfrick, appearing behind her.

His face was sullen and his great-axe was still sheathed. He was taller and bulkier than any of her men, but, at that moment, he looked like little more than a sulking child.

'Are you and I having a fight?' she asked, not looking at him.

'I think maybe just a disagreement,' he replied. 'I only have so much loyalty to go around.'

She felt for him. She really did. He was Alahan's axe-master and would be loyal to the house of Teardrop until he died. That was as sure as anything. As sure as the axe that had cut down Lord Algenon.

'I didn't challenge your young thain to a duel. I just said I won't swear fealty to him.'

'You owe him your allegiance.'

'Based on what? The ancient traditions of Fjorlan? Those traditions got my father killed – for what? For disagreeing with Algenon fucking Teardrop?'

He looked at her. His wide, hairy face was creased and emotional. He was almost a foot taller than her, but he shrank under her gaze.

'I'm your friend, Halla. I am. But I'm a man of Fredericksand. . . I'm axe-master to the house of Teardrop. I always will be.'

Falling Cloud took a step backwards. 'Err, Halla. . .'

'What?'

'One of those trees just moved.'

She broke eye-contact with Wulfrick and they both looked along the trench. Some distance away, on the edge of the ice, three black shapes began to sway against the white background. The trees had thick trunks and rope-like branches. They had appeared dead at first, cracked and dry, but their movements now, although strange, seemed organic.

'Those are not trees,' said Wulfrick, slowly reaching for his great-axe.

'Does anyone else have a sudden headache?' asked Falling Cloud. 'I think I feel sick.'

The three black shapes juddered and their branches reached downwards, pushing at the icy ground. Snow and rock flew into the air as they clamped on to the earth with bizarre strength.

'Halla. . .'

She didn't understand what she was seeing. Was the glare playing tricks on her eyes? They weren't trees any more. The branches were now legs and arms – no, tentacles. They lifted the trunks from the snow and exposed circular mouths, shaking snow and earth from needle-like teeth.

'Halla. . .'

Her feet wouldn't move. She wanted to turn and address whoever was speaking to her, but the black shapes wouldn't let her. They came together, writhing across the ice as one black blob of tentacles and grotesque mouths, crawling over each other.

She could hear Wulfrick next to her. He was panting and stamping at the ground.

'I think we need to leave,' she whispered.

The shapes darted forward, covering the ice with alarming speed while groping at the air with their tentacles and roaring. It was a guttural bellow that made her skin crawl. No natural beast could make such a sound. *What the fuck were these things?*

'Halla. . .'

She couldn't turn and she couldn't run. Her mind twisted before the monsters, as a hundred points of pain erupted in her head. It was more than a headache; it was a feeling of near-madness that rooted her to the spot.

'Halla!' screamed Falling Cloud, shoving her aside as the creatures approached.

The monsters were upon them quickly, barrelling Wulfrick to the floor. There was a scream of pain as Lars Bull, barely able to raise his axe, was lifted from the ground and torn in two. Another man was driven into the ice, his head smashed to a red smear. Wulfrick was vibrating with rage, leaping to his feet and frothing at the mouth. His eyes were now black and his knuckles had turned white against the haft of his axe. One of the beasts reared up at him, but he didn't flee.

'Run!' she ordered, her voice cracking with fear.

She turned and saw a clear path behind them. Everywhere else, the creatures loomed. They blocked out the light, reaching for men and swatting aside axes. She screamed in anger and swiped at a tentacle, but the flesh was tough and her axe barely cut the surface. Heinrich sent arrows into them, but they didn't slow. Rudolf Ten Bears buried an axe in the trunk of one, but it barely flinched. She stood with her back to the rocky wall, keeping her axe close to her body.

Then Wulfrick attacked. He seemed to have lost all sense of reason. He leapt at the creature before him, burying his axe in its trunk and pulling himself upwards. The rest of her men – four or five now – were trying to flee along the trench, but they were struggling, their bodies frozen in fear. Falling Cloud pulled at her shoulder, dragging her away from the wall.

'Run!' she repeated, shoving Heinrich backwards as a fleshy maw grabbed one of the fleeing men, dissolving his flesh into gooey pink liquid.

Wulfrick was roaring and pulling his way up the creature, chopping chunks from its mass as he moved. It flung him left and right as if he were a minor annoyance like a fly, grabbing at him using its tentacles. Black ichor sprayed from the tree as Wulfrick hacked at it, covering his axe-blade and running down his face. The other two beasts moved to block their retreat, stretching out, with their limbs whipping against the snow.

'Up!' shouted Falling Cloud, doing his best to marshall the remaining men.

He leapt on to a ledge, out of immediate reach of the creatures, and waved frantically at the others to join him. Heinrich followed, loosing an arrow behind him and slipping forward on the ice. Halla wrapped her arms round his waist and hefted him upwards to Falling Cloud's waiting hand.

'Get up there! All of you – now!' she screamed, trying to climb to the ledge.

A dead man was flung at them and a beast loomed. Its maw was inches from Halla when Falling Cloud launched an axe into its mouth, making it buck with alarm and pull back. The axe sliced open the circular orifice, but quickly disappeared into the mass of black.

'They won't die!' shrieked Heinrich, his eyes deeply bloodshot.

'They'll die!' replied Wulfrick, no sanity in his bellowed words.

Falling Cloud grunted with exertion and pulled Heinrich up out of the trench, stepping backwards on to the plateau to get clear of the beasts. Colm Tide Bound interposed himself between Halla and the closest creature, giving her time to tense her arms and heft her body up to the ledge. The man was swallowed whole, his feet disappearing in an instant. The creature's trunk rocked backwards and rippled, like a snake swallowing a rat. When it turned its mouth back to her she was on her feet, on the high ledge, being pulled away by Heinrich. Rudolf followed, but the others were cut off.

She turned. One beast was sluggishly trying to digest Colm; another was methodically tearing apart the last man. Wulfrick was still attached to the back of his creature, driving his great-axe into its black flesh with tremendous strength. He was in a deep frenzy, clearly thinking only of destruction. Retreat would be impossible for him, she realized.

'Halla, we can't get to him,' said Falling Cloud breathlessly.

One of the tree-things began to pursue them, climbing vertically up the walls of ice. The other loped towards Wulfrick.

'We need to leave,' snapped Falling Cloud, grabbing her by the shoulders. 'Now!'

They ran. Rexel, Halla, Heinrich and Rudolf. Five men were dead and Wulfrick could not survive against all three tree-things. She wanted to turn and help him, but once she'd begun running it was all she could do. Her mind recoiled from what she'd seen, hiding in a corner of her head, just wanting to scream and hide. *What the fuck were those things?*

* * *

Halla stood by the huge door to her great hall, looking nervously into the stark white morning. Her eyes were haunted and she refused any offer of a seat or a drink. Her men, still wearing their armour and clutching weapons, were all covered in a flaky, black substance, too thick to be blood. It clung to their skin, hair and under their fingernails, giving the appearance of them having rolled in mud and let it dry.

'They weren't trees,' mumbled Heinrich Blood. 'Tentacles. . . mouths. . . just black.'

'Talk sense,' snapped Brindon Crowe. 'Halla, please, come sit. Talk to us. What was it?'

'Halla,' said Alahan, 'is Wulfrick dead?'

She turned away from the door for the first time and looked at him with moist red eyes. With a shaking hand she pushed a stray tendril of red hair from her face and swallowed hard. 'I don't know. I – we – couldn't get to him.'

Falling Cloud stood and put a hand on her shoulder. She looked at him and then they fell into a tearful embrace. She broke down on her captain's shoulder, hearing Wulfrick's frenzied roaring in her head.

'Easy,' said Rexel, wiping away his own tears. 'We're still alive. . . we're still alive.'

She had seen so much, weathered so many trials and defeated so many enemies. But the trees. . . Could they kill Wulfrick? If a hundred men had attacked the axe-master, Halla would have put her bet on Wulfrick. What could a black tree do that a hundred men could not?

Brindon Crowe took charge. The old priest made sure Halla, Rexel and Heinrich were seated comfortably while Tricken directed servants to stoke the fire-pits, allowing warmth to flow over the hall and through shivering limbs. The last survivor of Halla's patrol, Rudolf Ten Bears, was still outside, clinging to his axe at the top of Kalall's Steps. He'd refused to move and appeared to be guarding something – perhaps himself.

'Rudolf's lost his mind,' said Halla. 'He ranted the whole way back.'

'He puked at the gates,' offered Tricken. 'He's thrown his axe. . . just give him time.'

Water and cloths were brought into the hall and they cleaned black ichor from their armour and faces. It came off only reluctantly and Halla scrubbed manically at her hands.

'It won't come off,' she mumbled. 'It won't.'

Rexel grabbed her hands. The cloud-man had a stoic expression, as if his mind was stronger than the others'. He held Halla's black-smeared hands and made her look at him.

'Halla, I've seen you fight and kill to defend yourself, your men, your land. . . I've seen you survive the dragon fleet, Ro Hail, the ice spiders, Jarvik, the Bear's Mouth – don't let a fucking tree bring you low.'

She tried to smile, but she couldn't tear her eyes away from her stained hands. 'It won't come off,' she repeated.

Heinrich Blood joined them and they fell together in a tight clinch, breathing heavily, with Falling Cloud whispering to his two battle brothers. It took a few minutes, but gradually her breath became less pained and the sound of Wulfrick's shouting faded from her mind.

'I need to know what you saw!' said Alahan, standing up as Halla finished cleaning her hands.

'And if I can't tell you?' she replied. 'If I don't know. . . if I don't want to think about it?'

'It was a beast,' offered Falling Cloud. 'Not a troll, not a spider, not the krakens themselves.' He bowed his head as if recalling the creature. 'It appeared to be a tree, black and dead. When it moved, it was fast. Branches became legs, tentacles. Its mouth was. . . just a hole. But the teeth – like needles.'

'It wasn't just the look of the thing,' said Heinrich. 'It felt worse than it looked.'

'That's the truth,' agreed Halla, finally able to speak clearly.

The three of them finished scrubbing themselves clean and slowly took seats opposite Alahan, Tricken and Brindon.

'Was it a darkwood tree?' asked Old Father Crowe. 'Black, with cracked bark?'

'Aye, it could have been,' replied Rexel. 'Never seen one. Do they usually move?'

Brindon leant forward and appeared to be taking his time. The atmosphere was still manic; the old priest slowed things down by moving his eyes from Rexel to Halla before answering. 'No, they don't usually move. Nor do they grow in Fjorlan. There are old, old tales of. . . dark things, dead gods and eldritch magic.'

'It's the Twisted Tree,' said Alahan, drawing all eyes to him. 'It's been reborn.'

CHAPTER TWELVE

QUEEN GWENDOLYN TIRIS IN NARLAND

THE LANDS OF the Twisted Tree, they were calling it. Each new group of refugees – clinging to saddles, pulling their worldly belongings in carts, or just walking in lonely stupor – told a tale. First there had been dozens, then hundreds; now there were thousands. They came from farms, townships. Some came from Ro Weir itself, those who had decided the new order was not for them. Some had family elsewhere or enough money to start afresh; others had left in the night, too scared to pack and too stunned to think of a direction to travel. The Hawks filtered them through the army, distributing as much aid as could be spared and picking up information from those who wanted to talk.

The Mistress of Pain was still alive and living openly as high priestess of her new world. They spoke of her as though her very glance could convey domination or death. She'd declared all the lands of Ro to be under the sway of her new religion, and south of Cozz she was largely correct. Rich men and women, nobles of Weir and Leith, and affluent merchant princes – they all cowered before her, changing their old world to fit her new one. And the Hounds – they were everywhere. Refugees spoke of death squads, purges, martial law and public burnings – which they called immolation.

Rham Jas Rami had failed. He was probably dead, and the Sister remained to direct her huge army. As she had feared, sorcery would still play a part in their battle. Swords may not be enough.

The Lands of the Twisted Tree. She thought the name bothered Xander more than the occupation itself. The bitch had seen fit to rename Tor Funweir. In doing so she'd pissed on centuries of history and tradition, kicking the house of Tiris in the face. The name went back to High King Dashell Tiris, the first man to unite all the cities of Ro. Before him, feudal lords had fought for territory and riches, taking and breaking alliances as their mood dictated. The house of Tiris and the Purple clerics who followed them had created a nation that had stood until now. It was Tor Funweir, not the Lands of the Twisted fucking Tree.

'You're from Hunter's Cross, my queen,' said Markos of Rayne.

'So?'

'So, why do you care?' replied the paladin. 'Your people are mongrels at best, godless yokels at worst. No-one has invaded the Cross.'

She was becoming tired of his pious horse-shit. The White Knights cared only for utter submission to the One. Anyone not constantly on their knees, praying for salvation, was a heathen. She could only assume that the Red Prince was the sole option available to them. Xander was many things: devout was not one of them. But after having their coronation blessed, she was sure that, whatever the One God wanted, it certainly wasn't prayer and austerity.

'Thank you for the insightful commentary,' she replied. 'Don't you have an evening prayer meeting to organize?'

He held himself upright, hands on hips and chest thrust out. 'A barbed tongue is the sign of an unchecked mind, my queen.'

'Again, insightful. Seriously, though, fuck off.'

The man didn't know how to react. She'd sworn at him before, but his mind could barely comprehend that anyone, even his queen, would dare to insult him.

'Anything else?' she asked.

'No. I will. . . fuck off, my queen.'

He left, returning to his Knights of the Dawn. They did not assist with the refugees, nor did they mingle with the rest of the army. When night came, they camped by themselves and refused all but the most essential coordination. Markos was the sole member to spend time away from the other knights. He wandered through their camp, sneering at the men and pointing out random acts of slovenliness or insubordination. He was largely ignored.

The Lands of the Twisted Tree. The more she sounded out the words, the more they angered her. The bitch couldn't enchant them all, whether they could kill her or not. Once her Hounds were routed, she could sway the odd warrior, perhaps put together some kind of rearguard, but— *shut up, Gwen,* she thought. There was enough bravado flying around the army without her contributing. Lords and mercenaries from Arnon and Du Ban had answered their king's call and given the army bulk, but many were treating the campaign as sport, not realizing how tenuous their lives had suddenly become.

A warm breeze drifted over the hills of Narland, sending her braided hair into a collar that wrapped itself loosely around her neck. The army was west of the King's Highway, camped in the endless, spider-infested hills north of Weir. Dokkalfar scouts were ranging in every direction between them and the city. All of a sudden it felt like a war – starving refugees, unlikely allies, slow troop movements. When those with power fought, those without suffered. Groups, mobs, collectives – citizens unused to combat, with crossbows held in untrained hands, fleeing from anything with a scimitar, turning Tor Funweir into a roiling mass of fear and confusion.

Standing on a hill, watching an endless stream of startled refugees, was not conducive to constructive thinking. The new queen of Tor Funweir left her isolation, striding back to the command tent, positioned on another hill in the distance.

* * *

The tent was octagonal and the table was circular. Round it sat the commanders of the armies of Tor Funweir. She knew some of them – Xander, Brother Daganay, Major Brennan, Tyr Sigurd, Lord Markos – but others were new to her. There was a watch commander from Tiris. Two landed knights, one with a large crossbow and another with an aged face, grey hair and heavy plate armour.

Lord Ronan Montague from Du Ban stood to the side, clad in a steel breastplate. He commanded yeomanry from his lands and had pledged his men to King Alexander Tiris. Other lords and ladies had sent oaths of fealty and what men they could spare. Animustus, the Gold cardinal of Ro Arnon, had pledged support to the new king but no men, claiming that the church city must remain protected. Other lords and rich men had provided supply lines to keep the army fed and equipped. Carts of grain, potatoes and salted meat arrived hourly from Tiris and Voy.

The new forces had doubled their number and close to forty thousand men now camped in the hills of Narland. Xander had welcomed each man with a smile, knowing that every warrior could make a difference. He'd assigned them to duties, made them assist the refugees and formed his men into a wedge, pointing south. The objective had been made clear – liberate Ro Weir from occupation, and pull down the banners of the Twisted Tree. For the first time, she thought they could do it.

'Is this risen man a joke, my king?' asked Lord Montague.

'He's our chief scout,' replied Daganay, patting Sigurd on the shoulder.

The lord of Du Ban looked along his nose at the Dokkalfar. 'I'm surprised to hear such words from a lesser churchman. This creature is a godless abomination. The Mandate of Severus remains as true today as it did when it was writ.'

'Well, technically,' began Daganay, 'they had a god long before we did – a Shadow Giant, if memory serves. Some histories even suggest—'

'There's not going to be a fight in this tent,' interrupted Brennan. 'And I don't trust either of you to keep this in words – there'll be a punch sooner or later. If the king wants Sigurd to stay, then Sigurd stays. Simple. He's in charge, you are not. This is rule number one.'

'Thank you, Major,' replied Xander.

Brother Daganay leant across the table and addressed Lord Montague directly. 'If you need any education in the histories of the Dokkalfar, see me later. The Kirin scholar, Vham Dusani, was particularly erudite on the subject.'

'Dag, give it a rest,' said Gwen.

'If we can begin,' grunted Xander, shaking his head.

'Of course, General,' agreed Brennan.

Around the tent, dozens of men now fell quiet to listen to their new king.

'Scouts and refugees are equally good at delivering bad news,' said Xander. 'It's been confirmed that Ro Weir fell several months ago, while the Red Army was in Ranen. At this point, over a hundred thousand Hounds encircle it. They are controlled by one of the Seven Sisters and they fly the banner of a Twisted Tree, thinking to remake Tor Funweir as a part of their new Tyranny.'

'Intolerable,' spat Ronan Montague. 'How has this been allowed?'

Half the room, judging by their expressions, seemed to want to laugh at the lord's naivety, but they checked their humour. Gwen imagined that Du Ban had remained free of the Sisters' influence and that Lord Montague, like many Lords of Ro, would have merely remained in his keep, hoping someone else would deal with the Hounds.

'My lord,' said the king, with a note of tolerance, 'this has been allowed by the complacency of the Lords of Ro and by the designs of the Seven Sisters. My brother and cousin were enchanted. Both Purple cardinals were enchanted. If I hadn't left Ro Haran, I'd have been fucking enchanted. We have a dead Kirin to thank for our current freedom, for one witch can cause much less mischief than seven.'

'Rham Jas Rami has given us a chance to win,' offered Gwen. 'Maybe just a fool's chance, but a chance nonetheless.'

'Numbers do not matter,' said Markos. 'The One is all the armour we need. Their swords will miss. Their arrows will glance from our faith as if it were the finest steel.'

Daganay rolled his eyes. 'Just to be safe, I think I'll still wear armour.'

'If they get through us,' offered Gwen, knowing that something needed to be said, 'then Tor Funweir falls. Arnon, Leith, Tiris. . . even Haran. There won't be enough true fighting men left to stop this Twisted Tree. Thousands of men, women and children need our help.'

'To that end,' said Xander, 'we deploy the army here and send out raiding companies to clear the surrounding area of Hounds. They're not organized and hopefully we can trim their numbers before we march on Weir itself. We don't know how many more Hounds can sail from Karesia – two million, three million? If we don't stop them at Weir, we won't stop them at all.'

* * *

The guard post was poorly made and the Hounds that occupied it were poorly trained. There were a hundred of them, flailing at the fifth cohort with wild abandon.

She parried a scimitar thrust and cut a man's throat. Her leaf-blade got stuck in his armour, but he died quickly and there was no-one close to take advantage. Either side of her, the wooden structure was alive with combat.

They'd closed in through the forest and attacked suddenly from the flanks. Whatever else the Hounds may be, they were clearly shit carpenters, and the guard post barely had walls. It was a series of wooden platforms and low fences, overlooking the King's Highway. It would have been a good spot if it wasn't so obvious.

'They're running!' shouted Symon. 'Pursue. No-one gets away.'

A wave of leaf-blades was launched from the trees, cutting down those running. Tyr Sigurd and his Dokkalfar were masterful at mopping up stragglers.

A company of yeoman from Du Ban, stationed with the forest-dwellers, rode from the woods and cut off the retreating Hounds, killing every last one that didn't already have a leaf-blade in his back. Everyone was dead in less than three minutes from when the Hawks had first broken cover.

She stood, cleaning her leaf-blade on her cloak and surveying the southern horizon. It was empty. Maybe ten miles south was Ro Weir; on either side of their advance, arrayed across the duchy, were the Hounds. The main force hadn't left Weir, but huge mobs roamed the countryside and every single one needed to be killed before they could push towards the city. It would be slow and violent, with many short battles and attritional losses to their vanguard, but it was preferable to being outflanked.

'Send word back, we're clear to this point.'

'Aye, my lady,' replied Symon. The young Hawk hesitated.

'Problem?' she asked.

'Why aren't they riding out to meet us? We've smashed all their patrols and pushed almost to their doorway – what are they waiting for?' He was not wounded and, though his sword was bloodied, he stood at ease.

'They don't make war like us. I'm not sure they make war at all. Think of them like an ant colony, stripping the forest floor of leaves and twigs, never thinking about things in their way. If an ant dies another takes its place. Each one is expendable.'

Tyr Sigurd rushed over to them. He was hugely tall and covered the uneven ground in long, graceful strides. His forest-dwellers were skulking on the horizon, as the Hawks pulled dead bodies into a pile next to the wooden structures.

'Take a rest, friend,' said Symon.

'Later,' replied Sigurd. 'Queen Gwendolyn, a small group of riders has been sighted to the south. Not these faceless suits of armour.'

'Not Hounds? Are they coming or going?' she asked.

'Heading this way,' he said.

Gwen narrowed her eyes. 'Symon, leave the bodies, get everyone to form up on the barricade.'

'As you say, my queen.'

'Sigurd, stay out of sight until they get to the ridge. See what they do.'

'Sensible,' replied the forest-dweller.

They parted. Symon snapped a few orders and the fifth cohort left a canvas of sprawled dead bodies on the grass and formed up at her back. The Dokkalfar remained in place, managing to be remarkably stealthy with nothing but a slight ridge to obscure them. Gwen herself, with Symon behind her left shoulder, strode towards the ridge.

She smiled as the distant riders came into view. Sigurd's eyesight was keen in the extreme. Gwen could barely make out horses, let alone armour. To her it was just a moving splodge of brown and black. Then a texture of white appeared above the splodge. As they neared the ridge, the lead rider came into view. He held a wooden lance, topped with a white flag. He was not a Hound and wore ornate black armour, with two wavy-bladed knives sheathed across his chest.

'That's a wind claw,' she muttered. Since Cozz, they'd met only Hounds. The former faithful of Jaa had stayed close to the Mistress of Pain, rightly thinking that she needed protecting.

'White flag,' said Symon. 'Does that mean we can't kill them?'

'It means they've got balls,' she said with a smile. 'If, at any point in the up-coming conversation, I give you a nod, cut them down. They can fuck their white flag if they think I'll put up with any shit.'

'With pleasure, my queen,' he replied.

She strolled across the grass, side-stepping a mutilated Hound and rising to stand on the ridge, with hidden Dokkalfar either side and Symon, sword in hand, at her back.

There were ten riders, on muscular warhorses, armed with scimitars and vicious knives. The wind claw was in the lead, but behind was a mixed group of Karesians and Ro. The natives of Tor Funweir shared the blank aggression of the Karesians and appeared to give no thought to the angry Hawks glaring at them.

'Rein in that horse,' said Gwen loudly. 'And tell your Ro pets to fuck off or they'll die within a minute.'

The forest-dwellers rose from concealment and the horses reared up in surprise. The wind claw stopped instantly, but the others had to wrestle their mounts into compliance.

'Give the order or they die,' she repeated, a growl barely contained behind the words. 'Seeing *your* face is bad enough – these are men of Ro, twisted by your craft. Bringing them here is an insult.'

The wind claw was a young man, but his eyes were still and penetrating. He didn't blink. 'I don't think you'd violate a flag of truce,' he said in a sharp, lyrical accent.

She nodded at Symon. He smiled and gestured to Sigurd's leaf-blade. The forest-dwellers, impassive and graceful, drew their knives and, with no apparent aim, launched them at the five men of Ro. Each traitor caught a blade in the chest and fell from their horse. Their chain shirts were poor protection against the razor-sharp Dokkalfar weapons, and three were dead before they hit the grass. The other two screamed in pain and thrashed around, spraying blood from his wounds as they feebly tried to pull the blades out of their bodies. The Karesians, still trying to control their horses, drew scimitars, but did not attack.

The young wind claw, staying impressively unemotional, raised a hand to his remaining men. 'Sheathe the weapons. I don't believe we are in similar danger of summary execution.'

'And them?' asked one of his men, pointing to the two dying men of Ro.

The wind claw locked eyes with Gwen and held her gaze even as they both listened to the gurgling death-rattle of his two men. His eyes were intense and she deduced that he was not a man squeamish of pain or death. The sounds slowly became murmurs, and finally silence as both men succumbed to their wounds.

'Time kills all men,' said the wind claw. 'Those with a blade in their chest more quickly than others.'

'What do you want, Karesian?' demanded Gwen. 'We have little time for flags of parlay.'

'Yes, that is your reputation,' he replied. 'Well, the reputation of the Red Prince. I do not know who *you* are.'

'I am Gwendolyn Tiris, Queen of Tor Funweir. And don't make me ask again.'

He smiled for the first time, though the expression lacked humour, not progressing much past a curl of the lip. 'What do I want? I want to speak to your husband, to the new king. I bring terms from my lady of the Seven Sisters.'

'Is this a fucking joke? We've hacked and slashed our way south from the ruin you left of Cozz. Do *you* think we'll accept terms from your mistress?'

'Just give the nod,' whispered Symon, his eyes low and angry.

She thought about it. Maybe it was curiosity, or perhaps some lingering sense of honour, that stopped her executing the young Karesian.

'You have a name, wind claw?'

'Ramazon Kadri,' he replied, 'of Kessia.'

'Follower of Jaa?' she asked.

'Of the Twisted Tree. The new and only world. A world you should embrace – or it will mean your death.' He paused, surveying the men and forest-dwellers who would gladly cut his throat if Gwen gave the order. 'But I am not here to deliver justice. That will come in time. I am here to deliver terms. I ask that you see me and my party safe to your king. We will peace-tie our weapons and trust in your honour that we will not be harmed.'

Again, curiosity took over. What did the witch have to say? What could she possibly have to say? Gwen knew that killing Ramazon was the safest course, but Xander would want to speak to him. . . and the husband was less charitable than the wife. The wind claw would certainly die; but there was no harm in hearing his words first.

'My queen,' prompted Symon.

'They live,' she replied. 'Six Karesians are no threat and Xander will want to decide their fate himself.'

* * *

Though the Karesians were not harmed, they had to weather countless insults as they were escorted through the forward ranks of the army. Ramazon looked to the front, sparing no comments and also appearing to spare no concern for the multitudes that wanted him dead. Pavilions, campfires, kitchen wagons, stables – each section of the army had its own reasons for hating the Karesian and his people, and each warrior let the wind claw know. If he was surprised at the size of the army camped only a few days' march from Weir, he didn't show it.

Lord Markos had met them at the lines, adding a hundred Knights of the Dawn in escort and announcing their arrival.

'Make way! We have an emissary from Weir. Clear the way for the queen!'

Everyone came to look. If the Karesians had not been surrounded by the knights, Gwen had no doubt that some overly eager Hawk would have sent a crossbow bolt or two into their ranks.

'This is how it feels to be outnumbered and surrounded by enemies,' she quipped, smirking at the wind claw.

'I am not perturbed by the stares of lesser men,' he replied, keeping his eyes forward. Luckily he'd not spoken loudly enough for the others to hear, so he remained alive after the insult.

It took time to move through the army, from the raven of Canarn to the white dove of the paladins and the red hawk of Haran. When the command pavilion appeared in front of them, they were deep within an army of Ro.

'Ho there!' shouted Markos.

From the large, octagonal tent, Xander, Daganay and Brennan appeared. They could not have been ignorant of the approaching riders. Word spread quickly among fighting men.

'A warm afternoon,' said Xander, smiling at the wind claw. 'Perhaps get off that pony and have a cooling drink.'

He directed Markos to withdraw and the mounted knights formed a protective barrier round the pavilion. Beyond them, hundreds of soldiers looked for a chance to attack the Karesians, but stayed back as Gwen dismounted next to Ramazon Kadri.

Symon and Tyr Sigurd stayed in close escort and led the emissary into the command pavilion, while the other foreigners were herded together nearby. Xander kept looking at the wind claw until he disappeared behind the pavilion's fabric. He then approached his wife.

'You found a wandering envoy?' he asked, kissing her fleetingly.

'He had a white flag and everything,' she replied, stroking his face. 'The Mistress of Pain has a message.'

Major Brennan coughed. 'Shall we just cut him up and send a few fingers back to Weir?' he asked. 'Maybe wrapped in his white flag.'

'Please!' objected Brother Daganay. 'We are still bound by the laws of war.'

They all looked at him. Gwen thought him sincere and that, in a perfect world, his way was the better way. But they didn't live in a perfect world and the war had moved far beyond rules and flags of truce.

'I'll at least say hello before I kill him,' said Xander, leading them all back into his tent.

Symon had put the wind claw in a chair and he was surrounded by men-at-arms. Maps and troop movements had been removed from the central table and the tent was sparse and stifling, the southern heat caught within the thick canvas. Daganay sat at the table and drank from a goblet of wine, while Brennan remained standing behind Gwen and Xander.

'King Alexander,' intoned Ramazon, spreading his arms wide and bowing his head. 'I greet you with respect and fear. . . and I bring terms from my mistress of the Seven Sisters.'

'Respect and fear?' queried Daganay. That's an evocation of Jaa, not your dead god.'

'Old habits,' replied the wind claw, maintaining his poise. 'Pleasure and pain are less useful when engaging in diplomacy.'

Xander stepped to a few feet in front of the emissary, and looked him up and down. 'You're unlikely to leave this tent alive. But be a good thrall and deliver your words first. If you speak without annoying me further, you'll die quickly.'

Ramazon showed a flicker of fear, just creeping into the edges of his eyes, but his stoic expression did not change. 'I'm here in peace, King Alexander, under a flag of truce. Please remain honourable!'

Xander let out a sinister chuckle. 'I wonder how many people of Ro surrendered. . . how many begged for their lives – how many of them did *you* spare? And how many did you burn? You lost the right to parlay when you used sorcery to enthral Tor Funweir. *You* broke the rules. Don't you dare impugn my honour for telling you to shove your flag up your arse.'

Brennan, almost as indignant as the general, drew his longsword and held it across Ramazon's throat. 'Do we need to hear his words, my lord?'

Xander appeared to consider it, but Gwen knew he'd already decided.

'Speak,' said the king. 'Deliver your terms.'

The wind claw could no longer keep his composure. Sweat began to form on his forehead. He looked from Brennan's sword to Xander's glare. 'You misunderstand my intentions. . . I am here to accept your surrender.'

Silence. Gwen couldn't believe that the Mistress of Pain would be so arrogant. Or that Ramazon would show so little concern for his own survival. He sat opposite an angry cleric, looking at an angry general and his angry wife, while an angry soldier held a blade to his throat – and he spoke of surrender.

'Please,' said the wind claw, 'allow me to continue.'

Xander gritted his teeth. 'Continue,' he snarled.

'We may appear to your eyes as nothing but monsters, throwing our Hounds at an obstacle until it submits. But we are not without wit – and not without strategy.' He was clearly scared, but his words were calm, arriving at their ears sounding like reasoned discourse.

'We've been killing Hounds since we left Cozz,' said Gwen. 'Your strategy is not working.'

A curl appeared at the edge of Ramazon's mouth. A nasty smile with too much confidence to be just bravado. 'While you were assembling your meagre allies, we were not idle. Before Cozz was destroyed, we had two whip-masters in position at Leith. When our campaign in the Fell ended, we had some spare troops. These Hounds – some sixty thousand – will be in position behind you within the week.'

Was it possible? In their haste to advance, could such a force have been waiting to the east? The hard glares that travelled round the pavilion – and the tightness that appeared on Xander's lips – told her that the others believed it was indeed possible. If they'd come from Arnon, Markos and his paladins would have seen them; if they'd gone north from Weir, they'd have marched straight into the bulk of Xander's army. But from the east, from the Fell and the Plains of Leith, an army could hold position, unmolested and unseen, until the Hawks had passed by and entered the hills of Narland.

'Sixty thousand,' muttered Brennan, his sword relaxing against Ramazon's throat.

'Do not fear, master Hawk,' said the Karesian. 'My mistress is generous. If your king surrenders, he will be allowed to return to Ro Tiris. His army may return to their homes.' Despite his smile, sweat still ran down his face; clearly, with a sword to his throat, his confidence was only so much consolation. 'If you allow me to return to Weir with your surrender you will all live. If not – you *must* know you can't win.'

Xander's eyes flicked from side to side as he thought of sixty thousand Hounds on his flank. Daganay glared at the Karesian, assessing his words and his manner. Brennan gradually let his sword ease away from the emissary's neck. Symon and Gwen just looked at each other.

'Is that all you have to say?' Gwen asked Ramazon.

The wind claw sat upright in the chair and slowly wiped a bead of sweat from his cheek. 'In Karesia, fear is a holy state. I find that I enjoy it. But, yes, that is the extent of my message.'

She killed him quickly, grabbing his hair and drawing her leaf-blade firmly across his throat. She wrenched his head forward until the blade cut his windpipe and he gurgled to death on his own blood.

'Listen to me!' she snapped at the others. 'Even if he's telling the truth, what's changed? What the fuck has changed?'

'Three are worth ten,' muttered Symon, drawing all eyes to him. 'In Cozz. . . when myself, Tyr Kalan and Queen Gwendolyn were fighting in dust and darkness. The three of us were worth ten of them – and we were wounded.'

Gwen let go of the Karesian's hair and his body slumped to the canvas floor. 'Three are worth ten,' she repeated. 'We beat them for armour, weapons, tactics, skill, morale, and we have nothing left to lose – they're calling it the Lands of the Twisted fucking Tree.'

CHAPTER THIRTEEN

FYNIUS BLACK CLAW
AT SISTERS' REACH

HIS DRAWING WAS rather good. He'd coloured in the grass and shaded the walls. On paper, from his imagination, Ro Hail looked different. In reality it was a miserable shit-hole, comprised primarily of ruined grey stone and rubbish weather. Rain, rain, wind, hale, rain, snow, and more rain. There was a lot of rain. They should have called it Ro Rain.

'What are these?' asked Vincent Hundred Howl, pointing at the drawing.

'They're walls, idiot. See? We don't need half this shitty ruin, so we use the rest to start building walls. East to South Warden, west to the sea. We'll need to establish quarries to the north.'

'That's a big wall,' he replied.

'Yup,' agreed Fynius.

He imagined Sisters' Reach as a fort, acting as a gateway through the wall he'd build.

'We need a name for the wall,' said Vincent. 'How about Vincent's Folly?'

'How about the Wall of Vincent's Gruesome Death. . . you fucking idiot.'

'Fair enough,' he replied. 'Just making a point.'

'A stupid point,' said Fynius. 'Go make it to someone else.'

'Don't need to tell me twice,' muttered Vincent, sloping out of the ruined building and into the rain.

As Fynius's cousin left, a hulking shape arrived. It loped across the rain-dappled cobbles, its huge head dipped and its stubby tail nestling between its hind legs. Warm Heart of the White Pack had decided that he would stay in Hail. The Volk war-hound had not yet shared his reasons, but Fynius had high hopes that his barks and growls would begin to make sense in a day or two.

'Did Lady Bronwyn feed you?' he asked, dropping his hand to let the hound sniff him.

The hound appeared happy enough. His mouth was open and he panted, seemingly unaware of his huge size and ability to intimidate. He didn't roll on his belly, but Fynius could imagine him doing so. The hound had a way of making everything feel calmer. Suddenly, when there was a dog to pet, there was no great struggle or stress of a war yet to win; there was just a wagging tail and a smiling man.

'You're going to ruin my reputation, dog. These bastards are used to a gruff captain, not a man who melts at the sight of an over-sized hound.'

Fynius took a deep breath and slowed down. His brain worked better when his thoughts were gradual and methodical. He rolled up his drawings and backed away from the forward battlements of Hail, letting the hound follow. Behind him, pulling down ruined buildings and helping the remnants of Wraith Company back to their underground havens, were the five hundred men of Twilight Company. They wore light blue and served their captain with a smile, never asking from where his wisdom appeared. They knew. They just knew.

Fynius leapt off the bare stone and landed in the paved courtyard, splashing rain water across his boots. Warm Heart looked at him from above, then calmly padded down the nearby steps.

He had cartfuls of stone and mortar to direct; hundreds of men to lead and a town to rebuild. But he could also hear a raven's caw and knew he was needed elsewhere. Leaving the burning torches behind him, he walked through the ruined gatehouse and on to the dark cobbles leading south into the Grass Sea. Outside the ruin was nothing but a cluster of trees. Nothing between Hail and Canarn but grass and emptiness. It was perfect. When Sisters' Reach was built and the wall complete, there would be a fortress ready and waiting for the dark future Fynius had seen. He knew the future wasn't set, but it pleased him to keep busy while waiting for the shades to assemble.

He walked further into the looming darkness, looking for Brom. The rain cut slices through the air, adding texture to nothingness. He stopped next to a thin tree that swayed steadily in the blustery wind. There were more trees like waving fingers in the distance, but everything else was black. Well, everything except the shimmering blue figure approaching him.

'Hello,' said Fynius, waving at the shade.

Brom nodded with a smile, showing how human he was becoming. 'It is time,' he said. 'We have found a place to meet and all the surviving Shade Folk have agreed to parlay.'

Fynius rubbed his hands together. 'Excited?' he asked.

The shade frowned, apparently confused by the question. 'I'm not sure I have felt excitement before. Yes, I believe I am excited.'

'You should smile when you're excited,' said Fynius. 'It reassures people.'

Brom absently petted Warm Heart, his ghostly hands passing through the dog's enormous muzzle. They could see each other, but Warm Heart looked at the shade with sadness, as if he knew something was on his mind.

'I had a sister and a father,' said Brom. 'I have been remembering them, and I find it difficult to smile when such thoughts appear.'

'Bronwyn would be happy that you endure. Ask Warm Heart, he knows her best of all.' The hound capered happily at Brom's feet, showing his agreement.

'Yes, but I worry that giving away our power to the other shades will cause me to forget them, to separate entirely from Bromvy Black Guard of Canarn. I would like at least to say goodbye.'

Fynius wanted to put a reassuring hand on the young man's shoulder, or to make him solid enough that he could stroke Warm

Heart properly for a few minutes, but he didn't know how and they had somewhere to be. 'If you don't get to say goodbye to your sister, I promise I will say it for you. And I'll tell her that you gave up your power to help the lands of men.'

'Thank you, exemplar,' replied the shade, now smiling weakly. 'We should go. It would not do for us to be late to our own parlay table.'

* * *

It was a Ranen hall, plucked from his mind as easily as he'd recall a childhood memory. Warm, golden light from a deep fire-pit split the room and the heraldry of Twilight Company swayed in the rafters. A raven flying over a half-moon on a pale blue field. The walls were stone, with a vaulted roof of thatch and wide, shuttered windows, allowing fresh air and glistening light to fill the hall. He didn't know if shades could eat and drink, but his mind had conjured barrels of ale and baskets of freshly baked bread. There was also a table. A table with six chairs. It was the only part of the hall that did not come from Fynius's memory. Brytag had decided that they needed six chairs.

'Well, *I'm* not standing up,' he stated, plonking himself at the head of the rectangular table.

Brom appeared first, as if he'd been there all along. It was strange to see him whole, for his form had always been ghostly and indistinct. Now, though, the former lord of Canarn was as real as Fynius. His face was still calm, but there was now texture to his pale skin and black hair. He was clad in a simple robe of pale blue, identifying him as a shade through which Brytag would speak.

'You look well,' said Fynius. 'It's nice to see.'

'Thank you,' replied the shade, 'it feels. . . nice. It is a strange thing to be one of the Shade Folk.'

'I don't think the gods thought you'd be needed again. You're just a remnant of a more primitive kind of worship. They've been spoilt with their armies of clerics and priests.'

'We are a purer form of devotee than any priest,' said Brom. 'Though we must now work together to be effective. A thing that has never happened in all the long ages of this land. The gods of men are prideful and arrogant; they remember slights, real and imagined, from thousands of years in the past.'

Fynius grinned, feeling excitement mounting. 'This should be very interesting then.'

Next to Brom, the air began to twist into a gentle vortex of cold, white mist. A moment later, a huge Fjorlander appeared. Even seated, he towered over Brom and Fynius. His hair was a golden mane of braids and matted curls, and his beard was woven into a fork. His robe was white, showing him to be a shade in the service of Rowanoco, and tufts of thick body hair poked out at the neck and wrists.

'Magnus Forkbeard, priest of the Order of the Hammer,' stated Brom. 'We were friends in life.'

'And our masters have been friends for aeons,' replied Magnus. 'An old raven and an old man of ice.'

The two shades smiled, sharing a quiet moment of reunion, both as men and as avatars of Brytag and Rowanoco. They might be the only true allies in the halls beyond the world, but Brytag had only so much power and showing favouritism to the Ice Giant would anger the other Giants, not to mention weaken their efforts against the Dead God.

'And you are?' asked Magnus.

'Fynius,' he replied. 'Brytag's exemplar. I invited you here.'

'I have not the power to help my exemplar,' said the huge priest sadly. 'He sits in Tiergarten with little guidance.'

'We can change that,' said Brom. 'If we have strength, we will not leave one exemplar to fight alone.'

'Strong words, old raven,' said Magnus.

Brom smiled, looking more like a man than he had yet. 'Thank you, old ice-beard. It will cost me mortal memories, but it's worth it.'

Fynius didn't know where the shades finished and the gods started, but in his meeting hall beyond the world, the lines were blurred. If he'd been a simpler man, he'd have been over-awed. As it was, he was merely curious.

The next chair shimmered, a rainbow of colours playing across the air. White, purple, red, blue, black, brown, until the light settled into a grey haze and a man appeared in the chair. He was dark-haired and clean-shaven, with huge shoulders, clad in a simple grey robe. He was a shade in service to the One God and the people of Ro.

'I am Brother Torian of Arnon,' said the cleric. 'I speak for Tor Funweir and the Stone Giant.'

Magnus gave him a hard stare and drummed his thick fingers on the table. The animosity was clear, especially as Brytag had seated them opposite each other. The One God and Rowanoco had a complicated history; they were past allies and mortal enemies in equal measure. Long ago they had fought together to defeat Shub-Nillurath but, more recently, the men of Ro had enslaved the Freelands. Rowanoco could forgive many things, but not the denial of his people's freedom. As for the One, he hated anything that threatened his carefully ordered laws of hierarchy. At least he used to.

'A Purple cleric,' stated Magnus. 'An appropriate choice.'

'A bearded barbarian,' replied Torian. 'How surprising.'

Brom was still smiling, letting the World Raven's good nature infuse him. He couldn't take sides, even if he had wanted to. He looked at Fynius and raised his eyebrows, nodding for his exemplar to speak. Fynius considered remaining silent and letting the shades air all of their grievances, but he didn't want old arguments to cripple their current efforts.

'May I speak?' he asked tentatively. Magnus and Torian didn't acknowledge him but kept their angry eyes on each other, pulling forth a hundred slights the other must answer for and putting them into their stares. 'I assume you have much to talk about, but the lands of men can't wait for you to make friends. Nor will Shub-Nillurath halt his attack so you can argue about who has inflicted the greatest wrong on the other. Your exemplars need help.'

'Brytag has never done us wrong,' said Torian, still looking at Magnus. 'But we do not trust this ignorant peasant. He is an apparition of a chaotic Giant, too unpredictable to trust.'

'And you are as cold and dull as the Stone Giant who speaks through you,' snapped Magnus.

A nimbus of icy air covered Rowanoco's shade, flaring outwards as if his form was not large enough to contain the anger he was feeling. Opposite him, Brother Torian snarled, his muscular arms pulsing and taking on the look of immovable stone. Fynius didn't know what would happen if they clashed. Would earthquakes rage across the earth? Would mountains fall and oceans rise? Luckily, he didn't have to find out; the remaining two chairs began to swirl with light and Magnus and Torian turned their hate-filled eyes from each other. Their divine anger dimmed.

Brom kept smiling, but a sadness appeared at the edges of his eyes. When neither of the swirling mists coalesced into a recognizable form, all three shades looked at Fynius.

'Strange,' he said. 'I feel Jaa from *that* one, but he's lost. . . adrift, as if he can't find his exemplar.' He turned to the other chair, upon which a robust swirl of mist was slowly churning. 'I don't know who that is. But it's old.'

Magnus banged his fist on the table. 'I know who that is.' He roared with laughter. 'I'd forgotten about him. What an absent-minded old Giant I have become.'

The thick mist rose higher and larger than all the others combined, until a wide, tusked face formed within the mist. It was a particularly large troll, densely furred with streaks of grey and black. It had a flabby muscularity and hooked claws. Even to Fynius, it was terrifying.

'We are the Breaking Storm,' intoned the troll, in a voice that sounded like rocks banging together. 'And we speak for Varorg.'

Torian stood and looked up at the huge beast seated next to him. The Purple cleric was not afraid, but it could well have been the first time either he or the One had seen a troll. 'Varorg and

Rowanoco are one and the same,' said Torian. 'A different name for the same god. How is this possible?'

The Breaking Storm directed his deep-set, jewelled gaze to the Purple cleric. 'We have endured in the ice for long years, man of the stone. Until this one summoned us.' He pointed a claw at Fynius. 'We thought we were the last of the Shade Folk. It is pleasant to discover we were wrong. We speak for the form Rowanoco took when he appeared to the Ice Men.'

'So the Ice Giant has two voices round this table?' said Torian. 'Perhaps it was foolish of us to come.'

'You had no choice,' replied Fynius. 'If you hadn't come, your power would slowly fade to nothing until the people of Ro were whistling in the wind as slaves of the Twisted Tree.'

Torian hung his head. He returned to his seat and gritted his teeth. 'If the World Raven wishes to share his power, we will gratefully accept.' He turned to the one obscured chair, where a tentative fingernail of Jaa's power was trying to make itself known. 'I certainly am more worthy of your help than the treacherous Fire Giant.'

'In that we agree,' said Magnus. 'Shub-Nillurath's survival is *his* responsibility.'

Fynius rubbed his eyes and shared an exasperated look with Brom. 'I think Jaa is weaker than any of you,' he said. 'The Shade of Dalian Thief Taker cannot even appear to speak for his god. He has no exemplar to anchor him to the world.'

'I knew him in life,' said Brom. 'His son was my friend. If we don't help him, he will drift forever.'

'Let him drift,' said Torian. 'We would not lament his passing.'

'Al Hasim would want to help,' offered Fynius. 'And we should not give up on Jaa so easily.'

'So your power is to be stretched thinly between each of us?' asked Torian. 'Will that be enough?'

Fynius considered the question, screwing up his face in thought. 'I honestly don't know. But I've seen the Tyranny of the Twisted Tree. It was as real in my mind as if I'd lived there all my life. Shub-Nillurath will choose Tyrants to control his land. He's already chosen some of them. I saw a cat-like creature of chaos in the Fell. I saw a unique Dark Young in Arnon. I saw a dismembered head in Kessia. I saw a brutal Bear Tamer in Fjorlan. I saw an immense spider in Far Karesia – and I saw a Mistress of Pain in Weir. Our power may not be enough, but it's all we have to give.'

The shades were silent, each form emitting a divine halo of varied colours, as if the gods were feeling sadness for the first time in aeons. It was called the Long War, but the battlefields had been empty and quiet for so long that the reality of Shub-Nillurath's move to power was hard to accept.

'We will accept your help,' said the Breaking Storm. 'Any help you can give.'

'Thank you,' said Fynius. 'I like you, Shade of Varorg.'

The others stayed quiet, processing the possibility of defeat and the need to reorder the world. The Dead God had too many tendrils, like a virus deeply embedded in the earth, too virulent to eradicate entirely. The world would never be the same.

'Yes,' said Torian. 'We also will accept any help. And we will accept truce. There is a real enemy here.'

'Agreed,' said Magnus. 'Each of our exemplars needs strength. I propose we take the old raven's gift and focus that strength where we can. You, man of the stone, what is your exemplar's name?'

'Fallon the Grey,' replied Torian. 'We plan to start a new order of knights. He will be the first. The time of the Purple and Red is coming to an end. I will reorder my followers and usher in an age of honour. And *your* exemplar, man of the ice?'

'Alahan Teardrop,' said Magnus. 'He is young, but strong. The last of his line. The oldest line in the lands of men. But I have nothing to give him.'

'Unrahgahr,' stated the Breaking Storm. 'Our exemplars fight on the same field, old ice-beard.'

They all looked at Fynius. 'And then there is you,' said Torian. 'And perhaps you deserve our thanks.'

'Not necessary,' he replied. 'I like the world; I don't want it to change any more than it has already. But don't forget Jaa. I think I can help him. A son is a powerful bond, perhaps enough to anchor the Fire Giant's shade. But that's for me to do. I think Al Hasim likes me.' He felt progress was being made for the first time. 'You, Brother Torian, we'll give you power enough to strengthen Fallon's sword arm and the arms of the other Grey Knights. We can't help his resolve or his honour, that will be left to him, but we can give him a sword arm that can change the world. Magnus, we will leave Alahan's strength to take care of itself, but we will give him the power to unlock the heart of Fjorlan. We will give him the power to remind the land of Rowanoco.' He grinned at the Breaking Storm. 'And Unrahgahr gets a change of diet.'

The troll returned the grin, smacking his pulpy lips together. 'Thank you.'

'This future you have seen,' enquired Torian. 'This Tyranny of the Twisted Tree. . . could we have stopped it? Was it our hubris that allowed the virus to spread?' His face, wreathed in divine power, twisted into a frown, as if a god was changing his mind or realizing he'd made a mistake that would rule the fates of many.

'Yes, you could have stopped it,' said Fynius. 'If you'd concerned yourself less with the Purple and noticed the suffering of the common folk, you would have more worship. As it is, many people of Ro were faithful because the clerics told them to be.'

Magnus roared with laughter, grinning at the One God's shade.

'You're no better, old ice-beard,' said Fynius. 'You told your people to be strong, honourable and free, but you never said how – or which was most important. You allowed a man of strength to convince others that freedom and honour were unimportant.'

The two shades shrank a little, both appearing to realize that Fynius was right. There was no anger or aggression, just sadness, perhaps even regret.

'Jaa may have let Shub-Nillurath live,' he continued. 'But it was you two who allowed him to come back.'

The wisp of wind where Dalian Thief Taker had tried to emerge was now churning like a tornado, as if the Fire Giant were roaring at the top of his lungs to be heard. He had no voice at the table, though Fynius imagined he could hear every word.

'Anger is not useful,' said Brom. 'Neither is self-pity. We are not defeated yet, though how much of our world remains will be decided when we leave this parlay table. I for one do not plan to surrender. If Shub-Nillurath has taught us anything, it is that killing a god is no small thing, easily done. If only a fraction of your followers remain, so do you.'

Magnus banged his fists on the table again. 'To remain is not enough. I will not be a lesser god, nor will I become a casualty of the Long War. I must be mighty or I will be nothing.'

'There is more,' offered Brom. 'There are soldiers of the Long War still fighting, with no allegiance to any of us. We can't help them all, but have assisted the oldest and the youngest. There is wisdom and luck in both. The Shape Taker and the little wolf are our gifts to you.'

'Who do they worship, if not us?' asked Torian.

'One is too young to have embraced a god, the other worships a dead Shadow Giant,' replied Brom.

'Dokkalfar?' queried Magnus. 'I thought they would have passed by now. Their time is surely over.'

'They cling on,' said Brom, showing Brytag's fondness for the forest-dwellers. 'Though not for much longer. We feel their might leaving the lands of men. Many have already left; the rest will follow. They have no more stomach to fight, they are too old.'

'But the Shape Taker endures,' said Fynius. 'He's been fighting for too long to know anything else, and we have seen his heart. This land needs Tyr Nanon, and thankfully, he has a dark-blood as a companion. They will cast a shadow for many years to come.'

For a moment the shades appeared peaceful. Perhaps acceptance bred peace, for everyone present now knew how far they had fallen and how fractured their power had become.

* * *

Then Fynius was back on the sodden grass of Hail as if he'd never left. His eyes flicked left and right as he tried to decide whether or not he'd imagined the entire experience. It was not impossible that he'd just been standing in the rain, talking to a tree for the last hour. . . No. Brytag wouldn't trick him like that.

Warm Heart panted at his feet, eliciting a smile. Fynius was not so arrogant as to congratulate himself, but he nonetheless knew that he and the World Raven had done their best. The war-hound knew it too, and he briefly heaved himself up on his hind legs in a show of friendship, so his heavy front paws enveloped Fynius.

'There are many people out there, my furry friend. People with families and friends, with personalities and opinions. So many are going to die. I could have joined an army and led men into combat, but I chose this instead. I hope I was right to do so. This way we save more people, more personalities and opinions. I'll never meet them all, but I can wish them all luck.'

Warm Heart whined, as if reminding Fynius that he still had work to do.

'Yes, yes, I know.' He looked south, through rain and darkness. 'How quickly can we get to Canarn, do you think?'

EPILOGUE

HE BOAT WAS fast and that was the nicest thing Brother
Lanry could think to say about it. He was part of the
third convoy, ferrying Malaki Frith's Red Knights from
Canarn to Ro Tiris. A few thousand men were already there,
and many thousands more were aboard ship or waiting outside
Canarn. It would be months before every man and scrap of
equipment was safely back in Tor Funweir. The country of his
birth seemed smaller, as if the edges were being squeezed by an
unwelcome guest.

'What happened to the sea wall?' he asked Captain Brook, the
man of Canarn in command of the ship.

'The new king blew it up,' replied the captain.

Lanry had seen the wondrous structure of stone and wood
many times, and had been amazed at it each time. Now, a huge
section in the middle was destroyed, and a hundred small boats
were attempting to clear the shipping lanes of the debris. The sea
wall would take years to repair and the low city beyond looked
very exposed.

'And the harbour?' asked the Brown cleric.

'The new king sailed his fleet into it,' replied Captain Brook.

Lanry grunted in disapproval. Surely there was a better way to
retake the city. Did Alexander Tiris truly have to attack Ro Tiris?

The boat lost speed as the sailors did a number of terribly
complicated things with ropes and sails. He remained at the side
of the sailing contraption, huddled in his thick brown robe and
looking forward to the opportunity to return to dry land.

'Nearly there, Brother,' said the captain. 'The Red Knights will go straight to the barracks. I assume you'll be headed back to Canarn in a day or two. I'll be here when you're ready.'

The boat glided slowly to a stop against a small intact section of the huge wooden docks. Lanry kept himself upright by holding on tightly to the railings of the boat. Once it had settled against the thick planks of wood, he felt far better. The subtle but unnerving roll had now stopped, allowing him to breathe out properly for the first time since he had left Canarn.

'Is there a ramp or gangplank of some kind?'

The captain smiled at him. 'Are we eager, Brother?' he asked, directing his sailors to lower the boarding ramp.

'No, just too polite to vomit on your delightful boat.'

'It's a ship,' replied Brook, still smiling.

Lanry took several offers of assistance and stumbled his way down the solid ramp, his simple leather boots making a satisfying clomp on the wooden dock of Ro Tiris.

Once on land, he instantly felt more like himself. He turned back to the boat and looked up at the captain. 'Good day to you, captain. I trust you'll enjoy the hospitality of the capital once General Frith's men are ashore.'

Brook frowned, looking at the city as a man would look at a closed tavern. He had much work to do helping the hundreds of knights disembark. Lanry smiled at him anyway and made his way slowly to the nearby gate, taking his time and getting a good look at the immense city walls. He stayed away from the main gate, preferring to enter the huge city via the less opulent Stone Town Gate. There were fewer workers and guardsmen, and the small doorway was tucked between stone buttresses, allowing unobtrusive entrance to the narrow streets and dilapidated buildings of Stone Town.

'Ah, the smell of pickled fish and effluence,' he muttered, 'how I have not missed thee.'

Lanry had spent much time in Tiris when he was a younger man. The House of the Kind, as the Brown church was known, had been his first posting after he had donned his robes for the first time. Cardinal Cerro was the chief of his order, and a man for whom Lanry had the utmost respect. He also knew how to make the best fruit tea in Tor Funweir.

Once through the gate, he quickened his pace. Stone Town was quiet, with few people wandering the streets and few windows with their shutters open. The people of Tiris had endured almost as much as the people of Canarn, but they had much less to rebuild. He guessed that the common folk of the poor quarter would simply remain in their hovels and wait until times improved. It was the way of the destitute to remain patient during the hardest times. This plan was sound right up until the multitudes of fleeing citizens arrived.

He reached the Brown church and took another moment to gaze up at it. It was a simple building, only slightly more decorative than the adjacent houses, but it was one of the tallest buildings in the city, and its significance made it, for him at least, one of the most important. Its bottom level was squat and wide, allowing hundreds of parishioners to seek food and shelter when needed. Currently the cavernous lower level was packed to the dark wooden rafters with slumped men and women of Tiris. It had been decreed that the multitudes of homeless were to be housed for the duration of the crisis. How long the crisis would last had not been specified, but Lanry thought it an open-ended situation.

A young woman, no older than twenty, with a muddy face and frail hands, approached him and fell to her knees. 'Will you bless me, Father?'

He placed his hand gently on her head. The poor girl looked exhausted and lost, and no doubt she was hungry. 'Don't kneel, Sister,' he said. 'I can bless you just as well when you're standing.'

She looked up and hesitantly rose to her feet. 'I'm hungry, Father,' she murmured.

'Then I will bless you with food,' he replied, smiling warmly. 'Come with me.'

He led her into the church, waving away the locals telling people that it was full. He couldn't help everyone, but he could help the young girl get some food. Small acts of kindness in the midst of such suffering could be mighty indeed.

'Please, a bowl of soup,' he said to the plump man in a white apron, ladling out portions of steaming broth for the occupants of the church. 'And would you make sure she has a place to wash and rest.'

'As you say, Father,' said the plump man, beckoning the young girl forward.

Lanry gave the girl a reassuring smile and left her to eagerly slurp a bowl of thick vegetable soup. He was stopped by townspeople several more times as he made his way to the nondescript vestry at the rear of the church. He blessed each of them with safety and full bellies, leaving a small wave of kindness in his wake.

'You look tired, Brother,' said a familiar voice. Cardinal Cerro of Darkwald emerged from his private sanctum. 'Perhaps a pot of tea.'

They embraced, chuckling to each other about the state of the world and their individual struggles. Lanry was younger by ten years, but both were old men and their banter was tinged with complaints about inexplicable pains in their legs, arms, backs and heads.

'Take the weight off, my dear Brother Lanry,' said the cardinal, pointing to a comfy-looking armchair in the corner of his vestry. 'Any demands on our time can wait until the water has boiled.'

Lanry sank into the plump cushions of the armchair and let out a contented sigh. The city of Ro Tiris was quieter than he'd ever known it, but the Brown church was busier than he'd ever seen it.

'You crowned the king?' he asked, imagining the advice he'd have given if he'd been at hand.

'I did,' replied Cerro. 'I believe the One has chosen well. He has good counsel and good men, but I didn't get the opportunity to make him a cup of tea.'

Lanry chuckled, taking a mug of sweet tea from his old friend. It was as good as tea could get, rich and warming with a smooth aftertaste that soothed the throat and stomach. 'I don't believe

I've met young Alexander Tiris,' he remarked, sipping at the deep mug of hot liquid. 'But I hear he's good at fighting. I imagine that's rather important for a king in such times.'

Cerro took a seat opposite with his own mug of tea. 'He's distilled everything down into fighting. Everything that has happened; everything that has been won and lost – it all comes down to a bit of a scrap. He's outnumbered and that has seemed to make him *more* determined to pick a fight.'

Lanry felt a slight tingle of warmth travel up his spine. 'Have you met Fallon of Leith?' he asked.

'I have not,' replied the cardinal, loading his wooden pipe with tobacco. 'Red Knight. Good swordsman, from what I hear.'

'Terribly nice young man,' said Lanry. 'Simple mindset, but determined in his way. He's also the exemplar of the One.'

Cerro spat out a mouthful of tea in surprise and leant forward, coughing. He controlled himself and straightened, placing his mug of tea on a small table and rubbing his chest. He didn't ask if Lanry was sure or what it could mean. Those of the Brown knew better than any other clerical order what the One God was capable of. They could also feel his dwindling power and the true depths of the current crisis.

'It's late in the day,' observed Cerro. 'Do we think he can make a difference?'

'He'll certainly try,' replied Lanry. 'If my old senses haven't escaped me, I know Sir Fallon is a warrior the likes of which Tor Funweir has never known. The One has seen fit to reorder the world. The Knights of the Grey will be the last of the old and the first of the new.'

Cerro puffed on his pipe, grumbling in thought. 'We should begin to plan for the future, my friend. The Purple, Red and Gold may resist, but we are of the Brown and mustn't let pride cloak our better judgement.'

'My better judgement keeps telling me the same things,' replied Lanry. 'That no number of Grey Knights or romantic ideals of victory can make a difference.'

'I have not heard the One's voice for weeks,' said the cardinal. 'Even when I crowned Alexander Tiris king of Tor Funweir. But I know that the Brown will have a place in the new order. *My better judgement tells me* that we are more important now than we have ever been.'

Lanry continued to sip his tea, though his thoughts turned to a world where the Ro had become a small nation of men, fighting to keep their freedom against a dead god and its followers.

'My friend,' said Lanry. 'You once described us as the mortar that holds the Ro together.'

'We are somewhat beyond soup kitchens, do you not think?' replied the cardinal.

'Perhaps. But if we must save the Ro from extinction, we should approach it as if we were saving a homeless man from starvation. With small acts of kindness.'

'Thousands of fleeing folk are going to start arriving in Tiris very soon. Do we minister to them here? Knowing an army of Hounds will be at the gates within six months?'

PART TWO

THE TWISTED TREE

THE TALE OF THE GORLAN

THE SPIDER MOTHERS were birthed before the Giants walked their paths of divinity. They were created from the void by Atlach-Nacha, an Old One who survived longer than any other. Through ages of deep time they endured, choosing followers and battles as their whim dictated.

They were priestesses and they were sentinels, tasked to endure beyond all the battles of the Long War.

When Rowanoco ascended and opened the way for gods of the earth, the Gorlan remained in the shadows, commanding those that crawl, until their mother was snared by Shub-Nillurath.

The Forest Giant needed sustenance as he clung to life, and he consumed Atlach-Nacha, using the energy of the Old One to sustain himself. Many Gorlan pledged to the Forest Giant, hoping to free their mother, but many more remained free, creating broods and enduring at the edges of the world.

As long as the Old One's power remained, so would the spider mothers. But every feast comes to an end, and all power fades.

PROLOGUE

THE GUARDIAN MISSED weather. In the void there was no wind, no rain, no warmth or cold. Everything was shimmering blue and neutral, flowing from one texture to the next, never rising too high or falling too low. It was possible, when concentrating, to discern landscape and life, but never for long. Above and all around was the void; below, through a tear, a sliver of rotten energy, was the real world, distant and mostly forgotten. The Guardian didn't know how long he'd been there. He even doubted that his memories of weather were real. Was snow as he remembered it? Was cold truly *cold*?

You will stand on the threshold. You will guard the tear. You will judge those who seek to pass, whether into the void or into the world.

The words were all that mattered. The Guardian was given instructions by the great Fire Giant himself, and he would stay and he would stand – until the halls beyond were blowing as dust in the winds of the void. But nothing had ever tried to pass, either into the void or into the world.

Why not close the tear? Let me return to the fire halls.

Because the tear was made by a Giant. . . a Giant now felled. No other being can undo what he has done.

The Guardian never questioned the wisdom of the great Giant. He waited and he watched. He constructed a labyrinth, using his great wit and cunning to form walls and twisted corridors between him and the tear. He learned to read the movements of the tear, the rotten energy, flowing to the real world below, and in its texture he saw mortals dance and contort. One moment they lived, the next they were ash and mist, to be replaced by more dancing and contorting figures. Nameless beings, Gorlan, Jekkans, Volk, Dokkalfar – and finally men. Every once in eternity, a blink of the eye showed him rain or a cloudy sky. These visions were the closest to happiness he ever felt.

Once his name had been Kaa. Now he was the Guardian. Once he had flown through the umbral sky of the void on immense red wings. Now he crouched on a plinth, waiting. He felt neither tiredness nor hunger. He couldn't remember boredom or anger. He merely waited – and he guarded the tear.

He wondered what the world was like. He knew the names and boundaries had changed, but the mountains and seas would remain. Once it was the Fire Lands. To the north, across the Hammer Sea, were the Stone Lands. What names did they have now? The Guardian didn't know. Nor would he ever. Even when he glimpsed the mortal world, its beauty, chaos and terror, he never heard a thing. He never learned what Jekkans talk about, or what Dokkalfar named their realms. Men talked a lot, their lips moving almost constantly, but the Guardian never learned what drove them to such animation or distress.

* * *

The shade was confused. With no guidance and vague memories at best, it drifted through the void, following a sense of purpose that drew him along pathways and across forgotten realms. There was an exemplar somewhere, but where? It should have been easy. When the shade gained consciousness, its sense of right was absolute, as was its pull towards the exemplar. Now something blocked it. Some means of control that the shade could not penetrate. It felt a vague pull, directing it up, down, left and right, gliding across endless tides of void energy, searching for the exemplar. It was all the shade could do.

Then it stopped, snatching at fragments of its former life. It was hovering on a shimmering wave of green energy, lapping gently at the shade's ethereal feet, as though it were standing in the wash of a mortal sea. The fragments came slowly, as awareness returns after a deep sleep. It remembered who it had been, the mortal of whom it was a memory. But the memories had not been lived and they gave the shade little guidance. He had been Dalian Thief Taker, greatest of the wind claws, but now. . . until he found the exemplar he was nothing. But still there was Jaa. The Fire Giant infused the shade with divine might, giving it purpose.

The shade trod on the air and a void path appeared. It shimmered through different tones of red and blue, always moving, never still. A few more footsteps and the path solidified, arcing away from him as a rainbow would cut a cloudy sky. The other paths appeared close, but to reach another would require luck or vast knowledge of the paths beyond the world. Each one led. . . somewhere. Powerful realms, forgotten halls, remnants of lost power or shattered divinity. And other things, things with neither names nor recognizable forms. Every scrap of belief went somewhere. Every god, spirit or urge that had ever been revered had a place in the void. The fire halls were here somewhere, but that was not the path the shade took. There was a new pull, one not of the mortal world.

Follow the flapping of wings, the smell of fire and smouldering rocks.

Was Jaa guiding its journey? Not to the exemplar; maybe to a way out of the void. The shade walked. It walked through epochs of might and majesty, fallen long since to dust. Huge, nameless spires of chaos whose inhabitants were gone. Fossilized tentacles, snaking into the umbral sky as corridors and halls of a dead civilization. The shade walked unseen. If the paths it trod had inhabitants, they were invisible. . . or perhaps they existed in the past or the future, too alien to be perceived.

Another footstep and the shade was walking on stone. The path became a tunnel. The sparkling blue of the void melted into cyclopean blocks of weathered granite and slate, pushed together by some craft unknown to mortal men.

Follow.

Openings and alcoves dotted the corridor, reaching into unlighted halls, too vast to truly comprehend. Shadows played in the air as wisps of darkness. They were glossy black, both sensual and terrible, but of no concern to the shade. It had arrived somewhere, stepped from the path and entered a hall – or a realm. The smell of ash and sulphur hung in the dusty air, and the distant sound of beating wings echoed softly through the passageway.

'To wander blindly is to invite permanent blindness,' said a gentle voice. 'What manner of being would think to wander here? Whether blindly or with intent, no being has entered this realm in memory.'

'I am the Shade of Dalian Thief Taker and I seek the exemplar of Jaa.'

The gentle voice let forth a thoughtful grunt, as an old man would think on a subject of importance. 'Then you may approach. Keep to the path. Look not too long into the darkness for things dwell in the shadowy places of my realm.'

The shade reached a stone precipice, beyond which was an endless vista of constantly shifting rocky passages. It appeared to be a labyrinth of some kind, with corridors twisting and turning in chaotic patterns far below. If the labyrinth had an end or distant boundaries, they could not be seen from the precipice. It rolled over leagues, sprawling like a corpse city with only the dead to walk its paths.

'What place is this?' asked the shade.

'It has no name. It has only a purpose.' The gentle voice was resonant, coming from every angle the shade could perceive. Up, down, left, right, within and without.

'Jaa showed the path to this place. Why?'

No answer. The shade could feel a presence nearby, but not an identity. Whoever spoke was infused with ancient divine power, though not hostile. To the contrary, the power, though immense, was welcoming – almost happy.

'What are you?' asked the shade.

Still no answer. The smell became more pungent and was joined by the earthy aroma of smouldering rocks. 'Forgive me,' said the voice, 'I have not conversed for. . . I don't believe I can finish that statement. The passage of time evades me, as does its meaning.'

'Do you have form? Or are you merely a mind and a voice?'

Overhead, a gust of wind almost sent the shade to the rocky ground. It was intense downward pressure, produced by the sweep of huge wings. The pressure abated only when the smell became almost overwhelming. At the downward entrance to the sprawling labyrinth, a giant platform rose like a single mountain peak against a stark sky. The plinth was carved into images of crackling fires, dancing this way and that in forms of glory and terror. A shape distorted the air, revealing glimpses of red scales and a long tail. As the form became visible, the shade dropped to the ground, averting its eyes from the enormous red dragon.

'I was called Kaa,' intoned the huge beast. 'Now I am the Guardian.'

'You're a Fire Giant!' exclaimed the shade.

'I am, but why do you not look at me?' asked the Guardian. 'I am not your god. In your terms, Jaa was my father.'

The shade tentatively looked up. The dragon measured a hundred feet from its fiery snout to the tip of its barbed tail. Segmented spines lined its muscular back, each one a subtly different shade of red, playing off each other like a strange mosaic. It perched on two legs, wings gathered behind into a spiny crest. An aura of flame surrounded it, crackling from gaps between scales and tumbling from wide nostrils. Most alarming was its face. The being was a Fire Giant, of the same order as Jaa, but its face was warm, as if it greeted an old friend or welcomed a new acquaintance.

'I know I appear intimidating,' said the Guardian, 'but I do not wish you to be afraid. I find that I crave discourse, and you are in need of my assistance.'

'I have to find the exemplar,' said the shade. 'I must anchor myself to the lands of men. All else is smoke and shadow.'

The Guardian's mouth opened wide and its huge, curved teeth parted. It could swallow a man whole, or bite him in two, but the shade did not feel under threat. The beast appeared to be laughing, its dark red tongue lolling over its teeth and its eyes shining, orbs of warm golden light. As the beast lowered itself to the plinth, it smiled – a subtle curve of the huge mouth, making it look almost feline. 'Your conviction is. . . refreshing,' said the Guardian, a guttural purr coming from the depths of its throat.

'Why did Jaa lead me here?' asked the shade.

A huge red tongue ran smoothly across the Guardian's teeth, leaving a film of spittle – red and smouldering – to fall from his scaly lips. As the phlegm hit the stony ground, it bubbled and steamed. 'The great Fire Giant led you to the tear. To the only true gap from the void to the realm of form.'

'Realm of form?' queried the shade, not fully understanding what he was being told.

'I don't know of any other name,' replied the Guardian. 'It used to be the Fire Lands, but I am sure the beings below would have named their own realms by now.'

'You mean the lands of men?'

'Men, Volk, Dokkalfar, Jekkans. . . perhaps the land of mortals.' The dragon smiled again, as if pleased with itself.

The shade looked again across the labyrinth. At the furthest edge, framed by distant shards of lightning, was a plunging sinkhole, wreathed in rotten energy and appearing to fall into nothing. He could feel the toxic power of Shub-Nillurath returning to the world.

'I can reach the exemplar from here?' asked the shade.

The wings flared. It was a shrug of uncertainty, but also a gesture that showed the dragon's size. 'No, but you still have a connection to the lands of men.'

The shade remembered a troublesome youth. Dalian Thief Taker had a son, perhaps the only tangible proof that he had ever lived. 'Al Hasim, but my memory is foggy.'

'Through the tear you can reach him,' said the Guardian. 'A dive of faith, reliant upon your son catching you. He can anchor you to your lands of men; give you time to find your exemplar.'

'I am glad of this information. Though. . . I am uncertain.'

'What is wrong?' boomed the Guardian, its eyes drooping into a pinched expression of concern. 'Perhaps I can help.'

'I'm surprised I can remember my son. I am of the Shade Folk; emotions should not concern me, but I feel hope that perhaps my journey continues.'

The dragon grumbled, slowly smacking its huge lips together. 'Lore exists telling of your kind. The first shade served the Stone Giant, long, long ago.'

'So, what ails me?'

More grumbling, then a guttural cough, sending more phlegm to smoulder on the rock. 'Nothing ails you. You are being nourished by another. A raven cawed in the distance as you arrived, telling me to help you. A shade, far away, is consuming itself to make you whole. You are becoming more than a memory. As long as the World Raven's power lasts.'

Chapter Fourteen

Lady Bronwyn in the City of Canarn

S HE HADN'T WORN armour for so long. The feel of tight leather and segmented steel plates was comforting, but made her feel strangely nostalgic; it made her think of her brother and endless hours sparring with him in the keep. She'd never developed great skill with the longsword, but was quick enough to be dangerous with rapier or shortsword. It was the latter that now held Hasim's scimitar at bay.

'You still wince before you parry,' said the Karesian. 'As if you expect to get hit.'

'Swords are sharp, you know,' she replied, stepping backwards and holding her guard.

'Granted, but don't enter a fight thinking you'll lose. What's your advantage?'

She twirled the blade, smirking at him. 'Besides a certain feminine elegance. . . I suppose, maybe my speed?'

'You're quick,' he replied. 'And I know about such things.' He made a figure-eight with his scimitar, skilfully cutting the air. 'I'm pretty quick myself.'

She lunged, taking a wide stance and forcing him backwards. 'Arrogance breeds overconfidence.'

'I'm still alive, sweetness. I must be doing something right.'

'Alive, but homeless,' she replied, feinting at his exposed chest.

He side-stepped, but didn't counter-attack. 'I don't know about that. . . Canarn is feeling a bit like home. Much more than Kessia ever did.'

She spun, slashing at him, only to be met by his raised scimitar. 'I happen to know that the duchess is picky about who she allows to stay in her city.'

'Well, I knew her brother,' he replied. 'He'd never forgive me if I left.'

She relaxed her guard, letting a wave of sudden emotion flow over her. 'I don't want you to stay because *he'd* want you to. I want you to stay because *you* want to.'

'I don't need to tell you why I'm staying, my love,' he replied, adopting his best sultry smile.

She was largely immune to his charms now. At least she told herself she was. Bronwyn liked to believe that she loved the Karesian scoundrel because of some inner connection rather than lust. *But is lust so bad?* she thought.

'We could just disappear for a few days,' he whispered. 'Forget about all of this and take a boat to a secluded island.'

'A secluded island?' she queried. 'What makes you think you can trap me so easily?'

'I will be nothing but the perfect gentleman.'

She grabbed his shirt and kissed him roughly. Hasim dropped his scimitar and wrapped his arms round her waist, lifting her off the ground. With her legs wrapped tightly round him, they fell back against the wall, tearing at each other's clothes.

'Don't be a gentleman,' she breathed. 'There are enough gentlemen in my life.' If she must live as an errant duchess, why not have a Karesian scoundrel for a lover?

* * *

On the wooden table was a pile of unread papers. She'd scanned the first few, but left the balance in a disorderly stack. An unexpected side effect of her return to the city was the abundance of paperwork that required her attention. Certain things she'd brought back with her – scrolls from South Warden and Hail, agreeing to peaceful

coexistence and mutual protection. Others were from the lands of
Ro, variously asking for alliances or land. It appeared that certain
lesser nobles of Tor Funweir wanted to relocate to the duchy of
Canarn. She knew little about how her city was perceived across the
sea, save that her father had commanded little respect. Brom had
not been in charge long enough to establish any kind of authority,
so it fell to Bronwyn to lead Canarn into an uncertain future.

Lord Hetherly of Chase, Sir David of Rayne and others had sent
her proposals of marriage, each hoping to make himself duke of
the city. The lords of Tor Funweir saw Canarn as a possible safety
net for when their lands were consumed by the Dead God and his
Twisted Tree. They showed little faith in the scattered armies of
Ro. She thought that their time would be better spent defending
their lands, rather than conspiring on ways to leave.

'I, Lord Hetherly of Chase,' she read, 'hereby make a most
respectful proposal of marriage. Lady Bronwyn, tales of your
wisdom and beauty have spread to my lands and I can think of
no better future for your city than to ally with the ancient house
of Chase.'

Ancient house? Bronwyn didn't even know where Lord
Hetherly's lands were, let alone how long they'd been there.
Somewhere near Du Ban maybe.

'I have five hundred men-at-arms and a household staff of
two hundred. I'm sure you will agree that these additions to the
beautiful city of Ro Canarn can only serve to strengthen our
respective positions. I eagerly await your letter of acceptance, after
which I will travel to your city and we will begin preparations
without delay.'

What a load of horse-shit, she thought. But at least he attempted
to be respectful. Others had acted as if they were doing Bronwyn
a favour by proposing marriage. Sir David had gone so far as to
write that she was his second choice, languishing behind a young
lady from the Falls of Arnon. Luckily for the young lady, she didn't
control a city or live sufficiently far away, so the Lord of Rayne
had accepted Bronwyn as a potential replacement. She imagined

a cleric or adviser telling their lord of the benefits of moving to a defensible city across the sea.

Other requests were more humble. Farmers and traders wishing to establish themselves in her duchy, offering a slice of their profits in exchange for small pieces of land, or property in the city itself. *These* requests would be met more favourably. Despite her stubbornness, Bronwyn welcomed new additions to Canarn. It was, after all, half empty. Dozens of taverns and shops, first closed when the Red Knights attacked, had remained locked up, with no-one to re-establish business or remove boards from windows and doors.

She rubbed her eyes and yawned, too tired to feel happy about her city's rapid increase in desirability.

'My lady, there is a man with a dog at the northern gate,' said Auker, shaking Bronwyn out of a half-doze.

'What? What man?' she replied, sitting up.

'A thin-faced Ranen in a blue cloak. Says you know him.'

She rubbed her eyes and poked the nearby fireplace into life, sending small sparks across the blackened wood. It was several days since General Frith and Brother Lanry had left for Ro Tiris and her keep felt empty. The Red Knights, waiting to leave, were camped outside the city, and would be gone in a few weeks.

'Did he have a sinister smile?' she asked. 'Looks like a gremlin who's pleased with himself?'

'That he did, my lady.'

She was tired and unfocused. 'How late is it?'

'Taverns are closed,' he replied. 'I can tell the gremlin to come back tomorrow morning.'

'No, no,' she grumbled, straightening her dress and wrapping her thick cloak around her shoulders. 'Go and tell Fynius Black Claw that I'll be happy to receive him.'

'Aye, my lady.'

She left her office, yawning loudly, feeling a tired shiver travel up her spine and across her shoulders. The room adjoined her bedchambers, where Al Hasim could be heard snoring. She had not moved to larger quarters and had left Brom's and her father's rooms exactly as they were. She hadn't yet decided if this was due to a mourning period or if she just preferred her old room.

She yawned again, this one stretching her mouth as wide as it would go and causing a more pronounced shiver. Hasim snored himself awake and grunted at her, his arms flailing from under the blanket and reaching for her.

'Why are you awake?' he slurred.

She rubbed her eyes and smiled at him. 'Well, I *was* awake because I was enjoying a moment of peace and quiet. I'm now awake because there's a mad Ranen at the gates who doesn't appear to know that it's the middle of the night.'

'What?' he coughed in reply. 'What Ranen?'

She frowned at him, shaking her head.

'Oh, *that* Ranen,' he said. 'What in the halls beyond does *he* want?'

'Why don't you come with me and ask him?'

She stood and composed herself. Luckily her clothes were in a side dressing room, so she could get properly dressed out of the way of Hasim's tentacle-like arms. Even Fynius Black Claw deserved a degree of formality when visiting with a duchess. He'd probably never been to Canarn and she wanted to make a good impression, perhaps even dissuade him of his notion that the people of Ro were his enemies.

'Do I have to get dressed?' grumbled Al Hasim.

She ignored him and entered her dressing room, where she began selecting clothes of an appropriate level of formality. Nothing too ostentatious, and certainly no armour or weaponry.

'You ignoring me?' he asked.

'No, I just thought you could answer your own question.' She looked back into her bedchamber and blew him a kiss. 'I suspect Fynius would not appreciate a naked man of the sun.'

'Then he's madder than he looks,' said Hasim. He slowly got up, groggily pulled on a pair of laced, leather trousers and searched for his sword belt.

'Leave the blade,' she said. 'Let us not confirm his worst suspicions.'

'I told you before, I'm not Ro,' he replied. 'I don't even know if he's got suspicions about Karesians. Didn't seem to at South Warden.'

She lowered her eyebrows at him. 'I'm not meeting him armed, so neither are you.'

Once dressed, she allowed him to fleetingly snare her in a tight embrace. He grabbed her rear and pulled her against him, latching on for a deep, passionate kiss. She stroked her hands down his back, then pushed him away with a devilish smile. 'Down, boy!'

He smirked and made a predatory snarling sound. 'Very well, my lady. I'll control myself.'

She turned away from him and looked in her full-length mirror. Not too bad. She'd developed more pronounced muscles since leaving home and her hands were no longer soft, but her bearing was still that of a noble of Ro. Her dress touched the floor and was of thick blue brocade, with a simple overtunic of the same colour. An appropriate ensemble for the occasion, but strange compared to the homespun clothes she'd been wearing in the Freelands.

She heard a dull thud from behind and spun round. Hasim was lying on his back, arms and legs spread. She thought he was joking, until his body began to convulse. She ran to him, cradling his head.

'What's— what's wrong?' she spluttered, as her lover's eyes looked right through her. Blood pooled at the corners of his mouth and his whole body shook. 'Hasim!' She kissed him and got no reaction. She slapped his face and he didn't stop shaking. His dark skin was hot to the touch and veins began to rise on his forehead.

She left him and flung open her door. 'Auker, come quickly!'

She shouted the guardsman's name three times before he appeared at the end of the torch-lit corridor and saw her stricken face.

'My lady?' He rushed to her side and saw Al Hasim, convulsing on the floor. The Karesian's chest was streaming with sweat. 'What happened to him?'

'I don't know,' she replied. 'Help me get him on to the bed.'

The guardsman obliged and hefted the lithe Karesian over his shoulder. Grunting with effort, he laid Hasim down as gently as he could on Bronwyn's bed. He didn't stop shaking, and his eyes still stared at the ceiling.

'Send men to the chapel,' she said. 'I need one of Lanry's acolytes, now. Anyone skilled in healing.'

He nodded and ran from the room, shouting for other guardsmen to join him. The keep servants, roused by her shouting, clustered in the corridor, asking what was wrong, but she closed the bedroom door and sat by the shaking Karesian.

'My love,' she whispered, stroking back his hair. 'What's happening? Hasim, say something.'

His eyes were not present, as if he looked at something far away. His face twitched as his stare intensified and his hands clenched into tight fists, forcing her to let go.

There was a jaunty knock on the door. 'Can I come in?' said a Ranen voice.

'Fynius? Now is not the time. Wait in the hall.'

The captain of Twilight Company ignored her and opened the door. He had ushered away the servants and stood with Warm Heart panting happily next to him. His thin face dropped from a smile into a frown as he saw the Karesian.

'Fuck, I'm too late,' snarled the Ranen, rushing to Al Hasim's side. 'When did this happen?'

'What? Five minutes ago, maybe a bit less. You know what's happening to him?'

'I do,' he replied, removing his riding gloves and unclasping his armour. 'He needs help or he's going to die and there'll be no-one to catch his father.'

'His father?'

'It's a lot to explain,' snapped Fynius. 'I can explain it or I can save his life. Your choice.'

He sat on the bed, rubbing his hands together as if he were a healer, feeling Hasim's hands and looking into his staring eyes.

The man was no priest, but she did not doubt his connection to Brytag.

'Help him,' she said. 'Please.'

Fynius held the sides of Al Hasim's head. 'Did you catch him, man of the sun? I'm sorry I couldn't prepare you. I rode as fast as I could. There is still a little power left for you and your father. We said everyone gets equal help.'

The Ranen stared down at Hasim, his thin face twisting into an intense frown. He then looked up suddenly, staring at the thin air between him and Bronwyn. 'I need more power to anchor him,' he said to the air. 'Hasim isn't strong enough on his own.'

For an instant, Bronwyn thought she saw another figure in the room, perhaps a man in a light blue cloak. She thought he spoke to Fynius before fading as quickly as he'd appeared. Something in the image was comforting, even familiar. Then the same blue light enveloped the room and a raven cawed from afar. She gasped, but couldn't move as the light began to churn like a stormy sea. Warm Heart sat in front of her, obscuring a rising wind from the middle of the room.

Fynius was now open-mouthed in the centre of a pale blue maelstrom of whirling wind. His hands were still clamped to the sides of Hasim's head, but he now pulled the Karesian upwards and blinding light passed between them. 'We've not abandoned you, Fire Giant,' he roared. 'Jump and we will catch you.'

She closed her eyes as the light became unbearable, but she imagined a man clad in black, falling from the sky to be caught by Al Hasim and Fynius. When she opened her eyes she saw an old Karesian man, with a high forehead and a stern face. He was ghostly and she could see the far wall through his body, but something about him suggested immense power. The blue light had not faded and she had no doubt that it was the only thing allowing her to view the apparition.

Hasim was no longer convulsing and Fynius sat next to him on the bed, panting with exhaustion.

'My son,' said the ghostly figure. 'I see you.'

Hasim coughed and sat up, wiping sweat from his face. He took in his surroundings and flashed a tired smile at Bronwyn before getting up from the bed and approaching the old Karesian.

'I felt you in my mind, Father. You were falling. I tried to catch you, but you were too heavy.'

'You caught me,' said the ghost. 'With help from this one.' He pointed a spectral arm at Fynius. 'Without you, my son. . . without the memory of you, I would have drifted forever.'

'It is a pleasure to meet you, Dalian Thief Taker,' said Fynius, looking drained of energy. 'Please accept this as our gift to you and Jaa. We can't help you find your exemplar, but we can give you the time to look.'

'We can feel him, but it fades. I will find him.'

Hasim and the ghostly figure of his father looked at each other. Both men's arms twitched as if they wanted to embrace, but knew it was impossible.

'I'm sorry I left,' said Hasim.

'I'm sorry I let you,' replied Dalian. 'I only ever wanted you to embrace Jaa and become a wind claw like your father.'

Hasim scratched his head, as if a thought suddenly intruded. 'I *do* feel him,' he murmured. 'Maybe it's just you, but I *do* feel Jaa. He's happy with me. I've never felt such a thing before.'

'If you feel him, you are one of few,' replied Dalian. 'And you cannot rest when the Fire Giant hangs on by a thread. I will find the exemplar, but you must rejoin the Long War as a soldier for Jaa.'

Bronwyn expected a witty response or a cavalier show of apathy. What she got was a nod of conviction. Something had changed in Al Hasim. He had felt his god for the first time, and it was not a feeling to be mocked or cast aside.

'We will meet again, my son,' said Dalian. 'For as we endure, so does Jaa. The Dead God can claim his lands and his followers, but *we* will keep the Fire Giant alive.' With a warm smile and a subtle bow of the head, the ghostly figure faded from view, appearing to slip into the gap between moments.

The blue light faded with him and Fynius sprang to his feet, looking again like a mischievous gremlin. 'No need to thank us, man of the sun. It was a pleasure.'

Hasim wasn't listening. He looked at the space where his father had been and his eyes appeared to burn with a distant fire. Bronwyn wanted to reach out to him, but she could feel heat from his body and smell the distant aroma of smouldering rocks.

Fynius stood and again addressed the air between them, as if someone was speaking to him. 'Really?' he asked. 'Is that even possible?' He paused, his mind processing something. 'Okay, but don't take too long. You've nothing left.'

He closed his eyes and his head went back as if some strong wind had suddenly hit him. His arms and legs twitched and his eyes shot open. He looked at her, his face dropping into a look of intense loss and sadness.

'Bronwyn!' It was not Fynius's voice. 'I have no more power, no more time. I fade into the void and I must say goodbye.'

'Brom?' She grabbed Fynius and saw her brother's love in his eyes.

'I remember you, sister. Before I leave, I wanted you to know that I love you.'

'Where are you? Can you come back like Hasim's father?'

He smiled at her, Brom's boyish charm showing through Fynius's face. 'No,' he replied, grabbing her in a tight hug. 'We have no more power. The World Raven can no longer sustain a shade. We have used every reserve of divine energy left to us. Brytag will endure, as his followers endure, but Bromvy Black Guard of Canarn must go. Goodbye, Bronwyn.'

She didn't let go of him, even as her twin brother roared with anguish and left Fynius's body. The man of Ranen slumped in her arms, and only Hasim's help stopped her from dropping him. They lifted the slender captain of Twilight Company and placed him on the bed, where Al Hasim had been minutes before.

'I can't feel Brytag,' murmured Fynius. 'I can't hear him. I just hope it was worth it. I just hope it was enough.'

* * *

She'd kissed Hasim a dozen times since Fynius fell asleep and he felt further away each time, as if he'd already left, drifting away as surely as Brom. But with Al Hasim she sensed that he was bound for Karesia and an exploration of his new faith. He looked across the sea, from the battlements of a high tower, with a pinched look of intense thought on his face. Bronwyn stood next to him, their hands clasped together, but she didn't say a word. The duchess of Canarn had said goodbye to her brother and she now had to say goodbye to Al Hasim. Now she had her own journey to consider. But hers would not take her far from home.

Fynius had curled up in her bed and entered a deep sleep, saying nothing more to them. They'd retreated to the great hall, and then to the tower overlooking the harbour of Canarn. It was a clear morning, with a bright blue sky threatening to intrude through patchy clouds.

'Kessia?' she asked, after several hours of silent meditation.

He nodded. 'I've not been there for ten years. I think I might start a cult of Jaa worship. The subterfuge appeals to my roguish side.'

'So, the Prince of the Wastes returns to Karesia. I feel sorry for the Dead God.'

Hasim smiled, returning to his old self for a moment. 'There must be thousands of people, languishing under this Twisted Tree, who could do with an alternative. Every person I turn back to Jaa is power stolen from the Dead God.'

She slowly put her arms around his neck and kissed him deeply. 'I won't ask you to stay, but I don't want you to die.'

He laughed heartily. 'People have been trying to kill me for years, my love. Karesians, Ranen, Kirin, mostly Ro. Perhaps my father brought me some extra luck, or maybe Jaa *was* watching. I feel him. For the first time in my life, I truly feel him. I have to do what I can.'

Bronwyn looked into his eyes and could detect no shred of doubt. 'I understand,' she whispered. 'You will always be welcome in Canarn.'

'Brom would want you to stay,' he said, stroking her cheek. 'This is your city as it was his – as it was your father's.'

'I'm staying,' she replied. 'I have a notion that I'll give a proposal of marriage to Vladimir Corkoson. He's one of the few Lords of Ro not to ask me. If we can establish a realm between Canarn and the Darkwald, perhaps we'll remain free for a little longer. Keep Brytag as our patron, maybe give back a little power.'

He raised his eyebrows. 'Brytag is a fine choice, and Vladimir is kind-hearted, but he uncorks a little too easily.'

'Well *you're* not going to marry me,' she said with a girlish smile. 'And Vladimir is more appealing than Lord Hetherly of Chase. I don't even know where Chase is.'

'Oh, the Lord of Mud is a far better match than me. I should just warn you that he can't stand straight without a bottle in his hand.'

'I'll live with it,' she replied. 'I doubt he'll see it as a proposal of love, and Fallon said to keep Canarn strong. That's advice you take to heart. The Darkwald is a large realm, given little respect by the rest of Tor Funweir. We have that in common.'

Hasim frowned, his thoughts appearing far away.

'Are you thinking about your father?' she asked. 'You never talk about him.'

He smiled, as if remembering a private joke. 'It's a long story. He was always obsessed with Jaa, and I always rebelled. It never occurred to me to actually listen to him. Though he helped me escape Kessia when Rham Jas got me in trouble. He could have had me killed. . . he *should* have had me killed. He just wanted me to be something I wasn't. But I knew he loved me and I always thought I'd see him again.'

She kissed him, letting his tears touch her cheeks. She loved him too, but she couldn't compete with Dalian Thief Taker. Hasim was one of the last followers of Jaa, and she was one of the last nobles of Ro. The world would not allow them the luxury of happiness, no matter how much they rebelled against the Dead God and his armies.

Chapter Fifteen

Alahan Teardrop in the City of Tiergarten

THE DREAMS NEVER stopped. Each night, Alahan fell into a deep pit of tentacles and despair. He was the exemplar of Rowanoco, but had nothing to show for it. He was the son of Algenon Teardrop, but he doubted everything. When the day ended and the cold cut through his limbs, he was just a young man from Fredericksand with an old name and dark dreams.

The tentacled woman had grown tall. She spread her arms round thousands of squirming figures in a tight embrace. Her arms echoed into dozens of tentacles, each one flailing at the figures, grasping and squeezing until all life was gone. She hugged the motionless bodies close, a gleaming smile all that was visible of her face. Why did Rowanoco show him this each night? It was as if the Ice Giant wanted him to know some truth but was too far away to make him understand. The shade of his uncle, Magnus Forkbeard, had been silent for days and Alahan's thoughts had turned to drinking in the ice halls after he felt the cold steel of Rulag Ursa's axe.

Then he was awake, his eyes snapping open to look at the grey stone ceiling. Something was wrong. Some nagging sound had reached his ears and pulled him from sleep. It was still dark, with a crackling globe of firelight the only illumination. He sat up and saw rolling shadows playing off the doorway. A slight wind caught the fire and it displaced the shadows for a second, showing a silhouetted foot at the base of the door. Someone was standing outside and Alahan had woken at a footstep. His eyes flicked to his axe, Ice Razor, leaning against a chair by the far wall. Then back to the door. The shadows had returned and the silhouette was gone.

Unsure whether he was truly awake, he froze, lying under a thick fur blanket, his eyes fixed on the shadowy door. The handle creaked and was then silent. Then it creaked again, slower this time, quieter. A sliver of dull light appeared as the door opened just a crack. The firelight from the corridor mingled slowly with the glow of his hearth and illuminated a man in the doorway.

He saw Alahan, saw that he was awake, and darted forward, drawing a curved knife. The young thain widened his eyes and threw off the blanket just in time to catch the man's arm and stop the knife entering his neck. The man was bulky, wearing thick furs and chain armour. He pushed down on Alahan's bare chest, gritting his teeth and pushing the blade downwards.

'Just let it happen,' grunted the man, using all his strength to push the blade to within an inch of Alahan's neck. Behind, through the dancing firelight, two more figures entered the room and closed the door, muttering to each other to be quiet. Before the door closed, Alahan briefly saw other figures, holding bloodied axes, in the corridor.

'He's awake,' said one.

'Not for long,' replied the man grappling with Alahan.

'Just get it done.'

Through the darkness, the sweat, the sudden waking and the men wanting to end his life, Alahan roared and shook his head, coming fully awake. He pushed the blade aside, unbalancing the larger man, and brought his knee up into his groin. The man flailed and the blade dug into Alahan's shoulder.

'Stop flirting and kill him,' muttered the man by the door, keeping his voice low and sounding as though he was keeping his temper in check.

The third man had his ear to the door as if he was terrified they'd be discovered. Both men, seeing their companion in trouble, now drew similar curved knives.

'Fucking coward,' spat Alahan, pulling the knife from his shoulder and driving it into his assailant's head. The would-be assassin had let go of the handle and was cradling his sore groin, but now he stared blankly, blood trickling from his mouth, nose and the fatal wound in his temple.

The other two men, similarly dressed in fur and chain, advanced just as Alahan sprang to his feet, keeping the bed between them. He wore only woollen leggings, but the cold was defeated by his adrenaline and survival instinct. His eyes flicked to Ice Razor, but the men blocked his path to it. He would remain unarmed.

There was shouting in the corridor as if the axe-men outside had been discovered. Steel against wood and strange growling. The men in the room looked at each other, alarmed by the sounds, but didn't back away.

'Your death needs to happen, Teardrop. The age of strength begins and we will take your life and your name.'

'Well, you'll have to,' he replied, reaching down to coil his fur blanket around his wrist. The knife wound in his shoulder had only caught flesh and was not debilitating.

They attacked together, one high, one low. They were big and determined, but their clothing made them slow. Alahan whipped the blanket into one of their faces and dodged the other. He was barely clothed and that made him fast, but one mistake and he'd bleed.

He moved away, trying to get to Ice Razor, but the blanket was now tangled and he had to let go, giving the men room to cut him off.

'Just die, boy!'

Outside, the sounds had risen in volume as running feet and roaring voices travelled along the corridor. The strange growling was now right outside his door, but the men still attacked again.

Alahan could avoid one, pushing his forearm into the man's wrist, but there simply wasn't enough space to avoid the second blade. It hit him in his exposed side, cutting deeply into his flesh.

A. J. SMITH

He howled in pain, punching the man in the face, but was barrelled to the floor by their collective weight.

It was now all arms and legs. The blade in his side remained, and the pain was extreme, but his strength didn't leave him. He was punched, kicked, his head was slammed into the stone floor, but he avoided the remaining blade.

'Hold him down,' barked the armed man.

Alahan got an elbow in the stomach and had the wind knocked out of him. They wrestled him flat and he saw a boot coming down to connect squarely with his face, making stars appear in front of his eyes. Then the bedroom door smashed inwards and Timon the Butcher appeared.

The Low Kaster was frothing at the mouth and his head, free of its leather strapping, was pulsing with red veins. His eyes were black, and blood dripped from a dozen small wounds across his bulbous torso. He held the limp arm of an axe-man, dragging the dead body behind him as a child would drag a favourite toy. He drooled and his flabby lips smacked together.

'Varorg!'

The huge berserker loped into the room and flung the dead body at the wall. Several more bodies were revealed outside as he left the doorway.

Alahan was kicked again, but refused to stop struggling. He had managed to keep the remaining knife from finishing him off, but he was now completely prone on the floor and pain from his side was gradually sapping his strength.

'Kill that flabby cunt,' said one of the men.

The young thain was pulled into a chokehold by the last man and they rolled over as Alahan struggled to breathe, his eyes fixed on his friend. Timon held a heavy battleaxe and his clenched fists seemed to be as large as a man's head. He ran at the knife-wielding assassin, ignoring the blade and driving the man into the floor with an immense strike. He was stabbed twice; once in the forearm as he advanced and once in the thigh as the assassin fell downwards. He didn't react, or even flinch from the wounds.

244

From the door, armed men of Tiergarten appeared and the sole living assassin, his arm still wrapped round Alahan's neck, swore under his breath.

'Better let me go,' grunted Alahan.

'Shut up, boy.'

Timon knelt down and pounded on the fallen man's head, until a dull crack and a spray of blood signalled his death. The Low Kaster then stood and vibrated, framed by a dozen new light sources from the doorway. Tricken Ice Fang appeared, joined by bloodied men-at-arms, and the arm round Alahan's neck loosened slightly.

'Keep back,' grunted the man, fear in his eyes. 'Keep back or I break his neck.'

Tricken put a hand on Timon's shoulder and the Low Kaster let him pass. Whatever frenzy Timon had been in, he now appeared calm, the grunting quietened and his eyelids drooping.

'Let go of him,' said Tricken calmly, picking at a blood stain in his dense red beard.

The choke loosened a little more and Alahan, fighting the pain in his side, wrestled an arm free and grabbed at the man's face. He dug his thumb into an eye and rolled free as his assailant groaned in pain.

'Friend Alahan,' wailed Timon, moving to help the young thain.

Tricken swung the haft of his axe and rendered the screaming man unconscious, just as blood started to seep out from his eye socket.

'Get him to Crowe!' shouted Tricken, seeing the knife wound in Alahan's side. 'Move!'

* * *

It was the second time Old Father Crowe had pulled him back from the brink of death. And the second time Timon had saved his life and delivered him to the priest.

'Do you know why the Ranen are given to fighting among themselves?' asked Crowe. 'It's because Rowanoco is a chaotic god.

245

It's a bold Order of the Hammer priest who'll say with certainty what our god values. We know strength, honour and freedom, but the order of importance is up for debate. You in Fredericksand generally value honour first; we in Tiergarten prefer to see freedom as paramount. Those in Ursa value only strength. No-one is truly right because no-one is truly wrong, and Rowanoco won't interfere; it's as if he wants us to disagree.'

Alahan was lying on a stone table, surrounded by globed candles and sweet-smelling incense.

'The Ranen will forever fight over which is paramount,' Crowe went on. 'But this is not just the latest disagreement. This is influenced from outside.' He chuckled to himself, more a grumble than a laugh. 'I'm strangely okay with us fighting for our own reasons – we've had a dozen minor skirmishes with Rulag's lot since he took over – but the Karesian witches getting involved; that I cannot abide. Make no mistake, Rulag's new religious convictions are not his own. He has not turned from Rowanoco. He has been pushed.'

The young thain sat up and rubbed his side. The wound had been healed into a small scar. It had felt far worse than it now looked. They were in a windowless room, somewhere in the Hall of Summer Wolf where the cold barely penetrated. The room was lined with shelves, upon which were strange items and old scrolls. It contained a cluttered desk and was warmed by a low-burning brazier. It was an odd sanctum, but well-suited to Old Father Crowe.

'So, the Greens tried to kill me?' he mused.

'They clearly didn't send their best. And you may have been an afterthought once they failed to kill Halla.'

Alahan wondered if Crowe was just being contrary for the sake of it; if the old man was testing him or throwing random insinuations into his speech in the hope that they'd be recognized.

'Why do you attack me so?' he asked, lying back down on the stone table.

Crowe's face wrinkled into a smile. The skin fell loosely from his cheeks and his eyes narrowed into dark creases. 'I taunt you so you may one day be worthy of your name.' He chuckled to himself, as if he'd said something funny. 'Did it not ever occur to you that I spoke the same way to your father?'

Alahan frowned. 'He spoke highly of you.'

'Because I stopped taunting him when he became worthy of his name. I am an old man. I have seen many thains, and I no longer feel the need to censor myself. Your family have given much to Fjorlan. Do you think you will give more if I am kind to you?'

He suddenly thought of his sister. He'd always promised to look after her. Promised her *and* his father. Crowe had never met Ingrid, but Alahan would welcome a grand confrontation. The Little Wolf would tear the old priest to pieces with grinning questions and naive wit. She'd ask him about his beard and make him feel bad if he was mean to her. Alahan was not blessed with his sister's subtle sense of humour. He'd always been more intense, more serious, more troubled. He was the eldest and he was the heir. She'd have been a far greater exemplar.

'I'm just a man,' he replied. 'My father should not have been killed. He should still be high thain. I should still be in Fredericksand, keeping Ingrid out of trouble. The dragon fleet should still be afloat – and Wulfrick should be standing by the door asking if I'm okay.'

'Fantasy is easy,' stated Crowe. 'Reality is hard.'

'So is life,' replied Alahan. 'Death seems the easiest of all.'

The old priest placed two brass cups on the table and poured liquid from an unadorned jug into each one. It was not mead. It had a pungent alcoholic odour that stung his nostrils.

'Drink this,' said Crowe. 'I save it for certain moments of contemplation. You're the first man to share it with me. But I think it appropriate.'

Alahan pressed a hand to his side and sat up, swinging his legs round to perch on the edge of the table. 'What is it?' he asked.

'Very rare stuff. I doubt there are more than a handful of bottles of it in all of Ranen.'

Alahan raised a cup to his nose and balked at the acrid smell. The liquid was clear, but a slight froth nestled at its edges.

'Frost whisky,' said Crowe. 'Brewed by the artisans of Sovon Kor in Volkast. The little berserkers from the north have been refining their craft far longer than any Ranen brewer of grain or honey.'

The priest took a slow drink, draining the cup, but not removing his eyes from Alahan. His body then shivered from head to toe as the liquor flowed down his throat. Even a hardened drinker like Crowe evidently swayed in his chair after a drink of Volk frost whisky.

'I feel I should keep my wits about me,' said Alahan, looking down at the unassuming cup of liquid.

Crowe closed his eyes and emitted a grumbled laugh. 'You have been unconscious for almost an entire day. I have kept you in and out of delirium and heard your heart stop twice.' He paused, taking a deep breath. 'It is the dead of night – you have no need of your wits until the sun rises.'

Alahan was speechless. He had imagined he'd been unconscious for an hour or two, kept alive by divine magic. He'd had no notion of how close to death he had been. Almost without thinking, he downed the liquid and felt it burn from his throat to his stomach.

'Fuck me!' he exclaimed. 'Are you sure this is supposed to be drunk and not used to clean axes?'

'You have to experience it, rather than drink it,' said Crowe, his eyes still closed and a strangely blissful expression on his face.

'A whole day,' mused Alahan. 'That means the betrayer is a day closer and we all have a day less to live.'

He felt a warmth across his entire body, ending as a pleasant crackle in each of his fingers and toes. His head lightened, but he did not feel drunk, just soft-limbed and peaceful, as if his arms weighed nothing and his body hovered above the table.

'I feel like I'm floating, is this normal?'

Crowe didn't open his eyes. He merely swayed gently from side to side. 'Anything you experience is normal,' he replied. 'That is

248

to say, the liquor affects men differently. Volk would say it was not meant for us, but I find that, if you add just enough dilution, it is rather drinkable.'

Alahan took several deep breaths. He'd been drunk many times and had never felt like this. The Volk liquor was probably poisonous and wreaking all sorts of mayhem in his body, but it caused his mind to quiet. It was the best he'd felt for months. Crowe had drifted away, presumably to seek his own answers in a gleeful state of stupor, while Alahan began to feel far away, as if his body was now an encumbrance to further thought.

He began to dream, his head drifting into a waking fantasy, as real as the table at which he sat or the stone room where Crowe had saved his life. He saw no tentacles and no dark woman, no Twisted Tree, not even the ever-present wisps of doubt. He saw his uncle and he saw an endless canvas of ice.

'I have returned,' said Magnus, taller and more solid than he had ever been. 'And I have a gift from the old raven.' His golden hair shone and his wide shoulders were made wider by a heavy bear-skin cloak.

Alahan looked into the vista of ice and saw what was waiting for him. A legion of men, shrouded in the same icy mist as Magnus, and ready to defend Rowanoco's land. They looked at him from ages past, their fists taut round hundreds of war-hammers. They were Order of the Hammer priests.

'We have been given the power to unlock the heart of Fjorlan,' said Magnus. 'And remind the world of Rowanoco's might. Rulag will learn the same lesson as the Ro.'

He felt power surge through his body, as if his every muscle had tensed at the same time. The Volk frost whisky had warmed his limbs, but it was barely a tickle next to the power that Magnus now unlocked. For the first time since his father had died, Alahan Teardrop did not doubt.

'The heart of Fjorlan,' he said, sitting forward and jolting Crowe out of his stupor.

The old priest looked at him and scratched his flowing grey

beard. He rubbed his eyes and looked again, sitting forward himself. 'What of it?' he asked.

Alahan breathed deeply, and gradually his face became a mask of calm. 'I am the exemplar of Rowanoco,' he stated, 'and I need to know about the heart of Fjorlan.'

Crowe rubbed his eyes again. 'Why did you not tell me this before we drank frost whisky?'

'Because I doubted. I don't any more.'

'Well, the Volk are the oldest followers of Rowanoco. It makes sense that their liquor would inspire a revelation.' He didn't question Alahan's statement or his request. He stood suddenly, shaking his head and leaning against the wall. 'Follow me.'

Alahan, unencumbered by the liquor, sat up and retrieved a tunic. The scar in his side didn't trouble him and he stood unaided, following Old Father Crowe out of the small room. The corridor was narrow and empty, with no other doors or windows. Small globes of firelight sat every few paces and a steep staircase emerged at the end of the corridor. Crowe stopped at the base of the stairs, holding his chest and groaning.

'Do you need to lie down?' asked Alahan.

The old priest glared at him. 'The day I'll take advice from you about drinking is the day I bury an axe in my own head.'

'In your own time then.'

The priest composed himself and ascended the narrow staircase, using both hands to steady himself. At the top was another narrow corridor. Alahan didn't know where in the High Hold they were, just that it was deep within the stone bowels of Tiergarten. They turned left, then right, passing no doors or windows, until they emerged on a stone precipice, looking over the Plains of Tiergarten. A chiselled staircase snaked its way round the side of Giant's Gift, with Rowanoco's Stone and the Hall of Summer Wolf visible below.

'I thought we were under the city, not above it.'

Crowe took a moment to bathe in the cold night air. 'The mountains and their vaults existed long before the city. Kalall Summer Wolf walked these halls, as has every high priest of

Tiergarten. Though you are the first man not a priest to ask me about the oldest vault.'

'The heart of Fjorlan?' he queried. 'What is it?'

'Come, it is close now.'

The chiselled stairs were exposed to the wind and lancing gusts of frozen air battered them against the cliff face. As they turned away from the wind, fissures in the rock revealed old vaults, hewn in forms of majesty, displaying ornate carvings and sealed stone doors. He imagined some were tombs, others ancient storerooms or perhaps forgotten mead halls. Crowe led him to one of these least ornate vaults, half-buried in the mountain. The entrance was tall, but no statues or carvings surrounded it. Strangely, given its obvious age, it showed signs of recent use and Alahan followed well-trodden footprints to the smooth stone doors. Crowe pulled the doors outwards and disappeared into darkness. There was no dust or smell of rot, just a sharp waft of clean air.

'Come in,' said Crowe, as a globe of light was sparked into life in the entrance.

Alahan stepped out of the wind and saw a long stone chamber in the flickering light. Either side of him, flanking a wide walkway, were weapon racks. The old priest closed the door and proceeded down the walkway, holding a globed candle in front of him. The light revealed hundreds of war-hammers, each one older and more ornate than the last. Under each was the name of a member of Rowanoco's Order of the Hammer, chiselled in stone. Thoin Hearth Fire, Mors Hell Fist, Dorron Moon Eye.

'The hammers all find their way back here,' said Crowe. 'Eventually. Your uncle's still drifts in the world somewhere, but it'll end up here. These last few will be of particular interest to you.'

Alahan stopped in the globe of light, facing a large statue of a helmeted head. The face was resolute, carved with intricacy and care, showing no weakness or doubt. It was a man of Ranen, locked forever in a stony mask of defiance. Beyond the statue, more war-hammers sat in discreet display cases.

Crowe, standing before the weapons, turned to face Alahan. 'When the men of Ro occupied the Freelands, and Fjorlan marched to war, it was the Order of the Hammer who liberated the land of Rowanoco. These two hundred hammers belonged to the men who fought the last time Ranen was threatened. They united the Free Companies and assaulted Ro Hail. If it wasn't for them, the Ro would still rule Tor Ranen. This is the heart of Fjorlan. A mausoleum for those who died to protect Rowanoco's land.'

Alahan should have felt over-awed, but instead he felt happy. Before him he saw the means to defend Tiergarten and remind Rulag's army that Rowanoco would not be felled so easily by a Twisted Tree. The war-hammers contained might and nobility beyond anything he had seen, and they wanted to be used. They wanted to once more defend the lands of Ranen.

'Where will you find men to wield them?' asked Crowe. 'As exemplar you can unlock their power. They can impart great strength, but they still need to be held by worthy men. The spirits of the two hundred priests will not give their skill to just anyone.'

* * *

Standing before the vaults were two hundred men. Not one was below fifty years of age and all had been judged unfit for combat, though many had protested. Their eyes showed just as much anger as any of Halla's defenders and their experience made each man valuable. Some had been warriors; others were skilled tradesmen or merchants. One or two had even been axe-masters or chain-masters in their youth. As the city prepared for war, they'd been spread across the higher levels, lending assistance with provisions and relaying words of comfort to the young. But the icy stare of Rowanoco had not left them, nor did they think twice when given a chance to fight for Fjorlan one last time.

The oldest, a former ship-master of Fredericksand named Arnulph Grief, was in his late seventies and needed a heavy crutch to stand upright on a crippled right leg. Even so, the old man had a stare to rival that of Brindon Crowe and his shoulders were huge from a lifetime of hefting dragon ships along wooden jetties.

'I will fight for you, my lord Teardrop,' said Arnulph in a raspy rumble of a voice. 'I have a few tricks left in my old bones.'

The man was taller than Alahan, even with a significant bend in his back from the crutch, and he would have been a fearsome opponent in his day. With Rowanoco's help he would be again.

'Thank you,' said the young thain. 'The same goes for each of you. I can't guarantee victory or single out Rulag for his treachery, but I can offer you a gift from the Ice Giant. I am Rowanoco's exemplar, his general in this fight – and you will be my company. Though youth has left you and you number only two hundred, with the heart of Fjorlan you will be mighty indeed.' He raised his head and smiled, feeling no doubt or fear. 'Follow me and meet those you will wield in defence of Rowanoco's land.'

He took a deep breath, continuing to smile as he turned and led the men into the vault. Crowe was already inside and had placed torches at the end, illuminating a silent company of stone figures, standing against the far wall. The statues were of the two hundred priests who had defeated the Ro and they stood guard over their war-hammers. Alahan approached the first figure, a towering man with a flowing beard rendered perfectly with hammer and chisel. Under the statue was inscribed the name Wilhelm Speaks in Silence.

'Arnulph Grief,' said Alahan, 'this will be *your* hammer.'

The old ship-master hobbled to stand in front of the statue and looked up with awe at the face of the priest. Wilhelm appeared to look back at him, as if he was assessing the old man. When Arnulph opened the simple display case and looked down at the war-hammer, a white light began to flow from the statue. The hammer was edged in deep ice, with a thick leather strap wrapped round the long handle. It was a two-handed weapon that would take great strength to wield.

'Arnulph,' prompted Old Father Crowe. 'You must touch the hammer. It may take a while for the weapon to accept you, and we have little time.'

The old man nodded at the priest, his eyes wide with anticipation as the white light caressed his hands. He closed his eyes and bowed his head, then grasped the handle firmly in both fists. The light flared and Alahan saw a spirit pass from the hammer to the man, as Wilhelm Speaks in Silence gave a portion of his power to Arnulph Grief.

'Exemplar!' boomed a voice, coming from Arnulph's mouth.

'I am here,' replied Alahan. 'We need your help. The lands of Rowanoco are once again threatened.'

'This one is strong,' stated Wilhelm, throwing away Arnulph's crutch and tensing his muscles. 'Why does he need *my* strength?'

'He is old,' replied Alahan. 'I suspect his strength is the memory of a man he used to be. You can make him that man again.'

Wilhelm screwed up Arnulph's face and flexed the old man's body. 'I will help this old man – and I will help you. But it will take time to repair his body.'

'Take the time,' said Crowe. 'The exemplar and I have another hundred and ninety-nine hammers to bestow.'

* * *

Horns blew from the forward defences and were picked up by each adjacent wall, the sound carrying up Kalall's Steps to be heard in the Hall of Summer Wolf. It was a single note, not the repeating warning of an approaching enemy.

Alahan had left the vault and allowed Crowe to help the old men bond with their new strength. It was a slow process and the young thain had needed to rest and think about his new role and the lack of doubt that it brought. After a few hours' sleep, he'd found himself drinking mead in the great hall, trying to make Tricken Ice Fang understand how two hundred old men could be useful. Then they'd heard the horn and paused.

'Someone approaches,' he said.

'Still morning,' said Tricken. 'I don't like visitors during breakfast.'

Alahan pulled himself upright. 'Let's go and see, shall we?' His words were now delivered with confidence.

'Aye, lad,' said Tricken, also standing.

From a side door, Halla and Falling Cloud joined them. They had slowly recovered from their battle with the trees, while Alahan and Tricken took charge in the city. He'd not yet been able to continue his conversation with Halla, nor tell her that he no longer doubted his power.

'What does the horn mean?' asked Falling Cloud, belting on a heavy, leather axe-belt, holding two razor-sharp hand-axes.

'Just going to find out, lad,' replied Tricken, scratching at his dense red beard and moving to the huge wooden doors.

The wind blew in a mist of snow from the High Hold, followed sharply by a gust of freezing air. Alahan hunkered up under his cloak and shivered, wishing he could take the fire-pits with him when he left the Hall of Summer Wolf. Halla didn't flinch at the cold breeze. On the contrary, she appeared to brighten under the freezing blanket, as if her city was saying hello.

Alahan and the axe-maiden were first after Tricken, exiting the hall side by side. She frowned at him as if she saw someone new in his eyes. He met her gaze, but didn't try to explain. She'd already said what she needed from him and he planned to deliver it in defence of the city.

The High Hold of Tiergarten was ringed by axe-men, all around the stone balcony, facing outwards with circular shields and heavy battleaxes. They were a new addition, commanded to stand by Alahan after he left the vault. The threat posed by the Green Men was not something he was going to ignore. Halla and her captains were too valuable to lose to a blade in the dark.

'Halla, they're signalling from the gate,' said Falling Cloud.

Tricken joined him. 'Aye, looks like. . . well, not an attack certainly.'

The axe-maiden narrowed her eyes and, without issuing any commands, began to descend Kalall's Steps. Alahan ordered men to follow her and increased his pace to keep up with the axe-maiden.

'Right, lads,' shouted Falling Cloud, 'let's go and have a look.'

The levels of Tiergarten revealed a city of people ready to die. Shops were closed, streets had been cleared and the city felt like a fort in enemy territory with the single goal of defending itself. The delay in Rulag's attack had helped Halla's men to secure the city, and allowed Alahan the time to unlock the heart of Fjorlan, but it had also increased the tension tenfold. These people were brave and would die for Fjorlan, but they were almost wishing for Rulag to just get it over with.

They quickly reached Ulric's Yard, passing people roused by the horn, and asking each other if the attack had started.

'Alahan, get down here,' shouted Tricken as he and Halla reached the bottom of the steps.

He took the last few steps three at a time, and joined them in Ulric's Yard. The battlements above them were now swarming with men, but they were not on alert. They'd come to see something, answering a call from their mates to come and have a look at whatever it was outside the gate.

The cloud-man, Rexel Falling Cloud, hopped up the nearby steps and shoved men aside to get a look himself. He stood aghast for a moment, his eyes widening and his mouth dropping in an expression of amazement.

'What in the fucking halls beyond,' he muttered. 'Get the gates open now.' Halla's captain had a thunderous voice, carrying far, with a note of aggressive authority.

The gate guards didn't ask for clarification; they moved quickly in response to the order and no-one contradicted Falling Cloud. Alahan strode forward with Tricken to the front of the group as the huge, wooden doors were pulled inwards by a heavy chain mechanism.

'I don't believe it,' said Falling Cloud, returning to Halla's side in Ulric's Yard.

A white sliver appeared, then a white expanse as the gates revealed the immense plains of Summer Wolf. At the base of the wood, silhouetted against the crisp blue sky, crawled a figure.

He was bloodied, cleaved and grunting, a mop of blackened hair sticking to and obscuring any recognizable features. But the huge man, growling like a beast and missing his right arm, was not what caused the alarm. Behind him, tightly grasped in his remaining hand, was a shimmering black creature. It was a cross between a limp, fleshy tree and a jet-black squid, with tentacles clustered together behind a thick body, tentacles that had been hacked to pieces by repeated axe blows.

'Wulfrick!' exclaimed Halla, rushing forward, ignoring the dead creature.

Alahan, like every man in Ulric's Yard, couldn't tear his eyes from the twisted tree. It was huge and monstrous, with a single, circular mouth dripping green ooze on to the cobblestones. Each tentacle left a film of sticky, black blood on the floor, trailing out of the gate and cutting across the snowy plains beyond. Wulfrick had dragged the creature from the Crystal Fork River to the gates of Tiergarten, on his knees, with a shattered leg and a missing arm.

The axe-master of Fredericksand suddenly stood up and roared to the sky. No words or meaning, just rage and pain. His eyes were black, though he was not in any kind of battle fervour Alahan had seen. He was covered in sickly patches of the creature's blood, drying on his bare torso and coating his face and wounds. The stump of his arm was cracked and split as if some eldritch infection had taken hold of him, and his muscles pulsed with red-raw veins.

'Get Crowe,' muttered Alahan.

'Yeah, I think you're right,' replied Tricken, staring in disbelief at the dead creature and the roaring figure of Wulfrick.

CHAPTER SIXTEEN

TYR NANON IN THE HALLS
BEYOND THE WORLD

T HE VISTA WAS covered in ruined stone of immense
proportions. The blocks were dusty and broken, falling
endlessly from breaches and large gaps, disappearing only
to re-form. Each crumbling fragment of rock was larger than a
mountain and further away than any earthly horizon. Beyond
the ruin was a spire of black and shadow, barely visible against
the shimmering blue sky of the void. Everything was vague and
unreal, as if barely more than a memory. In the far distance, he
imagined, there had once been other structures, perhaps towering
over the spire. Now it was a desolate expanse of nothing. True
nothing, far more barren than an earthly desert or the deepest
ocean. Just the absence of form and substance, long turned to dust
in the winds of beyond.

But the ruined wall and spire remained, a skeletal reminder that
the Shadow Halls beyond the world could not be felled so easily.
It had once been a great realm, a place where devotion flowed,
turned into divine energy and returned to the world. Now it clung
on to existence through the last spark of divine energy it possessed,
the blood of Utha the Ghost.

As the albino cleric grew into manhood, his heritage had been
all that kept the halls intact. He was unknowingly maintaining
the one the Dokkalfar loved, their lost Shadow Giant god, as he
followed the strict rules of Tor Funweir and walked the path of
the Black. If only Nanon had met him when he was still a child;

maybe more could have been done then, rather than at the end of the battle, when the final swords were being swung and the Long War prepared to claim more casualties and declare more victors. Was it too late for Utha to change anything? Was change even necessary? Or was vengeance all that remained?

'Does it help to see it?' asked Corvus.

'I don't know. . . I thought I should see it at least once.'

'The blood and wisdom of your people built that hall. In long ages past.'

'It's not really so long,' replied Nanon. 'I have a new appreciation of time since I came here. Ten thousand, fifty thousand, a hundred thousand years – it all seems so small, so short. When you see it in context.'

The raven cawed in his mind, singing a distant song of Brytag's wit and wisdom. Every sound gave Nanon new insights into the raven god. It appeared that even Giants could be understood if he spent enough time with them, and Brytag wanted to be known. Nanon thought the World Raven desired friends, as if they kept him rooted in the lands of men.

'You should try not to have context,' said Corvus. 'A true sense of perspective is a dangerous thing. Even you, Tyr Nanon, occupy such a tiny speck of reality as to be the definition of insignificant.'

'So. . . what? Significance isn't real?' he asked.

'Not at all. It is a delusion, and one that every creature is guilty of to one degree or another. If enough mortal beings hold the same delusion – such as significance – it becomes real. . . after a fashion.'

'And you?' asked Nanon. 'What tiny corner of Brytag's mind can comprehend a creature as tiny as me?'

'The World Raven likes your kind.'

'A god is capable of such a thing?' he queried.

'Brytag cares more than most,' replied Corvus.

Nanon felt the raven's boundless empathy, as if the god of luck and wisdom was the counterpoint to Rowanoco's strength and bluster. Brytag's personality was deeper than any mortal, more layered and textured than even the oldest Dokkalfar, but he was good-natured and caring. As the void paths faded and the gods of men snatched at empty threads of faith, it was the World Raven who fought back. Not the One, standing tall behind his clerics, sword in hand, blazing with righteous anger. Not Jaa, weaving fear into the minds of enemies and burning them to cinders. No! It was a humble raven, soaring from the shoulder of the Ice Giant to try to save the lands of men from Shub-Nillurath.

'Perhaps it is time to return,' said Nanon. 'I think I've seen enough of the realms beyond.'

A sense of happy completeness flowed from Corvus, almost smug but far too warm to be negative. 'I'm glad you have chosen to live and continue your fight.'

'I sense you knew I would,' he replied.

'We hoped you would,' said the raven. 'You have much yet to do, many more people to care about. You are good-natured and that is rare in a warrior. Rarer still in a soldier of the Long War.'

The thought made Nanon sad. Why was it rare? Why did people not care about each other? He'd met so many mortal beings, so many friends and so many enemies, but he could count the truly good-natured on one hand. Rham Jas was an assassin, Glenwood was a criminal, Dalian was a mass murderer. They were his friends, but all were dark men, as capable of evil as they were of good. Even his own people were most often too proud and haughty to care about anything but themselves.

'Perhaps Keisha,' he muttered. 'She was innocent. A hunter's daughter made a slave. Used, manipulated and discarded. She's always been a victim.'

'Until now,' offered Corvus.

'Now she just has a Jekkan and its servitor to worry about,' he replied, remembering the dire situation he'd left in the Fell.

He felt boisterous humour from the raven. A kind of knowing aggression that made Nanon smile. It appeared that Brytag was not concerned by the Great Race of Jekka.

'We were sent to help,' said Corvus. 'In saving your life we have taken you beyond. You will return infused with our energy – divine energy. The thing the Jekkans fear the most.'

'Their power comes from the Old Ones,' replied Nanon. 'The Giants came later.'

'But the Giants were creatures of the realm of form once, unlike the Old Ones. Rowanoco, Jaa, the One, Brytag, even Shub-Nillurath – their strength in your lands of men is far superior to the might of the Old Ones. Why do you think the Jekkans dwindled and died?'

It made sense, but Nanon was not schooled in such ancient lore. Perhaps Vithar Joror would know of such things, or have heard misty tales of the time before the Giants, when chaos ruled the realms of form.

'I have always feared them,' said Nanon, pausing as his head filled with memories. The Jekkans' claws, their luxuriant whiskers and, most of all, their sibilant, blade-like voices, sharp enough to cut flesh and destroy thought. 'The Dokkalfar were at war with them once, but we didn't win. We just made them leave us alone. It wasn't our might that saved us, it was the Jekkans' capricious nature. I think they just got bored and moved on to tormenting something else. And that was when they were already in decline.'

Brytag knew much about the Jekkans. Nanon could feel a thousand unspoken comments and observations, many of which were scornful in the extreme, as if the World Raven thought them interlopers or aliens of some kind.

'You can help me defeat it?' he asked. 'It's to be a Tyrant of the Twisted Tree.'

'Anything we need to do has already been done,' replied Corvus, the warm humour returning.

Nanon smiled. 'Take me back.'

* * *

He opened his eyes and saw tunnels of darkness between thick trees. The canopy blocked the sky and the ground was textured with logs and dense bramble bushes. To his left, Keisha was curled up in a ball, clutching her legs and rocking back and forth with a pained moan. On the ground before him was Rham Jas's katana and his own longsword, discarded in the long grass. He had returned to his normal form, slender and unassuming, but his extremities still crackled with the divine energy of Brytag.

'Some new sorcery, knife ears?' purred the Jekkan.

Nanon looked up and saw the creature. It hung in the air, swaying between trees, its long, slender body moving as a snake in the dark air. It looked different. The nimbus of chaos was gone, as was the radiating pain of its speech. For the first time, he could actually look at it without wincing. Its angular face was feline and sensual with sharp eyes and long whiskers, feeling at the air. Its slender fingers scratched towards him with curved claws, but it was no longer terrifying.

'Not new,' replied Nanon. 'And not sorcery.'

The Jekkan was bloated with the collective energy of the dead Fell Walkers, but its eyes now focused on the forest-dweller before it, a flicker of interest passing across its face.

'What power is this?' asked the Jekkan.

Nanon slowly leant down and picked up his blades. When he straightened, the floating creature before him had backed away, directing its servitor to guard it. The undulating beast had been hesitant, flowing forward only slowly, but now it was just a patch of oozing darkness, devoid of its maddening power.

'You have one chance to leave,' said Nanon. 'Your Old Ones have no more power. They – and you – are just smoke and myth, with no place in the realm of form. You will never be a Tyrant of the Twisted Tree. Return to your ruins and die quietly.'

The Jekkan hissed, swaying in the air, a spectre of ageless chaos. Its slanted eyes conveyed no emotion, but Nanon could feel its confusion. It did not understand fear or hesitation. It had only ever known dominance and absolute power. Now, if it would not withdraw, it would feel the might of true divinity. Nanon did not want to kill so ancient a creature, but neither would he cower and allow the Jekkan to feed on the energy of the Fell Walkers or dominate this land as a Tyrant.

'Back!' he said with a strength of purpose that could topple the greatest tree. 'I will end you if I have to.'

Nanon swelled back into his original form, rising in height and letting his limbs burn with power. He still held the blades, but they now shone with the collective energy of Brytag and the oldest of the Dokkalfar.

'You would be the tastiest morsel to finish my meal,' said the Jekkan, enunciating clearly, the words visibly slicing through nearby shrubs but sounding like nothing more than a wisp of wind to Nanon.

'If you understood fear, you would feel it,' announced the Shape Taker, striding forward down a dark tunnel of closely packed trees.

The servitor formed two huge eyes and looked at him with them. Hundreds of lesser eyes rippled across its surface. It didn't form any tentacles or weapons; instead the shapeless mass looked and acted like a timid dog that has been struck by its master.

Nanon felt the sudden need to restate his presence. He took a wide stance and swung the shimmering katana at the Jekkan servitor. An arc of frozen air followed the blade as it sliced into the creature, cutting it smoothly into two lesser creatures, howling from a thousand mouths and thrashing against the mossy ground. It wasn't dead, but Nanon knew it was primal enough to recognize a superior opponent and fear it as such.

The servitor parted and fell into two patches of black liquid, unsure how to react and powerless to defend its master. Nanon took two huge strides between the parted creature and approached the floating Jekkan, weaving his enchanted blades in the air.

The ageless creature glided further away, twisted confusion forming a strange expression on its face. It had no memories or knowledge to call upon to tell it how to react. Its only recourse was to flee – but it had something that didn't belong to it and Nanon wanted it returned.

'Give the energy back,' he snarled. 'It is not yours to take.'

'The knife-eared people need it no longer,' rasped the Jekkan.

'But the forest does,' he replied. 'The Fell can once again be settled – it can still bloom and greet the daylight with green leaves and good brown earth. If you take the energy of the Dokkalfar this forest will twist and wither, darkening with each day that passes.'

The Jekkan gathered its arms across its chest, tapping its claws together. It was still moving away, but its slanted eyes were focused on the ancient forest-dweller before it.

'You are a thrall,' spat the Jekkan. 'You are nothing to me.'

'Give. It. Back.'

The Jekkan opened its slim mouth and howled, sending a violent distortion through the air. It withered trees, obliterated shrubs and flowed harmlessly round Nanon. Keisha was far enough back to not have been touched by the howl, but she was still curled up in a tight ball on the grass.

'You are of the Great Race,' stated Nanon. 'You have seen what is and what will be, but you could not see this, for the divine is lost to you. You take the rotten energy of Shub-Nillurath, but cannot perceive your own end. Your world ended ages past and you are nothing but a relic that has not yet had the decency to die.'

'This is wrong. . . this is wrong,' shrieked the Jekkan, amazed that its words did not cut the forest dweller.

The Great Race of Jekka were not warriors. They used their servitors for war, and were, by nature, extremely cowardly. Nanon, on the other hand, *was* a warrior – and he was the first Tyr to attack a Jekkan.

He leapt at it, leaving the ground and sweeping his icy blades forward. The creature balked, but its face still didn't register fear, even as the blades struck into its sensuous body. It contorted around the weapons, curving like a snake in the branches. Nanon felt the huge impact of his attack, but there was no blood and neither sword had cut flesh. Even so, the Jekkan flailed in the air, its claws lashing out to cut Nanon's face. He withdrew the blades and struck again, smashing the katana and the longsword into the creature's head. Again there was no blood, but it reeled, as if dazed, and its feet hit the forest floor for the first time.

'You wish to end me,' said the Jekkan, doubled over against thick grass.

'No,' replied Nanon. 'I wish you to give back what you stole.'

He was done talking. For a moment, Tyr Nanon the Shape Taker was the mightiest being in the lands of men. He was the oldest Dokkalfar and he was infused with divine energy. For a creature who had never known a god, it was a power unlike any other. Brytag's energy wouldn't last, but while it did, it was enough to overpower even a Jekkan.

He dropped the blades and clamped his hands to the Jekkan's head, willing it to release the stolen energy. He had struck it four mighty blows that would easily kill any mortal creature. Now he was alarmed at how frail it appeared. Its skin felt like moist paper, folding and turning red under his fingers.

He could feel it trying to reach his mind. Its chaos magic lanced from wide, cat-like eyes, but he shrugged it off as if it were nothing more than wisps of smoke.

'Give it back!' he shouted, directing all his power into his hands and forcing the Jekkan to regurgitate the life-force of the Fell Walkers.

'It is mine,' wailed the creature, suddenly seeming to realize that it was not in control.

Stark white energy flowed from its mouth and its eyes, flooding the forest with untold centuries of power and will. As the light touched grass, it once more became a living green colour. It struck bark and returned life to ancient tree-trunks. Where there had been darkness and death, there was now a rapidly moving blanket of life and energy, giving the lost life-force of the Dokkalfar back to the Fell. Nanon saw faces he recognized flow as mist from the writhing Jekkan. Vithar Loth the Tree Father, his ghostly face as calm in death as it had been in life, rose slowly and settled into a peaceful repose on the forest floor, and then an instant later to nothing. Other faces followed, other expressions of tranquillity,

265

peace and acceptance, each one adding to the spreading pool of energy, returning life to the forest and denying power to Shub-Nillurath.

As the Jekkan withered to a desiccated husk, Nanon didn't let go. He closed his eyes and slowly drained the last spark of power from the creature, giving its vast wellspring of eldritch sorcery to help rebuild the Fell. Far away, the trees burned by the Hounds began to regrow. Close by, the dead Dark Young were obliterated into fertilizer. And somewhere, in the heart of the Fell Walk, several hundred Dokkalfar returned to the earth and gained a strange kind of peace. But the Jekkan was dead.

He stood and looked down at the creature. It was empty of power, nothing more than a broken vessel. But Nanon knew, even as its body was turned to ash by the might of the forest, that it was no small thing he had done. He may have killed the last of the Great Race. He may have extinguished a light that had burned for aeons. But the world did not shake, nor did his form catch fire in punishment. Time kept moving, the wind still blew, and the old Tyr slowly flowed back into his smaller form and turned away from the empty circle of grass where he'd killed the Jekkan. He tried to find the remains of the servitor, but there was nothing left of the inky black monstrosity.

'Keisha,' he said calmly, knowing that the revitalized forest would have cleared her head of chaos magic.

'I can't see,' she muttered, squinting up at him through her fingers. 'Is everything dark?'

He crouched next to her. 'Look again.'

She blinked rapidly and moved her hands from her face, arching her neck to look around the forest. It was night-time, but the swaying green trees allowed ample moonlight to shine through. The Kirin girl stopped blinking and frowned at him. 'What happened?'

He tilted his head. 'Deep time just coughed.'

* * *

The Fell Walk was strangely peaceful. Once they'd dropped beneath the forest floor and entered the ghost settlement, the air was fresh and clear, as if nothing evil could penetrate. Nanon's Kirin companion was amazed at the huge tree-trunks and the Dokkalfar's symbiotic engineering. Her wit had returned only slowly since they left the Jekkan and the most caustic observation she could muster was to say, 'Are your people trying to compensate for something?'

He knew she'd be okay, but he had to allow her time to reorient herself. Even for a dark-blood, a mental assault from a Jekkan was a mind-shattering experience. The power of the forest had healed her but the scars would remain.

'Up ahead, the long walkway,' he said, pointing to the centre of the settlement.

'How did you build this place?' she asked, picking at a vibrant green leaf sprouting from a staircase. 'And how do people not know it's here?'

'There were hundreds of settlements like this once,' he replied. 'Before the One God decided he didn't like us very much, the Fell Walk was just a small village. The Twisted Tree took over from where the Purple clerics left off.'

Keisha followed him up a staircase of wood and moss, and they moved towards the hanging platform where Vithar Loth had previously addressed the Fell Walkers. He tried to walk slowly, allowing the Kirin girl to process the high vaulted ceilings and winding walkways. She marvelled at the thick vines, connecting the levels and holding up the vast central amphitheatre. To Nanon, her reaction was amusing. He enjoyed the awe in her eyes and the way her legs stumbled as she tried to look everywhere at once. He longed for the gift of ignorance, to be able to see things fresh, for the first time. As it was, the old Tyr was fighting tiredness and desperately wanted to spend a few hours in quiet meditation. Try as he might, he couldn't share Keisha's wonder.

'Just up here, we can rest,' he said, quickening his pace along the walkway.

A little further and they ascended another staircase, rising above the amphitheatre to a row of small huts, formed from wide gaps in the bark of a huge tree. He led her inside and was amazed at the cleanliness. No dust or dirt sat on the simple beds or the low tables. The cleansing of the Fell had flowed over the settlement and washed away any stink of death that may have remained. Any personal belongings had been taken into the Shadow Flame with the Fell Walkers, and the hut appeared fresh and new.

She pulled her eyes from the spectacle outside and slumped on a long, narrow bed, used by the Dokkalfar for meditation.

'Nanon?'

'Yes, Keisha.'

'Is it safe to sleep here?'

He selected his own bed and crossed his arms over his chest, falling into an elongated stretch as his body felt relaxation for the first time in months.

'Yes, I believe it is,' he replied, closing his eyes. 'The Long War can wait for a few hours, while we rest.'

'Sleep well, Nanon,' she responded.

Within a few moments Nanon had entered a state of deep meditation. It was not like human sleep, but more a heightened sense of calm, all his external energy focused inwards. Dokkalfar could remain in meditation for weeks if needed, using their innate power to sustain themselves while their mind recovered its spark.

Quickly, Nanon shut out the external world and allowed his newly revitalized power to hug his mind. It was warm and soothing, like a hot bath that never cooled. It slowly washed away the stress of several months' frenzied activity. The deaths of Rham Jas and Dalian. The enchantment of Glenwood and the rescue of Keisha. Lastly, his journey with Corvus and the end of the Jekkan. All things, all movements, all actions – they left small points of memory and experience in his mind that, with appropriate meditation, would simply become a part of his being.

'Meditation is supposed to be relaxing, my friend,' said Vithar Joror, reaching Nanon's mind from the forests of the Heart. 'You'll need to remain motionless for weeks if you keep worrying so.'

'You know what's happened? Or do I have to tell you everything?'

'No, no,' replied Joror. 'I can sense much from your tumbling thoughts.'

The smell of jasmine and damp grass signalled that he had inadvertently let his mind wander north, to his most recent home in the Deep Woods of Canarn. Joror probably knew him best, but they'd drifted further apart the more time Nanon spent among men.

'You killed a Jekkan,' said the Heart's Hand. 'And you travelled beyond.'

'So mundane when spoken of in mortal language,' replied Nanon. 'Neither felt mundane at the time. I worry that too much has happened, that the world will struggle to process all of these changes.'

'It will,' said Joror, 'as will you. No-one, not even the fabled Shape Taker himself, can remain unchanged by such events.'

'Fabled? Truly?'

Joror was silent for a moment. 'Perhaps legendary is more appropriate. Especially since Vithar Loth's folly.'

Sadness crept across the calm of meditation, as Nanon felt the countless dead forest-dwellers who had followed the Tree Father into the Shadow Flame. 'I wanted him to tell you.'

'Well, he didn't,' said Joror. 'He sentenced hundreds of Dokkalfar to death, expecting me to follow him in reverent suicide.'

Nanon's mind hugged him closer, protecting him from the flood of pessimistic thoughts that tried to assault him. He could have been lying in the abandoned Fell Walk for hours, but each second was now a struggle, as his calm fought a bitter war with remembrance and sadness.

'Remove your doubts and allow yourself rest,' said Joror. 'For when you are done, you and the dark-blood will return to the Heart.'

Nanon felt instant dislike for this idea. It was slow, defensive and very Dokkalfar. It would no doubt involve a lot of sitting around and waiting, all the time observing a world that was slowly breaking apart. Perhaps there was a time when he'd have liked the idea. Resting, meditating, waiting – they were important to the Dokkalfar and had served them well as the men of Ro hunted them to near extinction and the Dead God ascended.

'I don't think I'll do as you ask, my friend.'

Joror was silent again, though Nanon could sense confusion and concern coming from the Heart's Hand.

'Please don't take my defiance personally,' continued Nanon. 'I find that I am now too impatient to belong with my own kind. You will always be my friend, but I can't condemn the Kirin girl to a century of sitting around.'

Joror's thoughts conveyed genuine sadness, as if he'd finally accepted that his old friend had changed. He was ancient, though roughly half Nanon's age, but he lacked the Shape Taker's curiosity. He was a Vithar, and had never joined the Long War, preferring to maintain his position as shaman and lore-master. When he spoke, the sonorous tones were resigned. 'Time destroys all things. But not your spirit, my friend. But, I must ask – what is left for you to do?'

Nanon was wrestling with something, a dark impulse that he tried to suppress. It was a very human urge, rising from annoyance and eclipsing any sense of Dokkalfar patience that he still possessed.

'Tyr Nanon,' snapped Joror. 'Tell me – what is left?'

'Vengeance,' replied Nanon.

* * *

When he sat up on the simple bed, Nanon had no idea how much time had passed. Keisha was nowhere to be seen and the glowing shards of sunlight suggested it was well past midday.

He stood and saw that his katana was missing. His longsword was leaning against the wall, but Rham Jas's blade and its scabbard were nowhere to be seen. He belted on the longsword.

Feeling a sudden jollity, he sprang to his feet and exited the small hut. The air outside was just as clear and fresh as it had been when he entered his meditation, and all things seemed peaceful. Vithar Loth had taken much from the Fell, but Nanon and the Jekkan had given much back. The balance was certainly in his favour. Outside he wandered downwards, on the branch of a huge tree, along a spiralling walkway to the forest floor. He could hear Keisha, grunting with restrained exertion, in the amphitheatre in the middle of the Fell Walk. As he followed the walkway she came into view, swinging her father's katana amidst the gentle blowing of leaves and the whistle of wind. Rham Jas had been here a few months ago, before everything changed. As had Utha, Randall, Glenwood and Dalian. All soldiers of the Long War in their own way – and all beyond Nanon's sight. Some in death, some in distance. The wide, circular space was sombre and empty, but his elevated mood remained.

'Try two hands,' he said, stepping off the branch and into the amphitheatre. 'It's got a long hilt for a reason.'

She looked at him, then pointed the slim, curved blade in his direction. 'Why do the Kirin forge swords like this?' she asked. 'It's not like a scimitar or that longsword.'

'I'm no expert,' replied Nanon, drawing his blade and standing en-guard. 'I know they are rare and take much time to forge. I believe your people designed them to be finer than the blades of Karesia or Tor Funweir. The metal is folded until all imperfections are removed.'

She swung the blade from high, to clash solidly with Nanon's longsword. 'I think I remember it,' she said, with sadness in her eyes. 'Did he have it before I was taken?'

Nanon deflected the katana and swung a controlled riposte from a low angle. 'Yes, certainly,' he replied, as she parried his longsword. 'I think your mother gave it to him when Zeldantor was born.'

She twirled backwards and grasped the katana in both hands. 'Don't talk about my little brother. I don't want to think about him.'

'You remember?' he asked, waiting for her to attack.

Her dusky face dropped into an expression of loss and anger as she crossed her feet nimbly and aimed a downward attack at Nanon's shoulder. 'I remember the smell,' she said, with a slight smile, showing no surprise that he side-stepped her attack. 'He was so small, and he smelled bad all the time. But Father told me he'd grow, and wouldn't smell as much.'

Nanon slapped down her follow-up attack and spun away. 'I think all human babies smell. Dokkalfar babies have a faint odour of moss.'

She launched a series of controlled downward strikes, showing minimal skill but incredible speed and strength. The katana suited her, but would take time to master. 'I've not thought about my family for years, until I met you. Now it's all I can think about.'

He kept his attacks light, fighting within himself to allow her time to get used to the Kirin blade. 'I met your father after you were taken. I often wondered what he was like before.'

She too appeared to be fighting within herself, unsure of how much speed and strength to bring to bear. 'He was funny. He made jokes and pulled faces. Sometimes the Purple men came and he'd scare them off. He was good with his longbow.'

'He was,' replied Nanon. 'But he was better with his katana. One-on-one, he was better than any I've known. Maybe even two-on-one.'

'I never saw him use it,' she replied. 'It was just. . . Father's sword – he kept it sheathed and made sure it was always at his side. Even when they slept, he kept the blade by the bed.'

'Is it nice to remember?' He allowed her to pull back the katana and disengage.

She hung her head and let the blade drop. 'I really don't know. It's like I'm remembering a life I never had.'

'You've endured much suffering since,' he replied. 'But you're now free to be whoever you want. You can remember and cherish whatever you want.'

'That will take time,' said Keisha. 'Like peeling off an old skin. I've been paranoid and on the edge of a knife blade for as long as I can remember.'

Nanon lunged forward and forced her to deflect his attack with her katana. 'But you have your own blade now. A finer blade than any knife. The question is, what do want to do with it?'

She kept the Kirin sword close to her, her hands apart on its long hilt. With her natural abilities, Nanon knew, she would one day be a fine swordswoman. Until that day, she'd rely on speed and a preternatural awareness of her surroundings. It wasn't perfect, but it would best many a skilled fighter.

'Where are we going next?' she asked. 'Will I need the sword?'

They clashed again, slower this time, as if they were engaging in a methodical sword practice. Her form was rough, but she attacked from strange angles and made it difficult to riposte. Nanon allowed her to advance, keeping his own form defensive.

'Where to next,' he mused. 'Well, as two soldiers of the Long War, I propose we rejoin the battle. But it's your decision.'

'I think I trust you,' she whispered, surprising him with a sideways kick. He avoided it, but nodded approvingly at the tactic.

'A hard admission, I would imagine.'

She shrugged nonchalantly, showing her endless capacity for taking things in her stride. 'I once vowed I'd never trust a man. . . you're not a man, right?'

Nanon tilted his head. 'I'm male, but not a man. Is this important?'

'I don't break vows I make to myself,' she replied. 'But since you're not a man, I can safely trust you.'

'So,' prompted Nanon. 'Do you want to come with me and finish what your father started?'

She screwed up her face. 'I've not really been anywhere. The boat from Kessia to Weir was the first time I'd been to sea. This is the furthest north I've ever been. But I like the trees, they remind me of Oslan. It's one of the nicer things to remember. Can we come back to the forest when we're done fighting?'

'If you like,' he replied with a smile. 'The Fell Walk is a bit big for the two of us, but the crops are already growing, the defences are in place.'

She considered it while they continued their sword practice. Her katana became a little less controlled, but there was no other sign that she wasn't fully concentrating on the duel. Nanon didn't rush her. It was a powerful thing to be given a choice for the first time and he wanted her to make it in peace.

'Do I get to kill the Mistress of Pain?' she asked.

He tilted his head. 'Yes. Yes, you do.'

CHAPTER SEVENTEEN

RANDALL OF DARKWALD
IN ORON KAA

Once they'd drifted south of Skeleton Bay, the sailors all retreated into a solemn silence, looking over their shoulders and keeping below decks as much as possible. Men coiled their ropes in seconds, not loitering or telling jokes, just doing their work and going back to their bunks. Ruth had been resting for a few days and looked more like her old self, but even she was less talkative. Only Vekerian remained on deck, stubbornly remaining at the helm of his ship, surviving on a few hours' sleep a night.

With no company from either Kirin or Gorlan, Randall stood alone at the fore of the *Black Wave* as the minaret of Oron Kaa came into view. As the young man of Ro scanned the still shoreline and the globe-shaped buildings, he could imagine a hundred things, each more terrible than the last. Spectres of fear were created easily in the mind of a man afraid, and Randall was very afraid.

To his eyes, looking over the ocean, the buildings appeared to be made of coloured glass, fragmented into a hundred sparkling shades. The burning sun formed strange patterns in the glass, dancing around the globes and glinting from the minaret. It was like no city he'd ever seen – like no *place* he'd ever seen. The water barely rippled, just a gentle surge as it hit the coast, but nothing he'd call a wave or a swell. It shimmered and sent dancing lights across the blue expanse. Distant plumes spiralled upwards across the horizon, nothing more than grimy clouds at the edge of his vision, stark against the light blue sky and dark blue sea. Water spouts maybe. Or clouds of insects.

The *Black Wave*, only its topsails in use, was gliding sedately round a craggy headland. When the rocks cleared, a low harbour came into view and a bell was rung from the forecastle of the ship. The sailors were reluctant to answer the summons, but slowly emerged from below decks when Jez Ran began shouting. They moved to the rigging and the heavy wooden winches that controlled the sails. Lines of thick rope criss-crossed the ship, each with an essential purpose unknown to Randall. They were pulled and coiled, and within minutes the wind spilled from furled topsails and the *Black Wave* slowed to a crawl.

The harbour contained no ships. It had two wooden jetties, secured to a shallow sea bed by heavy pillars. There were coiled ropes and a few barrels, but no structures until the spherical buildings began, a hundred feet or so from the water. The semi-circle of jagged grey mountains isolated the settlement from the northern deserts and looked unnatural when viewed close up. It was no kind of rock he'd ever seen, looking more like tightly compact ash or charcoal.

'I can't see anyone,' he said, moving to stand by the captain.

'And you won't,' replied Vekerian. 'Not until we go ashore.'

Randall felt a tingle at the back of his neck and turned to see Ruth approach. She was again beautiful, with the stark sky framing her slender figure and the sway of her hips. For a moment, Randall forgot where he was and his head filled with lusty urges that had no place at the edge of the world.

'You have been up here for many hours,' said the Gorlan mother. 'Does Oron Kaa not disquiet you?'

'It does, but. . . it's like it flows around me. Like I have some kind of armour.'

'It is exactly like that,' she replied. 'You are armoured by me and the fragment I have left in your mind.'

'Do I need to be afraid?'

She stepped against him, the minaret appearing over her

shoulder. 'Why do you always ask that? Surely you know the answer by now.'

He gulped, realizing that he was stronger than he imagined, but still hesitant to accept it. 'I – think that I shouldn't be afraid here.'

She smiled and kissed him softly. 'You are doing wonderfully, young Randall.'

He returned her kiss as the ship bumped to a gentle stop in the harbour of Oron Kaa. They were now at the very edge of the world, kissing as if nothing really mattered.

'If Utha's here, please help me find him,' he implored.

'The shadow is here,' she replied, 'and he needs us now. Know that I watch over you and that the power of Shub-Nillurath is as much based on smoke as it is on substance.'

The majority of Vekerian's crew assembled on deck, wielding katanas and longbows. A few would remain behind to guard the *Black Wave*, but close to fifty armed Kirin would join their captain ashore. Many carried large canvas sacks, hoping that the search for Vekerian's brother would also yield some plunder. They were not pirates, but the future held little possibility for making an honest living and pillaging a corpse city at the edge of the earth was less reprehensible than attacking a merchant ship. They clustered together, looking to Ruth for some kind of guidance. When she didn't give any, they turned to their captain.

'Great mother,' said Vekerian, 'I don't know why you wanted to come here. But I thank you. We will follow you ashore.'

Ruth strode away from Randall and gathered the hem of her dress, before gracefully climbing over the railing and down the gangplank. Randall followed, stepping swiftly on to the dusty ground of Oron Kaa.

'The first building, make it ours,' commanded Vekerian, swinging his katana and puffing out his chest. 'Kill anything that isn't already dead. Now, get off this fucking ship!'

'You heard him,' offered Jez Ran. 'We're here for the captain's brother, but they won't miss a few coins. Chins out, lads.'

Whether through fear of their captain and first mate or confidence in the Gorlan mother, the fifty Kirin sailors grunted and disembarked behind Vekerian.

Randall didn't draw the sword of Great Claw, taking his cue from Ruth's slow, considered demeanour. He didn't feel vulnerable or afraid and his hands didn't shake. He thought of Utha and the pride he'd feel in his young squire. And he thought of Ruth, and the strength she'd given him.

'Your thoughts show a new steel, young Randall. Is it possible you are beginning to trust yourself?'

He didn't answer. He felt it would be rude and unnecessary to do so. She knew what he'd say and a smile appeared as she plucked the answer from his mind.

Behind, Vekerian led a wedge of sailors in Ruth's wake, each man eyeing up the closest building. No-one had emerged to challenge them and Oron Kaa remained silent and still. Further inland the buildings were larger and sat, high in the air, on narrow pillars of the same fractured glass design. It wasn't a town and had nothing that could be a tavern or a shop. Only the central building stood out, much taller than the others and as wide as the *Black Wave*.

They reached the first building, a squat bulb of red and green with no obvious doors or windows. The sailors remained quiet and spread out to encircle the building, looking for an entrance. When none was found, Vekerian ordered them to break through the shimmering surface, sending small fragments of glass on to the dust. Tunnels connected the building to all the others, but they were too small for humans to use, and Randall could only guess at their function. Now he was closer, he couldn't see a single door or window in any of the buildings. Not that this deterred the Kirin. They smashed at the glass until a slender frame of metal was visible within. They found their voices, shouting and jeering at each other to make a useable hole in the building. One of the men poked his head and torso into the hole and shouted, indicating that there were people within. He pulled back and they continued to break the glass until a whole section had been destroyed.

'Get 'em out,' ordered Vekerian, spying two robed figures within the globe. His eyes were narrow and his face was pinched.

Two Karesian men with blank stares were pulled from the building. They didn't resist and their limbs appeared floppy and inert, as if they were half-asleep, though their eyes were wide and bloodshot. They were insulted as weak-willed whores and kicked bloody by the sailors, while Vekerian demanded to know where he could find his son. They wore only thin robes and made no sound as they were beaten up.

Randall narrowed his eyes, realizing that the Kirin were not acting normally. They had not appeared violent or aggressive up to this point. He'd seen them fight before, but only to defend against a Hound warship. This was different, as if some kind of fever had taken them.

'Remain calm,' said Ruth. 'Oron Kaa begins to weave its magic upon them. A crawling buzz will begin to infest their minds.'

'And us?'

She stroked her hand down his face and curled her lips into the thinnest of smiles. 'You and I are stronger than them. In time, perhaps they will look to *you* for protection. If I am successful here, Raz Mon Vekerian and his crew will remain free longer than many other mortals.'

The two blank-faced Karesians had been beaten nearly to death and the sailors now ransacked the first building, pulling out furniture and fittings, all made of the same fractured glass. None of it looked valuable and the Kirin smashed their way through the remainder, searching for anything to plunder. Vekerian stood back with Jez Ran, both looking towards the central minaret with watchful eyes. They fumbled at their ears and winced every few seconds, as if they could hear a distant buzzing.

'Finish up,' said Vekerian. 'We're moving on to the next building.'

The Kirin showed obvious distress, grumbling, presumably at the same sound heard by their captain. Randall could hear nothing but the sound of breaking glass and complaining sailors.

'Let us join them,' said Ruth. 'Stay close to me and do not draw your sword.'

The Kirin stayed at walking pace, though they were now drenched in sweat and gritting their teeth. They reached the next building, languishing in the shadow of the minaret. It was one of several in an outer ring round the central ground, which, when viewed from close by, could almost be called a town square. The other buildings, squat and spherical, were densely packed with claustrophobic streets too narrow for men to walk comfortably. From the complaints of the Kirin, it appeared the buzzing noise was growing worse the closer they got to the minaret. They now swore almost constantly, loudly doubting their captain's wisdom in searching for his son.

Before Vekerian or Jez Ran could exert their dominance, figures appeared from between the nearby buildings. They wore the same black robes and showed the same blank expressions. Men and women, mostly Karesian, but a fair smattering of Kirin, loped into view from every side of the bizarre town. Further inland, past the minaret, more figures appeared. Randall could see dozens and knew that dozens more were approaching. The settlement had appeared abandoned, but now it burst into at least a semblance of life. The frenzied movement of the sailors contrasted sharply with the solemn procession of men and women, each one more impassive than the last. Utha and Voon were nowhere to be seen and Randall stayed where he was, never more than a few feet from Ruth.

Fuelled by the growing pain in their heads, the Kirin sailors attacked, hacking the mindless figures to the stone floor. Vekerian was at the front, whirling his katana with controlled skill. Randall could see blood beginning to pool in the captain's ears as the buzzing made him scream. It was unnerving to see men cowed by a sound he couldn't hear and the young squire began to worry for the Kirin sailors.

'You need to trust me,' said Ruth. 'These men *will* survive if I am successful.'

The Kirin cut down any inert figure that stood before them, but they began to wail in ear-splitting pain as they did so. The buzzing was taking its toll and even Vekerian now struggled to continue.

'Desist!' intoned a cracked female voice. It came from the centre of the town and carried far in the still air. 'Do not let the mother manipulate you. Leave now and I will not eat your hearts.'

The Kirin barely heard the warning. They were now committed to killing the endless procession of robed figures. Twenty or thirty were dead and the sailors twitched, as if their fever had reached its peak. They scratched at their ears, many dropping their blades and flailing on the floor. Only the strongest remained standing, but they were enough to kill blank-faced people who weren't fighting back.

The distant voice began to laugh, the sound a whip-crack of pleasure and pain. The Kirin faltered against the weight of more and more blank-faced inhabitants. Then openings and doorways began to appear in the mottled glass of several of the buildings. Some were big enough for men, though others were small; these appeared well above head height. The sailors who could still move stepped back, pulling their mates away from the dead and dying bodies lying in undignified piles between buildings.

'Hold here,' said Vekerian, his eyes darting between the closest openings.

His men fought the urge to run and those who had been felled by the buzzing sounds were pulled to their feet. Eyes and ears were bleeding and many Kirin were wailing in rising panic.

Suddenly everyone turned from the openings to look at the dead bodies. The robed figures lying in their own blood began to judder and contort. Each body flipped over until they all stared blankly to the sky. The Kirin took another step backwards. Many were held upright only by the assistance of their fellows.

'What's happening?' whispered Randall.

Ruth stepped in front of him protectively and he saw fine, black hairs appear on the back of her neck. 'They were once called the Shan,' she replied. 'They are the Builders of Oron Kaa. The first and last slaves of Shub-Nillurath. I will free them this day.'

Each dead body – many with missing limbs and grisly wounds – shook violently, splaying itself as wide as it would go. Each head went back, each throat swelled and split, and each mouth opened.

The old woman's voice sounded again. 'You have killed much flesh. Luckily, you will be adequate replacements.'

From each dead body a creature emerged, scratching its way out of their mouths. They broke through teeth and distended jaws until three sets of thin, membranous wings emerged. They looked like long wasps, mottled in sickly shades of red and green, with large segmented bodies and clawed feelers sticking out from circular, sucking mouths.

The buzzing must now have been deafening; Randall could see the Kirin screaming in agony. Even Vekerian was on his knees, struggling to crawl backwards.

Ruth marched forward, through clusters of crying Kirin. Her skin was now flowing and twisting into a new form, her body elongating and each limb splitting into two smaller legs. The new appendages were long and narrow at first, but slowly thickened as they lifted her body off the ground.

'I have not seen you for many ages, great mother,' said the old woman, appearing from an opening high up in the central minaret. She looked as she sounded, hateful and wrinkled. Her pinched eyes were black, and widened as she saw the Gorlan mother transforming amidst buzzing insects and screaming Kirin. 'You are too late to change anything, old woman. Your power is not wanted here.'

Now fully transformed into a huge spider, Ruth swatted away the insects with her front legs, pushing forward with enough power to topple the smaller buildings. The buzzing creatures avoided her, focusing on the Kirin. Vekerian's men were now helpless as the insects latched on to their faces and clawed at their throats.

'Run!' screamed the captain, pulling himself backwards across the dusty ground. He appeared to have suddenly remembered something.

Within a second a dozen Kirin had their mouths ripped open by insects burrowing deeply into their throats. The men flailed and shook, but were helpless to resist the grotesque Builders of Oron Kaa. Some were stronger and had managed to crawl away, keeping hold of their katanas, but they mounted no defence and were merely trying to escape.

An insect fluttered towards Randall and he jumped backwards. The creature was fuzzy and emitted a foul stench that made the air distort. It reached for him but then pulled back at the last moment, hissing loudly. It seemed to have sensed something that scared it. More insects, on getting close to him, also hesitated and found themselves skewered by hairs from Ruth's colourful abdomen, a thick mist of them. The blade-like hairs surrounded him, keeping him isolated from the carnage. How she managed to control them and keep him from being impaled was a mystery, but a mystery he was happy to accept.

Randall felt like a passenger, viewing the madness of Oron Kaa from a place of safety beyond where the buzzing and the insanity could penetrate. He stared up at the old woman and gasped, realizing that Utha and Voon were standing either side of her. He didn't understand what he was looking at. They both wore black robes and were clearly not prisoners.

'Utha!' shouted Randall. 'What are you doing?'

The albino held two Karesian scimitars and Voon's ever-present spear was across his back. His master sneered at him from above and whispered something to the old woman. She began to laugh again, the same sharp sound, conveying no humour but rather depthless hate. She stopped laughing when Ruth reared up and hissed at her. The immense Gorlan was smashing her way through buildings and crushing faceless people beneath her eight heavy legs. She was past the Kirin, many of whom were now staring upwards as the Builders took control of their bodies.

The insects, the buzzing, the laughter – none of it affected Ruth *or* Randall. He stood, still protected by a mist of Gorlan hairs, starting to realize how powerful his companion truly was. Perhaps the most powerful creature in the lands of men. But more than that, he realized how much she knew and how much she'd given him. But still he looked at Utha and felt lost.

'Great mother!' screamed Vekerian, slicing an insect in two and retreating.

Ruth made no move to help the Kirin, but continued crawling over and through the buildings, crushing glass and hissing up at the old woman. The spectre of a dead son had brought the captain here and Randall hoped Ruth knew what she was doing. The alternative was that she'd simply used these sailors to get her to Oron Kaa.

'Master!' shouted Randall, his throat turning hoarse from the effort.

'He is no longer the weak flesh of Utha the Ghost,' said the woman. 'He is now mine, for this moment and forever.'

'Shut up,' he replied. 'I wasn't talking to you.'

The old woman balked at his manner, unable to understand how he was proving immune to the madness of her settlement. He was reminded of Saara the Mistress of Pain and how angry she had been when Ruth overpowered her. Time and again, the might of the Dead God and his enchantresses had been swamped by the ancient power of the Gorlan mother.

The opening on the high minaret began to close, gradually obscuring Utha, Voon and the old woman. Her servants and her insects had been unable to stop Ruth and the huge creature was now crawling up the central building, leaving a thick layer of silk attached to the adjacent structures.

Randall began to move after her, stepping over gyrating Kirin bodies and round buzzing insects. The mist of hairs followed him like a floating suit of armour, allowing him to enter the central square unmolested. He suddenly felt angry. He'd seen Utha and he'd seen that his master was in trouble. Though his journey had changed him, he was still here to rescue the caustic Black cleric.

He sped up and ran to reach the base of the minaret. He could still hear Vekerian, but forced himself not to turn back. The central square was made of dusty flagstones, octagonal and fitted together at strange angles that didn't appear to make sense. He reached the mottled glass pillar that supported the minaret and skipped left and right, looking for an entrance. He saw two round the base, rectangular openings with no door or doorframe, from which blank-eyed people were emerging. The fine mist of Gorlan hair dissipated, but the Builders still hung back, too afraid to attack him.

'Just so you're aware, I'm drawing my sword now,' he shouted up at Ruth. He could just see one of her back legs, disappearing across an adjacent building. Her silk ran in glistening lines up and down the minaret, catching insects in its sticky mass.

The sword of Great Claw had rarely met so little opposition when it struck flesh. No parry, no armour, not even a vague attempt to dodge it – the expressionless people just died, slumping downwards with barely a whimper.

'How dare you interfere!' screeched the old woman. He heard it echo around the clashing glass colours of the interior. He imagined she was talking to Ruth, but the sentiment was probably meant for him too.

Three more robed figures loped towards him from a spiral staircase and were cut down with two thrusts and a backhand. He didn't like killing these men, but diplomacy was impossible. When they were dead, he looked around for the first time. The interior was made of the same small glass blocks of clashing and sickly colours. Daylight cast a glow through the openings but was repelled within a few feet. Unnatural illumination came from somewhere but there were no lanterns or fires, just irregular rooms and bizarre refractions of light, ringing an ornate column that contained the staircase.

'Be gone!' screamed the woman, her voice cracking at the edges.

It was still hateful, but now it was full of fear as well. 'You have lost, Ryuthula.'

The building shook and he heard the smashing of glass from above. Then running and shouting. All at once, footsteps echoed down the stairs. Not the clump of boots, but the soft patter of bare feet. Three or four, or maybe five. He held his sword high and ready, taking a wide stance.

Young girls, not one older than eighteen, all wearing bloodied rags, ran down the spiral staircase. There were ten of them. They held each other protectively and froze in place when they saw him. Their faces were dirty and drawn, with bags under their wild, violet eyes. They appeared malnourished and tortured, barely filling the patchwork trousers and tunics they wore. And they all looked the same – they all looked like the Seven Sisters.

'Ruth!' he shouted, having no earthly clue how he should react.

She didn't respond and he slowly lowered his sword. 'It's okay,' he said, consciously softening his expression. 'I won't hurt you.'

The girls' faces were wild and unfocused, as if they couldn't hear the words. Then, with a high-pitched shriek in unison, they ran at him. Randall had killed men, he had fought, been wounded, and even gained a modicum of skill with his longsword, but he panicked as the young enchantresses assaulted him. They were just young girls, not like anyone he'd had to kill before, and his sword arm simply wouldn't move.

They scratched and kicked him, forcing him to use his free arm to cover his face. One of them dug her teeth into his hand and made him drop the blade. Then he fell and they were all over him, biting, kicking, scratching and slapping. One girl, one of the eldest, he thought, stood next to him and kicked her bony feet into his head. A tinge of embarrassment must have crossed his face as Randall was beaten unconscious by six young girls.

* * *

His body was unconscious, but his mind remained active. It was a strange experience, as if his physical form had not yet caught up with the new power Ruth had given him. He experienced the pain, but as a distant echo, like a past version of himself, squealing for aid. He saw the girls and the Kirin through closed eyes as faded ghosts, shimmering across a black canvas. Then three more figures plunged into view. A bent old woman and two men.

He was lying on the floor and would have felt exposed if his thoughts were not so clear. Utha and Voon were guarding the old woman and that made him angry. He began to focus and the figures came into view, though he could see more than flesh and bone. Within both of the men was a squirming insect, though Utha's appeared to have melted into the albino's flesh. Voon's had consumed his mind and was now in control of the empty shell previously occupied by the exemplar of Jaa. But the old woman was the most confusing. There was no insect in her, but she wasn't human and her power was barely contained within the shrivelled body she wore.

Suddenly a deathly scream made the ground shake and the glass windows shatter. From the sky, Randall felt a new presence, one not of form or substance but of divinity and rage. It strode downward, through glass and metal, as if descending imaginary steps, and came into view clearer and more solid than anyone else in his field of vision. The figure looked at him, sensing that, unlike the matron mother and her guards, the unconscious young man could see him. It was Dalian Thief Taker, a wind claw Randall had met in the Fell. And he was far angrier than the young squire.

Dalian, visible only in Randall's mind, approached the figure of Voon and stared at him. The exemplar of Jaa looked straight through the wind claw, awaiting instructions from the old woman. He gathered the young girls together, before a downward staircase that led away from the minaret. They were preparing to flee from Ruth, with Utha standing guard over the matron mother. Randall wanted to call out, but knew his body wouldn't respond if he tried. He wondered what would happen if he were to die. Would his newly awakened mind drift around Oron Kaa like Dalian, searching for a new body to inhabit? Or would he slowly drift away, following his mortal form into oblivion?

He felt his body twitch as he began to regain consciousness, but not before he saw Dalian Thief Taker ball his divine energy in a small globe within his fists and lunge at Voon. He emitted a powerful roar that made the earth shake again, causing all those who couldn't see him to reach for the stability of the outer wall, confused by what was causing the sound. Dalian struck Voon with a thunderous clash, causing the Builder within to hiss and writhe in pain. The creature died almost instantly, smashed to pulpy pieces by the divine might of Jaa and beginning to ooze out of Voon's mouth.

Utha, the old woman and the clustered girls backed away, confused by what they were seeing. Voon doubled over on the floor, coughing out pieces of the insect on to the mottled glass, as Dalian took control of the body.

As he felt his eyelids flicker open, Randall heard a violent roar. He couldn't be sure whether the sound had reached his mind or if he'd regained his hearing just in time, such was the power of the voice.

'I am Dalian Thief Taker. . . and I am the exemplar of Jaa.'

* * *

Randall awoke with his face pressed against a sharp, glass floor. Splodges of pain hit him in the arms, hands, legs, chest and face. He'd been bitten, kicked and scratched, but it was the sound of steel on steel that had shaken him awake.

He groggily turned over and tried to cry out to his master, but his voice was lost somewhere in a badly bruised chest. Utha was squaring off against Voon, wielding two scimitars against the Karesian's spear.

'Don't fight,' he croaked. 'Fight her.' He pointed to the old woman, fleeing with the young girls down the passageway.

If they heard him, they didn't show it. Voon's eyes were clearer now and a strange glow shone from his extremities, as if Dalian was infusing every inch of his new body. Utha looked no different, except for the hateful sneer on his bone-white face.

'Ruth!' he shouted again. 'Utha and Voon are fighting.'

They clashed in front of him, a blur of steel and arms as the scimitars searched for a way past the spear. Utha was as ferocious as ever, eschewing defence for frenzied attack, forcing his opponent on to the back foot. But Dalian didn't back away. Randall had seen Voon fight before, in Claryon Soong's mansion, but now. . . everything was different. He hardly moved his feet as he twirled Zarzenfang in tight circles with a serenity of motion that was barely human. A fire burned in his eyes as he met each of Utha's attacks with parries of dizzying speed.

'I do not wish to kill you,' said Dalian, through Voon's mouth.

'Jaa owns these lands no longer. You will bow to Shub-Nillurath,' spat Utha, confirming Randall's worst fears.

'You are the last Old Blood!' shouted Dalian, true anger sounding in every syllable. 'How *dare* you stand against me!'

'Utha, please!' said Randall, making them notice him for the first time.

His master still sneered, ignoring pleas for him to stand down, and attacked again. Dalian effortlessly blocked the scimitars, appearing to flicker from point to point with a tiny flash of fire announcing each movement. Utha's face was a twisted contortion of devotional mania, wide-eyed and drooling. Whatever had happened to him was beyond Randall's power to reverse.

'Fuck you!' shouted the young squire. 'Fuck you and fuck Shub-Nillurath! You drag me to the edge of the world and fall to a fucking insect.' He began to cry. 'You're Utha the Ghost. You're the strongest man I've ever known. . . you're stronger than Torian, stronger than Vekerian, stronger than Rham Jas, stronger than Ruth even – please!'

Dalian kicked one of the scimitars from Utha's hand, sending it to clatter against the glass wall, near where the old woman had disappeared. He then smashed the albino in the face with the haft of Zarzenfang, making him crumble downwards. For an instant Randall hoped that Utha would stay down, but he surged upwards with insane eyes fixed on the Karesian, swinging his remaining blade.

'So be it,' said Dalian with resignation. 'Your Shadow Giant will finally get to die – but *I* serve only Jaa, and his land doesn't need you any more. Not now I am here.' He twirled the spear under his arm and levelled the serrated steel point at Utha.

'Don't kill him,' pleaded Randall. 'This can't be the end.'

'He's gone,' was all Dalian said, before lunging forward and impaling Utha on Zarzenfang. Blood erupted from the albino's mouth as the spear emerged from his back. Before his eyes closed, he screamed insanely – he screamed with pain and he screamed with pleasure.

Randall just stared at his dying master, unable to think or cry out. The strongest man he'd ever known stretched his arms wide, craning his head backwards, then fell like a rag-doll to the floor as Dalian removed the spear from his chest. Utha was dead.

'Boy, look at me,' said the Karesian. 'You know who I am. I know you grieve, but answer me this – is the Gorlan friend or foe? Do I need to deal with it?'

The remaining glass at the base of the minaret suddenly blew outwards, exposing a thin steel frame, skeletal and rusted. Shards of coloured glass showered the interior, forcing Randall to curl up and protect his head. Dalian winced as needles of glass struck him, but he didn't cower or take cover. With the outside now visible, Randall saw web and destruction. Buildings were crushed, hundreds of insects were dead, dozens of Kirin were lying motionless, and an eerie calm had descended on Oron Kaa. From the devastation, walking on two human legs as if everything were normal, came Ruth, entering the minaret and walking directly at Dalian.

'Where is the Queen in Red?' she demanded.

Randall wiped tears, blood and glass from his face. 'Utha's dead!' he wailed.

The Gorlan mother glanced at the motionless albino, then at Randall. Her face softened as she locked eyes with the young squire, but re-hardened as she turned back to the spear-wielding Karesian.

'Don't test me, great mother,' said Dalian.

'Test you?' responded Ruth. 'You have killed the last Old Blood.'

She flickered forward and grabbed Dalian round the throat, lifting him like a small child and forcing him to drop his spear.

'Test you?' she screamed, tightening her grip and turning the Karesian's face a bright red. 'I will not test you. I will merely tell you what to do. Now pick up Utha and follow me.'

Dalian was losing consciousness, but was powerful enough to send two sharp punches at Ruth's face. 'I am a servant of Jaa,' he wheezed.

'And I am a servant of Atlach-Nacha. Your Fire Giant should remember his place if he is to survive.'

She spun round and rammed Dalian into the floor, causing the ground to shake with their collective strength.

Randall tried to stand, but all his body would do was sprawl on the floor, looking at Utha's corpse. He crawled, groaning in pain, to reach his master, trying to shut out the one-sided wrestling match playing out between the two mighty creatures. Tears still ran down his cheeks and it was only the pain of movement that tempered the wellspring of loss bubbling up from his stomach.

'I will fear nothing but Jaa,' roared Dalian, somehow managing to get to his feet under Ruth's vice-like grip.

The Gorlan mother was no longer serene. She exhibited rage in a way he had not yet seen. Her eyes were black and in every movement of her slim body was revealed raw power.

Randall's hands reached Utha and he crawled up his master's body, his hands balling into fists against the thin black fabric of his robe. He felt blood and sweat, but no movement. Utha's chest was still, with a jagged line where Zarzenfang had struck.

Ruth flung Dalian through the outer frame of the minaret and strode across to Utha and Randall. The Karesian got to his feet, but didn't immediately attack. Something in his burning red eyes showed that he was reassessing the situation.

'You will do as I say or I will kill you,' said Ruth. 'I care not for your Fire Giant or his Long War – I care for this young man and his master. And I care that the Queen in Red is utterly destroyed. Now pick up the Old Blood and follow me.'

Dalian hesitated but, taking note of his numerous wounds and the mighty creature before him, he lowered Zarzenfang and approached.

'You are stronger than the exemplar,' said Dalian. 'But do not trifle with Jaa or his shade. We will do as you ask, but your insolence will be remembered.'

She smiled. 'Do not test me, Dalian Thief Taker.'

A moment of tense mutual respect passed between them, but all Randall could do was cling to Utha's body and cry. Ruth knelt down next to him, her soft hands stroking his face.

'You are good-hearted, Randall of Darkwald. Perhaps meeting you was as important as meeting the Old Blood. I find I have learned more from you than from him.'

'You didn't need us,' he replied. 'Were you just playing a game?'

She kissed him. It was slow and gentle, but strangely reassuring. She waved Dalian forwards and the glowing Karesian wrapped his muscular arms round Utha's body and hefted him upwards. Randall pulled himself into a seated position and tried to stand. Ruth stopped him from falling and allowed him to lean on her shoulder.

'Where are we going?' he muttered. 'And what's he doing with Utha's body?'

'The power that resides here is pungent, but still it ultimately flows from the divine. Utha the Shadow *is* the divine. His mortal flesh is less important than you think – if we move quickly.'

Randall glared at Dalian, fighting anger, sorrow and confusion. He wanted someone to blame, but realized that he didn't know enough to be fair. He couldn't hate the. . . thing that looked like Voon, but acted like Dalian.

'Who's the old woman?' he asked, tearing his eyes from the glowing Karesian and Utha's corpse.

'The Queen in Red,' she replied. 'Here, she is called the matron mother. When I birthed her, I named her Nephila.'

'What?' was all he could think to say. 'She's a Gorlan?'

'One of the oldest still alive,' she replied.

The implications of this were too vast for Randall to wrap his mind around, let alone come up with any particularly intelligent questions. 'What?' he repeated.

She kissed him again, smoothing back her hair. 'Answers will take too much time.'

Dalian, effortlessly carrying Utha's body, moved to the downward staircase through which the matron mother and her girls had fled. He didn't ask where he was going or what Ruth intended. He moved with purpose, keeping his eyes still, just as Randall remembered from when he had met him in the Fell.

'Wait,' snapped the squire. 'I don't care who you are, don't take his body out of my sight.'

Dalian stopped, but he didn't turn. He waited as Ruth assisted Randall in joining him at the top of the stairs, then continued down, slowing his pace so that they could keep up.

'The tear is this way,' said the Karesian. 'I can feel it.'

'The tear?' queried Randall as they moved down a narrow, rocky tunnel, plunging into the earth of Oron Kaa.

'The Footstep of the heretical Forest Giant,' clarified Dalian. 'A doorway to the beyond.'

Randall was in pain, but, with Ruth's strength and his own adrenaline, he began to walk unaided, following his master in death as he had in life.

Chapter Eighteen

Fallon the Grey on the King's Highway

H E'D FALLEN ASLEEP on a thin bedroll, among trees, but he'd woken on a dusty training ground, standing ready and holding a pristine longsword. He wore plate armour with a grey tabard displaying his future heraldry: a broken longsword on a grey field, signifying that a Knight of the Grey would sooner break his blade than use it without honour. He was clean and washed, his short black hair closely cut and his face freshly shaved. He hadn't been this clean since he left Tor Funweir.

Looking around, he saw a ring of stone buildings and a statue, dominating the training ground. He'd seen it before. It stood outside the Red cathedral in Ro Arnon and showed a Purple cleric in a warrior's handshake with a Knight of the Red. Under the figures were the words, 'Where nobility and war meet, honour must be found.' It was the original motto of the Red and would be remade as the motto of the Grey.

'You have ridden far,' said Torian's shade, appearing as a fully armoured Purple cleric at the foot of the statue.

'Not as far as you,' replied Fallon. 'I feel strong; does that mean the World Raven was true to his word?'

Torian tensed his shining steel gauntlets and unsheathed a fine longsword. 'Defend yourself, exemplar.'

The shade launched a powerful series of attacks against Fallon's head. He parried, keeping his arm close to his body but taking a defensive stance. Torian was shorter, but his shoulders were huge and his balance excellent. In life, he had been a cleric of the quest and would have been a formidable swordsman. As a shade, his movements were too fast for Fallon to predict. The Grey Knight took a wide base and retreated from the rampant Purple cleric. He felt outmatched for the first time in his life. He received a glancing thrust to his chest.

'Stand,' said Torian, giving Fallon room to compose himself. 'There is much power to be had, but you must earn it. Perhaps another opponent would be more appropriate.'

The shade took a large side-step and revealed another figure, approaching from the statue. It was a Kirin man, slender with lank black hair. He held a katana in two hands and moved like a predatory cat.

'And this is?' asked Fallon, unimpressed by the new apparition's form.

'In life, his name was Rham Jas Rami,' replied Torian. 'He killed me.'

The Kirin had no expression, as if he was a body with little or no mind, but his movements became lightning fast as he attacked. He ran directly at Fallon, their blades clashing next to the Grey Knight's head, before Rham Jas disengaged and gave ground, moving across the dusty floor.

'I've heard of this Kirin,' said Fallon. 'An assassin. I believe we have him to thank for killing his share of enchantresses.'

The Kirin attacked again, another single attack, launched with speed and finished with a darting run, back out of range. Fallon only just managed to parry, avoiding a heavy blow to the chest. Rham Jas used disorienting tactics and didn't get involved in duelling. He was quick and strong, but his true strength lay in his reactions. Fallon could see his eyes assessing every inch of his opponent before he attacked, finding weaknesses while concealing his own.

'Am I supposed to kill him?' asked Fallon.

'If you can,' replied Torian. 'He is a fearsome opponent, even for you.'

The Grey Knight loosened his stance, letting the longsword hang loosely at his side. The Kirin took note and stepped closer, concerned that he might be drawn into a feint. He circled Fallon, staying on the balls of his feet, his katana held close. Then he attacked again. He didn't run, but took a wide stance and covered the ground in two steps, swinging for Fallon's head. As he approached, the Grey Knight moved to meet him and punched him in the face before his blade could strike. Rham Jas was stunned for an instant and lowered his sword. Fallon punched him again and kicked the katana to the ground. Two more punches and the Kirin dropped. He was dazed, but alive.

'Am I supposed to kill him?' repeated Fallon.

Torian smiled. 'Perhaps not.'

Rham Jas vanished from the dusty training ground and the Purple cleric faced him once again. 'We have limited power to give,' said Torian. 'We have chosen you over a hundred Purple clerics and ten thousand Red Knights. We need to know that you deserve Brytag's gift. We have seen your heart and know that your honour is unquestionable, but we need to see your sword arm, for that is where we will strengthen you.'

Fallon chuckled. 'My sword arm? The one thing I'm confident in?'

Torian attacked, hacking at his head with controlled strength. He retreated from the blows, deflecting most but feeling a sharp dislocation as he was struck on the left temple. Fallon dropped his sword and gasped for air that would not come.

'If you had been awake, you would be dead,' stated Torian, as the Grey Knight clutched the side of his head. 'It is not enough to be a good swordsman, even a great swordsman. We need your sword arm to change the world. Now, stand, and defend yourself.'

Fallon had been struck before, but never so badly. The pain surged through his body, making everything fluid, but the sensation quickly passed and his hand came away from his head with no blood. 'Please don't do that again. Real or not, getting a blade in the head is not pleasant.'

'You are the last of the old!' roared Torian, attacking again. Fallon side-stepped and avoided being struck, retrieving his longsword to guard the air between them. 'You are the first of the new!' Another attack, this time a lunge, avoided with a strong parry. 'We don't want a Knight of the Red!' Their blades clashed with dizzying speed. 'We don't want a Purple cleric!' Fallon kept his blade close and his stance defensive. 'We want a Knight of the Grey!'

Suddenly he felt everything slow down. The dusty training ground fell into the distance and Torian's shade became a flickering apparition. Fallon's body relaxed and he felt the duel happening at the corners of his perception. The clash of their swords made no sound and his muscles didn't tense as he fought.

'I've known nothing but combat,' said Fallon, parrying with speed he didn't know he possessed. 'I was a knight before I was a man. I'd killed before my sixteenth year. I tested my skill at every turn and I never found my match. If I'm to test myself against the One God, I fear for his survival.'

Torian did not slow, his sword now moving as a blur of steel, but Fallon met every attack with an effortless parry. As the duel continued, he realized where he had found the new power. Each time their blades clashed he took a little more from the shade, weakening Torian and strengthening himself. He found new moves, new ways to block and attack. Old weaknesses disappeared, like repairing holes on a well-used road.

As the shade's movements became clumsy and uncoordinated, Fallon launched a ferocious attack and drove Torian to his knees. The Purple cleric defended his head with a horizontal blade, but the Grey Knight effortlessly broke through the defence and split him down the middle, from head to chest. The body broke apart, revealing a bright light, and Torian again became a ghostly apparition, floating above his own dead body. His face was serene, but fading from view, as the last of the One God's power was passed to his exemplar and the Knights of the Grey.

'Lead them into battle, exemplar,' said Torian. 'Lead them and gift them with your strength. As the Grey Knights act as one, each of your sword arms can change the world.'

'Will I see you again?' he asked.

'No, but we will be watching as you form the new order. Always remember, Fallon, honour must stand at the fore. Do with those of the Red and the Purple as you see fit, but make them understand. Make everyone understand. As you endure, the One God will regain his strength. But you *must* endure and you must protect as much of Tor Funweir as you can.'

* * *

North of Cozz was a line of destruction. The enclave itself was a smouldering mess, and hundreds of wrecked and abandoned carts framed the highway. It didn't look like Tor Funweir – it didn't look like any place.

Two hundred Knights of the Grey camped round a small fire, to the west of the King's Highway, in a copse of trees. They'd changed mounts in Tiris, and again in Voy, maintaining their speed. They stopped for an hour to eat, then two to sleep. They'd seen no Hounds to fight, and few Ro to help, but the wilds of Tor Funweir were ravaged, with abandoned farms, homesteads and whole villages. It made Fallon sad to see what had happened in their absence. This was no joyful homecoming and each of his knights kept their own counsel during the journey. Even Verellian had been quiet, though Fallon could feel echoes of his new power passing to each of them. As he woke on the tenth day, he knew that there was no power left for the Red, the Purple or the Gold. Everything was within the two hundred men of the Grey. They were trained warriors and some of the most dangerous men in Tor Funweir, but now they stood, walked and rode with straight backs and strengthened muscles. Each one was now more dangerous than Fallon had been when he defeated Torian.

'Six days to Weir,' said Verellian. 'At good pace. I'd say the king is too far for us to reach him before he gets there.'

'I'd say you're right,' he replied. 'We'll have to pledge to him as he besieges the city – or retreats.'

'Alexander Tiris is not known for his piety,' grunted Sergeant Ohms.

'But he *is* known for his honour,' said Fallon. 'I think he's the right man.'

'Agreed,' said Verellian. 'One thing that binds the two hundred men here is that we were none of us the most pious of men before we took the Grey. The One God doesn't want piety.'

'Agreed,' said Ohms.

A whistle sounded from the flats, beyond their camp, where Lucius of the Falls was on watch.

'Check on it,' he said to Ohms.

The sergeant nodded and rose from the fire. The others held their sheathed longswords in a cautious display of readiness, but none were raw recruits and they all kept calm. Below, within sight of Fallon, the rest of his men all looked up the ridge and slowly stood. Each man wore a chain shirt, having discarded their heavy plate for the sake of speed.

'Slowly,' said Verellian. 'Nice and slowly. We're the hunters, not the hunted.'

'Aye,' said Fallon, who had been the first to stand. 'Remember, this is Tor Funweir. Anyone who says different is our enemy.'

They moved slowly away from their fires, past their picketed horses and over a small, craggy slope, to the flatlands surrounding Cozz. No features but distant trees, abandoned carts and the ruined enclave itself.

Ohms appeared from the south, with Lucius behind. 'Men approach,' said the gruff knight.

'About a thousand,' supplied Lucius. 'Black armour. . . look like chess pieces.'

Fallon considered it. A thousand men would likely be a straggling pack or some outlying patrol. But they'd know more than him about the situation in the south. 'Let's have a look,' he said, striding to the front of the men.

They fanned out across the grass, moving south between ruined carts and grazing horses, free of their restraints. The dust rolled gently from the King's Highway, signifying a small group moving towards the enclave.

'A thousand men is a lot,' said Verellian, falling in behind Fallon as they strode towards the dust.

'A thousand doesn't mean a thousand,' replied Fallon. 'A thousand means a hundred that can fight, a couple hundred more who will fight if they think they can win, and the rest barely know where they are. This is not a sophisticated enemy.'

He had no fear of Hounds. It could have been five thousand and he wouldn't have paused. He knew each Grey Knight felt the same. The One God would tell them when to be afraid. They formed up in a column, concealed behind the remnants of carts, displayed in chaotic piles of wood across the featureless plain. The Hounds appeared slowly, sauntering north in a loose mob. They all looked the same, encased in thin steel armour from head to toe.

The debris parted, allowing the two forces to see each other. The Karesians stopped marching. They pointed and showed alarm, clustering into a steel mass on the King's Highway. Their alarm turned quickly to confidence when they registered the two hundred men arrayed against them. It was as if they expected more to appear, perhaps a rearguard of Alexander Tiris's army or some kind of ambush.

'Hounds!' shouted Fallon, still moving towards the Karesians. 'We are the Grey Knights of the One God.' He gave them a moment to process this, a moment they spent swinging their scimitars suggestively and joking to each other. 'You will tell me your deployment to the south, and you may live.'

They laughed. The sound was strange coming from a thousand blank steel faces.

'Do you think I'm fucking joking?' boomed Fallon, drawing his sword.

The others formed a line either side of him, Verellian and

Ohms standing closest. All two hundred held longswords, though William's was held in two hands.

'You don't need to die,' shouted Ohms, spitting noisily on to the grass.

'But you're going to,' muttered Lucius.

'Easy,' offered Verellian, 'remember, nice and slowly. We're still the hunters, let's not spook the prey.'

'They don't look like pheasant,' whispered Ohms, 'and we ain't got no crossbows.'

Fallon strode forward, keeping his blade low, and crossed the grass quickly. The others muttered prayers or coarse words of encouragement, but all followed. All they saw were enemies of the One God and invaders of Tor Funweir. Their blades and armour meant nothing. Their orders and their commanders meant even less.

'You are foolish men of Ro,' replied a faceless Hound, standing in the centre of their lines. His accent was thick and an edge of humour cut through his words, as if he imagined he was in control.

The two forces were now close. The Hounds had no detailing on their armour or weapons. The only differences were in height and weight.

Fallon smiled at the Karesian who had spoken. 'You're a long way from home. It's a terrible thing to die on foreign soil.'

'And who will be killing us?' replied the Hound. 'Not you and your band of. . . thugs.'

'Thugs? Fuck off,' growled Ohms, standing behind Fallon's right shoulder.

Verellian laughed, though his eyes betrayed exasperation.

'Keep talking,' said Fallon. 'You'll just anger men who are already angry. Answer my questions and live – simple.'

They hesitated. The lead Hound turned his head left and right, confirming to himself that he commanded the larger force, but he appeared to have no idea what to do. Most of his soldiers held scimitars, but they didn't line up in any kind of formation. In fact, most were trying to skulk as best they could behind their fellows. Though their faces were concealed, their heads were uniformly pointed downwards. Fallon imagined that they were just as blank-faced under their helmets.

'I think we shall. . . kill you,' said the Hound, with no certainty or confidence in his words.

'Finally,' said Lucius of the Falls, taking two large strides and swinging his longsword into the neck of the leader. The blade cut between thin, black steel plates and, as the knight kicked his opponent to the grass, blood sprayed upwards.

'Kill them!' roared another Hound, his voice tinged with fear.

There were a thousand Karesians, but all of them were on the back foot, hoping that their mates would do the killing and they could survive another day. When faced with a solid line of longswords and men who knew how to swing them, the Hounds were just armoured bales of hay.

'In a line, boys,' commanded Verellian. 'Hold, defend, strike, advance as one.'

Each man knew his role. With shields held close and controlled swings, they cut down the first rank of Hounds and advanced over the bloodied grass, pushing the Karesians back. The scimitars that weren't being held defensively bounced off shields with hardly a cut or blemish. Fallon barely exerted himself as part of their line. He killed one, then another, each strike finding a gap in their armour or delivered with strength enough to sheer steel.

'Watch the flanks,' shouted Ohms, as a group of less-useless Karesians realized they could outflank the knights. 'Thin the lines.'

Men repositioned to cut off the manoeuvre, leaving those in the centre to defend against two or three Hounds each. Verellian favoured his shield, Ohms used brute strength, Lucius used superior skill. When their lines wavered under sheer pressure of numbers, Fallon broke ranks and strode forward. A glow of golden light enveloped him, flashing from every movement and arcing from the point of his sword.

The first man died easily. The second fell like dust. Before he knew it, he was hacking into steel armour and cleaving flesh.

He felt barely present, as if his glowing sword arm acted on its own, swinging the blade left and right as was needed. Parrying effortlessly, severing arms, legs and necks. He wasn't touched by their clumsy attacks. Wasn't cut, overbalanced, pushed back or surrounded. He stood tall, using strength and speed to cut down dozens of men. He could hear shouting and sounds of dying, but he didn't stop, using the energy flowing through his body to overwhelm these lesser men.

Then they began to run. Fallon's advance had cut a hole through the pack, stopping any chance of his men being outflanked. The Hounds withered before him, like grass in fire. He felt taller, looking upon his foes from a height as they died from grisly sword wounds. He bashed one man in the face with his shield and the man flew back, barrelling another three to the ground. He kicked a man in the chest and felt his ribs break beneath his breastplate. Ten men tried to surround him, but he killed them all with no effort. He severed a neck, impaled a Hound on another's scimitar. Two had their heads cleaved in with successive swings of his sword.

Running men now filled his field of vision. The Hounds were being routed. They ran from the exemplar to be cut down by the Knights of the Grey. Then, with a resounding snap, his sword broke against a steel breastplate. He frowned with annoyance and smashed the hilt into a man's face, then used his shield to throw Hounds out of his way. Their bodies broke against the hardened wood and steel, until the shield snapped across a man's head.

Then there was no-one left to kill. Around him lay dead and dying bodies. Along the horizon, glinting steel figures sprinted south. He was covered in blood and he panted heavily. His hands were scarred and felt sticky from sweat and blood.

'Hold,' shouted Verellian. 'Do not pursue them. Let the bastards run.'

Fallon turned his back on the retreating Hounds and faced his men. They were bloodied and their chests rose and fell with exhaustion, though each face wore an expression of joy, of victory

– perhaps even of redemption. And they looked at Fallon, showing awe and gratitude. Perhaps for the first time, they truly felt like Knights of the Grey.

Verellian approached him, cleaning his blade. 'You were always good,' he said with an ironic smile. 'Now you're a fucking nightmare. I feel sorry for the Hounds.'

'For Tor Funweir!' proclaimed Lucius of the Falls, raising his longsword to the sky and banging it on his shield. 'And for the Grey.'

None had died. All two hundred warriors of Ro were intact, with barely a handful of cuts to show for their victory. In that moment, their victory meant everything. They weren't cutting down Ranen axe-men whose only crime had been to desire freedom. They weren't besieging a city of women and children. They were fighting for Tor Funweir, protecting the lands of the One God.

'Wounded men need killing,' announced Verellian. 'A couple of hundred Karesians are breathing their last while we congratulate ourselves.'

Ohms sheathed his sword and ran a calloused hand down his bloodied face. When he had composed himself, he started shouting orders. 'Right, you lot, put these bastards out of their misery. Clean kills, let's not get creative.'

'Keep some alive,' ordered Fallon. 'The least wounded.'

* * *

No-one asked him to help, not even Verellian. Hundreds of bodies needed assembling into pyres, swords needed sharpening and armour needed bashing back into shape, but none of it was done with Fallon's help. He stood on an upturned cart, looking south, watchful for any pack sent looking for their lost Hounds. Enough had got away that a response party was not out of the question. But the fear he'd seen in their eyes made it unlikely. Maybe they'd just keep running until they saw the gates of Weir.

Behind him, Ohms had managed to marshal the ruined carts into some kind of defensive bulwark. It was the way of knights to want a wooden wall whenever they stopped for any amount of time. It was rough, but provided a line to patrol and a raised position from which to view the southern fields. They were exposed, but buoyed by their victory and showing no fear of additional Hounds.

'Fallon, we have survivors,' said Verellian, flexing his maimed hand.

'You sore?' asked the Grey Knight.

'Still getting used to the new strength. Happily, the Hounds are terrible swordsmen, but wonderful practice.'

Fallon hopped off the cart and faced his old friend. 'You're being more respectful than I'm used to. You've not called me a pig-fucker for days.'

Verellian screwed up his face. 'What do you want me to say? That you're exemplar and I don't feel right insulting you?'

'You don't feel like that,' he replied.

'No, I don't, but a lot of these men do. If they heard me treating you like the low-rent turncoat you are, it might affect your image.'

Fallon laughed, glad of the insult. 'Well, let's keep pretending,' he replied.

They returned behind the wooden bulwark, to where Lucius had restrained a dozen survivors. Ohms had the rest of the men at ease, resting as best they could with minimal rations and small fires. As soon as Fallon returned from the upturned cart, Ohms ordered two men to replace him on watch, making sure the southern plains were guarded.

'They all had pouches of some drug shit,' said Lucius. 'Black, squishy stuff.'

'It's what keeps them compliant,' said Verellian. 'You'd need drugs to make you fight if you were that shit at fighting.'

'What do they do with it?' asked Lucius.

'Smoke it, I imagine,' replied Fallon. 'Just get rid of it.'

'Aye, my lord.'

The prisoners were lying face down on the grass, stripped of their armour, with their arms restrained. Their wounds were minor – a cut here, a shallow stab there – and none were in danger of imminent death.

'How many got away?' he asked.

'Hard to tell,' replied Lucius. 'A couple of hundred at least. Two of these fuckers pissed themselves. I thought the Free Companies were poor soldiers, but these Hounds are a fucking disgrace.'

'I think they know that,' he replied. 'So do their masters.'

Lucius pulled one of the Karesians into a seated position and slapped him. The prisoner had a debilitating slice across the back of his leg, but was otherwise unhurt.

'He tried to run, but didn't get very far,' said Verellian. 'He talks better than the others.'

'Your name?' asked Fallon, keeping his tone calm.

The Hound looked at him with red eyes. He was older than Fallon and his face was scarred across the cheeks.

'Raza,' he replied, dried blood cracking on his lips.

'Well, Raza, my name's Fallon the Grey. Please understand that your life is in the balance unless you cooperate.'

The Karesian gritted his teeth and winced in pain as Ohms pulled him upright, standing on his wounded leg.

'I understand,' he grunted.

'Good. Now, tell me the Hound troop placement around Ro Weir – and anything you know about the Hawks.'

Raza spat bloody phlegm on to the grass and cleared his throat. He was in pain, but wore it well. Fallon guessed this was not his first battle, nor his first injury.

'Troop placements. . . hard to answer. Many packs, with more coming. We don't deploy like you, we just mass.'

'How many?' asked Fallon.

'A hundred thousand – many packs formed in a line round your Weir, clearing any citizens not yet under our domination.'

Verellian and Fallon shared a glance. The number was not a total surprise. It was all the Karesians had. They didn't have skill, discipline, honour or loyalty – but they could overwhelm most targets like an army of ants sweeping the forest floor. He spared a thought for the common folk of Tor Funweir, having to deal with the new order.

'You're a long way from Weir,' snarled Ohms. 'Why so far north?'

Raza tried to compose himself, but his leg wouldn't take his weight and even small movements made him wince.

'We were part of an advance force,' he slurred, spitting out more blood. 'We'd been killing risen men in the Fell; then we were ordered to outflank your king.'

This was a surprise. Everyone within earshot snorted with derision, doubting that the Hounds were capable of such strategy.

'With this mob?' queried Ohms. 'You ran from us.'

'No, master knight, we are a scouting pack. The main force is sixty thousand strong, moving west against your king.'

Fallon considered it. It was sound strategy, based on their advantage of numbers.

'Our forces are limitless, our strength endless,' said the Hound. 'You make war in lines, with order and discipline. We swarm you, choking your lines with dead men. Death means nothing to us. It means everything to you.'

'Raza, look at me,' said Fallon, drawing the Karesian's eyes upward. 'Where is the king?'

'South-west,' said Raza. 'Somewhere between Lob's Wood and the hills of Narland. Our scouting packs have all been destroyed before accurate reports could be relayed. All we have found are cartloads of fleeing Ro.'

Verellian grunted, screwing up his face. 'They're holding position?' he asked. 'He's got balls, our new king.'

'How many men has he got?' asked Fallon. 'How many warriors of Ro are you looking for?'

'Unknown,' replied Raza. 'Some forty thousand. Nothing to threaten us. Once we smoke them out.'

'You won't be smoking anything, son,' said Ohms, kicking the Karesian's wounded leg. 'Feel helpless, don't you? Feels shit, doesn't it?'

Raza shrieked and looked imploringly at Fallon. When he saw that no-one was going to stop the sergeant, he fell back to the grass and wept in pain.

'What do you think?' Fallon asked Verellian, giving the Hound a chance to compose himself.

The Grey Captain considered it. 'Forty thousand is the largest army of Ro I've ever heard of. But the Hounds are just too many. We'll have to trust they can get past the flanking move. Either way, we have to hope they can dig in around Weir.'

'If not,' mused Fallon, 'we'll have to save as many of them as possible. There is a time for fighting and there is a time for protecting. Let's hope we know the difference when we see it. But I need a new sword first.'

'You'd do better with a greatsword, something two-handed and heavy. A shield is a waste of an arm for you.' He scanned their men and saw two hundred longswords. 'Don't know where we'll get one out here, though.'

'A dead Hawk,' replied Fallon. 'I've seen a few.'

* * *

Fallon stood over the body of a dead man of Ro. He had a frail right hand and wore a red tabard, with a rampant hawk sewn into the fabric. They'd found him sprawled across a bramble bush, directly in their path. They were now in the hills of Narland, riding hard in the wake of the Hawks' advance. Their progress was just short of spectacular and Fallon allowed them a few minutes' rest while he picked up a new blade.

'Try it out,' said Verellian, reaching down and retrieving the two-handed sword. The dead man's crippled hand was strapped to the hilt, with his stronger hand doing all the heavy work. 'It's well-forged. The Hawks know about steel.'

Fallon took the greatsword and felt its weight. He'd trained with the heavier blades, but never wielded one in battle. It felt surprisingly comfortable, with a long hilt and parrying hooks on the cross-piece. The sword was at least four feet long and tarnished from years of use.

He turned it aside and knelt down next to the dead warrior of Ro. The man had two deep cuts to his neck and head. The second blow had likely been delivered when he was already dead. They were smooth cuts, indicating the curved scimitars of the Hounds.

'This is a good blade,' he said to the dead man. 'I'd like to take it.'

He heard the distant voice of Torian's shade, as if the words had been spoken in the distant past. 'His name was Boldin of Triste,' said the voice. 'He was born in a small fishing village in the river lands of Haran and he was a corporal in the Hawks of Ro, loyal to his general.'

'Where did he get the blade?' whispered Fallon, quietly enough that Verellian wouldn't hear.

'Alexander Tiris broke Boldin's hand in the training yard. The young swordsman never regained enough strength in his right hand to properly wield a shortsword, so his general had a greatsword forged and trained the man to use it. He used that sword for seven years. He favoured an aggressive style, using the strength in his shoulders to compensate for his crippled hand.'

'Would he want me to take it?' Fallon looked at the man's closed eyes, imagining all the things he'd done and all the things that had been taken from him.

'There are oceans of understanding that block a clear answer to that question, but yes, I believe he would.'

Then the shade was silent, as if it had never been there. Fallon stood and looked at Boldin's sword. It had streaks of blood on both edges, and the tip was covered in wet earth.

'It's a good sword,' he said, turning back to Verellian.

The old knight looked at him with a knowing glint in his eye. He then nodded slowly. Fallon retrieved Boldin's scabbard, unbuckling it from across his back and strapping it on.

CHAPTER NINETEEN

ALEXANDER TIRIS IN THE DUCHY OF WEIR

'KING ALEXANDER, MAY I speak to you?' asked the forest-dweller.

Xander smiled at his chief scout, suddenly realizing how little they had spoken. 'Of course, Sigurd. The fights are done for the day.' He motioned to the nearest chair and offered a mug of wine. Brennan remained, cleaning his hands in a standing water basin.

'Thank you, no,' replied Sigurd, taking a seat. 'I have no taste for the fermentation of grape.'

'I suppose it must appear strange that humans spend so much time drinking. Men say that if you drink enough, everything feels better.'

Sigurd didn't crack a smile. His face resembled a statue, hewn from grey rock. 'I find human habits interesting. I learned to treat them so from Tyr Nanon the Shape Taker. He said that humans either drink to forget or drink to remember.'

'Your friend is wise,' replied Xander.

'He is – and he wishes to speak to you, King Alexander. Though he is wise enough not to approach unannounced through ranks of warriors.'

Xander sat forward. 'If you trust him, he is welcome.'

'My king,' offered Major Brennan. 'Let me assess his intentions first. Even Dokkalfar can have ulterior motives.'

Sigurd's face didn't change, but he tilted his head, as if he took

310

offence at the Hawk's words. 'Tyr Nanon is a soldier of the Long War,' said the forest-dweller. 'He is above your suspicions.'

'No-one is above my suspicions. I don't know him, so I don't trust him near the king.'

'Easy, Major,' said Xander, standing up. 'Sigurd, is your friend waiting beyond our lines?'

'Indeed,' replied the Dokkalfar. 'He and a female companion are to the east.'

'Then we will go to *him*,' offered Xander, smiling at Brennan.

The Hawk major screwed up his face. 'Aye, my king, that sounds reasonable.'

He belted on Peacekeeper and wrapped himself in a heavy, woollen cloak. The sword had been cleaned and then cleaned again, but still a narrow streak of dirty black ran down the steel surface. It had been fired once, when first forged, and it had not liked being fired again in the inferno of Cozz. But it was still sharp and it would still serve.

The three of them left his command pavilion and entered the twilight haze of Weir. Gwen was seated outside, arguing with Lord Markos about what the One God wanted. It was a common argument among the army men, and had become background noise, almost humorous in the way it bounced around between men of different characters and levels of piety. Markos was the only man who took it seriously. The paladin still preached to Gwen, trying to make her understand that, as queen, she had been chosen by the Stone Giant. He told her that, if Xander died, she'd be monarch of Tor Funweir and would have to rule. He saw scathing words, contained behind gritted teeth, and knew his wife didn't want to think about it. In fact, she and Xander had agreed not to discuss the possibility of their deaths. Both of them hoped deep in their hearts that, if they died, they'd die together.

'Where are you going?' she asked, standing up.

'Sigurd wants to introduce me to a friend of his,' replied Xander.

Brennan called for horses and a guard of Hawks to accompany them. Gwen left Markos, intending to join them, and they mounted quickly, with armoured men in formation round their king. Being guarded as king was a world away from being guarded as general, and Xander felt increasingly awkward as they rode through the camp, with Brennan shouting 'Make way for the king and queen.' He thought how helpless he must appear, needing Hawks to keep him safe. He was in fact as good a swordsman as any, and better than most, but kings needed protecting in ways that generals did not.

'It's all for show, my love,' said Gwen, riding next to him within a circle of armoured men.

'Doesn't it bother you?'

She bit her lip and smiled. 'It does. And it *will* do, right up until someone aims a crossbow at their new king and queen and our guards stop them.'

They were not assailed by crossbow-wielding maniacs, and reached the eastern edge of the camp within ten minutes. The forces from Du Ban occupied huge pavilions of crisp, white fabric, all along the perimeter of the camp. Lord Ronan Montague did not acquiesce to the usual austerity of a mobile army, preferring to turn his portion of the camp into a palatial home away from home, tucked in next to a craggy line of rocks and overlooked by dozens of guards.

'Tyr Nanon is waiting beyond the rocks,' said Sigurd. 'The forces from Du Ban did not appear. . . friendly.'

The royal procession had garnered something of a crowd from around the white pavilions, but Brennan ushered away all the onlookers and led the company to a shallow ravine leading up and away from the line of rocks. Across the King's Highway, the wilds of Tor Funweir stretched into the distance, revealing nothing but grass, trees and darkness.

'Yonder,' said Brennan, nodding at a thin globe of light barely visible between the trees. 'Who camps so close to an army this size?'

'A man who isn't worried about that army being his enemy,' replied Xander.

'Not a man,' corrected Sigurd, lifting his face and making a subtle whistling sound, reminiscent of a calling bird.

From the distant campfire, two figures walked slowly into the open. Xander, flanked by his guards, rode in front of his men to get a good look at those who approached. The first figure was a dusky-skinned Kirin girl, holding a sheathed katana and wearing tight black clothing. She was attractive, but her face showed no trust and little compromise. The second figure was a Dokkalfar, though he was far shorter than any Xander had seen before. He was barely six feet tall, but carried himself like a predatory cat. He wore a Ro longsword and simple clothing of green and brown fabric.

'A warm night, friend,' said the king.

'Indeed,' replied the strange forest-dweller. 'The fire was so you could see us. I have found that being *too* stealthy unnerves people.'

'What are your intentions?' snapped Major Brennan. 'You are talking to our king.'

Gwen chuckled in Xander's ear, too quietly for anyone else to hear, though neither of them rebuked the major for his manner.

'My name is Tyr Nanon. I was friend to Rham Jas Rami, and this charming young human is his daughter, Keisha. We're soldiers of the Long War and we're here to help.'

Xander looked more closely at the girl's katana and realized he'd seen it before. 'Then you will accompany us back to camp,' he replied. 'I will allow no harm to come to you.'

'Form up,' commanded Brennan, directing men to assemble round the two newcomers. Tyr Nanon looked with interest at the mounted Hawks, nodding and smiling as he was surrounded by steel and horses. He showed no fear and far more expressiveness than Xander was used to from a Dokkalfar.

'Much as your camp looks delightful,' said Nanon, 'perhaps you'd care to join us at *ours*.' He looked back over his shoulder at the flickering globe of firelight. 'It is far less impressive, but requires far less ceremony. Your riding globs of metal can join us if it makes you feel safe.'

'All of them?' queried the Kirin girl, frowning at her companion.

Brennan nudged his horse forward. 'The king is free to rest

313

himself round any campfire he so chooses, but *I* decide where his guards station themselves.'

Gwen raised her eyebrows and muttered something to herself, before gathering up her horse's reins and riding towards Tyr Nanon's modest camp. 'Stay or go, Brennan,' said the queen. 'But I want to sit down.'

The major shook his head. 'Accompany the queen,' he ordered three nearby Hawks.

Xander followed his wife, with their guards close behind and the two newcomers jogging to keep up. Their army was visible only as a series of distortions in the twilight air, spreading across the low ground and coming to his eyes as glints of fire and flashes of colour. When night fell, forty thousand warriors of Ro would be hard to see unless you chanced upon their lines in the darkness. Nanon and Keisha had secreted themselves within spitting distance of the army, but had not been seen by patrols or guards.

Gwen, Xander, Brennan and Sigurd sat on the dusty ground, opposite Nanon and Keisha. Their guards remained mounted, forming a protective circle round the small copse of trees. The two newcomers had no baggage or supplies of any kind. No food or horses, just light armour and weaponry.

'You have a problem,' began Nanon. 'There is an enchantress in Ro Weir. All your swords and armour mean nothing to her.'

'But you can help?' Xander prompted.

'Yes, I think so,' replied Keisha, her voice deep and sultry. 'I'm a dark-blood, like my father. Nanon will get us into the city and I'm going to kill the Mistress of Pain.'

The short forest-dweller grinned, the first such expression Xander remembered seeing from one of his kind. 'We plan to dig in and besiege her out,' said the king. 'once we have seen the common folk safely north and have pushed through the Hounds. If you want to kill the witch first, that's even better.'

'Yes, I'd noticed you were holding position,' said Nanon. 'Sooner or later you'll have to meet them in open battle. If you march south now, you'll be flanked, but you'll reach the city and be able to dig in – assuming you kill the massive mob of black steel waiting to meet you.'

'You've seen them?' queried Brennan. 'What are they waiting for? We haven't moved in almost a week.'

'They don't know which way you'll go,' replied Nanon. 'I think they secretly hope you'll withdraw under superior numbers. If war is your goal, you mustn't stay here any longer. We can kill the witch, but you must reach Weir before the Hound Lands are emptied and Tor Funweir chokes. Otherwise your name will be lost amidst the limitless branches of the Twisted Tree.'

Xander shared looks with both his wife and his adjutant. Nanon was terse in his summary, but nothing he said rang false. The army had waited, protecting fleeing folk and clearing small packs of Hounds, but they'd won no decisive victories; nor had they pulled the Karesians into any significant battles. Despite a thousand theories and reports, in reality they could only guess at how many Hounds awaited them and how many more Karesia could provide. There were armies to the east *and* to the south. He could only march in one direction.

'My king,' said Brennan, 'he speaks wisely.'

'Aye,' agreed Gwen. 'Both sorcery and swords will play a part in this war. If Tyr Nanon and Keisha can deal with the sorcery, we should provide the swords. South?'

'South,' he agreed. 'Brennan, muster the vanguard and tell everyone else to make ready. Will you accompany us, Tyr Nanon?'

'Afraid not,' replied the forest-dweller. 'I never liked armies. Too little personality when you put men in companies and brigades. And we can move much faster on our own. But, before you go. . .' His grey face fell into a look of concern. 'Do you know of the Dark Young?'

Xander shivered, as if a sudden chill caught his limbs when he was reminded of the thing he had fought under Ro Haran. Gwen balked slightly and Brennan growled. Round the fire, only Sigurd and Nanon remained impassive. Even Keisha showed revulsion and fear at mention of the tree creatures.

315

'I see you do,' said Nanon. 'The priest and altar of Shub-Nillurath. I have been in the catacombs of Ro Weir and have seen what the Mistress of Pain has created. If I had a god I would thank him that her creatures were shrouded in darkness, but she has many.'

Brennan stood from the fire and raised his chin. His hand rested on the hilt of his old longsword and he tensed his muscles. 'We had ten soldiers and we burned one of those things to the ground. Imagine what we can do with forty thousand soldiers.'

Nanon peered up at the major, tilting his head and looking more like a Dokkalfar. 'You are brave, man of Ro. And I'm gambling a lot on you being right, but do not cast them aside so freely. They are the doom of my people, in more ways than you know.' He looked at Tyr Sigurd and a look of distant sadness passed between them. 'Take your army south and retake your city – but be ever mindful that Shub-Nillurath's children still have a part to play in this battle of the Long War.'

* * *

Xander hoped that the battle of Narland would be remembered. That tales and songs would rise from the hearts of the Ro in remembrance of a glorious victory against all odds. Perhaps even the king would be mentioned – either in praise or in mockery.

The army was mustered, well-prepared and facing south, having assembled into mixed columns and marched at speed to the largest concentration of Hounds they could find. Nanon was right; dozens of packs had been run over by their advance, but now, at the edges of the duchy of Weir, they faced off against a huge mass of black armour and scimitars. It was the biggest army he'd ever seen, perhaps fifty thousand strong. All he needed to do was punch a hole through steel and flesh and march to the gates of Weir. A simple proposition, made complicated only by fifty thousand warriors of Karesia.

Markos and his paladins were stationed on the left flank; Brennan and five thousand mounted knights were on the right.

In the centre, Xander and Lord Ronan Montague would follow the banner of Tiris, with their infantry behind. The lead riders fanned out, relaying orders to their troops and redeploying the army. Markos and his knights formed up into a wedge on the left. Brennan and four companies of mounted Hawks did the same on the right.

Daganay rode to the front, wheeling his horse next to Xander in order to address the troops. 'With your permission, my king?'

'Make your words strong, my friend,' he replied.

The Blue cleric held his mace above his head. 'Men of Ro!' he shouted. 'This is my country – this is where I was born. I like this land. It isn't perfect – it isn't any kind of paradise, unless you wear Purple.' The nearest ranks laughed at this gallows humour. 'But I like it nonetheless. I don't want it to change. I don't want this dead god telling me what to do. I may die here. . . I probably will, I'm a fat old bastard. But I'll kill anyone who tries to tell me that this isn't Tor Funweir – and we're not men of Ro.' Men cheered this, their desperation evident in their clenched fists and gritted teeth. '*They* say these are the Lands of the Twisted Tree. *I* say this is Tor Funweir. I have a mace, I have a king and I am not afraid. You all have weapons – and you all have a king. Are you afraid? Do you fear the faceless masses of the Dead God?'

'No!' came the booming reply.

'Each sword arm makes a difference. Each man you kill makes a difference. With every swing of our swords we will claw back Tor Funweir. When the dust settles and the dead swim in the waters of beyond, know that your sword made a difference.'

The men were roused, but their eyes remained steely as they let forth a grim cheer. The central ranks, mostly guardsmen, men of Du Ban and a few companies of Hawks, slapped each other on the back and shared words of encouragement, the most senior warriors using their experience to calm the newly bloodied.

'My king,' said Sergeant Ashwyn. 'Another fucking white flag.'

Xander looked south and saw a small party of horsemen

approaching, their flag of parlay swinging in high arcs as they stopped between the two armies.

Gwen nudged her horse next to his. 'Just more horse-shit,' she said. 'There's nothing they can say to us, not now.'

Brennan and Markos signalled that they were in position on the flanks, ready to charge when the order was given. If the day went well, the cavalry would dismantle the edges of the Karesian army and force them into the centre, making men flee and catching the rest in a meat-grinder on three sides. *If* the day went well.

'My king?' prompted Ashwyn. 'Orders.'

'Gwen, Ash, Sigurd, you're with me. If they want to talk, let's talk. Let's go and pick a fight. Everyone else – hold.'

He nudged his horse forward, but didn't press it into a gallop; he wanted to allow the opposing warriors to get a good look at him. Behind, the army of Ro held their ground, ready to attack if ordered to do so. Xander knew that each one of them was itching for a fight. Their eyes, their posture, their stillness. They were a coiled spring waiting to be released by their king. A frenzy of swords and patriotic rage could be unleashed at a word or a gesture.

They reached the Hounds asking for parlay and stopped, two small groups of riders between two huge armies.

'Speak!' said Xander.

None of these Hounds wore helmets and it was strange to see them as individuals. They had faces and expressions, though all looked half-dead and to be in some kind of trance.

'I am Whip-Master Turve Ramhe,' said an older man whose swarthy face was covered in small scars. 'I have an offer from the Mistress of Pain to the king of the Ro. You can have your life and the lives of your men. All you must do is withdraw to your city and give up your Tor Funweir. This land is no longer yours. We are prepared to give you the duchy of Haran, as long as you swear allegiance to the Twisted Tree.'

The man's gaze flowed across all of them. He frowned at Xander, sneered at Ashwyn, snarled at Tyr Sigurd and leered at Gwen. Everything about him was grotesque. His eyes were narrow, his face sweaty and scarred.

'Not acceptable,' said Xander.

The whip-master nodded, thrusting out his bulbous chin. 'If you reject this offer, I have been instructed to cut out your eyes and make your wife eat them, before I rape her with my scimitar.'

'I'm glad you said that,' Xander replied. 'It means I won't have to decide whether or not to kill you.'

Almost before he'd finished speaking, Gwen's leaf-blade had entered the space between them. She flung it underarm from a scabbard on her thigh, cutting the air with a whistle to lodge in the whip-master's throat.

'That's the second man I've killed under a white flag,' she observed as the remaining Karesians fled in horror.

Xander drew Peacekeeper and filled his lungs so he could be heard by both armies. 'We are the Hawks of Ro: stand down or die!'

Three horns sounded from behind and the thunderous roar of men unleashed filled the landscape. The Hounds, filling his eyes from horizon to horizon, stayed where they were, having no horses to meet the ongoing charge and little genuine will to fight.

'Stay alive, my love,' they whispered to each other as the wave of armoured warriors picked them up.

Sigurd broke off to join his forest-dwellers, skulking in the middle of the army, while Xander, Gwen and Ashwyn rode at the centre of the advance. The Knights of the Dawn made the most noise, their armoured chargers slow to pick up speed but unstoppable when they got moving. Brennan's cavalry covered the ground more quickly and both wings of his army fixed on the Hounds' flanks.

'This is the ground to die on,' roared Daganay from the mass of troops. 'This is the time – fight for your king!'

Xander was no raw recruit; he had fought hundreds of battles. But charging a pack of fifty thousand Hounds as king was new even for him. Such a battle had never taken place in the long history of Tor Funweir, and was only happening now because he had forced it. It would have been an unthinkable nightmare just a few short years ago. It was poor strategy, too rash, too aggressive – there was no territory to be gained, and a simple victory here would not make the Hounds abandon Ro Weir and the south. But it would mean they could win, if only for a day and only for a single battle. If only to give Nanon and Keisha a chance to kill the witch.

He rose in his stirrups and tensed his legs, balling his hand into a fist round the horse's reins. Peacekeeper was aloft, swaying in the air with the red hawk of Haran, the black raven of Canarn, the gold eagle of Tiris and the white dove of Arnon. Four of the great cities of Ro united.

'For the One God and for King Alexander Tiris,' intoned Markos of Rayne as the knights lowered their lances.

The sound of impact was deafening. The first few ranks of Hounds came and went, reaching him as barely a bump on the plains as warhorses rode them down. His world narrowed until all that mattered was the sea of black armour directly in front of him. They crashed into the pack, but even though they killed hundreds with hoof and steel, he could see that they had barely dented its mass. He couldn't see the flanks, nor Brennan and Markos; he could only see more men that he needed to kill.

Horses began to falter and riders were swarmed, pulled to the ground and run through. Hounds kept dying, throwing themselves at the warriors of Ro with no evident skill or training. Their sheer numbers blunted the charge. He'd lost sight of Gwen, last seen somewhere to his left, and only the stream of coarse language enabled him to locate Daganay. He tried to focus, keeping the Hounds back from his horse with Peacekeeper. He swung his mount left and right, clattering men to the ground and kicking others to death.

'General!' shouted Ashwyn, as the sergeant was thrown to the ground by a rearing horse.

Xander drove his bastard sword into a man's skull and swung

out of the saddle. His horse whinnied and began to gallop away, sending a cluster of Hounds to the muddy ground.

Ash was being mobbed by black armour. He lay on his back, holding his shield in both hands and swearing. Xander ducked a swipe, parried a thrust, killed a man at the neck, another in the chest. He headbutted a Hound that tried to tackle him, dragged a wounded man of Ro to his feet, and still couldn't see Gwen. The men attacking Ash all looked up at him through narrow visors. Two ran away, another two met Peacekeeper and Ashwyn killed the last.

'Don't die,' said Xander, helping the man upright. 'I need you to repair my sword after the battle.'

The blacksmith didn't have time to reply and Xander didn't have time to ask if he was okay. There were more Hounds – many, many more Hounds.

Stubbornness took over as the battle carried on, consuming time as well as energy. He imagined the men at his back staying alert through grit alone, dealing with each new life-or-death encounter in turn, not looking too far ahead or thinking too much about their fellows. The Hounds were poor warriors, but hard living; drugs and sorcery had given them a toughness and determination that was hard to break. In small groups they were easily intimidated, but a huge army. . . he feared they could not be overcome even with grit and superior skill.

Daganay became visible as bodies piled up on the ground and cleared his field of vision. The Blue cleric was roaring with righteous anger and clubbing men out of his way with his heavy mace. He stood in front of a wounded Hawk who was missing a leg and twitching on the ground. Another man, a guardsman of Tiris, lay nearby, trying to breathe through a severed windpipe and reaching for the churchman.

'They're wounded, leave 'em be,' grunted Daganay.

In the midst of so much death, the cleric was at his most dangerous when he was defending the helpless. Xander wanted to assist, but a chasm of black steel lay between them. He trusted his confessor to stay alive and save as many men as possible. But still he couldn't see his wife.

He grabbed a nearby Hawk. 'Give me a line, soldier – form the fuck up.'

He held an area of bloodied ground, driving his sword into any men who got close. Other warriors joined him, Hawks, guardsmen and a few Dokkalfar, pushing forward into a line and driving the Hounds back. Commands were relayed along the line, in grunted shouts and gurgled death-rattles, telling the army to assemble. In the distance, dust and blood flew at the corners of his vision and he saw riders at both edges of the Karesian army.

'King Alexander!' shouted Lord Markos of Rayne.

The White paladin was still astride his armoured charger and appeared with his knights, like a tidal wave, over the Karesians' heads. He had discarded his lance and instead wielded a huge two-handed greatsword, controlling his mount through the strength of his legs. His force contained many riderless horses and many more wounded men, but they hadn't faltered. They scythed through the Hounds, breaking the flank into steel blobs of fleeing men.

Lord Markos rode directly at Xander, ordering his men into an arrow behind him. The clatter of their charge displaced all other sound and suddenly the Karesians appeared less interested in fighting. They stopped and stared, looking at each other for guidance and finding none. Before they could decide on a course of action, they were ridden into the dirt by the White Knights of the Dawn.

'I have a horse for you, my king,' boomed Lord Markos, throwing down the reins of a riderless charger.

Xander killed the last obvious opponent and fell to a seated position on the grass. Ashwyn slumped next to him and they both looked up. From the right, Brennan's cavalry had broken the other flank and the Hounds were in disordered retreat. In the centre, all around him, he saw a thick column of bloodied warriors. With him at their point, they'd cut a hole in the Hound lines. He'd barely noticed how far they'd gone or how many men they'd killed. It was like waking from a nightmare to find yourself at peace, in a warm bed with a blazing fire. Battles, it seemed, were experienced in small chunks. You never saw the whole, you just saw the pieces in front of you.

'Gwen,' he muttered, 'where's Gwen?'

'The day is ours!' shouted Daganay.

The cleric pushed his way past weary men and leant on Xander, his breath coming in short bursts and his mace covered in a slick of blood.

'Shall we pursue the fleeing Hounds?' asked Markos, wheeling his horse and lowering his huge sword.

'No, hold your position,' answered the king.

Markos glanced at the waves of fleeing Karesians and sheathed his sword. 'Several thousand of the enemy are running, your grace.'

Daganay coughed and spat blood on to the ground. 'General, the grim work begins. . . men need killing and men need saving.'

He looked around. No point of the compass was empty of blood and death. Hounds, Hawks, guardsmen, paladins: they all bled the same. He didn't know how long the battle had lasted, just that his body ached like he'd been running for a day and a night. Time was just another thing he'd discarded while killing Hounds.

'A good day,' whispered a voice.

He smiled before he turned, letting her voice wash over him. She was bloodied and favouring her right leg, but she was alive and she was standing. For a moment, Xander wished he could ask her not to fight, but he'd made her a promise he'd never break. Who was he kidding. She was tougher than him anyway.

'My horse went down early,' she said, wiping blood from her face. 'The beast provided nice cover.'

'A good day,' he agreed, latching on to her for a lingering kiss.

'My queen!' exclaimed Markos.

From the press of standing warriors came Brennan and his column of riders. The Hawk major dismounted and shoved his way through them. He paused in front of his king, wiping blood from a deep sword wound on his armoured shoulder. Then he dropped to one knee.

'My general, my king!' stated Major Brennan. 'We have victory.'

Markos held his freshly cleaned greatsword aloft. 'My general, my king,' he shouted.

Then Ashwyn dropped to his knee, followed by every man close to him. In a ripple of battle-hardened loyalty, hundreds of men, many of them wounded, took a knee before him. 'My general, my king!' they shouted, sending a wave of conviction and victory across the bloodied fields of Tor Funweir.

* * *

Xander wandered the uneven field, stepping over bodies and round pools of blood, surveying the damage and gathering his strength. Over a thousand of his men were dead. The number had been told to him by Daganay an hour after the battle, and had been echoing in his head since he retreated to his solitary wandering.

The dead Hounds numbered more than five times as many. Much of the Karesian army had broken into scattered packs and fled in every conceivable direction. They didn't have the discipline or leadership to assemble as a single force and had been easily mopped up by Markos and his knights. The paladins acted with a tireless fury, following their leader wherever he beckoned. Only now, with no more enemies to fight and the sun beyond the horizon, did they take any rest.

The king of Tor Funweir did not desire rest. He didn't know what he desired. He wandered the battlefield, catching the globes of light from flaming torches and the occasional patch of clear moonlight. Daganay had men searching the fields of death for those still clinging to life and they did their work in silence, as the only light and movement in the darkness.

Brennan had taken the army south, occupying the shoddy bulwarks left by the Hounds. The warriors of Ro were more integrated than ever. Even the Dokkalfar mingled freely among the soldiers, beginning to understand humour and camaraderie.

The guardsmen from Tiris, Brom's men from Canarn, even Lord Montague's men; they were treated as equals by the Hawks. They shared weapons, armour, food, water and stories. He wondered how many of their stories were about him.

After speaking to Tyr Nanon, and emerging victorious from the greatest of battles, Xander was beginning to think they could win.

'Time to pray,' said a gruff voice from the darkness. 'I believe now is a good time to address the One.'

Xander saw Daganay meandering round the dead bodies, torch in hand. His breastplate was being repaired and he wore only his Blue church robes.

'You've never pushed me to pray to him before,' he replied. 'You always said the One didn't give a shit.'

The cleric nodded. 'Maybe *I* give a shit, your grace.'

Xander wanted to laugh, but it wasn't funny. 'Is that what you're going to call me from now on?'

'Not usually when we're alone, no,' replied Daganay. 'But I thought it was worth reminding you this once.'

'I didn't need reminding.'

They stood in a churned-up field, with the smell of death all around them and barely enough firelight to see each other's faces. He'd left his ever-present guards and wandered far enough from their camp that he could no longer even hear the nightly sounds of his army. Battles were strange things that made you exhausted, but denied you sleep through insistent memories and constant aches. Many warriors of Ro would do without sleep on this particular night, and many others would fall into a sleep from which they wouldn't wake.

'You are Alexander Tiris,' said Daganay, 'and you are king of Tor Funweir.'

'That's just the long-form version of your grace,' he replied. 'And I still don't need reminding.'

Daganay lowered his torch, illuminating their faces. Xander sometimes forgot that his confessor was in his middle fifties. The man fought like a beast, far beyond what his age would suggest.

'You're not even wounded,' Xander said with a smile. 'I thought the One didn't give a shit.'

'About *you*,' he replied. 'I'm a cleric, remember.'

They shared a laugh. It was his first since the battle and he felt as if he was releasing huge tension from his facial muscles. He'd been locked in a snarl of grim concentration for hours, glaring at everything in front of him. Now his face relaxed into a warm smile.

'Xander,' said the cleric.

'You've never called me that.'

'From now on, that's what I'm going to call you when we're alone. But you'll be my king when others are present.'

'You sound almost like Gwen,' he joked.

'I'm your other wife,' replied Daganay. 'Just not as pretty. Now, let's get it over with.'

Xander puffed out his chest and scratched across his shaven head. He hadn't bent in prayer since they left Ro Haran and Daganay hadn't mentioned it. Now, with battles fought and more death to come, they knelt on the sodden grass and spoke to their god.

'I am Alexander Tiris,' he said to the One God, 'and I am the king of Tor Funweir. I *know* you care. I saw you watching when we stood at Cozz. Last time we spoke, I was in Ro Haran, kneeling on a thick carpet. The world has changed since then. . . and I am struggling to keep up. If it weren't for Gwen. . . I don't know, maybe I would have turned back.'

'And,' prompted Daganay after a moment.

'Oh, yes – and sorry for cursing your name a few hundred times. In Haran, in Canarn, definitely a few times in Tiris. . . when I got blown up in Cozz. . . fuck, I can't remember.' He bowed his head, hating the honesty required of him. 'And, err. . . I've killed a bloody awful lot of men.'

CHAPTER TWENTY

INGRID TEARDROP IN THE REALM OF SUMMER WOLF

L EAVING THE TENT had been a big step, but she knew it
was time to end her captivity. Corvus convinced her with
his insistent flapping that she would be safe, but poking
her head through the canvas opening for the last time was still
a nerve-wracking experience, even though she already trusted
the big raven. Once outside, she skipped invisibly away from her
confinement, smiling with glee.

Rulag's men sat at their fires, drinking their ale and rubbing
their feet, apparently unaware that Ingrid walked within a few
feet of them, skulking in the morning gloom.

Corvus just looked at her, his beak somehow managing to
appear smug. The raven cawed every few minutes, reminding her
to hurry up, and she reached the first siege tower before the sun
had fully risen. She had nothing but a blanket and a small sack
of pillaged hard bread and salted beef.

The guards were all outside and the empty interior was bigger
than she had imagined, like a tall, thin house with no furniture.
The stairs were wood and snaked up through six levels of the
tower. There were slots for axes to be thrown, and hatches from
which to pour oil and throw flaming torches. It would be rolled
towards the city, loaded with men and used to mount the walls.
But before that, it was a perfect hiding place.

And now she slept at the top. . . and it was really horrible. The
extra height doubled the wind chill and her stolen blanket was no

protection. She'd been hiding in a cramped wooden compartment with her stolen food for several days. The top of the tower was divided into small sections, filled with axes, above which were platforms for axe hurlers. The level below held the drawbridge and would be the main route over the walls of Tiergarten for Rulag's warriors.

Rulag Ursa and Harrod were probably fuming with rage at her escape. They hadn't stopped looking for her. Throughout the day, taking no rest, a hundred men had been tasked with finding her. They scoured every nook and cranny of the camp, sending patrols as far south and east as they dared, trying to find Rulag's future wife. They searched everywhere, even the towers, but her hiding place was too small for them to thoroughly search without disassembling the structures. On the two occasions they *had* poked their bearded faces into the storage compartments, they'd appeared to look straight at her but hadn't reacted, eliciting a mocking caw from Corvus.

The raven had got her here and guarded her as she slept, but he couldn't make her any warmer, or provide her any entertainment. The most interesting thing that happened was the daily movement of the tower, when dozens of men and dogs strained to shift her hiding place towards the city. It was a cacophony of grunts, shouts, barks and armour. Her view was of swarming men, each nothing more than a sound and a shape, carrying an axe and clad in fur. But multiplied by a few thousand it was scary and humbling. She'd been with them for weeks, dragged along at the centre of their advance like a reluctant mascot, sabotaging their army and causing mischief whenever she could. But now she saw what she couldn't from the ground. She saw enough men to change Fjorlan.

She wriggled out of the wooden compartment, pushing past bundles of throwing-axes to emerge at the edge of the top tier. She lay flat, with her face just peeking over the edge. The warriors were formed up again, as they had been for the last two days, in columns and mobs, with the baggage to the rear and the sled dogs at the flanks. They didn't drink in the evenings any more; nor did they fight or gamble. A moving tavern had suddenly turned into an army. They still cursed, but now their vitriol was all aimed at the nearby city.

The tower juddered as the sled dogs took the strain, and once again she was moving along the rugged gully at the front of the army, one of a dozen siege towers. The landscape was the same, with sheer walls of rock and snow either side of them, until a break in the ice showed her Tiergarten for the first time.

'Wow,' she breathed, stunned into awe for a moment.

She had been born in Fredericksand and she loved Fredericksand, but Tiergarten was truly wondrous. It was taller than it was wide, cut into the side of a mountain as if it had been there since the land was formed. She smiled, suddenly confident that such a place could not easily be destroyed. Walls and towers and gates, of grey stone and thick hard-wood, were fixed together with a solidity that made it a part of the landscape, rather than a city of men. It looked out over a huge, open plain, stopped only by the Fjorlan Sea, which was suddenly visible over the gully walls. The army was moving towards the plain, but keeping well clear of the city.

Corvus had been quiet, perched atop the siege tower, but now he sprang into the air and his glossy wings took him quickly across the snowy vista. He didn't caw or flap, which made his flight silent but strangely ominous. He left the army and moved further inland, criss-crossing the gullies in smoothly curved lines. He wanted Ingrid to see something and she knew she wouldn't like it. She felt a surge in her stomach, a nasty feeling of nausea that made her grunt and sit up on the wooden planks. She recognized the feeling and stopped smiling. The ground appeared to rise, suddenly hitting her eyes and making her retch. Somewhere ahead of the army, the black trees were moving. A shimmer and a mist rose in their path, undulating towards the city, though she couldn't see the beasts themselves.

The columns of men below were now narrow, snaking along behind the siege towers, allowing the beasts to get ahead.

Perhaps they were just here to mop up after the trees had attacked Tiergarten.

'Everyone's going to die,' she muttered, putting a hand to her mouth as she retched again. 'Those horrible trees are going to kill everyone. . . even Alahan can't fight things like that.'

She crawled over the slotted wooden compartments to the front of the tower. As it moved, her view rose above the rocks to reveal the city, then fell below the gully walls, showing nothing but other towers and marching warriors. Even from the front she couldn't see the trees. The army was moving parallel to them, separated by walls of ice and rock. They'd been freed. She didn't know if they could be directed or just unleashed, but certainly the men of Ursa were confident enough to stay clear of the city and not rush an attack. Suddenly the walls of Tiergarten didn't look so high.

'Battle formations!' came the command from beneath, relayed to all sections of the army, making them redeploy.

The thin lines of men bunched up behind the towers as the gullies ended and the plains appeared before them. They were here, closer than she'd realized. Hiding in the tower had kept her ignorant of where they were and what they were doing. They'd been near Tiergarten when she'd escaped and, since then, she'd been too scared to speculate on how far they'd travelled. While she slept fitfully, pleased to be free but terrified of being caught, the men below had been preparing for battle. They'd camped just out of sight of the city and woken in the mood for a fight.

Corvus returned, landing close enough to make her jump.

'Don't do that,' she said breathlessly. 'I'm scared. I don't need any more surprises.'

The bird clicked his beak and hunkered down, slowly stepping towards her on curved talons. She wished he could speak, maybe reassure her or tell her a joke to raise her spirits. Alahan used to pull funny faces behind their father's back whenever his sister was miserable, usually about being told off or caught doing something naughty. But the bird didn't speak, just pecked gently at her hands, lightly fluttering his wings.

Caw

Quieter now, Corvus hunkered down and cuddled up to her arm. For a moment she thought he was pretending to be a cat, or some other furry animal. He hopped up and down, padding his feet across her thick blanket.

The tower began to lurch left and right as the ground changed from rocks to level plains of ice and snow. The gullies were now little more than small peaks, stretching inland as rocky crests, like the backbone of some huge lizard. The towers were lined up at the front of the army and now held position, a short distance from the huge stone monolith of Tiergarten and the mountain of Giant's Gift. The men of Ursa could finally spread out after weeks of being stuck in narrow valleys. The plains, pushing west towards the Fjorlan Sea, were the biggest open spaces she'd seen since leaving her home, and the army moved from clusters to thick lines, with glaives, spears and axes pointing at their goal.

Somewhere in Tiergarten, maybe watching them or planning the defence, was Alahan. He was strong, clever and determined. Ingrid hoped he was lucky too.

Caw contributed Corvus. The raven hopped excitedly and jumped from the tower, soaring ahead of the army. The black shape of his body became smaller and smaller, his wings still as he glided on updraughts towards the city.

From the gullies, well in front of the siege towers, shimmering black shapes crawled into view. Their sharp outlines cut into the white of Summer Wolf and a disquieting aura was carried with them. The darkwood trees crossed the ice slowly, spreading out into a line of twisted movement and writhing tentacles. Those below averted their eyes or gritted their teeth, fighting their fear of the creatures. She imagined the defenders of Tiergarten seeing them for the first time and their fear spreading like a virus up the stepped levels of the city.

Then a sound reached her ears. It was deep and booming, coming from all directions and displacing the hiss of the trees and the grunting of the men of Ursa.

From north and south, from Giant's Gift and the Crystal Fork River, from every angle of the realm of Summer Wolf, could be heard keening. The trees stopped moving, thrashing their black limbs against the ice, as if they had heard the sound but searched for its origin.

Ingrid knew the sound of trolls. It was imprinted in her ears from before she could remember. The Ice Men of Rowanoco gave voice to the anger of their god, making all true-hearted Ranen stand a little taller and feel a little stronger. Rulag's men were afraid, as if they suddenly knew how angry they had made their god. All their talk of strength was made petty when they heard the trolls, their feeble arms cowed by childhood fears made real.

From the base of Tiergarten, plumes of snow flew into the air and chunks of icy earth erupted upwards. Balls of dark fur emerged from the ground, stretching out their huge bodies, supported on bulbous limbs. A dozen trolls clawed their way from the ice of Summer Wolf and loped towards the trees. In the lead, at the point of an arrow of brown and black fur, was an Ice Man smaller than the others. He was on all fours, moving slowly and raising his tusked mouth every few steps to keen. The sound of the keening was beautiful to Ingrid's ears, expressing a primal sadness that made a tear fall from her eye. When all twelve trolls made the sound, the trees began to buck and scratch at the ice. One monstrosity broke away from the line and approached the lead troll, a single black figure meeting another against featureless white.

The Ice Man was less than half the size of the tree, which reared up, thrashing its tentacles in a bizarre dance of aggression. The troll just looked at it, as thousands of human spectators held their breath. The Ice Man's wide, hairy face tilted upwards at the tree-beast, his chubby jaw and fleshy lips squashing into a look of confusion. The keening stopped and the other trolls hunkered down on all fours, snorting and growling, spraying phlegm across the ice.

The tentacled beast gave voice to a hissing cry, sending shards of high-pitched whining across the plains. Ingrid's resolve was strengthened by the trolls, but still the sound made her wince. Below, Rulag's remaining army was on the back foot, unable to remain confident when faced with a family of trolls.

The shriek grew louder as the beast crawled towards the lead troll. It thrashed in the air, spraying a mist of white at the troll, but still the Ice Man didn't react with anything more than mild confusion. When the tree exposed its circular maw and splayed its needle-like teeth, the troll grunted. When the beast lunged forward and attacked, he barely moved an inch. The trunk of the black tree was thrust sharply into the troll's chest, a dozen puncture wounds appearing at once. Silence descended for a moment, then the troll looked down at the creature that gnawed into his chest, as if that should be enough to kill him.

'Varorg!' roared the troll, loud enough that Ingrid imagined a rockslide somewhere in the gullies.

The Ice Man reached down, wrapping his huge arms round the monster's trunk and, with a grunt, hefting it off the ice. Black tentacles shook violently in the air, trying to reach the ground, but the troll was hugely strong and appeared not to care about the seeping wound in its chest. The Ice Man squeezed the larger creature and dug its claws into its shimmering, black flesh, securing a firm grip. The other trolls then sprang into life, howling and running at the darkwood trees, even as the small troll moved towards the next monster, wielding the thrashing beast like a huge club.

The children of the Dead God faltered, unable to comprehend the ferocity of Rowanoco's Ice Men. Ingrid felt as if a conflict far beyond the petty struggle for Tiergarten was playing out on the ice of Fjorlan. Or maybe she was just afraid, and her mind conjured fantasies to keep her safe.

The lead troll began beating one Dark Young with the restrained mass of another. He spat and growled, smashing the two beasts together with awesome strength. His family, just as unconcerned by the monsters, charged, claws outstretched and muscles rippling. They set about the trees with chaotic ferocity, leaping on to their backs, clawing at their flesh and grabbing tentacles. They shrugged off attacks and ignored the sickly green mouths, sending out waves of triumphant keening with every hammer-blow of their over-sized fists and every swipe of their foot-long claws.

She sensed a wave of confidence travel across Tiergarten and heard distant cheering. It was the sound of angry triumph.

'Unrahgahr!' roared the small troll.

The trees had no answer. They were unused to the power of the Ice Men, unused to creatures that didn't feel fear and didn't care about wounds. Their tentacles thrashed left and right, but were grabbed by the trolls. One of the Ice Men was trying to eat one, swatting away its writhing branches and biting a chunk from its oily, black flesh. The small one still held one of the creatures, but it was now limp and covered with seeping black blood. It was smashed into the snow and the other trees, its dead mass being used as an over-sized club. Or maybe a flail, now that its tentacles whipped limply wherever the troll hefted the dead beast.

Ingrid could barely believe her eyes as the darkwood trees began to flee. As they'd approached Tiergarten, all madness and writhing limbs, they'd appeared unbeatable. Now, being thrown around like inert flesh by the trolls, they were far from intimidating. In fact, they were now just meals. But still they were fast, thrashing to gain purchase on the ice and pull themselves swiftly north to the relative safety of the gullies. The trolls pursued, sweeping after the trees, smacking their pulpy lips together and keening in ravenous triumph. Behind them, torn apart on the white plains, were five dead trees, tentacles and trunks splayed in messy piles.

Ingrid wanted to cheer. She wanted to jump up and down and give the trolls a massive hug. Even more, she wanted to see Rulag's face – and the Karesian, he'd be really cross. She chuckled, letting momentary elation fill her up. They'd won a victory. A huge victory, against fear and madness. If only she could have stood by her brother and felt the joy in Tiergarten, behind the walls that once again looked high enough to repel any army.

'Get these fucking things moving,' screamed a gruff voice from the ground.

She could see the men below moving hurriedly. They'd quickly regained their composure after watching the last of the trolls disappear into the northern gullies. Rulag's captains shouted commands and readied the army for attack. Their trees had been vanquished and, no matter what Kal Varaz thought, axes would still decide the fate of Fjorlan.

The tower lurched forward and she held on tight to the wooden frame, keeping her head away from the edge. She could distantly hear Corvus, and the sound kept a smile firmly planted on her face. Whatever happened, she knew that Brytag watched and she really liked Brytag.

'I'm coming, Alahan. . . I'm still alive. . . I escaped.' The smile became a grin. 'I was a real pain in the arse too. You'd be proud of me.'

She was only whispering, but she hoped that her words would float across the air, from the top level of the siege tower to the top level of Tiergarten, letting her brother know that neither her body, her mind nor her spirit had broken.

What felt like it *would* break was the siege tower. It creaked and groaned, brute strength the only thing that forced it over the last few rocks. Either side, the other towers, six in total, rumbled on to the plains of Tiergarten, followed by tight columns of men staying behind cover. The sled crews and their whips thrashed the dogs onwards, receiving barks and bites from the abused animals.

They were gaining speed, but kept in tight formation as they moved into the open. With no rocks or gullies to obscure the army, they stretched back as far as she could see, snaking behind each tower and clanking across the snow. There were still sleds and baggage at the rear, with several large tents set up on the high ground. Rulag was too scared to fight Alahan himself and would be sneering at his enemy from a safe distance. She knew how angry that would make her brother. How could the thain of Jarvik claim superior strength when he hid behind his men?

She was now level with the High Hold of the city and had a spectacular view of Tiergarten. It dug into the mountain in irregular levels, each level starting with a wall and a gate and ending with solid rock. Shapes scuttled across the walls, looking like nothing more than ants climbing over an anthill. Glinting metal and the rusty brown of ballistae shone from the bottom level as the defenders clustered, ready to meet the siege towers. Flaming braziers were placed along the wall and huge wooden arrows were flung around on cranes by ballistae crews. Hundreds of warriors, surely more than Rulag had expected. Her smile returned as she saw banners flying over the High Hold. A wolf, howling against a rising sun, fluttered next to a weeping dragon. The heraldry of Summer Wolf and Teardrop, defiantly aloft.

'Halla's in the city,' she muttered. 'She's made it home.'

If Ingrid had a heroine, it would be Aleph Summer Wolf's daughter. Men called her One-Eye the Axe-Maiden. She was the toughest woman Ingrid had ever met. With her *and* Alahan in the city, she thought that no-one could prevail against Tiergarten, though she wasn't naive enough to disregard the thousands of grubby warriors marching behind the siege towers.

Closer and closer they moved, spreading out into a sinuous web of black and brown. The men of Ursa roared at each other, relaying commands to keep behind cover and hold formation.

The towers were kept empty so they were light enough to move quickly, but men had now moved into the bottom level and she could hear them grunting beneath her. She huddled up as best she could in the compartments above the drawbridge. She'd be able to peer forwards and see the chain-secured wooden planks drop on to the walls and the axe-men rush out. If she continued to be lucky, they would be too busy to look above them. If she was *very* lucky, she'd be able to jump down and make good her escape before the drawbridge dropped.

At intervals, the huge ballistae sprang back as they unloaded fiery arrows at the towers. A long shaft of burning wood arced towards her and thudded into the tower, several levels below.

'No, no, don't shoot at me,' she muttered, wishing she could shout to the people of Tiergarten.

Other arrows struck other towers and fires caught on the wood. One tower was struck twice and rolling red and yellow flame quickly spread, causing panic among the sled dogs at the base. The crews tried to marshal the animals, but quickly retreated from the spreading flames and abandoned the tower to a rising swell of fire.

Buckets of water that had been stored in the towers were relayed from man to man in an effort to quell the fires. She heard men frantically running up the stairs and Ingrid's tower was quickly doused from below. A fog of woodsmoke obscured the city for a moment, making her cover her mouth to muffle a cough. Her eyes stung and she looked down, through gaps in the wooden plank-work to the drawbridge level. There were now men of Ursa just below her, but they were too busy with their buckets of water to look up.

When the smoke cleared, one tower was totally engulfed in flame and two more were full of men with water, struggling to control the blaze. The other three rumbled onwards with the men, not missing a step.

The walls gained more texture, as did the faces of the men and women standing on them. The defenders were stationary, meeting the oncoming army in three ranks of steel and grit. The front rank held throwing-axes and their arms were poised, waiting for the attackers to get within range. The ballistae crews reloaded and Ingrid lay as flat as she could as the huge wooden frames released their bolts a second time.

These bolts had barrels attached and were aimed at the thin tendrils of marching men, detonating into mushroom clouds of flame as they hit the ground. She forced herself not to look, but couldn't shut out the sound of men being burned alive. It was like nothing she'd heard, a cacophony of equal parts troll, wolf, pain, fear and gurgling vomit.

So many people were dead already and they'd not even reached the walls. In that moment, with men rushing into the siege towers and the gate of Tiergarten before her, Ingrid lost any romantic ideas she may have had about war. There was no honour or glory here, no sense of why they were fighting. She imagined the average battle brother wishing he could just throw down his axe and go home. Maybe he had a farm and some children. Maybe they were waiting for him. She believed that Rulag cared – and she knew that Alahan did; but the fifth axe-hurler from the right? Did he actually want to kill another man? She thought of her father, wishing he was here, his strong arms holding her and his bearded face smiling with a kind word and a silly joke.

The towers slowed and hatches were opened, allowing the exchange of throwing-axes to begin. From the city, two volleys came in an instant, as men and women released their tensed arms. From the towers, men were cut and cleaved, but released their own axes at the defenders.

She just lay there, pressed against wood, with her hands firmly on her ears as fire and death erupted around her. Everything was muted and hazy, as if her head was underwater. She dared not look at the other towers or behind at the army. Many would have died from the flaming pitch, she knew, but nothing had stopped or slowed down.

They were so close now. Tiergarten loomed, shutting out the crisp blue sky, appearing all at once as a stone mask in front of her eyes. Hundreds of battle brothers stood firm on the first wall and hundreds more covered the higher battlements. This was not the weak city of women and farmers that Rulag had predicted. It was a well-defended block of stone and axes, not budging an inch as Rulag prodded it.

A spray of blood splashed across her face. She gasped and flapped at the air, trying to wipe the sticky film from her skin. It came from below, from the split skull of an axe-man, preparing to lower the drawbridge. As she looked in horror at the dead man and her own blood-covered hands, the level below was filling with men. She didn't look up as the siege tower thudded into the outer walls of Tiergarten, making her world stop suddenly with a violent shake.

Any hope she had of escaping first was lost in a haze of dust and shouted voices. Battles were too big for one young girl to truly process and she had no idea what was happening. At least one other tower had reached the walls and death was flowing across the battlements, conveyed by axes, glaives, punches, kicks and lots of swearing.

She crawled back to the edge of the tower. It was a long drop to the walls below and the stone was swarming with warriors, with more rushing forward from the tower. They were met by ferocious fighters wielding small hand-axes. They were dressed in leather, not chain, and looked like cloud-men of Hammerfall. They used speed to blunt the advance, but couldn't stop the sheer weight of men attacking them.

'To the left!' roared a voice from the city. 'Plug that gap. No-one gets through.'

She couldn't see who had spoken or what gap he referred to. There were gaps everywhere. No attackers had pushed beyond the forward walls, but she could now see all three siege towers against the battlements, and another one rapidly approaching. She looked behind and saw the entire army of Ursa. They were poised and ready to take their turn ascending the towers and assaulting the walls of Tiergarten.

'Push back, hold those fucking walls,' screamed a man from the city with bright red hair, swinging his axe and trying to reach the front line of defenders.

'Tricken, get men to the left,' responded a female voice from along the battlements.

'Light up the towers!' came a command, signalling the launch of a dozen small casks of pitch.

They were aimed below Ingrid's hiding place, but she felt the sudden eruption of heat as more men were set alight. Water was thrown from the tower, dousing the flames, but the pause in the assault allowed the defenders to reinforce their line.

Ingrid noticed that she was crying. The tears had started at some point after the siege towers struck the walls, but she'd not registered them. Perhaps the blood on her face had obscured them or perhaps it was so natural a reaction that her mind ignored it. She had seen so many men die in so short a time. She'd seen blood and gore on a level beyond what she could stomach. As she retched and vomited on the wooden planks, the last thing on her mind was escape.

Caw

Somehow she could hear Corvus above the deafening sounds of battle. The sound of the raven eased the twisted knot in her stomach. The bird kept cawing, but she couldn't turn her eyes skyward to look at him. It was the loudest sound in her ears, but not the most insistent. *That* honour went to the endless whistling, thudding and scraping of axes cleaving flesh. The clank of armour was secondary; the desperate shouting and roared commands came a distant third. And it seemed to be going on forever.

With shaking hands and a sore throat, she pulled herself away from the wooden floor. Not high enough to be seen, but high enough to see Corvus, perched at the top of the siege tower.

'I'm scared,' she whimpered. 'I don't know what to do.'

The raven was still, looking at her through his black eyes. She wished he could speak, somehow convey Brytag's reassuring presence to a terrified young girl. But all he did was look at her.

'What do I do? Please tell me.'

She reached for him, not daring to sit up or move too much for fear of being noticed by rampant axe-men. Her fingertips crackled at the ends of her shaking arms, blood and sweat dripping on to the wooden planks.

Corvus hopped up and down, turning his beak to scan the walls of Tiergarten. He snapped at the air, as if searching for something or someone. She focused on him, trying not to look at the battle that raged all across the forward walls of the city. She couldn't imagine how many men had died in a shattering few minutes of steel and blood.

340

Caw

Corvus had spotted something. He sprang from the wooden frame at the top of the tower and flapped his wings, rising sharply into the foggy air. He glided away from her, over the heads of fighting men and burning wood. When he stopped, his wings fluttered rapidly and he hung on to the air above the battlements, cawing at something below.

Ingrid wiped her eyes and edged forward to see what her friend had found. Her hands still shook and vomit still scratched in her throat, but she suddenly hated her hiding place and trusted that Corvus would do his best to look after her.

'What have you found?' she asked, wincing at the pain in her throat and surprised by the croaky depth to her voice.

The raven began to fly in tight circles above the adjacent siege tower, where a frenzied battle was playing out on the wide stone battlements. She struggled to focus and discern any individual warriors; it was just a texture of men and fighting, spreading in a line to left and right of her.

'I just see more men dying,' she whimpered.

Corvus gave forth a shrill caw and rose higher in the air. Below him, a man of Ursa died, looking up for an instant, frustrated at the irritating raven. The axe that had severed his neck was held by an axe-maiden with red hair and an eyepatch. It was Halla Summer Wolf.

Ingrid fought the urge to cry out, to shout at Halla and wave her arms in the air. The axe-maiden was killing men like a farmer chopping wheat, but any distraction – such as the screaming of a lost girl – would mean her death.

She looked different, somehow larger and more imposing, commanding a section of the battlements with complete authority. On either side of her, her men were chopping down warriors of Ursa, fifty men doing the work of two hundred. But still the enemies lined up in front of them.

Four siege towers now rested against the walls of Tiergarten, unloading men in their hundreds, with more lining up to bloody their axes. The ballistae still fired and pockets of flame still erupted from the icy plains, but there were too many attackers. From the rear, more armoured men of Ursa had begun to heft a huge battering ram towards the city. They held circular shields above their heads and grunted in unison, forming part of a second assault, aimed at the huge wooden gates.

'Halla!' Ingrid shouted, suddenly frantic. 'Halla! They're going to attack the gate.'

The axe-maiden didn't hear her. Her voice could not carry over the sound of axes and death. Other defenders had spied the ram now and more casks of pitch were thrown, only to bounce off raised shields with small eruptions of smoggy flame. A few men of Ursa died, but the battlements were now too chaotic for any concerted attack on the ram. The huge wooden tree-trunk hung on chains from a framework, being carried forward with chanted grunts by a hundred men. It moved quickly, weaving between ranks of battle brothers and covering the last few paces at a virtual sprint.

The sound of wood on wood was dull at first, barely audible above the noise of steel on steel, but each successive strike of the ram caused more noise, much of it consisting of the shouting from the defenders as they moved wooden planks to brace the gate. She wanted to cover her ears again and shut out the battle, retreating into silence where death and struggle couldn't penetrate, but something in her stomach forced her to keep watching.

Corvus was hovering over the inner courtyard now, cawing at the column of warriors preparing to defend the main gate. They were led by two men, one impossibly tall, wielding a hammer, and the other— it was Alahan, it was her brother. He stood next to the Order of the Hammer priest and held an arm to the sky, signalling for his men to stand ready. Ingrid looked at him, smiling as if she was seeing him for the first time in many years. In reality it had been barely one year, but everything stretched and distorted when your world had been turned upside down and you'd lost everything you knew.

She wanted to leap from the top of the tower and run to him, but her path was blocked by hundreds of fighting men and spreading piles of the dead. The jump down wasn't too far, but she'd be landing on the heads of Rulag's battle brothers and they'd kill her before she had both feet on the stone of Tiergarten.

'Alahan,' she mumbled, over and over, her voice quivering. She was so close, but perhaps further than she'd ever been. Maybe she'd have to watch him fight. Maybe she'd have to watch him die.

The gates were buckling. Each thunderous blow of the ram was accompanied by more waves of splintering wood, reaching her ears as a horrible grating sound. She didn't know how old the gates were or if they'd ever been breached, but Alahan and his men took the attack seriously, standing behind circular shields and holding axes ready.

Along the battlements, Halla had disengaged and was signalling to someone behind her. Her men had cleared a section of the walls and were throwing bundles of burning pitch into one of the towers. The men still to mount the walls had faltered and were beginning to flee back down the tower, surprised by Halla's ferocious defence. The wooden structure had caught fire and was slowing, billowing more and more black smoke into the crisp air. The battle brothers of Ursa redeployed, focusing their efforts on less well-defended sections of the wall, or lining up to flood through the gate.

'Alahan,' she mumbled again, not knowing what to do and hoping that he'd happen to look upwards and see her terrified face at the top of the tower.

He didn't see her. He just stood, axe in hand, glaring in front of him. She couldn't see the gates, but imagined her brother was staring at broken wood, trying to calm his mind for the battle to come. The old priest next to him was more stoic, his long, white beard barely ruffling in the breeze. His war-hammer was still, held casually across his chest, but she'd known enough priests not to underestimate the old man. Her uncle Magnus had told her of Old Father Brindon Crowe, a man of Rowanoco wiser and more powerful than any other who had lived. Magnus had also told her that he drank too much mead and was a miserable old git. Ingrid didn't care about the last bit, as long as the priest stood next to her brother and kept him alive.

Then the gate exploded inwards. She saw planks of wood flying into the air and men dying from huge splinter wounds.

'This is our ground!' screamed Alahan, charging at the gates.

He didn't look back or wait for men to follow him; he just ran, his face a mask of focus and anger. He disappeared beyond her sight and Ingrid held her breath. She could hear fighting and shouting, but not see the battle itself.

'Don't die, don't die!' she cried.

She glanced back and saw hundreds of men of Ursa queuing to rush the broken gates.

'Now!' roared Halla, leaping atop the battlements and swinging her axe high in the air.

Nothing happened for a moment, then a series of guttural shouts echoed from the north of the city. The paths leading up to Giant's Gift erupted with warriors, tattooed in blue and frothing at the mouth. They were like no men of Ranen Ingrid had ever seen. Most were bare-chested and swung strange axes, not made of metal or wood.

'Varorg!' screamed the leader, soundly unnaturally like a troll.

They were few, maybe two hundred, but they made an almighty mess as they sliced into the columns of men, arrayed before the city. They moved in a wedge, from north to south, following the arc of the city walls and taking the attackers by complete surprise. The two remaining siege towers were suddenly empty of warriors as the blue men caused havoc on the plains below. Each of them carried only a huge axe, forgoing a shield and relying purely on strength. Some died and most were wounded, but they didn't seem to care. In fact, they screamed louder and appeared happier every time they were cut. There were still many thousands of men on the plains, but enough had worked against them that they were now on the back foot.

But the real advantage came when the line of men by the gate was severed. With no reinforcements, the attack faltered. The brute shock and suicidal frenzy of the blue men's attack had allowed Alahan's men to clear the gateway and they now rushed forward to assist the blue men outside the walls.

A horn sounded from the rear, carrying from the gullies of the Crystal Fork to the walls of Tiergarten. Rulag was signalling a withdrawal. Both sides had lost many warriors, but the defenders had proven far more obstinate than the lord of Jarvik could have expected. Even Ingrid, shaken out of her confidence by the realities of battle, had been surprised by the resistance on display.

'They're running,' boomed Old Father Crowe. 'Stand fast, let 'em have the plains. We keep the walls.'

'Get rid of those fucking towers,' commanded Halla.

The battlements were still alive with combat, but the defenders now rallied behind the axe-maiden and, with no reinforcements, the attackers were quickly pushed back or killed. Flaming torches and more pitch were thrown at the towers and Ingrid took a final look behind her. Before she jumped down, on to blood-red stone, she flashed a grin at the fleeing men. They weren't beaten, but they were bruised enough to prove a point. She hoped that Rulag Ursa, skulking somewhere out of danger, now believed her. Alahan really wasn't that easy to kill.

CHAPTER TWENTY-ONE

SAARA THE MISTRESS OF PAIN IN THE CITY OF RO WEIR

S HE IMAGINED A huge tower, built in the centre of Weir. It would be narrow, black and featureless, commanding awe and fear from any who saw it – and it would be seen for miles inland and miles out to sea. Within, she would build unlighted chambers and twisted corridors, the angles and turns of which would be known only to her. On the top level, she would sit on a throne and look out across her Tyranny, through the only window.

If her thralls braved the dark labyrinth of her tower, she'd allow them to seek counsel, but all other lesser creatures would remain as ants, crawling this way and that as her whim dictated. Some would be enchanted, others would serve out of fear, most would be compliant for the depraved excess she allowed. In time, the Tyranny of Weir would be as a hand, fitting delicately into a glove of pleasure and pain. It would become the only reality she would allow.

Her vision was crystal-clear, as if the tower was already built and the land already subdued. Shub-Nillurath pulled her close and showed her the future, whispering of pleasure and pain. She no longer doubted. The Forest Giant embraced her, clutching her to his chest and strengthening her mind. People called his name in rapture and she felt his infectious power returned to the world, like insects crawling on her skin. Soon, enough of his might would have returned for the sky to split, and the Forest Giant to claim his land in person.

She had no illusions of unity between Tyrants. Her position

346

would be given by Shub-Nillurath, but he would not lift a tentacle to support her. Nor would he care to support the Jekkan Tyrant of the Fell or the Aberration, in whichever corner of the land it ended up. She imagined that rivalry between the Tyrants would define their existence.

* * *

Back in the dusty vault, she willed the cloud-stone into life. The glassy orb had been vibrating for hours as someone desperately tried to contact her, but she'd remained unmoved, concentrating on her own needs before those of her thralls. With a wave of her hand, a rugged face appeared in the stone, framed by a dirty brown beard and angry eyes of the deepest green.

'Finally. Do you see me, bitch?' barked Rulag Ursa, communicating with her from half a world away. He backed away from the stone and revealed a semi-circle of bloodied warriors, all scowling at her. On the ground before them, nursing the stump of his arm, was Kal Varaz, the wind claw she'd sent to Fjorlan. 'And do you see him?'

Rulag grabbed a fistful of the wind claw's hair and showed his badly beaten face. Both eyes were swollen closed and his jaw was a deep crimson. 'This man lied to me about your fucking trees,' snapped the lord of Jarvik. 'That means you fucking lied to me.'

She tried to remain composed, but small twitches of irritation kept appearing at the corners of her mouth. 'Speak plain, my lord Bear Tamer,' she said with an ominous purr.

'Your risen men, darkwood trees. . . Dark Young, whatever the fuck they are. They're being torn apart all along the Crystal Fork River.' Absently, the loathsome warlord kicked Kal Varaz in the face and rendered him unconscious. 'Trolls ain't never had so good a meal.'

'The city stands?' she asked.

'Yes, it fucking stands,' he shouted. 'It stands and it fights – like the Ice Giant himself has sharpened their axes. Bad luck has plagued us since we left Fredericksand.'

She thought quickly. Her campaign in Ranen had not gone smoothly since the day Rham Jas Rami killed Ameira in Ro Canarn. Every thrall she had had in the lands of Ranen, phantom or otherwise, had been killed. She had no generals to suppress the peasants and lesser men of the Freelands, but still Rulag could be useful. If her Dark Young had been bested by Rowanoco's Ice Men, she'd have to rely on the axes of brutish ignorant men.

'You must take the city,' she insisted. 'You must eradicate every drop of blood from the family of Teardrop. Only then will you truly be the Tyrant of Fjorlan.'

'Fuck you!' screamed Ursa. 'I'll take the city, but we're through. I don't need you *or* Rowanoco to make me thain of Fjorlan. I'll take it with strength.'

To punctuate his point, he stomped violently on Kal Varaz's head with a heavy, steel-shod boot. Three, four, five times he stamped downwards, until the wind claw was a twitching mess with half a head, splayed on the bloody ice of Fjorlan. With a roar he then drew his axe and smashed the cloud-stone into a thousand pieces.

'Fool,' she muttered, once her own stone had returned to a cloudy sleep. 'He destroys an item more valuable than his life in a fit of pique.'

She took some deep breaths and calmed her mind. She lamented the failure of her campaign in Ranen, but it didn't sting like it might once have done. One day, when Tor Funweir was firmly under her heel, she'd lead her host north and conquer the lands of ice properly. Perhaps Rowanoco was indeed stronger than the One or Jaa. And perhaps she had been naive to trust in the fool of Ursa. The Freelands had stubbornly repulsed her attack, and Fjorlan was clearly more dogged than she'd predicted. Let them have their ice and their Earth Shaker. Their time would come when Shub-Nillurath had returned to his true might and majesty.

She left the vault and tucked the cloud-stone away in a thick canvas pouch, tied to her belt. She was at the base of the knight marshal's barracks, in dusty catacombs unused for decades, where stone vaults plunged away into impenetrable darkness. She'd sent trusted aides into the dark bowels of Ro Weir and found lost dungeons and vast passageways by the score. In the furthest of the vaults, behind a circular door of chiselled stone, Saara went to visit her last remaining sister.

Isabel the Seductress was motionless, chained to the floor with her eyes rolled back in her head. Her mind was reduced to a globe of lost consciousness, smashed into submission by phantom thralls. She couldn't think clearly enough to move, or even to scream. She could laugh and she could drool, but nothing more.

'Sleep well, sister,' she said, stroking back Isabel's matted hair. 'You will be here for centuries, shouldering this burden for me. I hope you know how much I love you – how much I need you. Your pain is a gift from Shub-Nillurath. Do not flee from it.'

She wished Isabel could be at peace, but she was writhing in sharp internal torment and Saara knew it.

'Your sacrifice is necessary. As sanity leaves you, know that *I* will remain. And, as more Sisters rise in Oron Kaa, I will insist they pay their respects to your inert body. You will be an altar to pleasure and pain as the Tyranny of the Twisted Tree claws into this land.'

Within Isabel's mind was a cage, a maelstrom of faces and names. Everyone enchanted by the Seven Sisters dwelt in the bowels of her consciousness, howling in resistance. Each thrall was met by a barrier of divine might, blocking their attempts to reach Saara. Instead they had consumed Isabel and were now locked away in an empty vessel.

She backed away from her sister and left the vault. Flickering red torch-light danced across the grey stone, providing minimal illumination. The catacombs were vast and labyrinthine. It was the only place she could truly be alone. No-one followed her down here, not even Elihas. Many levels above, her followers fucked and drank and smoked drugs, revelling in their new-found freedom. Ro and Karesians, lost in pleasure and pain – each one was a shell, with nothing to offer Saara but compliance. They were people of influence, wealth and power. Now they gave all they had to the new order. To the Lands of the Twisted Tree.

She walked down a long stone corridor, lost for centuries underneath Weir. From the wall, rotting weeds thrust from every gap, and a thick dampness permeated the air. Towards the end of the passageway, she turned a sharp corner and entered the catacombs. The Dark Young swayed in the fetid air somewhere in the darkness, beyond her sight. She held her arms wide and closed her eyes, drinking in the divine energy dribbling from the trees. She couldn't see them, but their presence was enough to elicit a tinkle of pleasure, travelling up her spine to caress her mind.

'We are as one,' she intoned. 'Bless me with your strength.'

She felt a rumble and a vibration in the air. The Young swayed, left to right, shimmering through the veil of darkness. She knew they felt her. They stayed planted in the earth, not moving to attack or investigate. They would be her final triumph. Far above, tunnels were prepared, leading from the Hawkwood Gate of Weir to the deep catacombs. When the time came, the thousand Young would take the slow journey upwards and into the light of Tor Funweir.

Then the Aberration howled. She could feel it in the darkness, not moving like the others but hunkered down and hissing. It had a savagery and bloodlust that set it apart from the lesser Young. It was the only creature she feared, as if a part of Shub-Nillurath's hatred scratched within. It had eaten hundreds of men, consumed them to the last shred of bone, but still it hungered.

* * *

When she was appropriately dressed in a high-collared black dress of thick satin, she rejoined the thralls, fighting her war in the stark daylight of Ro Weir.

'My lady, please watch your step,' said a nearby wind claw, offering her his hand.

She reached the top of the regular stone steps and approached the duke's balcony, above the King's Highway, from where her senior aides directed their forces. Suddenly her senses were assaulted by thousands upon thousands of warriors. Below her, on the forward battlements of Weir she saw ranks of Hounds, wind claws and soldiers of Ro; on the muster fields of Weir were tens of thousands more, and on the horizon, low to the dawn sky, were the armies of Ro, sending flashes of red and steel across the open ground.

'Have we sent emissaries?' she asked.

The wind claw pointed to a cluster of dead men and three white flags, heaped on the grass between the two forces. 'I don't think these Ro want to talk, my lady.'

She smiled, finding the brutality of her opponents intriguing. In a different life, she'd have got to Alexander Tiris first and ensured his loyalty. He and his Hawks would have been fearsome allies and this battle would not be necessary. As it stood, Saara saw the coming conflict as little more than a theatrical opportunity to unveil the Thousand Young of Shub-Nillurath.

From an adjacent staircase, Elihas of Du Ban emerged. The Black cleric of Ro, encased in his plate armour, was as stoic as always, sparing not even a glance at the armies before Ro Weir.

'Our little war reaches its end,' said Elihas. 'Just a few more people to kill and Tor Funweir will be under heel.'

Reports were delivered by a dozen whip-masters and Ro commanders, chattering in her ear about this thing or that. She discarded much of what they told her, listening only to the information she deemed important. The king of Tor Funweir had some fifty thousand warriors, formed up into mixed companies, with at least a third of them mounted. They had some risen men in their ranks, and the army flew many different banners. Canarn, Haran, Tiris, Arnon, and others she didn't recognize.

'How sweet,' she muttered. 'It appears they have united against me.'

'My lady,' began Elihas, 'we have assembled as many Hounds as can be spared without leaving Arnon and Leith vulnerable. They number eighty thousand. They're awaiting orders.'

The Hounds were everywhere on the dusty green plains of Weir, squeezing into every corner of the muster fields and eclipsing the outlying farmsteads. The glare from their armour created a distortion and played tricks on her eyes. It looked like nothing more than a carpet of black metal, some new addition to the landscape where once there had been grass and trees.

'Hold position,' she said. 'They are to encircle the city, covering every inch of the wall – with one exception.'

'The Hawkwood Gate?' offered Elihas.

She nodded. 'Keep it clear. And have only heavily drugged Hounds near it.'

'And if Tiris just charges?'

'Hold position,' she repeated. 'If they want to reach the walls, let them dig their way through eighty thousand Hounds who can't run away.'

Elihas smirked. It was the only humour his face seemed to allow and conveyed more scorn than amusement. 'I can feel thousands of lives about to end. The Black aspect is happy this day – and my life's work reaches its end.'

'And when your work is done?' she mused. 'Will you finally submit to me?'

His smirk disappeared and he looked her in the eye, perhaps the only man in Weir who would dare to do so. 'I'll make you a deal,' he growled. 'If you can enchant me, I'm yours. If not, you're mine.'

For an instant, Saara considered entering his thoughts then and there, taking time out from the war to start to weave her enchantments into the cleric's mind. But it wasn't possible. To enthral Elihas would be the work of many months' patient endeavour. She resolved to use him as a treat when the killing was done.

'Their deployment is ragged,' said Elihas. 'They're not following their fabled battle-tactics. It'll take a while for them to muster for a charge.'

'Prepare a few packs to pursue when the king is dead and the Hawks run away, but until then hold position.'

Saara felt a surge of pain enter her head, as if a thin needle drove its way into her troubled mind. Somewhere below, scratching in the catacombs, the Dark Young were calling to her and, in the centre of the cacophony, the Aberration screamed. She winced, reaching forward to lean heavily on the balcony's edge. A dozen men moved to assist, but she waved them back and composed herself.

'You have your orders,' she snapped, rubbing the sides of her head. 'All you have to do is stand still – surely you can do that without my assistance.'

Elihas hadn't moved to help her, but he now took over, shouting orders at wind claws and whip-masters. He cast a sideways glance at Saara, but otherwise ignored her as she hurried to the nearby stone steps. She tried to maintain her poise, but the stabbing pain in her head made her flinch every few steps. She was a slender woman in a dress among dozens of heavily armoured men, but each one fled from her, not daring to catch her eye or even stay in her field of vision.

At the bottom of the spiral steps, she thrust her arm against the nearby wall and edged along it. With a few deep breaths, and a moment of calm, she pushed the pain to the back of her head and entered her private sitting room, slamming the door behind her. The surge of the Dark Young was powerful but not aggressive, almost as if they cowered before the sharp voice that rose from among them.

She lay face down on her bed and flailed on her dressing table for her pipe. With the pain making it scarcely possible to see, she loaded the pipe with rainbow smoke and pulled the thick vapour into her lungs through quivering lips. The drug took the edge off the pain, but mostly just made the call sharper and more distinct. It was summoning her.

* * *

Saara stood in the huge stone entranceway that led to the dark catacombs, and stopped. The way behind her was open and clear, leading from the depths of the city to the Hawkwood Gate. The city streets were like a ghost town, as if awaiting the Thousand

353

Young of Shub-Nillurath. They were restlessly on the move. They'd scuttled through vast, stone vaults and crawled upwards to meet her, displacing the air as a noxious flood of tentacles and madness. They called to her, but their voices were a murmur next to the roar of the Aberration. She beckoned them upwards, fighting the pain in her head and trying to focus on the work to be done.

She walked through a misty line where darkness eclipsed daylight and saw a texture of writhing, black bodies. They filled the passageway, crawling over each other to bubble forward as an eruption of fleshy madness. At the front, with clear stone between it and the rest of them, was the Aberration that had been Rham Jas. For the first time, it appeared in the open, allowing her to see it.

It shared only its cracked, black flesh with its brothers and sisters, being different in every other way. It had a small, muscular body, suspended on four thick tentacles, each ending with a mass of wriggling feelers. From the cleft where its two front legs met rose an elongated head, sharp at both ends and split with a mockery of a human face. It moved like a sinewy panther, with hundreds of feelers padding on the stone like paws.

'Come to me, creature,' she said, arms beckoning, 'come into the light.'

It paused in front of her, making the mass of Dark Young stop dead in the tunnel. They swarmed over each other, reaching forward but apparently too afraid to pass the Aberration. Saara thought it worrying behaviour, but was determined not to show any fear in front of the creature as it craned its lithe body to look down at her. The face was locked into a black scream of anguish, just as it had been when the Kirin first died. The eyes, mouth and nose were all stretched across the middle of its pulpy, angular head, clad in a hundred different shades of black. It wrinkled and contorted, twisting into pain, then hate, then pain again. She wanted to feed off its suffering, but it wouldn't let her. She wanted to feel its mind and caress the divine spark of Shub-Nillurath, but it was closed to her.

The eyes became suddenly white, as if milky orbs had thrust upwards through the flesh of the face. She gasped as they looked at her, showing a maddening awareness of where it was. Its head swayed from side to side, then up and down, slowly assessing her.

'We are both of us servants of Shub-Nillurath,' she whispered, hesitantly reaching for the creature. 'The Twisted Tree has claimed these lands. But lesser beings say otherwise. They have risen up against our power. You must rise into the light and obliterate them. Will you kill the king for me?'

She touched its face and it let her, blinking its bone-white eyes and hunkering down, level with her. She stroked its head, moving her palm across a grotesque doppelganger of Rham Jas Rami. Her movements were tentative; she expected the Aberration to rear up at any second. But it stayed at eye-level, regarding her with chaos in its eyes.

'The battlefield awaits. Reveal the Twisted Trees to these lesser mortals.'

The creature shook with a sudden mania, its legs rippling with a glistening muscularity. The face split as sticky tendrils snapped apart to reveal a gummy mouth, from which guttural sounds began to spew. The creature was trying to speak. The orifice puckered and spat, but she could discern no meaning in its spewing, just strange syllables connected by throaty gurgles. As the mouth pulsed and formed simple lips, the sounds became clearer. She stood transfixed, unable to scream or leave as the Aberration spoke through gnashing, glass-like teeth.

'We are the priest. . . we are the altar.'

The words could have come from no mortal mouth, and the meaning carried a sea of emotion – raw, unhinged emotion. It snapped forward, its newly formed mouth inches from her face. She jumped backwards, but the Aberration didn't attack. The creature rose back to its full height and screeched. It was high-pitched, like fingernails on glass, and made the other Dark Young flail madly and pull themselves forward.

The white eyes turned back to her and Sara felt her mind being penetrated. All of her power, all of her years – none of it meant anything as the Aberration took control. But it didn't harm her. She could instantly feel that it was somehow unable to. It wanted to show her something and she had no choice but to see it.

* * *

She saw the Tyranny of Arnon. A hundred black spires, slicing into the air and a thousand voices, rising in exquisite pain. At the centre of the massed towers, sitting astride a many-faceted throne, was the Aberration. As it festered in the catacombs of Ro Weir, the creature had imagined its future. It knew much, having taken knowledge from the dark-blood, and had already decided that Ro Arnon would be its future domain. It liked the rocky pinnacles and felt the towers of the Gold church were worthy of the creature's majesty. It thought much of itself; it felt that it was a superior form of life.

She looked closer. The Aberration had an army of thralls spread throughout its land, informing, and infesting everyone with paranoia. It would control them through brutality, but never reveal its motivations or allow them to see its designs. Saara was amazed at how far ahead it had thought. To the creature that had been Rham Jas, the king of Tor Funweir was already dead and the Tyranny of the Twisted Tree was firmly under heel. It hadn't considered defeat for an instant, never doubting that it would rule its own land as Tyrant. Its subjects would understand that it was absolute ruler and would do as it wished: without law, without morality and without consequence.

Saara wanted to see herself in the creature's future, but it had no regard for her. Perhaps it had chosen Arnon because Saara already ruled in Weir. But there was nothing in the Aberration's thoughts to suggest this. There was nothing in its thoughts regarding her at all. It thought her barely superior to the peasants and lesser men of Ro. She imagined the only thing that kept it from killing her on a whim was her tireless service to Shub-Nillurath, for even in its imagined future, she could sense the creature's devotion to the Forest Giant of pleasure and blood. Or perhaps there was more: behind the hatred and arrogance, Saara realized that the Aberration saw her as an equal and that the thought was disturbing to the creature. It made them rivals.

The vision was so real, giving her a clear picture of a world where the Twisted Tree held absolute authority. The remaining warriors of Ro were a minor problem, insignificant in the span of centuries she'd have to rule. If only they realized. . . if they could see the future she'd seen, they'd surrender.

* * *

The Aberration gave her a final, spite-filled glance, then pounced over her head and towards the light of Ro Weir, shimmering into a barely visible shadow as it moved. She remained a helpless statue, as the thousand Young of Shub-Nillurath writhed past her, squeezing their fleshy, black bodies round her and after their master. She closed her eyes, letting the sea of thick tentacles wash over her. She was buffeted, but only gently, and after a maddening few minutes the column of thrashing beasts had passed by.

She opened her eyes and turned back towards the daylight. The last few Dark Young were just crawling out of the catacombs and seeing the sky for the first time. She could hear muffled screams, as a few stray pairs of human eyes dared to look upon the creatures.

She did not feel powerless or mundane; far from it. She felt as if a future rival had revealed itself. A creature as malevolent and cunning as she herself was.

'Matron mother,' she whispered to the air, 'can you hear me? I have news of our triumph. And news of an enemy.'

CHAPTER TWENTY-TWO

DALIAN THIEF TAKER IN ORON KAA

HE KNEW WHO he was. His sense of identity had returned and the greatest of the wind claws walked again in the realms of form. He had flowed into his new body not knowing what would happen. Anger and faith had driven him on, driven him to possess the mindless shell of the exemplar, driven him even to kill Utha the Ghost. But now, as every wisp of his divine energy settled into the mortal body, he knew that he lived again. Voon was gone, but Jaa now had an exemplar of true might and conviction; and Dalian had a much younger body, with feet that did not constantly hurt. He chuckled to himself.

'What's funny?' asked the young man of Ro, limping along next to him.

'I appear to be Dalian Thief Taker,' he replied.

'That's not funny,' said Randall.

The Thief Taker had barely noticed that he carried a dead body down endless stone steps with a young man and a Gorlan mother. His thoughts were so vibrant and alive, as if Voon's relative youth had rekindled a spark of energy in the old wind claw. He couldn't help but imagine all the wonderful things his youthful body was now capable of.

'Can you hurry up?' said the young squire, fixating on the limp figure, hanging from Dalian's powerful arms.

'We have time,' said Ruth. 'As long as the Shan within him lives, his human body is sustained. However it may look.'

'The Shan didn't live in his chest, did it?' asked Randall. 'Because that's where the spear went.'

Dalian glanced over his shoulder at the finely crafted spear across his back. He knew it was called Zarzenfang, and that it was far less appropriate than two kris knives, but Voon had greatly valued it and the Thief Taker would honour the weapon.

As he briefly looked back, he saw hateful eyes glaring at him. Randall was a powerful young man – perhaps more than a man – and all of his ire was directed at Dalian.

'We met in the Dokkalfar settlement, didn't we?' he asked, gradually increasing his pace down the steps.

Randall screwed up his face, surprised at Dalian's manner. 'Yes. You were with Nanon and the bloody Kirin.'

'Rham Jas, yes,' replied Dalian, enjoying the flood of familiar memories. 'Unfortunately, he is dead. We failed in killing the Sister.'

The young man of Ro just twisted his mouth into stupid, gormless expressions. Dalian felt a modicum of sympathy; Randall *had* been through much, without the benefit of divine certitude.

'We are nearly at the tear,' he stated, feeling a crackle across his skin.

'Then hurry up,' said Randall, focusing on the only thing he cared about.

The stairs levelled out and Dalian carried Utha's body along a wide, jagged passageway. Left and right, the stone was adorned with intricate carvings of thrashing beasts and wailing supplicants. Something about the sweep of the designs made him think they had been carved by the insects, perhaps using their wings to scrape the stone and their puckered mouths to refine the details.

'I don't understand the need of wicked people to display their wickedness,' he mused. 'Such heresy belongs in unadorned darkness, gawked at by its ignorant followers and those that brave the shadows.'

'*What* are you talking about?' asked Randall. 'Why are you talking at all?'

He decided to keep his musings on heresy for a later time and concentrate on getting the Ghost to the tear. Though he felt no guilt for killing the Old Blood, he understood the Gorlan's desire that it should not be Utha's end. For want of any immediate alternative, Dalian was prepared to ally with the ancient creature – if it meant the death of the matron mother.

He felt a crackle at the back of his neck. His new body was less hairy than the previous one, and Voon's smooth skin made him shiver with an unearthly chill. The air was alive with energy, dancing from jagged rocks and shimmering in their wake. Everything was a dull green, with sharp edges of sickly light touching their arms and legs. Randall gasped with surprise and scratched frantically at his crackling hands, but the Gorlan calmed him with a thin smile.

'It is divine energy,' said the woman.

'It is rotten energy,' replied Dalian. 'Seeping from a tear in the world.'

'You are in no position to make judgements,' she said. 'It was your Fire Giant who allowed this to happen.'

He was too controlled to lash out and too wise to think a sudden rebuke would make any difference, but her words were deeply insulting. Jaa did what he did in the distant corners of deep time and his actions were not to be questioned by lesser creatures, even a Gorlan mother.

'I said that your impudence would be remembered. We are equally good at remembering blasphemy.'

'Spare me,' she replied, raising her arms and revealing that the rotten energy did not touch her or Randall as it did Dalian. 'Do you know what an Old One is, Dalian Thief Taker?'

He'd heard the term, but only as a vague mention in heretical accounts of the time before Jaa. 'What relevance does it have?'

'If you had occasion to converse with your Giant, you should ask him if *he* considers me blasphemous or if he knows the name Atlach-Nacha. I think he would show due respect.'

He didn't change expression. Voon's face was naturally dour and Dalian was glad of the stony expression. He didn't like admitting that he didn't know things and Jaa had not thought to bestow upon him any knowledge of the Old Ones or the importance they played. In the short term, it was the wise course to comply with the Gorlan's wishes.

'I don't wish to interrupt,' said Randall, 'but Utha is still dead.'

Dalian looked down at the limp body he carried. He was strong enough that the albino weighed virtually nothing, but his expression, even hanging in a death mask, showed a strength worthy of respect.

'I apologize, Randall. I forgot who it was I carried.'

'Just hurry up!' snapped the squire. 'And stop arguing about Giants and Old Ones. I don't give a shit. I only give a shit about Utha – and you put a spear through his chest.'

'Then let us hurry,' said Dalian, quickening his pace along the divinely charged passageway.

The crackling green energy thickened and spread like mould over the floor and walls. He could ignore it, but felt that Randall would be more vulnerable to the rotting power of Shub-Nillurath. This concern disappeared when he saw how the Gorlan mother stood over the young man. Dalian could sense a protective barrier, flowing like spider silk from the woman to envelop Randall in an invisible cloak, through which the corruption of the Dead God could not penetrate. Dalian hoped that their collective immunity would anger the matron mother, perhaps drive her to do something foolish.

The passage widened and the walls became more jagged, with pits and tunnels cut into the surface. It was as if the stone itself was rotting.

Ruth moved ahead, emerging into a large, glowing cavern. A globe of rotten energy was repelled by her presence, darting backwards into darkness. Randall followed into the cavern and his eyes widened as he saw the tear for the first time. The cave was high and deep, ringed with stalactites and pitted rock, plunging into deep tunnels and dark fissures. The tear itself was a sharp cut in the air, wavering like a flag in the wind and belching forth fetid green energy. It had no front, back or sides. It was a rend in reality, a gateway through which one world touched another.

It was the first time Dalian had seen it as well. When he'd passed through, in search of Voon, he'd been merely a shade, unconcerned by the tear, or perhaps in too much of a hurry. Now, seeing it through mortal eyes, he was repulsed by it.

'Remain here,' said Ruth, indicating the cavern entrance. She then strode down the wide terrace to the cave floor and raised her head to breathe in the stagnant air.

Randall obeyed Ruth without question, skulking in a greenish shadow at the end of the stone passageway. Dalian didn't hide or cower, nor did he drop the Old Blood. He did as the Gorlan mother asked purely for the sake of ease. If the old spider was here to kill her daughter, who was the exemplar of Jaa to argue? The old woman had twisted the faith of the Fire Giant and deserved to die for her heresy.

Ruth was a small figure, gliding smoothly across the pitted stone towards the tear, though her eyes were constantly moving from one dark cave entrance to another. Then she stopped and began to change shape. Dalian narrowed his eyes to see through the black shadows and crackling green energy. The woman began to stretch, then swell, then contort, until a huge, brightly patterned spider crouched in the cavern. She was thick-limbed and hairy, with vibrating feelers and huge, downward-curving fangs.

'This visit is overdue,' croaked a voice from the darkness. 'You look old, my mother.'

The huge spider reared up, raising her front two legs off the ground and baring her fangs. It was a threat display that would terrify a lesser creature or one not already blessed with the divine fear of Jaa.

'I warned you,' said the matron mother. 'But you stayed in your hole and ignored me. It is *I* who have done this thing, for my own power, and you may not take it. You will wither and decay while I am queen of this world.'

Ruth hissed at the air, her vibrating feelers producing a shrill echo around the cavern. Slowly, the sound formed into recognizable words and the Gorlan mother replied to her offspring. 'Madness has infected you, daughter. A madness borne on the wings of fear – fear of your end.'

The matron mother laughed, the sound appearing from darkness and displacing Ruth's hiss. Dalian couldn't tell in which hole she skulked, nor if she was alone, but there was confidence in her laughter, as if she'd lured them into a trap.

'Your games of intimidation are lost on me,' hissed Ruth. 'Face me: now!'

Dalian heard a strange clacking sound. He turned sharply to see that Randall's teeth were chattering. The young squire had a hand clamped round the hilt of his old longsword and his feet shuffled nervously.

'Easy, lad,' said the Thief Taker. 'I don't think you or I have a part to play in this struggle.'

Randall scowled at him, his eyes drawn to Utha's dead body, before he managed a response. 'Just shut up,' he mumbled, embarrassed.

In the crackling cave, Ruth moved further away from them, spreading her thick legs wide, but keeping her fangs bared. She passed the shimmering tear and planted her front legs before a patch of muddy, green darkness. Her feelers twitched in the air, using a sense not available to Dalian to locate her errant daughter.

'You have nowhere left to run,' hissed Ruth. 'Your dead god cannot help you.'

When the matron mother appeared, she had shed her human form. Long, slender legs of black and gold reached out of the darkness, planting their spiked ends on sickly green rock. A wide face and a long, tapered abdomen followed, revealing a huge, golden spider with flashes of black dotted across its body. There was nothing of the cracked old woman, no sign of her wrinkled body or hateful eyes. Her leg-span was as large as her mother's, but she was far more spindly. Ruth was thick-bodied with heavy legs, whereas the matron mother was light and nimble, with a fragility not seen anywhere in Ruth's huge, hairy form.

'I hate spiders,' said Randall, through quivering lips and chattering teeth.

'They're Gorlan, not spiders,' replied Dalian, echoing the squire's own words. 'Perhaps the first time for a millennium that two of this size have been seen together.'

The two Gorlan mothers circled each other amidst arcs of rotten green energy. Ruth stayed in the centre of the cavern, watching closely as the matron mother moved over the higher, pitted rocks around the tear. Dalian didn't share Randall's fear, but still found the creatures awe-inspiring. They were true beings of deep time, all but forgotten in the lands of men, but mightier even than the reborn wind claw.

When they clashed, it was the matron mother who attacked first, causing a dark distortion between them that even the green energy could not penetrate. Her long legs snapped downwards at Ruth's head, to be swatted aside in a flurry of dizzying movement. Their legs met in the air, flashing more darkness across the cavern each time they clashed. It was as if small pockets of ancient energy erupted in the air, signalling to the cosmos that two Gorlan mothers fought. Each attack, each defence, each time their fangs flashed forwards, there was a surge of blackness. It was impossible to tell who had the upper hand. Ruth was slower, but much heavier, and used her thick legs to keep the nimble black and gold spider at bay. Though their fangs were bared, neither landed a bite as they maintained a stand-off from the tips of their flailing legs.

'Can we help?' murmured Randall, largely to himself.

'Be my guest,' replied Dalian. 'However, I believe *I* will remain here.'

He could sense the young man's head whirring. He still kept half an eye on his dead master, but was not so distracted as to step out of the shadows, or get too close to the battling Gorlan.

Ruth was still hissing, filling the cavern with ancient anger, while her daughter remained silent, striking out from the pitted rock with dizzying flicks of her front legs. Her movements forward and back were too fast for Dalian to follow closely, but he saw Ruth's reactions struggle to meet every attack. Even so, the older Gorlan did not appear to be in any distress, as if she were conserving her energy while letting the matron mother exhaust herself. It was a brand of combat unknown to the Thief Taker, its ebbs and flows incomprehensible to a man who relied on blade and armour.

Then Ruth leapt upwards. Four of her thick legs pushed down and extended, like the release of a powerful spring, propelling her at her daughter. The matron mother tried to shuffle sideways, but Ruth's mass was difficult to avoid. A hiss and a squeal followed, accompanied by the frenetic clicking of opposing legs. Half their struggle was lost in shadows, but it appeared to Dalian that Ruth had pushed her daughter against the wall. The older Gorlan's huge, hairy abdomen twitched up and down, sending flashes of red and yellow hair through the rotten green twilight of the tear. Then a sickening pulpy sound filled the cavern as Ruth pivoted to fling her offspring back into the light. The matron mother writhed on her back, exposing two shallow bite marks in her underside as she tried to right herself.

It was the closest he had been to the lesser Gorlan. In the light, he thought her gold and black markings were strangely beautiful, giving her abdomen the appearance of a flower with its petals yet to open. Her legs had the same banded pattern as they clicked inwards, trying to gain purchase on the pitted stone floor. Ruth approached slowly, spreading her eight huge legs, but her movements were now lopsided and a pulpy wound above her eyes oozed pus on to the green rock.

Randall gasped in pain and took a step out of the darkness, feeling the distress of the Gorlan mother.

'Stay back, boy,' warned Dalian, but the young man ignored him and unsheathed his old longsword. His remaining wounds had disappeared, either through the obscuring darkness or some eldritch ability to heal. The fetid green light whirled around him, but was repelled. Not by Ruth's power, but by Randall's own slowly emerging might.

'It's my fault,' murmured the man of Ro. 'If she'd not given of herself to save me, she'd be stronger.'

The matron mother ignored the approaching young man and managed to pull herself upright, facing Ruth. The larger Gorlan rubbed her feelers across her eyes, trying to clear blood from her vision. Her movements were jerky, as if her legs struggled to support her bulk. Her daughter was also wounded, but had less weight to carry, and raised her front legs in a final, defiant challenge. The two huge spiders circled each other, warily keeping their wounds out of range of attack. The matron mother turned until her forked spinnerets faced Randall, flickering in the air like a hand with missing fingers.

Dalian didn't know if the young squire was afraid. He certainly didn't show any fear as he gripped his longsword in both hands and hacked at the Gorlan's abdomen. The creature stood twice as tall as Randall, but the savage cut in its black and yellow body drove it downwards, until its belly pressed against the green-lit stone. It hissed and twitched, its spindly legs drumming loudly against the ground as it tried to turn. Randall backed away, narrowly avoiding being struck.

Then Ruth seized her opportunity and pounced. She plunged her vicious fangs downwards into her daughter's fragile-looking body. Again and again she struck. Shiny droplets of venom oozed from her fangs and bubbled within the matron mother's dying body. The attack was frenzied and terrifying, causing huge blobs of black energy to blink into being and disappear around the two Gorlan mothers. The green lightning from the tear suddenly darkened, as if afraid of what was happening. Shub-Nillurath's high priestess was dying, her body slowly dissolving from corrosive venom and curling upwards into a skeletal hand with eight twitching fingers.

When the matron mother stopped moving, Ruth backed away, though the rotten arcs of green light did not return. The Gorlan mother was badly wounded and it took time for her to pull her bulk back into her slender human form. Randall stood by her until she was fully transformed, and helped her up. She had no obvious wounds, but she clearly needed the young man's strength to stand.

'Hurry,' said Ruth. 'Bring Utha.'

'I must commend you, great mother,' replied Dalian. 'I have never seen such an expression of pure power.'

She glared. 'Commend Randall, he will soon be all that is left of my power.'

'Just hurry up,' snapped Randall, approaching the tear.

Dalian made his way to the bottom of the cavern, staying well clear of the dead Gorlan mother. Even with her legs turned inwards and green pus oozing from her body, she was intimidating. But he focused on the tear and joined the other two, basking in its grotesque, rotten energy. It was glassy, like a distended orb of green and black, ripping through reality in a single, gaping slice.

'The power of the Dead God is weakened,' said the Thief Taker, as the fetid green energy retreated to the tear. 'Perhaps if we collapse the tunnel—'

'Throw him through the tear,' snapped Ruth, wiping hair from her snarling face.

'What?' enquired Randall. 'Can I go with him?'

She straightened and put a hand on the young man's shoulder. 'Your journey with him is over, young Randall. *I* will have to look after him from now on.' Her words were suddenly kind and her eyes betrayed genuine feeling for the squire. 'I didn't predict your involvement and I have no answers for you. You are a complication – a delightful, spirited, innocent complication.'

Dalian hefted the dead body towards the tear and prepared to throw him into its glassy surface.

'Wait,' snapped Randall, running to his master's side. He placed a tentative hand against Utha's forehead and a single tear trickled from his left eye. 'I'm sorry, master, I've got to stay here. Ruth will look after you from now on. I wish I'd got to you sooner; we could have talked some more. I'll miss you, Utha. You were my friend.'

When Dalian was sure the young man had finished saying goodbye, he flung the dead body through the tear. The inert form twisted slightly in the air, but disappeared soundlessly, as if breaking the surface of a millpond. A moment later, the slight ripple had faded and Utha the Ghost was gone.

Randall faced the Gorlan mother with tears flowing freely down his face. 'Please tell me you told the truth. That he will live.'

'He will live,' replied Ruth. 'He will live many lives and see many things, both beautiful and terrible. But I must go; my time is now short.' She left Randall and strode towards the shimmering barrier between worlds. 'You will live too. You will live as I endure, as the last shred of my power – and all that remains of the Gorlan. I name you Gorlan father, Randall of Darkwald. Do not be afraid to explore your power once I am gone.' The young man reached for her, as if he had far more to say, but she ignored him and closed her eyes. With a single wide step, the Gorlan mother glided through the tear, disappearing just as Utha had.

Then everything was still. Dalian wiped his hands, shrugging off a dried smear of Utha's blood. 'Fascinating,' he remarked, aware that Randall was glaring at him. 'I'm sorry, should I be in some way reverent?'

Randall wrung his fists and shouted. No particular words or meaning, just an expression of frustration and anger, echoing around the jagged cave. It was unfocused and emotional, conveying loss that moved even Dalian to feel empathy. The young man began to kick the dead Gorlan. He shouted and swore, driving his boot into the slender abdomen of the matron mother until the huge dead spider rocked over and deposited a viscous pile of blood on the stone.

'You've killed it once,' said Dalian. 'Do you intend to kill it again? Perhaps that would further weaken Shub-Nillurath.'

Randall dropped to his knees and cried. He looked at the tear, at Dalian, at the retreating green glow, but none of it lessened his grief. The young man didn't seem to realize that he now emanated power, making his tears strangely out of place. Dalian thought of a crying shark or some other terrible beast moved to tears. Ruth had gone, but she'd left something dark and ancient in the young man of Ro. Something Randall did not yet understand.

'You would be welcomed as a servant of Jaa,' said Dalian. 'I have many battles yet to fight and you would be a mighty ally.'

'What?' spluttered Randall. 'I'm a lot of things, but mighty is not one of them. I've known and served mighty beings; I've been friends *and* enemies with mighty beings. I've seen them fight and die – I lost my virginity to one, in a dusty cabin on a Karesian ship. But I'm just a confused squire, too far from home.'

Dalian stood over him, considering and deciding against a reassuring hand on the shoulder. The boy hated him and would not appreciate it, but he needed to compose himself. 'That may once have been true,' said the Thief Taker. 'But no longer. Do you not feel it? The power racing through your veins?'

He looked at the subtle energy crackling across his fingertips, but before the young man could respond, the sound of hesitant feet reached their ears. From the darkness, near the matron mother, a number of young girls appeared. They varied in age by about ten years, with not one above late teens. Each swayed on her feet, leaning on another for support.

'Greetings,' said Dalian, inclining his head.

Randall stood and joined him in the centre of the cave. He wiped tears from his eyes and glared at the young enchantresses.

'The matron mother is dead,' said Dalian. 'Her power has invested and sustained you. Without her, you will wither and die, unless you allow Jaa's divine fear to save you. The Seven Sisters were once devotees of the Fire Giant. They can be so again.'

The girls staggered forward and he saw blood creeping from the edges of their eyes and the corners of their mouths. Perhaps he was wrong and they had no future but to return to the dust of the world. As they moved, the youngest, a girl yet to see her tenth year, fell forward on to the rock. Blood spread from her small body as she died, convulsing behind her sisters.

'I don't think they can be saved,' observed Randall. 'It feels like their power is draining from a broken cup.'

The eldest girl bared her blood-stained teeth at them, snarling like a starved beast. 'We need your energy, your blood – give it to us.'

All the girls licked their lips and reached out with shaking arms. They looked at Dalian and Randall as if they were sides of meat. There was little sanity in their eyes, just depthless hunger. The blood increased its flow as they slowly approached, seeping from under their fingernails and tumbling from their mouths. They didn't charge or run, just walked on frigid legs across uneven ground, seemingly unable to move quickly.

'Stop!' shouted Randall, drawing his sword. To Dalian, he muttered, 'Go back to the steps.'

The Thief Taker slowly removed Zarzenfang from its sling and backed away, finding the young man's confidence intriguing. Randall remained in the cavern, pointing his old sword at the eldest girl, but he was gradually side-stepping towards the nearest wall.

'Give me your blood,' growled the lead girl as the young enchantresses encircled Randall. They ignored Dalian, focusing on the nearest source of energy.

'Last chance,' said Randall, keeping away from the girls and reaching the wall.

The girls were now covered in their own blood, frenzied hunger on their faces. Randall showed no fear. He gritted his teeth. His hand was against the wall and the subtle glow rose in intensity, making cracks appear around his fingers. Small stones began to fall from the ceiling as the young man made a jagged fissure travel quickly upwards.

'Dalian,' he said. 'Run!'

The cavern groaned and a large stalactite fell, to smash on the floor and send one of the girls flying. From Randall's glowing hand a web of cracks spread outwards, causing boulders and dust to fill his vision. The stairs shook and Dalian backed away. The whole cavern was starting to collapse. From where Randall stood, the destruction spread quickly, crushing the matron mother's body and dispersing the blood-covered enchantresses. Three were killed, mangled under fallen rocks. Two more flung themselves at Randall to be killed by his longsword.

'Time to leave,' said Dalian, shouting to be heard above the sound of a dozen cave-ins happening all at once.

The young man of Ro darted away from the wall, though the boulders and stalactites did not touch him. A spray of gravel covered his head, but he reached Dalian unharmed. They sprang up the first few steps just as the cavern ceiling fell. In a single show of power, Randall of Darkwald had killed ten enchantresses and buried the Footstep of the Forest Giant beneath tons of rock. It would take decades, perhaps more, for the chamber to be unearthed.

'I think we should get to the surface,' said Randall, looking with alarm at the spreading cracks in the rocky ceiling.

'Can you not control this?' replied Dalian as chunks of rock fell from above.

'Err, apparently not,' said the young man. 'I just. . . did it.'

The destruction was spreading and the staircase was beginning to shake. They stowed their weapons and rushed upwards, chased by a collapsing tunnel of fractured stone. They outdistanced the cave-in quickly, leaving just a rumble, far behind them, but they didn't slow down. Dalian was amazed at the young man. Not only could he strike at a Gorlan mother and collapse an ancient cave with little apparent effort, but he could keep up with Voon's powerful body as they ran. He wasn't even sweating or out of breath when they sighted the clear blue sky of Oron Kaa.

Outside, both men blinked in discomfort as the blazing sun assaulted them. They'd been in a dark, cold cave, with fetid green light the only illumination. Now the heat and light returned, dizzyingly. They moved away from the top of the stone staircase just as rock and dust erupted outwards. The jagged archway that marked the route downwards collapsed in on itself, leaving barely a crack to indicate it had ever been there. The matron mother was forever entombed beneath the mountains.

Ahead, through dust and shimmering air, Dalian could see the ruined settlement of Oron Kaa. Half the bulbous buildings were crushed, or had toppled over. Against every surface, twisted in dense web, were motionless insects, and on the far side of the central square, hundreds of human bodies were sprawled on the ground. Ruth had torn the place apart, and the death of the matron mother had robbed it of much power. It felt like a battlefield, with a curious silence hanging over a conflict that few men could imagine. The rampaging Kirin, the faceless acolytes, the maddening insects, the immense Gorlan – a conflict of time and power, as much as death. But now, just the curious silence.

'Survivors,' said Randall, striding away from the cave-in.

A handful of figures, heads bowed, wandered among fallen sailors and between destroyed buildings. Their arms and legs appeared heavy, as if they struggled to walk. At first, Dalian thought they were wounded or perhaps hampered by the heavy webbing, but as bodies began to move and sit up, he knew some other device was at work. Those standing knelt to help their fellows, until dozens more heavy-limbed Kirin stood in the ruins of Oron Kaa. Each had had a Builder force its way into their mouth; they now stood and looked with fearful eyes.

He turned sharply in response to a sound, and saw a Builder plummet to the irregular cobbled ground. Then another, until all the remaining insects fluttered their last and twitched downwards. It was strange to stand among the dying creatures, tumbling off buildings and flopping limply around them.

'Why do they fall?' he asked Randall. 'And why do the Kirin rise?'

The young squire was smiling. He spared a glance at the dying insects, but his eyes were focused on the Kirin, most of whom were now standing. 'Ruth's freed them,' he replied. 'The Kirin *and* the Builders. The matron mother kept the insects enslaved and I think they are glad to finally die. They weren't wicked by nature; they were used, like the Dokkalfar, like the young enchantresses, like the Karesians. Imagine being a slave for thousands of years – you'd gladly embrace the beyond.'

'You sound happy for them.'

Randall nodded as a group of Kirin approached through the ruined buildings. They looked tired, skin slick with sweat and limbs shaking. The man in the lead was taller than the rest, with a leather waistcoat covering his muscular torso. Randall gasped and took two large strides forward to meet the tall Kirin sailor.

'Captain Vekerian!' said the young man. 'Do you know me?'

'I do, great father,' he replied, an echoing hum sounding in the depths of his throat. He looked human, but there was an alien glaze across his eyes and a twitchy unease in his movements. 'Vekerian? Is that my name?'

Randall looked at him closely. 'It was, when you were just a man.' The other Kirin assembled behind their captain, each sailor displaying the same awkward movements and faraway stare. 'You are now part man, part Builder. An alliance has been struck in your flesh and a newly freed creature nourishes you.' The young man of Ro put his hand on Vekerian's shoulder and smiled. 'You can call yourself whatever you like. You're free. That goes for all of you.'

Dalian could feel the growing spark of power in the young man. Since Ruth departed, her strength had spread to every inch of Randall's body. It might take years for him to fully understand his might, but he'd taken a large first step towards true power – and everyone who saw him knew it.

The fifty Kirin were gradually joined by dozens more figures. The inhabitants of Oron Kaa, newly freed by the death of the Queen in Red, looked at the burning sky as if they'd never seen it before. They walked on legs that seemed to confuse them and exchanged interested looks with their fellows. Dalian wondered if this was a new kind of life.

'Will you protect us, great father?' asked the creature that had been Vekerian.

Randall blushed, glancing over his shoulder as if looking for Utha or Ruth and some words of encouragement. All he saw was the Thief Taker. With a hard stare at the floor, the young man appeared to realize he was alone, with no-one remaining to hold his hand. 'I'll try,' he replied.

'Randall, can I talk to you?' asked Dalian. 'We are not finished.'

Vekerian and the other Kirin glared at him, as if offended by his manner. They looked to the young man of Ro, who smiled awkwardly back at them. Dalian doubted that such mighty power had ever been contained in so meek a form. The new creatures looked to him as their master, their protector. They didn't question his manner or what he looked like, and Dalian had no doubt that they'd kill for him if he wished it. Luckily, Randall of Darkwald was a rather nice young man and he waved them back.

'I have few answers, if that's what you were hoping for,' said Randall, leading the Thief Taker away from the increasing mob of confused people. 'I know things I shouldn't know. . . I can do things I shouldn't be able to do. The rock of the cavern – it just obeyed my command.'

'I believe Ruth told you not to be afraid of your power. That is good advice, young man. But *your* journey is not *my* journey, and it is not what we need to talk about.'

Randall chuckled to himself, his intelligent eyes, sharp jawline and thin beard making him look far older than he was. He ran a hand down his face and yawned, turning to look out to sea. 'My journey,' he said, knowingly. 'It started in a tavern in Ro Tiris and ended at the edge of the world.'

'Ended?' queried Dalian. 'This is not the end for you. Oron Kaa is now yours; you will be its guardian. Ideally you would be a devotee of Jaa, but other than that you are the perfect ally.'

'I don't think I care much for the gods,' replied Randall. 'But I can accept what you say about Oron Kaa. I promised these people I would protect them – and I think I can.' He narrowed his eyes and took a deep breath. 'Ruth tore this place down, but there is plenty of rock, and trees to the east. We can rebuild, and guard the tear.'

Dalian smiled at him.

'That's what you want, isn't it?' continued the Gorlan father. 'You know devotees of Shub-Nillurath will be drawn to the tear. They'll try to unearth it and let his power flow. We've corked the Footstep of the Forest Giant, but we've not destroyed it.'

They faced each other, two beings of power establishing that they were not enemies. Dalian did not wish to challenge the powerful young man. At the very least he deserved time to process the loss of his friends and the surging power in his body. At the edge of the world, Dalian was prepared to ally with the Gorlan father and the new creatures that now looked to him for guidance.

'I think we have an understanding,' said the Thief Taker.

'There's a ship at dock,' replied Randall. 'It can get you back to civilization. If that is your destination.'

'I plan to meet with my son in Kessia. We are due a quiet drink of desert nectar, and we must rebuild the faith of the Fire Giant. As we endure, so does Jaa.'

The young man of Ro scanned the ruined city and the low coastline. There was confidence and resignation in his eyes, and a hundred stories of things he could or should have done differently. Eventually he smiled. 'I imagine I'll be here a long time. And I imagine you and I will meet again.'

CHAPTER TWENTY-THREE

GWENDOLYN OF HUNTER'S CROSS IN THE DUCHY OF WEIR

SOMEWHERE, IN A bright corner of her mind, Gwen thought of another life, a life now lost to her. She was in Ro Haran, relaxing in a small sitting room next to her husband. An open window, framed by billowing red curtains, revealed a crisp blue sky and a dark ocean. Things were peaceful and neither of them wore armour or held swords. Their hands were soft and the wounds of war were long healed. It was strange that her mind retreated to this kind of peace. A simple kind of peace, with no demands or thoughts of the past. Perhaps her mind was a gentler place than she had thought.

Slowly, the soft skin of her hands became rough, and the leather of her sword hilts replaced the soft touch of her husband. The relaxing feel of a cushioned sofa merged slowly into the feel of the harsh canvas of her saddle. In increments, her fantasy shattered and she was again on the crowded fields of Weir, staring with uncontrollable terror at the swarm of rippling black tentacles that swept towards them. They moved like a relentless wave of black water, with texture coming as breaks in the rippling surface, rising as a swell and falling back to the flowing mass. Every so often, in an insane moment of clarity, she saw a creature appear in the wave of black. It was the same as the thing in the catacombs of Ro Haran; the thing that had killed four men and taken a dozen more to kill it. There were hundreds of them, or maybe thousands.

She just looked, not thinking to shout or flee. She didn't even know how long she'd been looking, just that she couldn't turn away or conjure any words of alarm. She was next to Xander and Daganay, mounted at the front of their lines. Thousands of warriors stood like swaying blades of grass either side of her, similarly rapt by the spectacle of horror before them. The Hounds, despite their numbers, were now merely a slight distraction, nothing more than a background to the black wave that approached.

Silence was everywhere. No-one could summon the gumption to shout or even speak. Forty thousand warriors – men who had killed their way south through endless Hounds – were suddenly turned into frozen statues. None of them looked towards Ro Weir; none of them cared about Tor Funweir or their struggle for freedom. The Twisted Tree had revealed itself and it was more than their minds could take. The battle would not be decided by swords *or* sorcery; it would be decided by thrashing tentacles.

The first of them to summon enough strength to speak was Daganay. The Blue cleric wheeled his horse, blocking her view of the rising swell of Dark Young. He shook his head vigorously and rubbed his eyes. He'd turned away but could still not speak in more than a whisper. 'Run,' he murmured. 'We need to run.'

His strength of mind was only marginally stronger than Gwen's, and she managed to speak just after him. 'Xander, we can't win,' she stated, grabbing her husband's shoulder and turning his face towards her.

Tyr Sigurd and his forest-dwellers, assembled behind them, had dropped to their knees and all had looks of unimaginable horror on their grey faces. 'The priest and the altar, the priest and the altar, the priest and the altar,' they chanted together.

The Dark Young approached the left flank, where Brennan's cavalry waited. The horses regained their senses before the riders did, and the armoured mounts began to whinny and buck; held firm by their riders, they were unable to turn away, and shuffled backwards in an ungainly attempt to flee. The forest-dwellers continued to chant, their sonorous voices the only sound she could hear.

Xander just looked at her. A tear appeared in his eye and his expression turned to one of extreme sadness. Not anger; not even fear. She saw the complete loss of hope creep across his face. From the moment they'd retaken Haran, they'd been pushed, kicked, battered, blown up – but they hadn't broken. It was before the walls of Weir that the armies of Ro would break, before a sword had even been swung. No commands or redeployment would allow them to hold their ground, and it was this loss of hope that crushed Xander's spirit. All he could muster were the words 'Stay alive, my love.'

Everything was now in slow motion. The tide of black was taking its time to reach them, rolling from the eastern side of the city directly towards their left flank. Some men were backing away, some horses had thrown their riders, some commanders tried to shout or scream, but the bulk of the army remained more or less as it had before the Young appeared. An enemy that removed your ability to run was powerful indeed.

'Knights of the Dawn!' roared Lord Markos of Rayne from the right flank. 'We die this day!'

A horn was blown from the far side of their lines and the sound of armoured horses suddenly filled the air. Gwen couldn't see them through the sea of terrified soldiers, but the high pennant of a white dove slowly emerged, bobbing on the wind as it moved across her field of vision. Some men looked, but most were rooted to the spot as a wedge of armoured knights charged across the open fields before their lines. The paladins' chargers wore blinkers, now closed across their eyes, and were being driven forward by the strong thighs and skill of their riders. The knights themselves appeared calm and at peace, with no hint of fear or doubt crossing their pious faces.

With Markos in the lead, they hunkered down, shields locked forward and lances lowered. On the open fields between the two armies they accelerated into a sprint, covering the ground in a blur of strength and steel.

Daganay shouted, 'Markos! For the One!'

The paladin saluted his brother cleric by unsheathing his huge greatsword and rising high in his stirrups.

The tide of black slowed, showing for the first time an awareness of the company of horsemen bearing down on them. The swarming mass of Dark Young flowed like a flock of birds, away from Brennan's cavalry and towards the White Knights. There was no cheering or shouts of encouragement, just thousands of faces watching impassively as a sea of black met a sea of white.

The clash was thunderous. A thousand steel-tipped lances, moving in a wedge, cut a sudden hole in the black wave. The sheer weight of the charge displaced dozens of Dark Young, sending them backwards in a blur of tentacles and shrill wailing. The wedge kept moving, digging into the tide like a knife into flesh, until their momentum was halted.

Markos was still visible, standing high enough in his stirrups to be seen through the melee of tentacles, gaping maws and rampant paladins. With supreme horsemanship, he kept control of his warhorse while hacking at black flesh with his two-handed sword.

From their lines, enough sense had returned that an order to fall back had been relayed, but it happened only slowly, with no-one wanting to turn from the eldritch spectacle before them. The paladins' charge was a thing stories would be told of, but the reality could not be ignored: they were being overwhelmed. The white tabards were now all but invisible within the swarming sea of black. Each Dark Young took a dozen cuts or more to bring down, whereas the knights could be felled with a flailing tentacle or a reaching maw. Horses were battered to the grass, men were thrown around like crushed rag-dolls and, within moments, only a small cluster of mounted knights remained. Five thousand of the toughest fighters Gwen had ever seen were being eaten up by a frenzied wave of death, the surface of which their charge had barely scratched.

She looked at Xander, then Daganay. All three wanted so much to have the right words or a sudden moment of clarity, but with their flickering eyes and pursed mouths all they could convey was sadness. The paladins had bought them time, but everything was so strange and muddled that no-one could think clearly.

'Not today,' said Gwen. 'We're not going to die today.'

'Who can fight that?' growled Xander, his sword hand flexing against Peacekeeper's hilt.

'We need to run,' offered Daganay, nodding as if his mind had hardened just a little. 'Full retreat!' he shouted, directing his words towards all the warriors of Ro within earshot.

The command was relayed and the withdrawal gained some momentum. The army, even the kneeling Dokkalfar, pulled their eyes from the dying paladins and broke into a jog, fleeing north. Those on horses had a harder time, but gradually the army moved backwards. There were no Hounds anywhere close and the withdrawal was quieter than any other she'd been a part of, with just the wailing of the trees and the death-rattles of the paladins providing any noise.

'Look,' said Daganay, gesturing towards the edge of the bubbling black tide.

She saw Lord Markos, still alive, standing on the flank of his dead horse. All around him the body parts of his company were being flung left and right as a feeding frenzy ensued among the Dark Young. It was as if a thousand sharks attacked a handful of helpless swimmers. At first they ignored the last paladin, too busy eating horses and men to consider him relevant. But he quickly reminded them that a Knight of the Dawn was not to be ignored, by jumping from his horse and charging the mass of tentacles. He swung from a high guard, hacking downwards in a frenzy.

'Run, my lord, run,' she muttered, searching the field of battle for a way the White Knight could withdraw.

Markos advanced a few broad paces but was swept up in the black wave, pulled into the air, then smashed into the ground, before his constituent parts were torn from his chest by a dozen feeding Young. The creatures swarmed into strange circles and bubbled outwards like a bizarre water spout, grabbing any chunk of flesh as yet unconsumed. It was only a matter of time until they would finish their meal and turn back to the army of Ro.

'Run!' shouted Major Brennan from the left flank. He was now on foot, chasing a fleeing horse.

Other men echoed his shout, pulling their fellows away from the battlefield to join the mass of running warriors.

'The hills of Narland,' shouted Xander. 'Make for the hills of Narland!'

Order had vanished and the retreating army became a mob of horses, men, steel and shouting. Gwen stayed close to Xander, with Daganay and Sergeant Ashwyn behind them. Their horses were startled, but eager to be facing the other way, and needed little encouragement to run.

Then a shout from behind and a high-pitched gurgle of pain. A horse whinnied and then fell silent, and a fleeting black shape darted past her. A man tumbled to the grass, his head annihilated in a flash of movement, and another was flung into the air by a tentacle that was barely a shadow.

'Form up,' shouted Xander, pointing Peacekeeper at the black distortion that appeared to be circling them.

'I can't see it – what the fuck is it?' shrieked Ashwyn, his horse sprinting desperately beneath him.

The nearest riders, unable to control their horses, could do little but flick their heads left and right, searching for the shimmering, black creature that was hounding them. Men continued to die, dragged from their saddles or turned into sudden flashes of bloody meat and torn steel.

She couldn't see it clearly, even at a distance. Just the occasional glimpse of a cat-like distortion in the air and a sharp, elongated head. Its movements described a ghostly circle around them, keeping its distance, with Gwen, Daganay and Xander in the centre.

Everything moved so quickly. It felt as if they were on an unchangeable course, being taken north at a speed and in a direction they couldn't control. Away. . . just away. . . that was the only direction the horses knew or the men could remember.

'Just stay alive,' she muttered, talking as much to herself as to her husband. In fact, she wasn't even speaking loudly enough for him to hear her. Or maybe she wasn't speaking at all and the words were in her head.

The cat-like creature moved closer, its circle shrinking with each man it killed. Then, in a moment that seemed to happen in slow motion, she saw the creature. It was black and sinewy, appearing to be made of the same stuff as the Dark Young, but utterly different in form and movement. It had four legs, each ending in a globe of tiny tentacles, providing it with a speed of movement that, when in motion, made it almost invisible. Its head was a thick, vertical spike, split in the middle by a fleshy mouth and a grotesque face.

'Rham Jas,' she muttered, seeing the misshapen face of the Kirin assassin protruding from the monster.

It broke its circle of movement and pounced towards them, its maddened face flashing with hate and hunger. She heard a hundred voices shout in alarm and a hundred faces twist into terror. The creature that had been Rham Jas leapt at Xander. It moved like a predatory cat chasing a mouse as it sprang at the king.

She wanted to be anywhere else in the world as she reached for him. She didn't even want to be closer so that she could help – she just wanted them both to not be there. She didn't care if they were in Haran, Tiris, Canarn or a rat-infested tavern in the back streets of Weir. She just didn't want to watch him die – but die he did.

Alexander Tiris, the Red Prince of Haran and King of Tor Funweir, was snatched from his bolting horse and torn into three pieces in mid-air. His body was thrown upwards, twitching as life disappeared in an instant of dislocation.

Then a hand was wrapped round her shoulders and her face was pulled away from her dead husband. 'Don't fucking look,' screamed Daganay. 'Don't you dare fucking look.'

Their horses twisted and turned in panicked lines as they fled from the creature, but it didn't pursue. Struggling to look back through the Blue cleric's restraining arms, Gwen saw Xander's body, sprawled on the ground in pieces, and the beast that had been Rham Jas crouched over it. . . feasting. It had sought him out, killed him, and now it ate him, giving his army time to run away.

Gwen's world turned as sharp as a blade, as clear as still water. She couldn't experience the pain that awaited her; all she could feel were pinpoints of focus telling her to run, to live, to fight another day.

* * *

The hills of Narland were dark and quiet. They'd fled from the beasts with not a thought to when they should stop, but exhaustion and mental exertion had forced them to rest.

Gwen had ridden in silence, and silence was all she heard from the other riders. The bright corner of her mind that allowed a future where they could be at peace was gone. All she had left was a wall of pain and anger – and something else, maybe guilt or shame.

'Sit down, my queen,' said Sergeant Symon, helping her down on to a half tree-stump.

All around them, faces and bodies, too troubled to speak or act with alacrity, slumped round lazily built fires. They'd seen nothing of the creatures since leaving the duchy of Weir, but not a man thought they were safe. Even so, no barricades were raised and the army that had limped north used only the hills and endless craggy valleys of rugged green for cover.

Symon wrapped a blanket around her shoulders and eased open her clenched fists, taking each of her leaf-blades and returning them to their scabbards.

'At least say something,' mumbled the sergeant. 'Any words will do.'

She'd tried to speak several times since the sun disappeared over the horizon, but nothing got as far as her mouth. Everything she could think to say was hijacked by the recurring image of Xander being torn apart without even the chance to swing Peacekeeper. Defeat was difficult enough, but to have been routed so completely had sapped each warrior of energy, conviction – even hope. All Gwen felt was a heightened version of what each of them felt. Was her loss of a husband truly so profound next to so much death? But still she could conjure no words.

'Please, my lady,' said Symon, tears rolling down his face as he made sure she was wrapped up. 'We need. . . I don't know what we need.'

'It's okay, lad,' said Brother Daganay, plonking himself on to the grass, next to their small fire. 'I'll take over. Go and have some food and check the south. We still need guard detail; you see to it.'

'Aye, Brother, thank you, Brother,' replied Symon, hastily standing and leaving them.

Daganay leant in and warmed his hands. 'You don't need to say anything, Gwen. Brennan's got things in hand. We're clear with good visibility south. We'll see if anything appears.' He let out a hoarse cough and patted his stout chest. 'Sorry, I think I might be getting old.' He took some deep breaths and wheezed with each intake. 'As I was saying, you can stay silent as long as you want. I'm not going anywhere. In fact. . .' He looked around the wooded valley they sat in. 'I might just stay here. I could build a house and raise chickens. I'd have to hire some hands to keep the Gorlan away, but it could be a nice life.'

It did sound nice. A simple farm, a simple life, maybe some peace. It was good country, with rich brown earth and thick trees that had stood for a hundred years. At least, it had been good country before the Dead God started a war. Now it was a graveyard, from Cozz to the gates of Weir, streaked with retreats, advances, battles, skirmishes and, most of all, death.

'If we *do* choose to leave,' continued Daganay, 'will you be coming with us, my queen?'

She didn't reply. She wanted to, but she still felt oppressed by the spectre of her dead husband. It was making her throat tight and refusing her the luxury of speech.

'That's okay,' said the Blue cleric. 'You can decide when we leave. I'm sure you're not the only one who doesn't want to think right now.'

A signal bolt was fired from the north, indicating something approaching, and both of them looked up from the campfire.

'Shit,' exclaimed Daganay. 'Stay here, I'll see what it is. It's the wrong direction for the Hounds and their beasts, so don't panic.'

She threw him a sardonic stare, indicating that panic was not really in her nature, dead husband or no dead husband.

'Very well,' conceded the cleric. 'I won't be long.'

He stood, wheezing heavily and flexing his back. Within a moment he'd left her small globe of light and joined other men, those with enough strength left to answer the warning bolt. Something was happening to the north. The valley opened into a wooded depression in the green expanse of Narland and more bolts were aimed skywards from the trees. Then shouting, fearful from her own men, and calm from whoever was approaching.

Symon rushed back to her side, his longsword held at the ready. 'Men approach,' said the young Hawk sergeant. 'From the trees.'

She heard, but didn't respond. Then Daganay appeared, his drawn face gliding into the firelight. 'My queen, come with me.'

She paused, but her stupor did not extend to her legs, and she rose to join them. Her movements were faltering and she required Symon's steady hand to walk in a straight line. Outside of her isolation, Gwen saw a long camp of deathly pale faces, each man yet to come to terms with what they had seen. It didn't make her feel any better to see that she was not the worst affected. Some cried, others shook uncontrollably. One man repeatedly sharpened his blade in a compulsive frenzy; another just wandered back and forth, muttering to himself.

'My queen,' said Major Brennan, coming to meet her. 'You are well?'

She still couldn't speak, but Daganay nodded to him and indicated that they should keep moving.

Through the low vista of silent warriors, a few still moved with a purpose, escorting a group of men into their isolated camp. The newcomers wore tarnished leather armour, but appeared to be something more than simple mercenaries. Especially their leader. He was a tall swordsman with a greatsword sheathed across his back and a subtle air of power about him.

'Identify yourself, stranger,' demanded Brennan, not thinking to chastise the rearguard for letting the men into their camp. 'This is not a good night to be wandering around in the dark.'

The group of warriors numbered two hundred or so, but their swagger conveyed more strength and confidence than their numbers alone suggested. The tall man who led them had a sureness of foot and a solidity of bearing that made him appear larger than any other man she'd seen, but still his eyes showed concern for the thousands of stricken men around him.

'My name's Fallon,' said the leader. 'What happened here?'

She'd heard of him; they all had. Fallon of Leith was a Red Knight, reputedly the best swordsman in an order of master swordsmen.

The rest of his company crouched down next to crying Hawks and shaking guardsmen, lending a comforting hand and a calm word. They hadn't seen the waves of Dark Young and had no comprehension of what could have cowed so many warriors.

'What happened,' muttered Brennan. 'We ran away, that's what happened.'

Next to Fallon, a hawk-faced warrior with a crippled hand spoke. 'Where's King Alexander?'

'Dead,' she replied, speaking for the first time in several hours and making Daganay move next to her protectively. 'He died at Ro Weir.'

'We had no choice but to fall back,' offered the Blue cleric. 'Staying there would have been a simple waste of life, with or without King Alexander Tiris.'

She couldn't make them understand or show them what she'd seen, but it felt good to speak again. If only to state that Xander was dead.

'Well, we need to get you moving,' said a third newcomer, a gruff man with serious eyes and the snarl of a sergeant major. 'You can't stay here.'

Brennan glared at the man. 'Do you know who I am?' asked the Hawk.

'Don't care,' said the gruff newcomer. 'It doesn't change anything; you still need to move.'

'Easy,' said Fallon. 'I know who you are, Major Brennan. This is Sergeant Ohms and this is Captain William of Verellian. We are Knights of the Grey and we're here to help, but you're being surrounded.'

'What!' exclaimed Daganay. 'Not now – we need to rest. These men cannot fight, they need to calm their minds after. . . what they've seen.'

'I don't think the Hounds care,' replied William of Verellian. 'They've been moving into position since the sun went down, a fair few, but not their full force. Keeping far enough back that you wouldn't see 'em.' He glanced around the army of broken men. 'Not that it appears you've been looking.'

'Watch it, Captain,' spat Daganay. 'Don't judge what you don't know.'

'I wouldn't think of it,' replied Verellian.

'There's something else,' said Fallon, narrowing his eyes. 'Something dark. . . I think it's circling you. We need to get this army north, into the trees.'

* * *

It took so much time to muster the army of Ro. Men refused to stand, some clinging to the ground as if it was their only chance of survival, others wandering blindly out of the gully and into the darkness. Brennan and a handful of officers carried on giving orders, but they were followed only reluctantly, as if every movement involved climbing a mountain. Tents that had only been half-assembled were slowly packed away, and the remaining horses were saddled, though the majority of the men simply stood around in silent clumps, reacting to commands only slowly.

Gwen stayed with Symon at the edge of the trees, watching Daganay assist a startled group of Montague's yeomanry. A few companies had managed to move north into the trees, but the retreat was happening far too slowly for the Grey Knights.

Fallon's men did the best they could to help, but two hundred men could only make so much difference to twenty thousand. Especially when most of those twenty thousand were struggling to stand. The hawk-faced knight, William of Verellian, stayed on the high ground, keeping a watchful eye on the eastern plains. They believed that the Hounds were surrounding them, and with the extreme slowness of the army's withdrawal, they were being given plenty of time to get into position.

'Too slow, too slow,' grumbled Verellian, whenever he looked back down into the gullies. 'You, cleric.' He pointed at Daganay. 'Get those men moving.'

Daganay frowned. 'Bloody knights,' he muttered, doubling his efforts to get the yeomanry into the trees. 'They always think they know best.'

Fallon appeared through the army, his face a beacon of calm and tightly controlled anger. 'You're Gwendolyn, yes?' he asked. 'The queen?'

She just nodded.

'A lot of people are worried about you,' he said. 'The Hawks particularly. They want you to know that they loved their king, and they grieve with you – but they're simple soldiers and they don't know how to tell you. So I will.'

She looked at Symon, and saw the young Hawk fighting back tears. 'It's true, my lady,' he murmured. 'A piece of me died when I saw King Alexander fall. I don't know who or what I fight for any more.'

She was too sad to cry, too tired to scream, but she heard every word. If only she could reply. If only she could summon words of inspiration for the young Hawk – for all of them.

'Queen Gwendolyn,' said Fallon, dropping to his knees, 'I pledge myself and my knights to you and to Tor Funweir. Know that the One God is not dead, though he *is* weak. In the years to come, remember that he blessed you as his queen and me as his exemplar.'

'Fallon!' shouted Verellian from the high ground. 'We've got a problem.'

The tall swordsman rose and made his way to the side of the gully. The hawk-faced knight offered his hand and helped the larger man to the dark grass above them.

'Hounds,' said Fallon. 'Does that mean they're attacking?'

'I think it might mean just that,' replied Verellian. 'South and east.'

Gwen couldn't see the Hounds, but a corner of her mind had heard every word Fallon had spoken. Many nearby warriors had heard as well, and looked at her with silent conviction.

Sergeant Ohms arrived from the south, with other members of Fallon's company. 'They're coming,' said the gruff knight. 'A lot of them.'

'Get these people moving,' shouted Verellian, frustration showing in his words. 'Do they not care that they're being surrounded?'

Fallon looked down, casting his dark eyes over the faces of Xander's broken army, until he locked eyes with Gwen. She echoed every hopeless sentiment felt by the army of Ro. All of their angst and grief could be seen on her drawn features. Again, she wanted to speak. To make him understand. But she couldn't.

Fallon turned to Verellian, placing a hand on the old knight's shoulder. 'We need to cover them,' he said gently. He dropped his head for a moment, as if thinking deeply. 'Wait.'

In two long strides, the swordsman was standing at the edge of the gully. He addressed Gwen directly. 'My queen, if you have an ounce of survival instinct left, I invite you to take my hand. You too, cleric.' He leant down and stretched out his arm.

She looked around, but found herself taking his hand and allowing herself to be lifted to the grass above. A sharp breeze of cold night-time air stung her face for a moment, before she managed to focus on the eastern darkness. All along the rugged plains of Narland were globes of firelight, travelling as a broken worm of movement above innumerable Hounds. Her eyes moved slowly, without a flicker of fear or murmur of alarm, across the distant line of Karesian warriors. They filled every corner of the dark plains, advancing in lockstep. There were so many of them. . . but all she could think of was how blank they appeared.

Verellian clicked his fingers in front of her face. 'Are you seeing this, my queen? Or are you still in a trance?'

She ignored him, finding nothing in the dark corners of her mind to tell her how to react. At that moment, watching a slow advance of men – too many men to fight – all she wanted to do was die. She swung her head back to look at the ghostly shell of the army, and saw thousands of faces that thought the same. Though a sharp feeling of doubt entered her mind, as if she should maybe not carry on fighting.

'My queen,' snapped Fallon, forcing her eyes back to the dark fields and endless column of Hounds.

Then the murderous distortion appeared, darting from one shadow to the next. It was harder to see in the darkness, with its black flesh barely displacing the shadows as it moved. If it hadn't been for the Karesians' torches and the imprints left in the grass, she might not have seen the creature that killed her husband. She nearly screamed, but anger took the edge off her rising panic. All the other men who saw it, aside from Fallon's company, reacted with fear and alarm, hastily pulling themselves back into the relative safety of the low gully.

'You can't fight it,' whispered Gwen.

Fallon, Verellian and Ohms exchanged glances, then peered into the darkness, trying to get a good look at the cat-like Dark

Young. It was well ahead of the Karesian army, who had slowed their advance, and was describing a tight circle of movement that got closer and closer as the knights looked.

'Stay back,' ordered Fallon, advancing a few huge strides towards the creature. His men drew their weapons, but remained between him and the slowly retreating army of Ro.

Fallon drew his tarnished greatsword. The moonlight danced across his face as he advanced, but his expression was incomprehensible to Gwen. There was no fear, or even concern. His breathing was not heavy, his hands did not shake – and a subtle mantle of warm, golden light began to emanate from his body.

'The fucker's glowing again,' remarked Verellian, sharing the apparent confidence of his friend.

'You can't fight it,' repeated Gwen, the image of Xander's dismembered corpse flashing before her eyes.

Verellian looked at her with a combination of concern and confusion. She knew he hadn't seen what it could do. He hadn't even seen its face, the mocking caricature of Rham Jas Rami. She wanted to shake him and force them to flee, but she was rooted to the spot; and the corners of her vision were assaulted by the pouncing, black distortion that approached Fallon of Leith.

The tall swordsman stopped moving and narrowed his eyes. A moment later, creating no more sound than a whistle of wind, the creature leapt at him. The writhing feelers on the end of each of its legs tickled at the air, and its sharp head angled downwards, aiming its gummy mouth at Fallon. Everything happened so quickly. She could barely follow the creature's movements, let alone the dizzying parry raised by the knight of Ro. His sword swung as his feet moved, side-stepping the attack with supreme balance and speed. The creature snapped at thin air and received a deep cut to the side of its shimmering black head.

'What the fuck is that?' shouted Sergeant Ohms, taking an involuntary step away.

Fallon pulled back his blade and looked at the feline monstrosity, assessing its sinewy curves and stretched, human face. The creature

391

was still for the first time since it had appeared before Ro Weir. It shook its head, as if the wound was a minor irritation; it pawed at the ground, its feelers digging small furrows in the earth. But it was bleeding. The wound had caused a steady slick of black ichor to drip from the thing's head. If it could bleed, she thought, it could die.

'So you're the Twisted Tree,' said Fallon. 'Look more like the twisted fucking pussycat to me.'

He attacked, drawing stunned gasps from everyone within sight. Defence was one thing, but attack. . . it was unthinkable. But still he attacked. His greatsword was an extension of his glowing body, arcing forwards with a light unlike any other she'd seen – a blinding spark of gold and silver, covering the huge swordsman, the grass, the creature, even the air. He hacked at it, the creature appearing utterly bewildered and unable to do anything but howl and flinch backwards.

'This is the One God's land,' roared Fallon, 'and I am his exemplar.'

The creature's howl became deafening and she had to cover her ears. Its body was now criss-crossed with deep cuts from Fallon's sword, and its feelers vibrated against the grass. The glowing knight raised his sword in both hands and drove it downwards with a rush of strength that could cleave a mountain in two. The aberrant Dark Young flailed forward in a last-ditch effort to deflect the attacks, and the blade sheared through one of its rear legs. It was severed halfway up and sent a dense spray of blood across the glowing grass.

The creature gurgled, almost a cry of pain, and pulled itself backwards. Fallon's sword was embedded in the earth, which allowed the beast to flee, manically flailing its remaining limbs and flickering away in ungainly surges of movement. With nowhere to go but through the Hounds, it crashed into the waiting army, flinging dozens of men out of its way as it fled south.

Then silence returned. Men gawped; others swore under their breath. To her left, Gwen noticed that Daganay was standing there, watching the glowing man with a look of awe on his face.

'Knights of the Grey!' commanded Fallon. 'To arms.'

His company, less astonished than the others, moved quickly to flank him, forming a thin line of blades in front of the waiting Hounds. A section of the Karesian army was clumsily regrouping to cover the large gap made by the fleeing creature, but the rest remained still, forming an unbroken line of black steel.

'Lots of men to kill, lads,' shouted Ohms. 'Plenty for all. Stand on Sir Fallon and keep those fuckin' eyes open.'

Their leader, still glowing, raised his sword. Gwen was suddenly aware that many Hawks of Ro, previously crippled by fear, were now poking their heads above the gully and watching the huge swordsman. She shook her head rapidly, feeling like she was waking from a dream. Suddenly she felt the cold night air and flexed her hands. They were stiff, as if she'd not used them for days. Her vision seemed to change from muddy glass to clear water, showing her the reality of their situation. Thousands of Hounds, arrayed in a horseshoe, stood ready, able to annihilate the broken army when and however they wanted. There was little fight left in the army of Ro. But still there was the glowing knight, standing taller than any other man, his light making the Hounds flinch backwards.

'I will kill any pig-fucking Hound that comes near me,' boomed Fallon, his voice echoing across the low plains of Narland. 'I know you're all on drugs, a few of the most important might even be enchanted, but I know you bastards feel fear – and you should fear *me*!' He took a step towards them and the closest Hounds took a step back. 'Go back to Ro Weir and tell your enchantress to send more men. This mob is a fucking insult to the One God.'

If the force of Karesians had been smaller, they would have screamed and run away. As it was, their drugged oblivion was enough to push them onwards. Hesitantly, starting with the ranks furthest away from Fallon, the Hounds advanced. Their movements showed no confidence and their advance was more of a saunter than a charge. There were maybe ten thousand of them, an insultingly small number, intended to mop up a demoralized army. But the Grey Knights were not demoralized.

'He's exemplar,' said Daganay. 'I wish I had something to write with. This needs recording.'

'The Hawks would follow him,' she whispered.

'And his Grey Knights,' replied Daganay, seeming to have an idea what the term meant.

There were only two hundred of them, but their formation – a single line, allowing each warrior room to fight – said much about their prowess. Not only did they show no fear, but they laughed and beckoned the Hounds forward with insults and challenges. Fallon was not part of the line but stood alone, dominating a large circle of muddy grass. His glow announced a killing zone in which his greatsword had complete control, and the Hounds appeared reluctant to approach him.

'You can still run away,' shouted William of Verellian, flexing a heavy shortsword, strapped to his crippled hand.

The Hounds were silent. Gwen guessed that they had been given their orders before they left Ro Weir and were continuing in an obedient haze. The knights were hugely outnumbered and Gwen's hands began to twitch. She was no longer comfortable being an observer. The image of her dead husband was no longer crippling, and she'd seen Fallon defeat the worst of the Dark Young. Her mind cleared and she saw hundreds of Hawks who felt the same.

She found her voice. 'Hawks of Ro,' she commanded. 'I am your queen. To arms!'

As if waking from a terrible nightmare, those warriors of Ro who had not already fled into the trees clambered out of the gully to stand on the muddy grass. They were a grim bunch, wielding an array of well-used blades, spears and maces, but they answered her command as if they were glad of it.

The Hounds had been expecting to mop up after the creature that had been Rham Jas. After a second assault from the maddened beast, the Hawks would have been a quivering mass of crying men, an easy victory for the Hounds. But the creature was gone and the army of Ro was strengthened by the Knights of the Grey.

Daganay tightened his fists round his mace, and Major Brennan, appearing along the gully at the point of the massed Hawks, grunted orders to those behind him. With the addition of the new warriors, the dark fields of Narland were now dominated by soldiers of Ro.

'Not looking good for you lot,' roared Fallon, grinning at the Hounds. 'Last chance to run – or every one of you dies.'

The Karesians were close now; the uniform texture of their black armour shone clearly in the moonlight. When they stopped barely ten paces from the line of Grey Knights, Gwen – and every warrior of Tor Funweir – was ready to tear them apart.

'Boo!' shouted Sergeant Ohms, loud enough to make a huge cluster of Karesians jump backwards in surprise.

In a spectacle that would have been funny at any other time, ten thousand Hounds turned and fled, their plate armour clanking through the night air the loudest sound she'd heard since waking from her stupor. The Hawks strode forward to join the line of Grey Knights, jeering at the retreating Hounds. It was a strange kind of victory, fuelled by anger, grief and desperation, but seeing the Hounds flee gave a jewel of hope back to the defenders of Tor Funweir.

* * *

They called themselves Knights of the Grey, but Gwen thought Protectors of Tor Funweir was more appropriate, for that is how they were seen. When the maddening delirium of the Dark Young had passed, the army of Ro looked to the knights as shimmering beacons of the One's favour. Their word was obeyed without question, and their stated intention to protect the surviving people of Ro had galvanized the army.

Unfortunately for Gwen, the death of her husband had doubled her already considerable cynicism and she struggled not to find reasons to argue with Fallon the Grey.

'I don't understand why we can't march south and assault Weir a second time,' she said. She hoped that the knights would be enough to turn the tide.

'Because we would all die,' replied Fallon.

'You don't know that,' spat Gwen.

He leant in, his head entering the globe of light under their thin canvas roof. The pavilion was modest, but kept off the rain as she argued with Fallon and his knights.

'I know that the queen lives,' said the exemplar. 'I know that her army lives – and I know that countless people of Ro still live free. Victories and defeats are fluid both. You win here, you lose there. All that matters is who lives when the battlefield is quiet. But the One God will pick no more fights until those who live are cared for.'

'The Walls of Ro,' said William Verellian. 'We hold north of Cozz and use the Walls as they were intended. General Frith will fortify Tiris and—'

'And Tor Funweir will stand a little longer,' offered Fallon.

They were right and she hated them for it. Surely there was a last-ditch plan, a desperate gambit that would ensure victory. Even without Xander, she struggled to accept defeat. They were giving up the south to the Lands of the Twisted Tree. Perhaps, in time, they'd be forced to give up the north as well. Her mind leapt forward, thinking of the men yet to take the field of battle. Malaki Frith and his Red Knights. Could ten thousand more make a difference? She couldn't imagine so, not when the Dark Young could annihilate five thousand Knights of the Dawn with no apparent effort. And the other great cities of Ro? Leith was already firmly under heel, but Arnon could be defended, for a time at least. Eventually, they'd have to choose between the church city and the capital at Ro Tiris.

There was nowhere for her mind to go but back to the peaceful sitting room in Ro Haran, perched next to Xander on a comfortable sofa. With no battles to fight and no struggles to endure, they were alone and at peace.

CHAPTER TWENTY-FOUR

TYR NANON IN THE
CITY OF RO WEIR

H E DROPPED SILENTLY into the water and pulled himself
along wooden pillars, under the small jetty. Keisha
followed and they swam through shadows towards the
eastern harbour of Weir. The guards above were watchmen of
Ro, given the easy job of patrolling the coast while the Hounds
secured the muster fields and pursued the fleeing army of Ro.
Hundreds of troop transports were at anchor in the bay, forming
a constantly moving supply of reinforcements from Karesia. The
clank of steel armour and the crack of whips filled the air and
he imagined Weir was now little more than a waypoint from
which to subjugate Tor Funweir. Or perhaps it would be the new
capital of the Twisted Tree, with its Mistress of Pain as Tyrant.

He stopped at the edge of the jetty, looking along the low stone
walls for a way into the city.

'I don't like the banner,' said Keisha, treading water next him.
'Can we pull it down?'

'That's not why we're here,' he replied. 'And we need to get
into the city first. There's a Tyrant in there somewhere and we're
going to kill her.'

'You mean *I'm* going to kill her?'

He smiled at her. 'Yes, I do mean that.'

'Let's get moving then,' said the Kirin girl, swimming past him
to the rocky coast, beyond which the southern walls rose.

It was dark, and the ripples they made in the water were too gentle to be seen by any patrol or lookout. They were distant from the arriving Hounds and approaching the port side of Weir. He was searching for the enchantress, but his mind didn't show him an easy path. The Mistress of Pain was stronger than when he had last felt her, though she was not yet the invincible force she wanted to be.

'Do you think the king got away?' asked Keisha, gliding along next to him.

'I don't know,' he replied. 'I wish I'd known there were that many. Not that I could have persuaded the king to turn back. For now, just be glad there are no more Dark Young in the city.'

Sloping walls of interlocking rocks rose above them, with water lapping at the base. Algae and seaweed made the lower rocks slippery, but it was a short climb to the docks above. They waited, treading water until the coast was clear. It was a strange thing to be infiltrating Weir again. Nanon had done it only recently, under less restrictive circumstances, just before Rham Jas died. On that occasion, an old water pipe had provided an ideal point of entry. That water pipe was now deep within a military camp and was inaccessible.

'How many men are we going to have to kill to get in there?' asked Keisha nervously.

'As few as possible. Killing people makes noise.'

He saw a gap in the patrolling men and pulled himself out of the water, sprawling as close as possible against the lowest rocks. Silently, he crawled upwards on his stomach, his limbs spread wide like a lizard leaving the ocean. His hands and feet found small gaps in the rocky incline, allowing him to scuttle to the wooden docks above. He gradually raised his head and scanned the eastern harbour of Weir. There were swaying lanterns, positioned along the huge docks, but many were broken, and there were dozens of gaps between globes of light.

He heard moaning from Keisha as she struggled to follow him. Though inhumanly dextrous, the dark-blood was not yet comfortable with her abilities. She worked too hard, using too much effort and not trusting her body.

'Just relax,' he whispered. 'Your blood will look after you.'

'Like it looked after my father?' she replied, crawling level with him.

He looked at her, her dusky skin barely visible in the darkness, but her face was locked in an intense stare. She was nervous. 'Your mind needs to relax more than your body, Kirin girl.'

'Just let me relax in my own time,' she replied, clasping the wooden platform with both hands and springing upwards. She landed in a silent crouch on the wood and darted across to disappear into shadow behind a line of barrels.

Nanon chuckled. Keisha wasn't the best at climbing, but skulking in darkness appeared to be second nature. He followed, jumping behind the barrels just as three guardsmen walked across their field of vision. Keisha was lying on her stomach, scanning the nearby gates and the port side of Weir. The city looked smaller from the south, with the sloped highways of the Old Town obscured behind high walls. But still the banner was visible. He imagined he'd be able to see the Twisted Tree no matter where he stood in the city of Weir. He liked it no more than did his companion, but while it still flew it was good motivation to carry on.

'Gates are guarded,' whispered Keisha. 'Where does that door go?' She pointed to a smaller entrance, further along the walls. It was unguarded and sat beneath a stone balcony. Though dozens of men patrolled the area, their route was haphazard and they paid little attention to the smaller door.

He pushed out his mind, trying again to find a route to the enchantress. He saw beyond the walls and the lattice of streets and alleys that snaked within, but the Mistress of Pain was somehow guarded. He winced as a point of pain flashed across his eyes. 'Damn,' he exclaimed, rubbing his face. 'She's strong. Stronger than she should be. Something has changed.'

'You said you could find her,' said Keisha, still looking at the small door.

A. J. SMITH

'Maybe if we get closer,' he replied. 'That door leads to silos, above the catacombs. It's where they store their grain.'

'I don't think their grain is worth guarding.'

He nodded and they edged forward, crawling flat across the wooden planking. They were distant from the main gate and the multitudes of arriving Hounds, but still they crawled between scattered patrols of Ro guardsmen. From one sliver of darkness to the next, their short journey took time and patience. Nanon didn't need to instruct Keisha on how to stay hidden, but she needed reminding to stay patient. She tried to cover the ground too quickly and he had to stop her several times, reiterating that waiting was often the best policy. The guards were not looking for two people trying to sneak into the grain silos. They weren't really looking for anything. They were just a fingernail of an enormous hand, given a random assignment to keep them busy while the Mistress of Pain planned her next move.

'You're enjoying yourself,' he whispered, feeling sparks of elation flying from the creeping dark-blood.

'I'm sneaking into a city to avenge my family. It's exciting.'

He smiled, making her frown at the wrongness of the human expression on his grey face. 'I'm enjoying myself too,' he replied. 'Usually I'd just fly over the walls and perch on a building. It's nice to try it the hard way for a change.'

'What?' Her face screwed up.

They were close to the door now, and clear of any meaningful patrols. The doorway was wide, with solid oak, barred in the middle. Sacks of grain were piled outside, but no-one stood watch.

'Shall we go?' he asked.

'You can fly?' she replied.

He tilted his head, but didn't answer. It was a simple kind of humour, but he enjoyed the look on her face. Keisha had not yet seen him take other shapes and he planned to surprise her at some point. He was sure that it would be funny. Once she'd stopped shouting at him.

He darted across the last few feet of darkness and stood beneath an arched canopy, dug into the outer wall. The door wasn't locked, but removing the bar would not be quiet; nor did the huge, steel hinges appear oiled. Nanon imagined there would be a sharp creak were he to simply pull open the door.

Keisha stood next to him in the shadowy doorway, her face still locked in confusion. 'You have to answer my questions. That hasn't changed.'

'Yes, I can fly,' he replied. 'When I'm a bird – or a bat, or a griffin. I'm sure there are other shapes I could take that have wings, though I've not tried them.'

'You can change shape? How?'

He tilted his head and realized that he couldn't remember his training. He couldn't even remember who had taught him about other shapes, nor how he had acquired the ability. 'I'm very old. There are lots of things I struggle to remember. Now, how shall we open this door?'

She shook her head in frustration and turned to inspect the door. He felt her mind churning with possibilities as she assessed the hinges, the bar, the weeds growing from gaps in the stonework, but she'd largely stopped thinking about Nanon's ability to change shape. This was good. She was able to keep focus and remain in the now, no matter how strange her surroundings. She frowned, then smiled, poking her head out of the alcove and taking note of nearby patrols. 'Just open it,' she said.

'And the noise?' he queried. 'They'll come and check a sudden creak from a door that shouldn't be creaking. And they'll find an unbarred door that shouldn't be unbarred.'

She didn't appear to consider these things important. 'So they hear a creak and see an unbarred door. These aren't elite soldiers. If they look inside they'll see a dark silo. In such a place I'd bet on you and me being able to evade any man who pokes his head inside.'

He considered it. Perhaps his slow, methodical approach was not always correct. Perhaps just opening doors sometimes was the wise course. 'I'd bet on us too,' he replied. 'If I fully understood the concept of gambling.'

She tested the bar and found that, with a little effort, it could be coaxed out of its niche on the rusted doorframe. She lifted it only as high as was needed and then waved him back to keep an eye on the patrolling men. 'The next bit makes noise,' she whispered, taking a firm hold of the door handle.

Nanon held up a hand, telling her to wait. When the nearest men reached the most distant point of their patrols, before they turned back towards the secluded door, he lowered his hand and nodded. She grunted, and strained against the handle. For a second nothing happened, then there was a grating of metal, and a thin dusting of rust covered the ground. The hinges emitted a sharp creak and the heavy door groaned outwards. She swung herself through the narrow opening, followed quickly by Nanon, and an instant later he'd pulled the door closed behind them. The sound of the door had been a murmur, not a shout, but would certainly be investigated.

The silo was in complete darkness, visible to his Dokkalfar eyes as a grey twilight world of barrels and sacks, piled from the sunken floor to the vaulted ceiling. Keisha, unable to see as clearly, had quickly edged along the wall and found a line of broken crates to move behind. He was impressed. She grasped things quickly, more than just how to hold a katana or stay hidden; the girl was perceptive and adaptable – and would become increasingly dangerous to her enemies.

'Nanon, hide,' she whispered once she was well concealed.

He could hear men approaching the door, complaining about the need to investigate. A few seconds before they opened the door, he hopped to the side, silently took the shape of a rat and crawled under a thick pile of burst grain sacks.

Moonlight streamed into the silo as the guards flung open the door. Three men holding torches, with a handful more staying outside. They scanned the cobweb-ridden warehouse from the doorway.

'Probably nothing,' grunted a man of Ro.

'*Someone* opened the door,' replied another. 'But I don't want to go rooting through this place. If it was thieves, they lucked out – as much rotten grain and mouldy bread as they can carry. If they find a way out.'

The guardsmen shared a laugh and retreated outside. They seemed to have little desire to do actual investigative work. The moonlight disappeared and the bar was replaced, leaving the silo in darkness. Nanon snuffled out from his concealment and scampered across, still in rat form, to give Keisha a nice surprise.

* * *

The silo was one of dozens, and adjoined hundreds more underground warehouses and countless vaulted chambers. Weir was almost as large underground as it was on the surface, but far darker. Once Keisha had stopped shouting about Nanon's ability to turn into a rat, the two of them made good time through the underground highways, encountering nothing but insects and vermin.

Travelling from the port side to the Old Town had been tricky, and required crawling through tunnels that provided water to the poorer areas of the city, but getting wet was the worst inconvenience they faced. As they took rest in a former wine cellar, Nanon considered how close he'd have to be to locate the Mistress of Pain. He'd tried every hour since they'd entered the city, and it was now well past midnight. Each attempt had been met with the same lack of success and the same sharp pain.

'Try again,' said Keisha, looking impatiently up a vertical passageway, at the top of which was a sewer covering. 'We can't just wander around the catacombs all night.'

He hadn't told her, but he was becoming concerned. When last he'd sensed the enchantress she'd been weak and steadily going mad, unable to keep her mind in order or understand the twisted contortions of thought caused by so many thralls. Now her very presence was elusive, as if she was being actively protected from his scrying. And there was something else, something causing him pain, something old and dark, festering in the Mistress of Pain's shadow.

'I've been trying since we got inside the city. I'll try again when I've rested. Each time I try I. . . brush against something. It takes much effort.'

She came and sat next to him on the lower shelves of a disused wine rack. Her expression was a cross between concern and tolerance. 'I'm not stupid,' she said. 'I know there's a problem. If you tell me what it is, I might be able to help.'

He groaned, unsure how to explain the restrictions he was feeling. She certainly *wasn't* stupid, but she *was* human. He understood her as much as any human he'd spent time with – more so in some ways; certainly as much as he ever understood her father. This did not make the explanation any easier.

'Something's protecting her,' he replied. 'She might be protecting herself. But she couldn't have done it the last time I sensed her. I'm worried that if I push too hard. . . I'll see something I don't want to see.'

Keisha nodded, but her eyes were narrow and Nanon could tell she didn't really understand. 'If you can't find her we might as well go back to the forest. I'm not trying to be mean, but we can't kill her if we can't find her.'

It was a logical assessment of their situation and far more direct than he was used to from a human. If he calmed his mind and remained still while he searched, perhaps he *could* find her. 'Okay,' he conceded. 'But you'll have to watch over me. My body will be vulnerable while my mind searches.'

She looked at him as if he'd said something utterly incomprehensible. 'You're going to do something strange, aren't you?'

He smiled and closed his eyes, swaying gently against the stone wall. His mind glided away from the frowning Kirin girl and left the wine cellar in search of the enchantress. He was now committed, with the trivialities of walking and talking just a discarded distraction. He moved upwards, through layers of stone and open, dusty chambers, until his mind felt the nightly breeze and saw the dark streets of Ro Weir. There was no trail to follow, no obvious direction or shining light, telling him where to look. He could feel the thoughts of a hundred thousand men and women, but the enchantress was not among them. A background hum of equal parts despair and malevolence infused the city, but it had no focus he could discern. It was a huge spider's web with an invisible spider. Where was she? He looked to the centre of the Old Town, to the castellations of the knight marshal's barracks and the squat opulence of the duke's residence. He couldn't sense the enchantress in either building. All he felt was a dull pain and a shadow, just out of sight.

He pushed his mind out further, extending tendrils of thought into the city. Soldiers, nobles, merchants, slaves; the hidden, the afraid, the confident, the insane. But no Seven Sister. He finally admitted to himself that he knew what obscured Saara the Mistress of Pain. On some level he'd known since he had first failed to locate her. The shadow that caused him pain was divine. It was a tentacle of the Dead God and it was wrapped round the enchantress like an iron blanket. He couldn't touch her – or even find her. To try would be to pit his strength against that of Shub-Nillurath. He doubted that even a dark-blood could strike at her, so powerful had she become.

The pain became unbearably sharp and all-encompassing. Something had seen him. Something knew where he was. Another presence had sent its mind into the darkness of Weir, looking for the enchantress. Something dark, filled with hate and hunger. It looked from every angle at once, using senses unknown to Nanon. It was not man or Dokkalfar. It was like nothing he'd ever felt and it looked at him with interest. He gently pulled back the edges of his mind, afraid that any sudden actions would startle the hate-filled presence. It let him retreat, making him aware that it could snap at him if it wished, like a bird of prey eyeing a mouse.

He opened his eyes and was back in the dusty wine cellar, breathing heavily. His senses felt raw and exposed, as if the strange presence had scraped its teeth across his mind. Nanon rubbed his eyes and coughed, feeling drained and naked. He suddenly looked up. Where was the Kirin girl?

'Keisha!' he said, as loudly as he dared.

'Over here,' she replied, a catch of breathless awe in her voice.

Nanon staggered to his feet, using the wall as support, and edged towards her voice. In the gloomy cellar, surrounded by broken wood and dusty bottles of wine, the girl stood motionless, looking up at something in the darkness. The pain returned to his head, though now it was merely dull and uncomfortable.

'Keisha!' he repeated.

A throaty growl seeped from the shadows and Nanon's hand went to his longsword.

'Don't,' snapped Keisha. 'It won't hurt me.'

Before he could ask what *it* was, the darkness slowly retreated like an insidious curtain to reveal shades of black, formed into a feline aberration, towering over the young dark-blood. As its head and limbs came into focus, Nanon saw a creature – almost a Dark Young, but somehow different – hunkering down and inspecting Keisha. The thing had four muscular limbs, three of which ended in a mass of clicking feelers. The fourth – its right back leg – appeared to be severed at the knee, though the injury did not hamper its movements. Its head was stretched in the middle and sharp at each end, with its mouth nothing more than a horizontal slice.

Keisha reached out towards the creature and it did not retreat, growl *or* attack. It lowered its strange head and allowed her to touch its flesh. She gasped, stroking her hand across the shimmering black head. The surface shifted and flowed under her touch, forming into a mockery of a human face all too familiar to both of them. Nanon didn't know how to react. He'd sensed the death of Rham Jas, and he'd known some defilement had plagued his friend in death, but he had never imagined this.

'Father,' said Keisha, in barely a whisper.

The creature didn't react, though the face gained texture and expression as it looked at her through her father's eyes. It slowly padded round the girl, ignoring Nanon and appearing almost protective.

'Be careful,' he warned. 'That is not your father.'

The creature snapped at him, showing a line of jagged, glassy teeth and crouching between Nanon and Keisha. It didn't attack, but the old Tyr knew with certainty that it could kill him if it wanted to.

'I won't hurt me,' repeated Keisha. 'Don't make it think you're a threat.'

He tilted his head, staying on the balls of his feet and preparing to move if needed. He could feel nothing of Rham Jas within the beast, but he did not extend his mind to look closely. He feared the creature was beyond him, perhaps beyond everything.

'If you can sense something in this thing, you should tell me,' said Nanon, keeping his dark eyes on the shimmering black creature.

'I feel its blood,' replied Keisha. 'Its heat, its strength. It's a dark-blood, like me. It wants something. . . to tell us something. . . to show us something.'

Nanon could feel nothing but hate coming from the beast and he was scared for his companion. The creature had certainly once been Rham Jas Rami. It had once been Keisha's father and Nanon's friend. Now it was a servant of Shub-Nillurath. That at least was beyond doubt.

'We can't trust it,' he whispered. 'We need to leave.'

The creature opened its mouth, hissing between gnashing teeth. It reacted to Nanon's words, showing anger but still not attacking. It crept backwards until it stood over Keisha's shoulder, pointing its sharp head at the forest dweller. He didn't doubt that it meant Keisha no harm, but he had no such certainty about himself. He pushed his mind out a little further, trying to find something to trust in the aberration. It let him, keeping its malevolent power in check, until Nanon located a tiny speck of a familiar mind. Rham Jas *was* in there, though twisted and primal and barely a memory of the man he'd been. But enough to sense the blood of his daughter.

'I'm sorry for you, Kirin man,' he said, stepping towards the malformed head. 'I know who you now serve, and that you have no choice.'

'What does it want to show us?' asked Keisha.

Nanon was hesitant to delve any further into its mind, until it approached him closely and bowed its head. Close up it was terrible and beautiful in equal measure. The lines of its body suggested a Dark Young mixed with a predatory cat and a sentient shadow. It was a servant of Shub-Nillurath that did not consider them enemies. The conundrum of its thoughts was enough to make the old Tyr curious and he reached out just a little more. He felt its depthless hatred and hunger, and glided round their sharp edges to the tiny speck of humanity that remained. Two faces dominated the speck, both women, one wreathed in love, the other in hatred. It had come back to Weir for the Mistress of Pain, but, like Nanon, had been unable to find her. Instead it had found its daughter – and it was confused.

'It appears Shub-Nillurath fosters little unity among his followers,' he said. 'This creature wants to kill the Seven Sister as much as us, but it can't. They're rivals for their god's affection. It wants to help us kill her.'

'What of my father?' asked Keisha.

Nanon hesitated. Perhaps the tiny speck of Rham Jas still had power, but everything else he sensed from the Aberration was infused with devotion to Shub-Nillurath. 'Your father is dead, but his love for his daughter is not. He died looking at you, thinking about how he'd let you down. It was his last and only thought when they removed his head. Such thoughts linger. . . such thoughts are powerful indeed.'

Keisha's lip quivered and tears formed in her eyes. She turned round, not wanting to look at the creature that had been her father. The Aberration padded after her, whining like a wounded animal. It nudged at her shoulder, hissing in agitation, but she shrugged it away. It gnashed its teeth together, splitting the face of Rham Jas in two, but she didn't turn. Then it roared, a vile gurgle, wreathed in anguish.

'Quiet!' snapped Keisha, turning to face the creature. 'If you will help we will let you help – but you are *not* my father. My father

was killed by Saara the Mistress of Pain. *You* are just a monster.'
She drew Rham Jas's katana. 'I will cut off your remaining three
legs if you do anything I don't like.'

Nanon's eyes were wide. He held his breath, ready to arm
himself, but the creature remained silent and still. In fact, as strange
as it was, the creature appeared meek, as if cowed by Keisha's
reprimand.

'You will show us what we need to see,' stated Keisha. 'Now!'

The Aberration obeyed. It didn't know why, it only knew that it
loved her and that it must keep her safe. It skulked away, through
the dusty wine cellar, to a downward staircase, covered in cobwebs,
where it waited for them.

'You have hidden depths, Kirin girl,' Nanon said with a wary
smile. 'Shall we follow?'

'At a distance,' she replied, wiping tears from her cheeks.

* * *

The Aberration led them through forgotten chambers and vast
catacombs. They followed up, down, left, right. Whenever it
stopped, so did they, and the distance between them remained.
They were far beyond the moonlight, and relied on Nanon's keen
senses to orient themselves in the darkness. The creature shifted
through a hundred different tones of black, and was strangely easy
to locate from its outline. He didn't know if this was deliberate,
but it allowed Keisha to see in near total darkness. Even so, both
of them stumbled multiple times in the forgotten bowels of Weir,
until the Aberration stopped and directed a hiss ahead of him.
Nanon judged they were beneath the knight marshal's barracks,
among a collection of vaults he could never have found without
help. The creature had led them up from beneath. Three burning
torches provided a muddy light, illuminating a corridor and a
dozen or more vaults.

Nanon and Keisha remained at the end of the corridor, shielding
their eyes from the sudden light, while the creature scratched next
to the furthest vault.

'Footprints,' said Keisha, pointing at disturbances in the dust. 'People come down here. One person at least.'

The still air was sliced through by an eruption of insane laughter. As one, Nanon and Keisha drew their weapons and crouched. The laughter continued, cracking and breaking until the female voice was hoarse. The creature was looking at something in the furthest vault, something it wanted to show them. Nanon sheathed his longsword and smiled, realizing how foolish he'd been.

'Your father didn't kill all of them,' he said. 'She may wish it so, but the Mistress of Pain is not the last of the Seven Sisters.'

They joined the Aberration, getting as close as they had when they left the wine cellar. In the last vault, chained to the wall, was a woman draped in rags. The tattoo of a coiled snake was just visible on her cheek. Nanon had seen it before, when she'd inched Rham Jas in Ro Leith.

'Isabel the Seductress,' he said, with a shallow bow. 'You are less well-attired than when last we met.'

The enchantress had no mind. Her eyes had rolled back in her head and the only things coming from her mouth were insane laughter and drool. Her sister had raped her mind and used it to protect herself. Nanon had been unable to find Saara because she now possessed the power of all her dead sisters, and was using the remaining one to store her thralls. She was more powerful than any enchantress who had gone before her and believed herself untouchable.

'Can I kill this woman?' asked Keisha, still holding her father's katana.

He nodded. 'You can. And doing so will allow you to kill the Mistress of Pain.' He turned to the Aberration. 'She's your equal. A Tyrant in the Lands of the Twisted Tree. That's why you can't kill her. You need us to do it for you.'

The creature backed away until it was half in darkness. Keisha followed its movements, the katana resting across her shoulders.

'Where are you going?' she asked.

Its mouth puckered and spat, forming deep grunts and

elongated syllables. The noises rose and fell in pitch and volume, until recognizable words formed. 'I will never harm you, daughter,' growled the Aberration. 'You will be welcome in the Tyranny of Arnon.' Then it was gone, melting silently into the shadows to spread the will of Shub-Nillurath to the lands of men.

'Until we meet again,' muttered Nanon.

They were both silent for a moment, processing what they'd seen. A friend and a father had a new life, but a life devoted to their enemy. In the years to come, the Aberration would be at the front of his mind, but now, in the vaults of Ro Weir, there was an enchantress to kill.

'Are you ready?' he asked Keisha. 'When it's done, we'll have to move quickly. I should be able to sense the Mistress of Pain and we'll need to get to her.'

Her eyes were distant, but there was a focus that he had not seen before. She still looked at the darkness where the creature had disappeared, but she did not cry and her hands did not shake. 'I'm ready,' she replied, turning and pointing her katana at Isabel the Seductress.

CHAPTER TWENTY-FIVE

HALLA SUMMER WOLF IN THE CITY OF TIERGARTEN

S HE HAD THREE new wounds. A long nick to her left cheek,
a deep cut across the back of her right hand and an irritating,
but shallow, puncture wound in her lower back. She'd been
blindsided when the siege towers first dropped their drawbridges
and had missed the glaive-wielder behind her. Only a thrown axe
from Rexel Falling Cloud had stopped the wound being fatal. As
it was, exhaustion was proving a bigger problem than blood. They
had committed every warrior and sprung every surprise to defend
the walls of Tiergarten. Only Alahan's mysterious company had
yet to be used, and she was sceptical about the newly confident
young thain's plan.

Unrahgahr and his family were gone, pursuing the trees north,
and could not be relied on to return. Rorg and the Low Kasters
were a nice surprise, but they were now within the walls and had
lost too many men to be used again in such a fashion. When Rulag
came again – and he would come again – it would just be steel on
steel. Unless the two hundred old men in the vault were as mighty
as Alahan and Crowe believed.

'Halla,' said Rexel, cleaning his hand-axes. 'Look at that.'

He pointed at the furthest siege tower. It was slowly falling
away from the walls, as fire turned the wood to ashen planks.
A small figure crouched on the battlements before it, gazing
down into the city. Halla's battle brothers stopped in surprise
at the small person, pausing in the grim task of throwing

dead bodies back over the wall.

Alahan was below, directing men wheeling carts across the exposed gateway, and he seemed to be the focus of the small figure.

'That's a girl,' said Halla.

'I didn't think even the bastard of Jarvik would use children in war,' replied Falling Cloud. 'But he has fewer warriors than we thought; maybe he had no choice.'

'You, girl,' shouted Halla, pointing across the battlements at the small figure. 'Stay there.'

The girl stood up and froze in place, standing amidst bloodied men and cleaved bodies. The dim light around her seemed to shift focus as a large, glossy bird dropped on to her shoulder. The girl didn't flinch, though the men around her backed away.

'Halla,' called the young girl, hurrying along the walls with the raven firmly planted on her shoulder.

With an excited hop in her step, Ingrid Teardrop ran towards her and flung her arms round the bloodied axe-maiden. Halla paused, unsure how to react and sending a confused frown towards Falling Cloud. The raven glided to the battlements, pointing his yellow beak at their embrace.

'Erm, how did you get here?' she asked, eventually lifting her arms to return Ingrid's hug. 'Are you hurt?'

The young girl buried her head in Halla's chain mail, her slender arms wrapped tightly round her waist. She was crying and her whole body shook.

Heinrich Blood, the young priest, ran to them, slinging his short bow across his shoulders, the quiver on his back empty of arrows. He crouched next to the girl and assessed her. 'Girl, are you injured?' he asked.

'*That's* Alahan's sister?' asked Falling Cloud. 'Thought she was a prisoner in Fredericksand. How the fuck did she get here?'

'Shush,' replied Halla. 'Watch the language. Heinrich, she doesn't appear to be wounded.'

He stood and shook his head. 'Well, she's not letting go of you. I'd say she's just in shock.'

413

The news was relayed quickly. Ingrid Teardrop was alive and had somehow found her way to Tiergarten. It gave a strange escalation to their already elevated feelings of resolve. Rulag had a smaller army than they'd imagined, the defenders had repulsed the first attack *and* they'd recovered Algenon Teardrop's daughter.

'Ingrid! Where is she?' shouted Alahan, running up the stone steps and appearing on the forward walls.

The young girl pulled herself away from Halla and her weakly smiling face turned towards her brother. They met, surrounded by blood and smoke, in a tight embrace, Alahan dropping to his knees and Ingrid howling with joy.

'I saw you running at the gates. I saw the trolls. I was hiding in a siege tower. I escaped from my tent. Rulag said he was going to kill you, but I caused loads of trouble and made lots of his men leave. I hate them all. I'm glad you made the trees go away. I saw them, they were horrible. They made me sick.'

She babbled about things and people, telling her brother everything that had happened to her in no particular order and with little clarity. She spoke of their father, their home, their uncle, a Karesian called Al Hasim, another called Kal Varaz, a raven called Corvus. None of it made sense to Halla, but Alahan listened to every word, clutching his sister's ragged clothing with tears springing in his eyes. In among the babble, it became obvious that Ingrid had thinned the ranks of Rulag's army through a nightly campaign of sabotage. How she'd remained unseen was a mystery.

'Halla, there's work to be done,' said Rexel. 'Tender as this scene is, it won't get done if we don't do it.'

'There are many dead and many wounded,' offered Heinrich.

She paused, watching the children of Algenon Teardrop reconnect. She had no brothers or sisters and had never experienced the bond she was witnessing now. It was the only beautiful thing for miles in any direction and she didn't want to look away, fearing what her eyes would show her.

'Halla,' repeated Falling Cloud. 'Tricken is over there shouting at us.'

She looked round, beyond dead bodies and burning wood, and saw her full company. They spread out across the battlements and covered every walkway. Each man was looking to Halla for orders. They had killed hundreds of men and lost friends to axe and glaive, but they were still tougher than anything Rulag could conjure.

Tricken Ice Fang, standing beside Old Father Crowe by the gatehouse, was waving his arms at her. 'How many dead?' shouted the red-haired chain-master. 'We've got at least a hundred down here.'

She leant on Falling Cloud and took a few deep breaths. 'What do you think?' she asked.

'I'll get men on it,' he replied. 'You go and fetch some water.'

She smiled, suddenly feeling how dry her mouth was and how bloodied her hands. Beneath her, young boys and girls of Tiergarten ran across the cobbles, delivering buckets of water and hard bread to exhausted warriors. She let Heinrich help her down the steps and then she sat heavily against a convenient barrel, stretching her legs out to relieve their stiffness. All around her, battle brothers did the same, taking rest and refreshment as best they could. She shouted a few orders to a few men and let the rest relax.

Falling Cloud eventually counted fifty-two dead warriors from her company, and a further twelve who were too wounded to fight.

'I killed men, Daughter of the Wolf,' said Timon the Butcher, appearing over Halla with a hunk of brown bread in his hand. He had many wounds, old and new, but none appeared to bother him.

'I saw,' replied Halla. 'You and Rorg made the difference, my friend. From now on, you and the Low Kasters stay on the walls with me.'

She didn't move from the barrel. Within an hour she was joined by Crowe and Tricken, both with a similar appraisal of the situation. They'd made Rulag's army flee mostly through ferocity and surprise. They were still outnumbered and, when the men of Ursa came again, there would be no surprises. The broken gates had been replaced by piled carts and braced with huge wooden planks, but the courtyard was dangerously exposed. The only truly good news, other than the appearance of Ingrid, was the destruction of Rulag's siege towers. He'd have to rely on ladders, though reports from the forward walls indicated that catapults were also mingling within the army of Ursa.

The day was drawing to a close, with a crisp wind signalling the arrival of a cold night. Hundreds of defenders took their rest wherever their weary bodies would take them, with many slouching against battlements or sprawled across Ulric's Yard and the bottom few landings of Kalall's Steps. Halla and her commanders now sat round a campfire, eating from bowls of steaming soup. Tricken and Earem Spider Killer debated troop placements; Falling Cloud, Heinrich and Lullaby argued about where best to tend to the wounded; Crowe sat next to her in silence. She hadn't seen Alahan or Ingrid since she left the walls, but word was that the young thain of Fredericksand was seeing his sister safe to the High Hold of Summer Wolf, after which he'd return to the vaults.

'They'll come again at first light,' muttered Crowe. 'Rulag will need a night to reprimand his commanders and shout himself hoarse.'

She slurped down a mouthful of thick vegetable soup, rich with onion and carrot. 'We can hold him off once, maybe twice more. Assuming his catapults don't make too much of a mess.'

Tricken contributed from across the fire. 'They'll try for a breach. There's no point sending boulders into the city. They might dent a few houses, but it won't help them get past us.'

'Is there any mead?' asked Crowe, squinting at a nearby serving boy running back and forth with a cauldron of soup.

'I'll get some, Master Crowe,' replied the boy, placing his cauldron on the cobbles and disappearing towards Kalall's Steps.

* * *

The old priest was right. As the first slivers of sunlight crept in from the rolling Fjorlan Sea, Halla saw the army of Ursa begin to deploy. She was fed and rested, but her limbs were tight and a dozen small cuts were giving her grief. Falling Cloud, below, commanded the cloud-men of the Wolf Wood round Ulric's Yard and the main gate. They were the most mobile troops she had, relying on hand-axes and light armour, and would hold the gateway. Tricken and Crowe stood with her above the ballistae yards, all looking west from the battlements.

'Ballistae are sighted, my lady,' said Tricken.

'I know,' she replied.

'Men are holding firm,' he said.

She looked at him. 'Tricken. . . I know.'

The red-haired chain-master shrugged. 'Didn't like the silence.'

'I'll go and tell Rulag to hurry up,' she quipped.

Across the plains, the men of Ursa began to move. They held shields, locked in formation, and advanced in columns. Behind them, pulled forward by sled dogs, were the catapults. There were a dozen or so artillery pieces, each one a tall wooden frame with a single, tightly wound arm of thick timber.

'Good,' said Tricken. 'I fucking hate waiting around to fight.'

Halla and Crowe both gave him dark looks, but hers was tinged with amusement. If the past year had taught her anything, it was that humour was often the best defence when your axe didn't feel sharp enough.

With no siege towers for cover, the attackers moved slowly, keeping together behind their wall of shields. As they approached the first ruined tower and entered ballistae range, the army broke up and spread into thin lines, marching over the snow with a rhythmical thump of boots and clank of chain mail.

'Start some fires,' she said quietly, making Tricken turn to the ballistae crews and start shouting.

Huge arrows were pulled taut and loaded with casks of pitch. From along the forward walls, a dozen fuses were touched with flame and a dozen huge bowstrings were loosed. The artillery was pointed upwards and the arrows arced towards the edge of their range, thudding into the snowy ground with a snap.

417

Small globes of fire flared and mushroomed amidst Rulag's army, sending men and steel into the air. Burning warriors shrieked and broke formation, but the bulk closed ranks and the advance continued. The ballistae fired again and more men were set aflame, but the attackers now broke into a jog and fanned out, bringing their long siege ladders swiftly to the front of the advance. The catapults jumped into life and sent boulders towards the city, covering the warriors of Jarvik and forcing the defenders to take cover.

'Heads down!' screamed Tricken, as a thick line of warriors ducked behind castellations and raised shields.

The boulders were aimed at the walls, but several overshot and smashed into buildings. The rest clustered in a small section next to the gate, sending chunks of stone in all directions. The battlements filled with dust and a thick spray of snow and ice. When Halla rose from concealment and looked over the walls, she saw a thick press of warriors assembling before her city. The catapults had caused no practical breach, but had smashed a portion of the battlements, and the army of Ursa was bringing its ladders and focusing on this area.

Halla moved quickly to the most likely point of contact, followed by Old Father Crowe and the Low Kasters. Rocks and hand-axes were thrown from the walls, striking the upturned shields below.

'Hold the walls,' she shouted as she ran. Below, she could see Falling Cloud viewing the advance through the makeshift gates. He looked up at her, his hand twitching as if he wanted to join her. 'Rexel, stay down there,' she called.

All along the walls, ladders struck stone, concentrated in the centre where the catapults had broken a section of the battlements. Spears and poles were levelled by the defenders and ladders were pushed away, toppling backwards on to the plains. Others were harder to dislodge and shouts came from below as men began to climb.

'Get rid of those ladders,' she shouted.

She reached the centre and stood, exposed on a broken section of wall, faced with five ladders. She assisted the men trying to dislodge them, wedging her axe under a final rung and heaving upwards. With Timon's help, one of the ladders was flung away from the wall, but she could see dozens of men ascending the other four, dangerously close to the battlements.

'Steel on steel it is,' announced Crowe, swinging his war-hammer into the head of the first man to reach the top of the wall. The man's skull split and he fell limply downwards.

'These walls are ours!' she roared, leading a mixed group of Low Kasters and her toughest battle brothers.

Men reached the walls and died. All along the battlements, brutal close combat raged as defenders struggled to kill an endless stream of attackers. More ladders were brought to bear and more men formed up for their chance to ascend the walls of Tiergarten. The ballistae kept firing, sending more fire into the columns of attackers, but the crews were now occupied with defending the walls and their firing was sporadic.

Halla chopped at anonymous heads and faces, each one that emerged atop the broken section of wall falling to join a growing pile of cleaved bodies. They kept the stone clear for what seemed like hours, until the first man of Jarvik set foot upon the battlements. A huge axe-man, wearing the red bear claw of Ursa, hacked his way through men to stand atop the walls. He roared and froth bubbled from his mouth, but he was sane enough to hold his ground and allow other men to join him.

Crowe stepped away from her. 'He needs killing,' said the priest, moving towards the berserk man of Ursa.

Halla stayed where she was, keeping a steady stream of climbers from getting to the walls, but half her eye kept track of Crowe. The tall, bearded spectre of a priest glided through defenders, swinging his war-hammer in tight circles, until he reached the huge axe-man.

A group of attackers now held a small section of the walls, their shields held close in a semi-circle. Crowe kicked out, driving a shield into its wielder's chest and crushing the man's head with his hammer. Other defenders joined him and the semi-circle was slowly crushed. The huge berserker split a man in two with his axe, but turned to face the old priest and was kicked in the groin.

'You're big, but you're stupid,' roared Crowe as the man stumbled backwards, cradling his crotch in pain.

He tried to raise his axe, but repeated blows from the priest's war-hammer crushed his defence. He took a blow to the face, another to the forehead. When his axe slumped to the stone, Crowe clubbed him to a messy death, using strength far beyond his years.

'Hold the walls,' repeated Halla. 'This is not the day we fall.'

Roars of agreement sounded from the walls and the warriors of Tiergarten doubled their efforts, fighting beyond exhaustion to defend their ground. They were severely outnumbered but conviction spurred them on. She saw Timon battling four men; she saw axe-maidens facing off against berserk warriors; she saw duels, mismatches and slaughter on both sides.

Below, Falling Cloud was marshalling the cloud-men to keep the gates clear. Whenever Rulag's men started moving the upturned carts, they were cut down by throwing-axes. The nimble warriors of the Wolf Wood were in loose formation, acting as skirmishers to blunt any attempt at breaching the gatehouse.

Just when she was starting to lose track of time, a horn sounded from the plains and the attackers withdrew, fleeing in chaotic lines across the plains of Tiergarten to their waiting rearguard. Cheers and shouts chased them from the city, accompanied by axes striking stone in a mocking salute.

She leant on her axe and smiled, trying to slow her laboured breathing. As the adrenaline faded, she checked herself for new wounds and found none except a nasty cut to the back of her hand. For a brief moment, with no sounds of combat to assault her thinking, Halla wondered how many men she'd killed.

* * *

Two hours later they came again. This time, the catapults were loosed first in a series of concentrated barrages at the centre of the wall. Tricken assessed every boulder's impact, shouting to her about the widening breach in the battlements, until, with another horn, the army rushed the walls and were once again turned back.

As the day dragged on, the defenders became a battered line of hyper-alert warriors, waiting for the next attack and the next man to kill. She stayed with Crowe and Timon, always at the point of contact on the forward walls, driving their battle brothers to fight through their relentless example.

Alahan joined them during the day. The young thain was now a different man. With the safety of his sister and the memory of his time in the vault, he now had something tangible to fight for. Even Halla was impressed at his skill and ferocity. He was arrogant about so many things – his father, his name – but not about his prowess in battle, and this was where his true might shone through. She didn't care about anything else; she was simply glad to have a fearsome warrior standing next to her, exemplar of Rowanoco or not.

Rulag's men attacked twice more, each time driving their bodies a little further through the breach and on to the walls. Falling Cloud kept the gateway clear, but his force was dwindling as more and more men were needed on the walls. As the sky began to bruise and the day drew to a close, their losses became obvious.

'Run, ya bastards,' snarled Crowe as the attackers withdrew from their latest assault.

She slumped to the dusty stone battlements and winced in pain. 'My back feels like there's still an axe in it.'

The priest wiped blood from his face and smiled at her. It was the only smile she could see among the defenders. The others were standing as statues, looking at dead friends and relatives, unable or unwilling to stand down and take rest. She didn't dare look closely for fear that she'd see Tricken, Rorg, Falling Cloud, Timon or Heinrich, slumped dead at their post.

She could hear Lullaby below, as the wise woman scuttled forward lending aid to wounded and dying men, and she could see Alahan, glaring at the running men of Ursa, but everyone else was beyond her sight.

'They won't come again 'til the morning,' said Crowe.

* * *

She slept. Bedrolls had been packed into the Riverman's Exchange building, off Ulric's Yard, and hundreds of men and women were snatching a few hours' troubled sleep. Only Brindon Crowe and Alahan had taken the walk back up Kalall's Steps to the High Hold. The few non-combatants did the job of clearing bodies, bashing dents out of breastplates and repairing links in chain mail. Several old men, former blacksmiths and stonemasons, had come out of retirement to lend their skills to the defence of Tiergarten, but everyone else tried to sleep. None of her captains were dead, though all had new scars to show their fellows. Her company had been at the front each time an assault came, using their experience to drive the less-skilled defenders to greater and greater deeds of valour. Even with Rulag's reduced force, Tiergarten was punching well above its weight.

Somewhere across the plains of Summer Wolf, she imagined the lord of Jarvik raged. He'd thrown everything at the city, believing a swift victory would be secured by his darkwood trees and his advantage of numbers. He had not known about Halla and her company. He hadn't known about Unrahgahr and the Ice Men, nor about Rorg, Timon and their Low Kasters. But still he had the advantage of numbers, an advantage that would slowly kill the defenders. Unless Alahan and Crowe were right, and the Ice Giant would lend his support.

Alahan was different now. He no longer averted his eyes from Halla, nor did he show anxiety or doubt. He'd become a commander, as respected as any man in Tiergarten. She tried to look past him and see the big picture, but her resolve was faltering.

After three hours of restless sleep, a nagging itch at the back of her neck caused her to wake and leave the Riverman's Exchange. The battlements were quiet, the breach well-guarded and skeleton crews remained on watch by each ballista. Ulric's Yard was dotted with fires and clusters of resting defenders. Tiergarten was deathly quiet, with just whistling cold air plummeting down Kalall's Steps. The sky was sparkling black and beautiful next to the snow-capped buildings.

An explosion sounded from behind her and she jumped in surprise as a column of fire rose suddenly in the city. In Starshold, the second level of Tiergarten, a large building was now aflame, sending muddy soot into the clear air. She froze for a moment, uncertain of what to do or what the explosion might mean. Citizens ran from the second level, heading to Kalall's Steps to avoid the fire. Defenders emerged from dozens of buildings round Ulric's Yard, strapping on armour and gawking at the flames in confusion.

Then dozens of men appeared from Starshold, rushing downwards in tight formation. They wielded glaives and wore expensive breastplates, covered by green bear-claw tabards. They appeared well-rested and ready for action, driving their serrated pole-arms into any man they encountered on their way down the Steps.

'With me,' shouted Halla, directing men to form up.

A few dozen men answered her command, holding their axes in a protective line. To the right, a cluster of cloud-men and Low Kasters, including Timon the Butcher and Falling Cloud, joined the line and they went to meet the advancing warriors. They were Green Men. Sons, cousins, brothers and retainers of Halfdan Green. A small army, kept loyal through coin and the promise of power in the new Tiergarten. Perhaps two hundred warriors.

'Shall I kill these men?' asked Timon, bubbling froth appearing at the corners of his mouth.

'Yes!' she replied. 'They have betrayed Fjorlan, they are worthy of your axe.'

The Low Kaster bellowed a challenge and bounded up the Steps, barrelling into the first rank of Green Men. Halla and Falling Cloud followed, and a defensive line was formed.

A horn sounded from the walls and she paused.

'They're coming again,' shouted a man from the forward gatehouse as Rulag's army began its first night-time assault.

'Fuck!' exclaimed Halla.

'I think we're in trouble,' offered Falling Cloud.

The Green Men roared with joy, hacking into any man who stood before them on Kalall's Steps. The defenders were dragged from their stupor only slowly, coming alert in increments as the burning building, attacking men and repeating horn intruded upon their rest. Tricken Ice Fang bellowed commands from Ulric's Yard, pulling lines, wedges and formations from the tired warriors of Tiergarten.

'We kill until there is no-one left to kill,' she roared, throwing herself at the Green Men. She drove up until she stood next to Timon, holding the line against the Green Men.

'She's right,' shouted Falling Cloud. 'We know how to kill – maybe we know more about it than them.'

She pushed away thoughts of tactics and defeat and focused on her axe and the power in her arms. She leapt upwards, leading a small group of defenders. Behind, the horns didn't stop and she heard Tricken take charge, directing the warriors of Tiergarten to meet the army of Ursa one more time. Low Kasters and cloud-men flooded across the battlements and Greta's ballistae crews loaded as fast as they could, but the remaining warriors of Ursa had stolen a march on them. With the Green Men consuming defenders, Halla simply didn't have enough warriors to hold the walls.

Distantly, Tricken's orders reached her ears and she knew the army was approaching the walls. She heard the hasty release of a dozen ballistae and the rallying cries of a hundred defenders of Tiergarten. They were being attacked on two flanks, just at the point where tiredness and attritional losses robbed them of their edge.

'Halla, they're committing everyone,' shouted Tricken. 'I can see Rulag. This is it!'

She gasped as a rolling bank of icy air swept down the steps. The Green Men didn't falter and appeared oblivious to the frozen air about to envelop them. Halla saw figures in the churning ice, each one taller and wider than any normal man. They held war-hammers and strode down Kalall's Steps two at a time, emerging like a wall of divine power. As the snowy air covered Ulric's Yard, she shielded her eyes, trying to see the figures through the glare. They appeared to be priests of the Order of the Hammer, clad in old armour of bronze and cold iron, with ornate, but tarnished, heraldry across breastplates and greaves. The crying dragon of Teardrop, the howling wolf of Summer Wolf, the sparkling emerald of the Green-Eyed Lords, even the black claw of Old Gar.

The Green Men turned in horror, barely able to raise their glaives as the spectral priests approached. But, when Halla's eyes became used to the icy glare, she saw that they were not priests, but old men of Fjorlan, cloaked in divine power. Each man carried with him a nimbus of strength from ages past, looming behind him like an extra skin. She recognized Arnulph Grief, an old warrior of Fredericksand, usually to be found in the taverns of Low Edge, leaning on his crutch and complaining at the state of the world. Instead of a crutch, he now wielded a huge war-hammer, edged in deep ice and held in steady hands. Before the old men stood Alahan Teardrop and Old Father Crowe, a tale of anger and struggle writ plain on their faces. Halla didn't know what the young thain had been through to raise the heart of Fjorlan, but she could no longer look past him or deny his power. He had no priest looming behind him – he didn't need additional power, she thought. He was exemplar of Rowanoco, and every warrior of Fjorlan who saw him knew it.

The Green Men, mostly now fighting to get away from Alahan and the priests, threw themselves at Halla's men, fighting furiously in an attempt to link up with Rulag's main army. Their plan had been sound: surprise the defenders at rest and push to Ulric's

Yard as the main force assaulted the walls. But the exemplar of Rowanoco had other ideas.

Halla's first opponent was bulky and strong, but his skin was soft and his hands unsure. She parried a downward swipe and killed him with a powerful slice to his throat. A thrown axe cut down a man to her left and the line of defenders struck. Alahan and his company hit the rear of the Green Men with snarled aggression and a deafening crack of ancient ice. War-hammers, used with inhuman skill, battered their way through expensive armour and bone, leaving a decimated line in their wake. The priests shouted, carrying a wave of divine conviction with them, as if Rowanoco himself had entered the field of battle.

'My land! Our land!' roared Arnulph Grief.

The Green Men were now caught in a vice, pushed into Halla's defenders by Alahan and his company. She directed every man who could be spared back to the breach, hearing Tricken's pleas for additional warriors. She could only guess what was transpiring behind her. The sounds that reached her ears spoke of a fierce battle as Rulag's men launched their final assault. Tricken was directing men to the gateway, and men on the walls screamed in defiance as the attackers began to mount the breach. But, looking ahead, all she saw were priests of the Order of the Hammer, each one more impressive than the last and each one the match of five men. Despite the strength of his company, Alahan stood out. Whatever else he might be, the young thain was a fighter of considerable skill and was himself the equal of three or four Green Men.

'Halla, we need to get back to the walls,' barked Falling Cloud, using his speed and skill to duel two heavily armoured men. 'They'll break through.'

Halfdan Green's small army began to melt in front of them in a haze of blood and metal. War-hammers did not cut or slice flesh; they crushed bone and smashed armour. Broken bodies toppled down the Steps, with limbs crushed and heads no more than a mess of blood.

Timon, almost as ferocious as the priests, began to grin broadly as he reached Alahan, cleaving two men out of the way to meet his friend. The remaining Green Men broke, but with nowhere to run they died quickly by the axes of Halla's defenders or the hammers of Alahan's company.

'Halla,' said the young thain. 'I hope we're not too late.'

'We are pledged to the city,' offered Arnulph Grief, speaking as a rumble of falling rock and cracking ice. 'This is Rowanoco's land and we will see it free.' It was impossible to know where the old man ended and the priest began, and Halla felt as though both men were speaking at once.

The last of the Green Men were killed and Falling Cloud joined them. 'The walls,' he said, averting his eyes from the spectral priests.

Behind, in the midst of dust, swearing and howls of pain, the walls of Tiergarten had been overrun. Rulag's army held large sections of the wall and were slowly driving into the gatehouse. They'd seized the ballistae and were cutting defenders from the battlements as they advanced. Tricken, along with Rorg and his Low Kasters, were now at the front, defending Ulric's Yard and stopping the attackers from gaining victory.

She wiped blood from her face and looked at Alahan. Behind him, Arnulph Grief and two hundred old men carried immense strength. Was it enough? She looked into Alahan's eyes, searching for confidence that she was lacking. Deep within the glinting blue she saw Rowanoco. The Ice Giant raged within his exemplar. He raged within his Order of the Hammer. He raged that his land teetered on the edge, and he raged with honour, strength and freedom.

'Will you follow me?' asked Alahan.

The old men advanced, their priestly passengers swelling into a line of swirling ice and wind. Broken and maimed limbs had been repaired; bent and infirm old men now stood straight and true, looking down Kalall's Steps towards the gates of Tiergarten. None appeared wounded from their fight with the Green Men.

Perhaps they *would* be enough. She had no choice but to trust in Rowanoco's exemplar.

'No,' she replied. 'But I will fight at your side.'

'Good enough,' he said. 'Let us go and kill Rulag Ursa.'

Side by side, they strode down the Steps towards Ulric's Yard. Falling Cloud cleaned his axes, Timon whipped himself into a battle rage, and the two hundred priests – Rowanoco's company – muttered prayers of anger and commitment. Brindon Crowe stayed at the back, surveying the dense melee of men they needed to clear.

As the nimbus of divine power swept down the Steps, a lull in combat flowed across the fighters and an odd silence descended. They saw who marched on them and intuitively felt the wrath of their god. The defenders were glad of it, the attackers terrified by it, but all paused in mid-strike to gawk at the two hundred priests of the Order of the Hammer. The pause gave Tricken a chance to pull his men back to a defensive line, forming a semi-circle round Ulric's Yard. The Low Kasters were slower to move and stayed on the flank, the madness of frenzy numbing their minds to the spectral priests.

Even at the head of Rowanoco's company, Halla gasped at the state of the walls. The battlements and gatehouse were lost and Rulag's army flowed into Tiergarten like ants over a forest floor.

'The ice halls beckon,' roared Falling Cloud, breaking the silence and banging his axes together. 'Oleff will have the drinks ready. But let's kill some cunts first!'

'Charge!' commanded Halla, leaping down Kalall's Steps.

Alahan and Timon ran on either side of her, with Rowanoco's company behind. Thousands of men fought in Ulric's Yard, but it was a group of two hundred who drew all eyes. Tricken's men parted, giving them room to charge. Halla saw shields raised and a hasty line formed by the attackers, but they were hesitant and allowed a thunderous attack to cleave through their first rank. She was distantly aware that her axe met resistance and that blood sprayed across her arms, but she was caught up in the intense charge and was barely able to breathe out. She heard Rowanoco's company smash into terrified men of Jarvik, and she heard Tricken order men to the flanks, but everything else was distilled to a five-foot circle round her.

The warriors of Ursa recovered quickly, spurred on to fight by shouted commands and the meagre force of defenders who faced them. Their fear of Rowanoco's company remained, but the mass of warriors still pushed into Ulric's Yard. The battle had swayed back and forth, but now came down to a single, dense melee in the courtyard of Halla's city.

Alahan fought to her left, Timon to her right. She could hear Falling Cloud, but not see him, and she had no idea where anyone else was or how they fared. If Rowanoco's company had turned the battle, she couldn't tell from where she fought. Certainly the defenders held their ground, spurred on by the spectral priests; but they gained no territory in Ulric's Yard.

The icy winds accompanied them, churning across their lines and getting in the eyes of Rulag's army. Snow and ice appeared in their beards, and hands were raised to shield against the glare. It was a slight advantage, but allowed Halla to kill three men quickly and push forward, alongside Alahan and Timon. Together, they formed the point of the defence, with Rowanoco's company spreading out either side of them. The priests now mingled with the defenders, fighting side by side with Low Kasters, cloud-men, warriors of Tiergarten and survivors of the dragon fleet.

Then she saw Rulag Ursa. The melee parted momentarily and she saw him. Just within the gate, at the rear of the vanguard, strode the Lord Bear Tamer himself. He looked as she remembered – barrel-chested, green-eyed, blond-haired and tall, clad in thick bear furs and wielding a great-axe. At his flank stood a priest of Jarvik who Halla recognized from her youth; he was named Harrod. Algenon Teardrop had taken his name and his honour, refusing to accept his hate-filled sermons.

'Ursa!' roared Tricken Ice Fang from the left flank. 'Decided to show yourself, troll cunt?'

She couldn't see the red-haired chain-master, but Rulag took note of the insult and strode from Halla's field of vision. But she had no time to worry for Tricken; she had men to kill and a newly inspired force of defenders to lead.

Alahan was less restrained. As soon as the exemplar saw the Lord Bear Tamer, he broke ranks and chopped his way into a small gap, ahead of their lines. Timon the Butcher followed him, causing a bulge in their lines as Halla and others moved to cover them. To their left, a towering priest crowned in a flowing mantle of ice clubbed two attackers to the cobbled stone. To their right, Rorg and two frenzying Low Kasters threw themselves forward. His men died, but the chieftain reached Timon and the two of them covered Alahan's back, their bulging heads seeping blood across their faces.

'You've betrayed the Ice Giant,' boomed the young thain.

The priests delivered similar admonitions, and Halla found herself caught up in a frosty wave, where all that mattered were axes, hammers and blood. They might win, they might lose – she no longer thought about it. Rowanoco had spoken and every defender of Tiergarten was now prepared to die for the Ice Giant. Either they would break or they would break the forces of Ursa.

She spared a glance across Ulric's Yard and realized that they had blunted Rulag's advantage of numbers. Everywhere across the courtyard, Rowanoco's company fought groups of axe-men. Each priest was a giant among men, towering over their opponents and keeping five or more attackers at bay. She saw one fall, hacked apart by a dozen axes and returning to the form of a broken body of an old man on the bloody ground, but the company had pushed them forward and pushed Rulag's army back.

The melee had broken up sufficiently for her to see Tricken and Rulag. The two warriors swung immense blows at each other, standing toe-to-toe on the left flank. The lines had moved and Halla was now a little way behind Alahan. The exemplar was fighting right-to-left, killing men who stood between him and the lord of Jarvik. Tricken kept the Betrayer busy, but Halla could tell

430

her chain-master was outmatched. Harrod, to Ursa's left, stood guard over his lord, clubbing his war-hammer into the head of any man who got too close to the duel.

Rexel Falling Cloud appeared by her side, a small trickle of blood coating his thigh. He'd been covering her back and a cluster of dead men lay in his wake. 'Tricken's going to die,' he said in a hoarse rumble.

'Let's move,' she replied, taking two large strides forward.

The defenders now advanced in a fork, with Halla and Alahan at the two points. At the corners of her vision she saw men of Ursa hesitate. They would kill a man of Tiergarten and then pause, faced with an enormous apparition of the Ice Giant's anger. The pause was enough to see them dead, and each hesitation allowed Rowanoco's company to drive them further back. The other defenders travelled with the priests, covering them and, in turn, using them as cover.

She gasped with anguish as Rulag dealt Tricken a fatal blow to the back of the head. Her chain-master went limp and toppled forward, even as Alahan tackled the thain of Jarvik to the ground.

'Fight *me*, you treacherous bastard,' screamed Alahan, smashing the haft of his axe into Rulag's face. The Lord Bear Tamer didn't fall and swung his great-axe defensively, keeping Alahan back as he recovered from the blow. He shook his head and growled like a hound. The hardened wood of Alahan's axe-haft had broken his nose, but anger and adrenaline pushed away the pain. A clear section of Ulric's Yard, soaked in blood, became their battleground. Timon covered Alahan and the priest, Harrod, covered Rulag.

The Betrayer's men were on the back foot, pushed against the walls as larger and larger clusters fled from Rowanoco's company. Even so, they still held the walls and the gatehouse. Warriors on both sides kept an eye on the duel, knowing that everything came down to Alahan and Rulag, but having one eye gave Halla the luxury of ignoring them. All she knew was that they fought on the left flank.

She wearily swung her axe for the thousandth time, driving a man to his knees and feeling tears on her cheek. Another man died as she drove her axe into his face. Maybe they weren't tears; maybe blood was seeping into her eyes from the cleaved flesh of every man she'd killed.

Then the points of the fork met and she stood before Rulag and Alahan. The duel consumed a large section of Ulric's Yard and dominated the line between attacker and defender. Even Rowanoco's company stood back from the duel, though they still killed any attacker who dared to face them. To her left, Falling Cloud decapitated a berserker. Far across the courtyard, she saw Heinrich Blood, standing on a barrel and loosing arrows at the gatehouse. All along the forward battlements, cloud-men launched throwing-axes at men of Ursa. There were now as many men running back across the plains of Summer Wolf as fought in Ulric's Yard. She suddenly thought they were going to win. But still, Alahan fought Rulag.

'I stand for strength!' shrieked the Betrayer, swinging his huge axe from high.

'Then I stand for honour and freedom,' replied Alahan, dodging the attack. 'And I stand for the Earth Shaker. You stand for nothing but betrayal.'

Their axes clashed high and low. Rulag was bigger and stronger, but let his rage cloud his skill. Alahan appeared untouchable, stepping left and right, his battleaxe used as much to deflect as to parry. The larger man grunted each time he swung his huge axe and Halla knew he'd exhaust himself before he'd land a blow.

Harrod, the priest of Jarvik, appeared to recognize that his lord would lose and took matters into his own hands. He glanced across the clear ground and clenched his teeth. Timon and Halla were close, but not close enough to stop the hammer-blow striking Alahan in the back. The exemplar grunted and flew forward, landing at Timon's feet and writhing in pain.

Halla didn't hesitate. She engaged Harrod, forcing him to raise his hammer to block her axe. She followed up with a kick to his groin and a punch to his throat. When he flinched in pain and dropped his guard, she drove her axe into the top of his head and kicked his corpse to the floor.

Timon stood guard over Alahan as men of Ursa lined up to kill the prone exemplar and Rulag backed away, breathing heavily. The Lord Bear Tamer saw that half his men were running. And then he saw Halla.

'One-Eye the Axe-Maiden,' he snarled. 'A man should have taught you your place by now.'

Halla thought him foolish for taking the time to insult her before attacking. She used the pause to dart forward and drive her axe at his face. He managed to keep the edge at bay with a hasty parry, but was too surprised to see the follow-up attack. The haft of her axe swung round and smashed into the side of his head, sending him reeling. Before she could deliver a killing blow, she had to turn to face another attack as Rulag's personal guard came to his aid.

'Coward!' she shouted, dropping into a defensive posture.

She could now see clear moonlight through the press of bodies. Rowanoco's company was smaller, with peaceful bodies and scattered war-hammers paying silent tribute to their sacrifice. The remainder acted as moving bulwarks, from where defenders fought for Tiergarten. They appeared as engines of war, larger, stronger and louder than any other warrior fighting in Ulric's Yard – and she dared to think that they had won the day.

'Get the fuck out of my city!' she shouted, splitting a man's head in two and kicking another between the legs.

'Kill me if you can, troll cunts,' roared Falling Cloud, ignoring his wounds and covering her flank.

'Varorg awaits you,' shrieked Timon, frothing at the mouth and standing over his wounded friend.

They were no longer defenders. Rulag's army was on the edge. Sections had already broken and fled from the city, while others, cornered, threw down their weapons. Even Rulag's personal guards were teetering, their loyalty not strong enough that they were willing to die. The lord of Jarvik just stood there as his army melted away, wide-eyed astonishment assaulting his grizzled face.

At that moment, as the army of Ursa began to break, a large, glossy black raven plummeted from the sky and struck Rulag in the face. He wailed in pain and grabbed at the bird, its claws scratching viciously at his skin and eyes. The bird cawed as Rulag smashed it against the cobbled stone and flailed at the gruesome wounds where his eyes had been. His men, already on the back foot, stared at their lord, but none sacrificed their own retreat to help him. Within a second, he knelt alone on Ulric's Yard, his bloodied arms held apart and his mangled face turned to the night sky.

'I am Rulag Ursa,' shouted the man, blood streaming from a face scratched beyond recognition. 'And I claim these lands. I will be the Tyrant of Fjorlan.'

They were his last words. Halla ended the battle and the Lord Bear Tamer's life with a single downward swing of her axe.

CHAPTER TWENTY-SIX

UTHA THE SHADOW IN THE HALLS BEYOND THE WORLD

'**R**ANDALL, YOU'RE ALIVE!' He looked at his squire through a glassy orb of blue and green light, large enough for him to see the young man from head to toe. 'Randall. . . can you hear me?' He banged on the orb and felt his hand being repulsed by crackling surges of raw energy. 'What's happening? Where am I?'

He remembered the buzzing, coming from all around him. He remembered Voon's blank face, staring at him, but he didn't recall how Randall came to be in front of him, or why he was behind an impenetrable barrier of energy. Or why his chest burned with pain.

'Randall!' he shouted, pounding soundlessly on the orb.

The young man was peering at the orb, but didn't register Utha, as if the barrier was solid on the other side.

'He cannot hear you,' said a sensuous voice from behind.

Utha didn't turn round at first. He leant forwards against the orb and took a deep breath, trying to orient himself. Whatever he'd been through left a sickening taste in his mouth and a dull thud at the back of his head. He could see the face of a cracked and twisted old woman, infused with hatred and power. He felt that he had met the Queen in Red and that he had not had the best of the encounter. The pain in his chest revealed a strange new scar, as if he'd been stabbed, but he didn't remember the wound.

'You are still alive,' said the female voice. 'You have passed beyond the petty indulgences of mortality.'

435

'And I'm stuck with you,' he replied wearily. 'After all this distance and all this death, I'm left with a fucking spider.'

He quickly admitted to himself that he was trying to pick a fight with Ruth. He felt a crackle flow over his skin and a waft of unnatural energy, but all he wanted to do was argue, or maybe punch someone.

'We have passed beyond. Matters of annoyance are now irrelevant.'

'Shut up,' replied Utha. 'Why didn't Randall come with me?'

His squire looked at the orb with sad eyes slanted into a weary frown. Over his shoulder, Voon stood. The exemplar of Jaa looked brighter and more alive than Utha remembered.

'What happened to him?' he asked.

'I apologize,' said Ruth. 'Do you wish me to shut up or answer your questions?'

Utha closed his eyes and took a few deep breaths. At least he was still alive. 'I'd like an answer,' he murmured.

'Very well,' she replied. 'Randall did not accompany you because he would have died. And Voon looks different because he is no longer Voon. His body has been claimed by Jaa.'

'What the fuck does that mean?'

'Do you remember Dalian Thief Taker? Well, he lives again, in the body of the exemplar.'

'Good for him,' grunted Utha apathetically. 'Just tell me where I am.'

She laughed. It was a horrible sound, suggesting irony, scorn and self-righteous horse-shit. Utha dared not look around and answer his own question, for fear that he wouldn't understand what he saw.

'Where am I?' he whispered.

'Look, Utha the Shadow. . . look at your prize.'

He slowly turned, tearing his eyes from Randall. Ruth stood, petite and human, in the foreground. Behind her, through unimaginable distance, he saw beyond the world. At first no shapes, just colours and light. Then, as he focused, his mind began to interpret the view and show him what looked like stairs of flickering red stone. Above, lightning flashed against the black and blue sky, showing glimpses of far-off lines and structures, perhaps halls, perhaps something else.

'The staircase, the labyrinth and the Guardian,' he said, looking up the immense steps taking form in front of his eyes. They were wide and irregular, large enough for ten men to walk abreast.

He looked down and saw no weapons, no armour, just a black robe and tinges of shadowy light. He didn't know if a sword or an axe would be of any use, but he wanted one, if only for illusory peace of mind.

'You do not need weapons of metal here,' said Ruth. 'Your body and mind are enough. Do not think of yourself as an interloper. You are more a creature of this realm than of the other.'

'Voon said he'd teach me,' said Utha, not turning from the ethereal staircase. 'Before I lost him in the Jekkan causeway.'

She shook her head. 'You do not need instruction. I have seen into your mind and seen all the strength I needed to see. In the realm of void, *you* may need to protect *me*.'

He stared at her. She was as he remembered, just a small woman of uncertain heritage. Thin, with long black hair and dark eyes. She didn't shine or sparkle. There was no energy crackling from her limbs as there was with him, no sign or clue that she wasn't just as she appeared.

'And how does a Gorlan mother fit into my journey?' he asked. 'Other than to make a man of Randall.'

'I imagine it will come as no surprise that I have not been entirely honest. I had my own reasons for accompanying you.'

'In the Fell you said you'd guide me,' he replied. 'Was that a lie too?'

'No. I will be your guide, but not for your sake – for my own.'

He glared, sick of ambiguity. 'Explain.'

'I am dying, Utha, last Old Blood of the Shadow Giants. The power that sustains me is gone. It has waned, faded, dripped through the gaps of the world, and I can feel it no longer.'

'That is a poor explanation,' he replied. 'What does your death have to do with anything?'

For a moment, Ruth's face fell into an expression of vulnerability, making her appear smaller and younger than before. She looked around at the bare, ethereal landscape before the staircase, then wove a sinuous pattern in the air, calling into being a pair of sturdy, wooden chairs. He didn't ask how she'd done it, nor did he marvel at the display of power. He had no doubts that he could do similar here in the void. All she had done was will the energy into a new shape, a lesser version of building a hall or forming a pathway.

'Be seated,' she said. 'This is as good and as safe a place as any.'

They sat at the same time, eyes locked together, two small beings in the midst of enormity.

'Are we going to tell stories now?' asked Utha. 'Because I have no stomach for your tales of woe.'

'My tales are your tales,' she replied. 'For your power comes from beyond just as mine used to. We are both of us infused with unearthly energy, though yours grows mighty, while mine infuses me no longer.'

He flinched as a huge spider beast flickered across Ruth's shadow. It had eight thick legs and a sleek abdomen, but from its midriff rose a feminine torso and two sinewy arms. The shadowy head was wreathed in fleshy feelers, forming a grotesque beard to a face blessedly obscured.

'Her name was Atlach-Nacha,' she continued. 'An Old One from before the time of Giants. She, like all mighty creatures of the void, fed her energy into the realm of form. As the One God blessed his clerics with conviction, and Rowanoco gave his priests strength, so Atlach-Nacha gave her Gorlan mothers immortality and power over mind and form.'

'You're a fucking priest – cleric? Whatever?'

'I was,' she replied. 'Before the Jekkans arrived, before the Volk walked from their stone, while the lands still roiled with chaos. Your Giants were still building their halls when I was sired from the void.'

She spoke of things not known to Utha. He doubted they were known to the highest Blue librarian of the great library in Arnon. Jekkans, Volk – he had a passing understanding of these things, but a time before the Giants?

'How old are you?' he asked, unable to conjure any particularly profound questions.

'Do not try to understand deep time, Utha. It is not measured in years, but in the movement of the earth's plates and the rising of mountains. I have seen a thousand million creatures come and go, and I find that I am not yet ready to die myself.'

'Are there others of your kind? Dying somewhere in the lands of men?'

'There was one other,' she replied. 'My insane daughter. You met her. The Queen in Red.'

Utha winced as images of the cracked, hateful old woman flooded his memory. 'Yeah, we met,' he whispered, feeling ashamed for something he didn't truly remember. 'She's gone?'

Ruth nodded, but her fists clenched and her eyes were sad. 'She sought to prolong her life by pledging to a dead god. A dead god who enslaved Atlach-Nacha and slowly ate her. Many of my kind pledged to him long ago. She hoped, like other Gorlan, that she could leach enough of his power to free our mother, not understanding the madness that would infect her. Over time, she thought only for her own survival. She orchestrated the corruption of Jaa's faith to strengthen Shub-Nillurath.' She paused, as if remembering things best forgotten. 'When the Dead God finished consuming my mother, my daughter knew she would die. She did not want to die. As Shub-Nillurath gained strength and she prayed at his Footstep, the Queen in Red believed she kept herself alive.'

'What?' he exclaimed. 'Do you realize what you just said? That the Karesians are destroying Tor Funweir because a fucking Gorlan doesn't want to die.'

'Yes. The destruction of the lands of men has been a side effect of my daughter's misguided belief that Shub-Nillurath cared about her enough to keep her alive.'

'That's insane!' he exclaimed angrily.

'It is the Long War,' she replied, as if that made everything okay. 'You still view it from the point of view of an ant, staring up at an ancient tree. The lives of men are less than nothing to a creature of deep time. My daughter was beyond morality as you know it. Though she *was* insane; the thought of death had driven her so. She would have seen the world a carpet of blood if she could have been its queen.'

His hand twitched. Somewhere, in another life, Utha the Ghost was on a battlefield, wearing his Black tabard and fighting for the freedom of Tor Funweir. If a hundred things had happened differently, he would still wield his axe, Death's Embrace, and would be fighting Hounds for the sake of the Ro and for the One God. He'd still be an ant, blind to the ancient tree, swaying above him and viewing things at a pace he could never comprehend.

'You want me to save you?' he asked, fighting anger. 'Why should I?'

A warm smile appeared on her face, a relaxed expression of utter confidence, in sharp contrast to her vulnerable appearance. 'Because you have no choice,' she replied. 'And by entering the tear, so that I could follow, you have already saved my life. But without me, you will never traverse the labyrinth. And what I ask is a small thing.'

'I don't even know how my power works,' he said, now snarling the words. 'I feel it, like an extra layer of skin giving me strength and knowledge, but it's primal and unfocused. I could obliterate you as soon as help you.'

She stood, her chair disappearing into the shimmering air. At the base of the staircase, she absently picked a speck of red dust from the shadowy stone and gazed upward into the lightning-filled sky. 'I am pregnant,' she stated. 'Randall of Darkwald will be a long-distance father, but his spawn still grows in my body.'

His anger disappeared in a moment of sudden laughter. Even in the realm of void Randall could bring him back to reality. He glanced behind him, hoping to catch a glimpse of the squire through the tear, but the rift was now empty, with nothing but dense rock on the other side. 'That's my boy,' he said quietly.

Turning back to Ruth, he tried not to show his distain. 'So, a good, solid man of Ro has given you a full belly. As long as *he's* still alive, I couldn't give a shit what happens to you.'

'You're not the ant any more, Utha,' she said, with an audible cough in her throat. 'You know your responsibility. . . you can hide behind petty indulgences of mortality, or you can embrace what you are – a demi-god of the void, a true Old Blood of the Shadow Giants.'

He was still sitting down and hadn't noticed the crackle of divine energy that now crowned him. It rippled across every inch of his body, but was most concentrated around his head. 'I want to go back,' he muttered. 'I want to go back to the lands of men.' He stood and faced the tear, letting his chair disappear. He peered through the globed barrier, but could see no-one, just rock, as if the cavern had collapsed.

'That is not possible,' replied Ruth. 'Not yet.'

'Why not? I know I have power. Can I not make my own choices of how to use it?'

She glided from the base of the staircase to stand next to him, looking through the tear to the realm of form beyond. Then she nodded. 'You can. You could focus all of your power and, through pain and exertion, dig your way back to Oron Kaa.'

For a moment he considered it. The compulsion in his blood to continue was powerful, but his stubbornness was no easy foe to defeat. He gritted his teeth and internally threw a curse at the Shadow Giant. The bastard had died ages before Utha was born, and yet the God's influence cast its shadow over everything he'd done since. 'I have free will,' he snarled. 'If I want to go back, I can go back.'

'And do what?' asked Ruth. 'You don't know what's happened since you've been gone.'

He glared at her. 'Yeah, a lot can happen in ten minutes,' he replied ironically.

'Deep time is as chaotic as it is deep. Ten minutes is not a useful concept here. While we've been talking, a hundred years could have passed, or no years at all. That is the nature of the void. By stepping through the tear, you are now adrift in time. There is no telling the kind of world you will see if you return now. Turn away from your past, Utha. You could waste centuries just staring at a land now lost to you.'

He tried to slow his breathing and not unleash a torrent of curses at the Gorlan mother. It was a struggle, but he bit his lip and managed to respond without swearing. 'So, my only road is up the stairs and through the labyrinth? And my only companion is you?'

She slowly swept her arm towards the base of the red-tinged stairs. He followed her movements, taking in the spectacle once again. If the staircase ended, he couldn't see where. If there was a gap in the charged, blue sky through which he could ascend, it was hidden behind a curtain of lightning and barely glimpsed shapes. 'And the Guardian?' he mused. 'I have to fight it with no weapons?' His eyes were drawn down to his crackling fingertips.

Ruth turned her back on him and strolled towards the staircase, her footsteps leaving a slight glow in her wake. 'If you have to fight it we have done something horribly wrong,' she replied. 'Are you planning to join me?'

He didn't want to. He really, really didn't want to, but he was still a practical man of Ro at heart and knew when he'd exhausted his options. He took a last look through the tear and muttered, 'So long, Randall of Darkwald. You're a good lad. . . and you deserved better than me.'

It was the best he could do. Not quite an apology, but better than a cuff to the back of the head or a barbed insult. As a final statement to a man he trusted above all others, it was fairly weak, but it was truly the best he could do.

* * *

The red staircase was endless. At least, its end was nowhere in sight and time had slowed to a tedious crawl. Utha had spent the first hour or so in stunned awe, trying to make sense of the towering structures that appeared, drifting in the void. But even endless vistas of eldritch power could get boring. Especially when you didn't understand what you were looking at. The bright blue shards of light that cut the sky as lightning were void pathways, travelling in unknowable lines between realms, halls and dark places. Ruth said that they were also adrift in time, and could be the echoes of journeys undertaken a thousand years ago. Utha stopped finding them impressive after an hour or two.

What was the point of the fucking staircase? Was it symbolic, or just designed to kill through tedium? Why not have the labyrinth at ground level? If ground level was a useful concept in the lands beyond. Certainly the slow walk upwards did him good, physically if not mentally. The power returned to his limbs and whatever he'd endured in Oron Kaa was slowly washed away by his divine blood. But his returning power did nothing to soften the boredom. A bit of him wanted a swift spiritual kick to the head, after which he'd suddenly know what it truly meant to be a demi-god. As it was, he was left with the same cynical human edge he'd always had. A distrust of authority, a hatred of being told what to do – and most of all, an abiding pessimism that everything was ultimately fucked up.

'Is there anyone out there I can talk to?' he shouted to the crackling blue sky, unconcerned by whether or not Ruth thought he'd gone mad. 'Maybe a reception area, where newcomers are given a guidebook?'

'Have you gone mad already?' asked Ruth. 'I thought you'd last longer.'

'Do these fucking stairs ever end?'

'Sometimes,' she replied.

'Well, what does that mean? If you're all I've got, you have to stop being so bloody obtuse.'

'It means that the staircase has no fixed height. I expected you to have stepped from it by now, but you appear content to keep walking upwards. Is it because you find the view calming?'

He hung his head. 'I'm still thinking as a man, aren't I?' He turned from the sky and looked up the endless red stairs. 'I see a staircase and I walk up it until it stops. I expect to see a door or a landing. But it's not really here, is it?'

'It *is* here,' she replied. 'But it is not solid in the way of mortal structures, form versus void. Nothing here is made with stone, wood or metal, even if it appears to be. It is made of will and memory, or sometimes simply raw power. But all is changeable.'

Utha placed a hand on the red stone banister. 'So, I can—' He interrupted himself by twisting the banister into a strange new shape, folding it like ethereal clay. 'But how do I know what to do with it? Do I just imagine a door leading where I want to go?'

'If you wish,' she replied. 'Though it lacks elegance.'

He wove a pattern in the air, displacing the wide staircase.

'Slowly,' offered Ruth. 'We do not want to find ourselves plummeting downwards through void space.'

For a change, her words didn't annoy him. In fact, they were almost helpful. He concentrated on the area under their feet, making sure the solid, red stone remained. Then, with a flick of his wrists, he sent everything else away. The red turned to blue, then black, and finally grey, as it rushed through the crackling sky like a new structure, perhaps a bridge or a new void path. It appeared to be made of solid blocks of grey stone, a pleasing testament to his previous life in Tor Funweir. The Ro built everything in grey blocks and he nodded in approval when it was done. 'A good, solid bridge,' he said with a smile. 'Now that's much better than a door.'

'I said you didn't need instruction,' said Ruth, the corner of her mouth curling into the smallest of smiles. 'Just a pointer here and there.'

Utha swept his arm towards the bridge, mimicking Ruth's earlier gesture. 'After you, my lady,' he said, taking her by surprise with his mock formality.

She frowned at him, but stepped off the red circle and on to the new bridge. Railings appeared under her hand and a high, stone canopy, reminding Utha of the Black chapterhouse in Ro Tiris. It was gratifying that the styles and engineering of Tor Funweir were evident as he forged his first structures from the void.

'There'll be a balcony at the end,' he called after Ruth. 'We'll be able to see the labyrinth.'

It was strange to know these things, but they just appeared, as if he'd always known them. He now understood that, if he willed it, it would happen. At least, that was the case when in the void. When in the realm of someone or something else. . . he didn't know.

He ventured along his bridge a few paces behind Ruth, and instantly felt better. It looked, felt, even smelled like a castle of Ro. He resolved to use a similar template for anything else he might build. It was a small way to remember who he had been, and the land now lost to him. At the end of the bridge he joined Ruth on the simple balcony and looked out into the realm of another. At first it was hard to see beyond the dense flashes of lightning, but slowly a sprawling grey maze appeared. Crackling black and white clouds rolled across the structures, obscuring any fine detail, but it was unmistakably a labyrinth, criss-crossed by shallow passages and spirals. From above, it looked like the kind of bizarre abstract painting an insane Karesian might paint.

'Who built it?' he asked. 'Jaa?'

Ruth was scanning the maddening lines of the labyrinth, perhaps searching for the exit or a safe route through. 'I don't believe so,' she replied, not looking at him. 'It would have the reek of fear and malice. No, this was built by something else.'

Utha knew that stepping from his balcony would place him within the realm of another. Could he still twist its energy to his will? Or would he have to match his power against the Guardian? 'If you know what guards this place, you'd better tell me now.'

'All I know is that it was built to defend the tear. The tear was caused by Shub-Nillurath's footstep. . . so it follows that nothing less than a Giant would be master here.'

He stepped from his balcony anyway, despite the lack of reassurance from the Gorlan mother. He created some more steps, leading down to the edge of the realm. Standing tall and pushing back his shoulders, Utha entered the labyrinth.

Suddenly the smell of ash and smouldering rocks filled his nostrils. It was hotter than Oron Kaa and he was glad that he wore only a light robe. Anything else and he'd be drenched in sweat within minutes. The walls were moss-covered, and formed of huge, interlocking boulders. At ground level, all he could see was a single corridor, passing beyond sight in both directions. High above, the void sky still crackled with energy, giving a sense of distance unlike anything he could glimpse in the lands of men.

Ruth appeared next to him, travelling into the labyrinth in Utha's wake. She poked at the dusty stone walls, pulling forth a small, yellow flower. 'Charming,' she said. 'A trifle warm for my tastes.'

'Not much of a labyrinth,' he replied. 'There are only two directions. Or can I change things here?'

She admired the flower, tickling its petals with her fingertips. 'It is the domain of another. To attempt to alter it means pitting your might against the realm's master.'

He thought it unwise to try, and decided to simply pick a direction. The way he was facing seemed appropriate enough and, saying nothing more to Ruth, he started walking. It was the first realm he'd visited and even the sparse walls and sprouting weeds held considerable fascination. Had it been willed into being like Utha's bridge, or meticulously fashioned, an inch at a time? The walls were irregular and the dotted flowers made him think there was a thoughtful mind behind its construction. It didn't loom over him and there were no disquieting sounds or whistle of wind. Despite its harsh outward appearance, the labyrinth was not a hostile realm.

'You are interesting,' said a rumbling voice from far away.

Utha stopped and instinctively reached for a sword that wasn't there. Ruth joined him, but her face showed that she did not know who or what had spoken.

'Well, your labyrinth isn't,' replied Utha, gritting his teeth and preparing to fight. He didn't know if he could punch the Guardian, or perhaps wrestle him into submission, but he'd give it a try.

'Do you not like it?' asked the voice, booming as a thunderous echo, and coming from all directions at once.

'I like the flowers,' offered Ruth. 'A nice touch.'

'How nice of you to say.' The voice brightened, as if the mouth it belonged to was smiling. 'The flowers are a recent addition. I tired of looking at dark things. I wanted to see something pretty.'

Utha straightened, lowering his clenched fists. He remained in a seemingly endless stone corridor, but he still felt no hostility, from either the realm or its master. If anything, he felt a benign, almost warm, presence, floating over him, like a welcoming blanket. 'Is this a trick?' he asked, letting cynicism take over. 'Are you some kind of sly beast that lulls your prey into complacence?'

Ruth put a hand on his arm, gently suggesting he remain calm. It was perhaps the first time she'd touched him and made Utha think she was just as anxious as him.

'Do you know what this thing is?' he whispered.

'We have reached the limits of my knowledge, I'm afraid. From here on in, *you* must be *my* guide.'

The voice rumbled into an immense growl, as if a huge monster was clearing its throat. 'Am I a sly beast? Yes, I believe that could be said to be correct. However, I do not wish to lull you, and nor are you my prey. You are a visitor, the first visitor to enter my realm from the land of form.'

Utha stood in the middle of the passageway and looked off into the distance. It was impossible to tell how far he was from the Guardian, but he felt that the master of the labyrinth could be wherever he wished; he might be speaking from a few feet away, deciding the fate of the visitors. 'There's no fight here, is there?' asked the Old Blood, almost disappointed.

'Oh, no,' replied the rumbling voice. 'Fighting is largely the province of mortals. Here, life ends through destruction, obliteration, disintegration. . . fighting is very rarely involved.'

447

Utha suddenly felt naive. He'd always used violence as a way of easing his passage through life. He was better at fighting than talking or negotiating, and had hoped that any obstacle, even in the halls beyond the world, could be punched into submission.

'We merely wish to pass through your realm,' said Ruth, now a small figure in Utha's shadow.

Another rumbling growl, this time with a questioning note. 'Why do you have a Gorlan attached to you?'

Utha shot a glare at Ruth and raised an eyebrow. 'I think she may have saved my life,' he replied. 'So I'm being kind.' He spoke loudly, but felt that he had little need to. The Guardian would hear, no matter how quiet the words.

'That is also interesting,' said the Guardian. 'I find that I am almost overwhelmed by interesting things. I like the spider-folk, though I'd not thought to see one again. She must be a true friend for you to protect her so.'

Utha knew that Ruth had travelled in his wake, but was suddenly aware that she was reliant on him for survival. His divine blood gave him access to the void, and power over its substance, but she was still a creature of form and had no such advantages. For all her age and knowledge, the Gorlan mother was only alive because Utha allowed her to be. But it took no effort, so he felt it a small matter when weighed against the intangible benefits of having company – no matter how irritating that company may be.

He shook his head, finding it strange that he was letting his mind wander Whether by intent or not, the Guardian exuded calm. 'So, what happens now?' he asked, again speaking loudly. 'If we're not going to fight. . .'

'I must assess you,' replied the Guardian, 'and decide whether or not to let you out of my realm. If I decide in the negative, you will wander the labyrinth forever. If the positive, we can have a nice conversation and you can go on your way.'

'Why do you get to decide?' he queried, stubbornly not wishing to cede control.

'Hmm,' purred the immense voice. 'Because my realm lies above the tear and the great Fire Giant bid me to guard it.'

'So, get on with it,' snapped Utha. 'Make your decision.' He was sure that his aggressive impatience would appear strange to the Guardian, but his confidence was shaken and, with nothing to punch, it was all he could think to do.

'Perhaps a little more respect,' said Ruth in a sharp whisper, again clutching Utha's arm. 'You are not demanding a drink from a tavern keeper.'

'Of that I am sure,' he replied.

A strong downdraught of wind passed overhead, accompanied by a waft of pungent, smoky air. The huge boulders making up the maze gave off a rippling warmth and a smell that made his skin tingle. No shape appeared with the wind, and no sound, except the constant rumbling of the Guardian. It emitted purrs, growls and grumbles, managing to meld the deepest notes of a lion's roar, a dog's bark and a lizard's hiss.

Both of them felt their hair being ruffled by the wind, but it passed, as if a door had opened to let in the warm air, and then quickly closed.

'It would not be proper for me to detain *you*,' boomed the Guardian. 'You are of divine lineage and you follow your destiny.'

'And me?' queried Ruth, her face dropping into an expression of fearful apprehension. 'I am neither divine, nor following my destiny.'

Utha thought he should care about Ruth's fate, but any concern he may have felt was eclipsed by his own sense of relief. He was divine. . . and he followed his destiny. This was the clearest expression of his journey that he had heard, and he liked hearing it.

'You should not be here, Gorlan,' said the Guardian. 'Your folk have no further ties to the beyond.'

'Can she travel with me?' offered Utha. 'I owe her that much.'

More grumbling, no doubt linked to a deep thought of some kind. The immense voice said nothing without first ruminating upon it through a filter of animalistic sounds. It was evidently in no hurry. After a few minutes that felt like a few hours, the voice emitted a final grunt, as if it had decided upon something. Gradually, the walls began to change. To Utha's left, the boulders parted and the ground beyond arced upwards, out of the labyrinth.

'Do I get to see what you look like now?' Utha asked.

'Would that please you?' responded the Guardian.

'I like to know who I'm talking to. It might make me less anxious.'

A concerned purr filled the air. 'Then you must approach. I do not wish you to be anxious. Though I must ask that you do not fear me.'

Utha turned and began to walk towards the voice, now coming from a definite direction. The lightning remained, but it now appeared far off, as if there was an invisible roof. The master of the realm had created a passageway through which the visitors could reach it. Once above the boulders, Utha could again see the chaotic lines of the labyrinth, spiralling in and out of straight passages and sharp corners. Most alarming was his view of the tear. From his elevated position, floating at an unimaginable distance from where he'd first entered the void, the rift was a plunging vortex of rushing energy, a thousand times larger than before. It was not simply a slice in reality, moving from void to form, but a divine scar, created by an enraged god. The tear was merely the way his mind interpreted the Footstep of the Forest Giant.

'Utha, slow down,' said Ruth, struggling to keep up with him. 'I am not as swift here as you.'

He stopped and spun round, glaring at the Gorlan mother. 'What the fuck do you want from me? I've kept you alive, not knowing I was doing it; I've taken you with me. . . I don't even know where the fuck I'm going.'

'But you feel a compulsion,' interrupted the Guardian, sounding closer than before.

Utha turned from Ruth and strode upwards with purpose. Within a few strides he glanced down and saw the edge of the enormous labyrinth. A huge distance had been covered in a few minutes, demonstrating that the rules of the void were subject to change. Ahead of him, looming over the ethereal horizon, was a towering plinth of dark red stone, upon which perched a smouldering silhouette. The shape swayed and shifted position, as if getting comfortable on an armchair. It was still distant, but it must have been the size of a Kirin galley. It got larger with every step he took towards it.

'Yes, I feel a compulsion,' he replied. 'Towards you and beyond. Somewhere out there are the Shadow Halls and I would reach them. I believe they only still exist because of me.'

'You believe correctly,' replied the enormous shape, now appearing to be sitting up on its haunches.

As the crackling lightning framed the silhouette, Utha got a glimpse of what he'd been speaking to. There was a rippling coat of flame that provided just enough illumination for the scaly reptile to be seen. Its head, the size of a large cart, was long and expressive, reminiscent of an old alligator. Its hind limbs ended in sharply clawed feet, though its front two stretched into sinewy wings that it gathered behind its spiny back. In the oldest tales of Tor Funweir, scribes would have called it a dragon, but Utha had thought them mythical beasts like unicorns and fairies. To see the fiery monster smiling at him through a mist of steam was both alarming and strangely amusing. A thousand swear words entered his head all at once, but all he could vocalize was, 'What the fuck?'

'My name was Kaa,' boomed the Guardian, its long mouth enunciating each syllable and showing a ring of hooked teeth, larger than longswords.

Utha approached the plinth and had to keep raising his head to look the beast in the face. He was aware that Ruth ran to keep up with him, but couldn't see her expression. Perhaps she was less awed than him. . . but he doubted it.

'I am Utha the Ghost, last Old Blood of the Shadow Giants. I have been haunted by the staircase, the labyrinth and the Guardian for so long. I find that the reality – such as it is – is not haunting in the slightest. Though perhaps it would have been a year ago.'

'Do you not fear me?' asked Kaa, a strangely innocent glint in his warm, amber eyes.

'I do not,' replied Utha. 'Though perhaps that is foolish. Whether through your sorcery or my own strength, I know you are not a threat to me.'

'You speak truth. To you I am no threat. But your companion seeks to cheat death. Would you allow her to?'

He stopped walking a good distance from the plinth. Beyond the seated Guardian he saw a mismatched structure of arches and tunnels, leading out of the realm. He'd have to forge his own path from here, perhaps dotting the umbral sky with good, solid Ro bridges of grey stone. But the question of what to do about Ruth was not one he could brush aside. 'That's it, isn't it? You're trying to cheat death. Your time has come and you refuse to accept your end.'

'Would *you* welcome death?' she replied. 'Or would you struggle for life?'

The Guardian sat up and his rumbling breath travelled, like a warm gust of wind, across the two small visitors. 'An unfair question. He has not lived through strata of deep time as you have. He will also become a god, and should get used to solitude.'

Utha stared up at the huge, red dragon. A distant chime sounded in his mind, like an alarm call responding to the Guardian's words. 'A god? Truly?'

Kaa looked down at him, his reptilian face rippling like a contented feline. 'The Shadow Halls beyond the world are yours to rebuild. The great Fire Giant would consider you an ally and would want your forest-dwellers to regain their strength. As the halls grow, so will you grow, and your followers will find their purpose once more.'

'Forest-dwellers? Oh, yeah,' he said, with resignation. 'The one we loved and all that shit.'

Ruth hovered over his shoulder, concerned about her fate but too interested to interrupt. Kaa just looked at him with his brassy eyes, smiling broadly.

'So, I'm going to be the god of the Dokkalfar?' he asked. 'I hope they like alcohol and women.'

The dragon hunkered down on his folded wings, looking at Utha from a lower position. He was still immense, but even though he had a mouth that could swallow ten men whole, Utha felt that he meant no malice or hostility.

'And the Gorlan?' asked Kaa. 'What part of your hall will you give to her? You will be ages building your hall and regaining your strength before any mortal creature calls you a god. Would you have her as company?'

He looked at her. She was small and unassuming, though always, at the back of his mind, loomed the image of the huge spider. He had never liked her, from their first meeting in the Fell. She had trailed along with them, to Kessia and beyond, providing little more than a warm place for Randall to sleep. But her advice had never been wrong. For her own reasons, the Gorlan mother had given good counsel and contributed much to his journey.

'I'm not fooling anyone,' he muttered. 'I can play at being a bad guy all I want, but I'd never condemn her to death.'

Ruth closed her eyes and breathed out, as if she'd been genuinely worried that he'd dismiss her.

'Interesting,' rumbled Kaa. 'You are good-hearted. That, along with your power, will serve you well.'

'My power?' queried Utha. 'If you know of it, you know more than me.'

'Hmm,' murmured the enormous dragon, padding on the plinth with his rear legs. 'Let me tell you a story. There was once a Giant of Shadows – his name is lost to deep time, but he entered the void as a shy creature, nurturing the hope that kindness would allow him to prosper. Over time, his people, the Ljosalfar, became mighty in the realm of form. But kindness took him only so far. When the great Forest Giant, Shub-Nillurath, attacked his folk, the Shadow Giant sought peace and was denied. His beautiful Ljosalfar became the dark Dokkalfar, and his mind was shattered. But, as Shub-Nillurath has proven, killing a god is not easy, and the Shadow Giant kept his mind, but lost his might. He was struck down to the realm of form and denied his memory, forced to be born and grow as a mortal being among his fallen brethren. I believe he yet lives, fighting the Long War, with no knowledge of his past.'

'And I'm his last descendant?'

'You are the last drop of divine that is left to him. A dilution of a dilution, a thousand times removed, but still as powerful. Your blood travelled a long way to reside in your simple body. There is truly no limit to the might you can achieve, assuming you make the right allies.'

* * *

For every step he took, a hundred years and no years at all passed in the realms of form. Nothing that he understood had any meaning: up, down, left, right, solid, fluid. Nothing was locked in place or consistent in form. If it weren't for his grey stone corridors and comforting fire-pits, Utha would be rather disoriented. He'd built a void path from the edge of the labyrinth to. . . somewhere. His instinct told him that the Shadow Halls were in a certain direction, but the pull was vague, as if it expected him to know the way. He was far from the realm of form, beyond battles and wars, and travelled further than the imagination of the oldest mortals with each step.

'I can't imagine Randall as an old man. Married with kids perhaps, in a shitty hut in the Darkwald.'

'*That* is what occupies your mind?' queried Ruth, reminding Utha that he was not alone.

'It's the last pleasant thought I have,' he replied, resting on a comfortable sofa, next to a roaring fire and under an arched window. Beyond him, through the window, the void crackled with endless energy, but it did not intrude upon his creation. He'd created no doors and the room was almost cosy. When he had leisure, he'd add a nice bed, and maybe some water to wash with. But, for now, he was happy to be sitting down.

'We're still moving,' said Ruth, sitting on a second sofa that Utha had been nice enough to create for her.

'I got sick of walking. Think of this room as a void boat.' He craned his neck to look out of the window and saw the rushing blue sky.

She smiled. 'You see? You need no instruction. Your hall will be mighty and creatures of the beyond will learn to fear you. You will become a Giant, Utha the Ghost.'

He willed a frothing mug of ale to appear in his hand. It was rich and cold, gliding down his throat, the best drink he'd ever had.

'May I have one?' asked Ruth.

He looked at her across the froth as he took a deep swig. He wiped his mouth and nodded for a similar mug to appear on a low table next to her sofa.

'Thank you,' she said. 'What shall we drink to?'

He paused, taking a deep, clear breath and feeling his mortal concerns fall away like leaves from an autumn tree. 'To Randall, to Voon, to Torian, to Nanon. . . fuck, even to that scumbag Kirin, Rham Jas.'

They shared a drink of good Ro ale, before a better toast came into Utha's mind. 'One day I'm going to shove my booted foot up Shub-Nillurath's arse. Let's drink to my foot.'

She raised her mug after a small, demure sip. 'To the boot of the Shadow Giant.'

EPILOGUE

I NGRID WORE A thick green dress and boots with fluffy
socks. It was still cold, but her happiness was enough to
provide a cosy warm glow that even the lashing winds of
Tiergarten couldn't penetrate. Corvus was dead, but she knew
he'd want her to be happy. She smiled, thinking of her friend
and all the things she wouldn't have done without him. She
knew he was still there somewhere, maybe watching her from
a cloud and cawing with glee. He'd be watching Alahan too. . .
and Halla, and everyone who lined Kalall's Steps, looking
up at them. Hundreds and hundreds of people; everyone
who hid during the battle and everyone who survived it. The
remaining old men and their hammers had returned to the vault
to give back the old weaponry, but they'd be honoured upon
their return.

Her brother was hurt, but stood unaided, wincing and flexing
his back every few minutes. Wulfrick was there, and had been
within arm's reach since the battle ended, though he didn't seem
to realize that he was now a dark-blood like Rham Jas Rami. She
remembered Al Hasim telling her about his Kirin friend and the
power he'd stolen from the horrible trees. She'd tell Wulfrick at
some point, when they were safely back in Fredericksand. For
now, the huge man was just cross that he'd missed the battle.

'Brothers and sisters,' shouted Old Father Crowe, the scary
man with the long beard. 'We have won.'

A cheer rose from the city, travelling as a wave of relief as
much as victory. Ingrid joined in, jumping up and down at the

edge of the High Hold and making her brother smile. Behind her, an honour guard flanked Halla and Alahan.

'My friends,' continued Crowe, waving his hand and quietening the cheers. 'Beyond our victory, I see great work that needs doing. There are men of Ursa who have surrendered and need attention. There are others who have fled to the Crystal Fork and need pursuing. But above this Fjorlan needs to be rebuilt, a new age of freedom, strength *and* honour. Rowanoco's land is once again free.' His cheeks were red from the effort of shouting, but his eyes did not waver. The old priest turned to face Halla and Alahan. He nodded at each of them, then turned back to the crowd. 'I am a mere messenger, a humble servant of the Ice Giant, but I will bear witness to the words of the house of Teardrop, as will each of you.'

Alahan took a deep breath and strode forward. At the last moment, Ingrid grabbed his hand and made him turn back; he smiled broadly. She let go slowly, allowing him a minute without her to look after him. He joined Old Father Crowe at the top of Kalall's Steps and rested his arms on the ornate stone railings.

'I am Alahan Teardrop Algeson,' he shouted, throwing his name into the air with defiance. 'And I am the thain of Fredericksand. From this day forth, that is all I will be. I renounce the office of high thain; we have no further need of it.' The crowd hushed, aware that he was discarding a title from the first days of Fjorlan. 'I will look to Halla Summer Wolf Alephsdottir, thain of Tiergarten, as my equal – and my battle sister.'

The cheers were now deafening. These people loved Halla before she returned with an army and defended her city. Now she was their talisman and represented all they had won against Rulag the Betrayer. She still didn't smile, but she looked less like an angry storm cloud as she joined Alahan at the railings, looking down Kalall's Steps. The first female thain in Fjorlan's history was dressed in a flowing golden cloak, over a thick leather jerkin and form-fitting trousers. Her long red hair was washed and formed a mantle across her shoulders. It was the first time Ingrid had

seen her without armour and she actually looked like a woman.
Behind her, grinning broadly, came Rexel Falling Cloud, his body
a canvas of bandages and a thick crutch wedged under his armpit.

Halla allowed the citizens of Tiergarten a moment to look
at her. The cheers had died down, but were now renewed in a
surge of warm applause and shouting. She finally smiled. Perhaps
her stoicism was swept away by the realization that they'd won.
Ingrid hoped so.

With a raised hand, Halla quietened the crowds enough to
be heard. 'You all know me. You may have travelled with me
from Hammerfall; perhaps from Jarvik, perhaps even from the
wreck of the dragon fleet. Or you may have fought alongside
me to defend Tiergarten. I thank each of you – some of you have
saved my life.' She glanced at Falling Cloud, then at Wulfrick.
'Some more than once. And this victory belongs to all of us,
and to all of Fjorlan, for a betrayer has been beaten and a land
has been freed. All I did was kill our enemies until there were
no more to kill. I wonder if I can finally address you in peace,
as your thain.'

The resultant cheers were deafening and the crowd chanted
her name. Alahan, smiling next to her, took a step to the side
and clapped, causing a wry shake of the head from the new thain
of Tiergarten. Ingrid joined in, whooping and hollering at the
top of her lungs. Wulfrick swept her up in his huge arms and
deposited her on his shoulders, giving her a spectacular view of
the cheering masses. Somewhere in the distant air, hovering just
inside her hearing, the World Raven cawed and Ingrid knew that
Brytag was happy.

* * *

Saara the Mistress of Pain could feel many things. As she stood
on her private balcony, she could feel that the matron mother was
dead. She could feel that the Jekkan Tyrant of the Fell had been
killed. She could feel the hate of the Aberration. And she could
feel that Shub-Nillurath had been wounded.

459

But Saara's power remained. Something had happened in Oron Kaa, something that left her completely alone but more powerful than she'd ever been. There would be no more Seven Sisters, leaving her to revel alone in the collective power of seven enchantresses. As long as Isabel lived, Saara could enchant anyone she wished with no fear. If she was to rule the Tyranny of the Twisted Tree alone, so be it.

Shub-Nillurath wanted to split the sky and claim his new kingdom, but he had been dealt a blow that weakened his connection to the world. But it was of no moment. Saara had won her most immediate battle and she looked forward to the construction of her tower and the adulation of her subjects.

'Do you remember *me*?' said a sudden voice from the darkness.

She spun away from her balcony's edge and saw the spectral figure of Kale Glenwood, the door visible through his ghostly form. He was grinning broadly and Saara had no earthly idea how he could be standing there. She looked at the dead forger from Leith for what seemed like hours, letting everything else fall away and feeling pressure rise in her mind.

'I saw you die,' she murmured.

The figure slowly flowed into the likeness of Cardinal Mobius. 'You didn't see *me* die,' said the Purple cleric. Then King Sebastian Tiris. 'Nor I,' said the former monarch of Tor Funweir.

Faces came and went, faster and faster. The first few spoke, but the rest quickly melded into a hypnotic dance that made her feel drunk. What was happening? Something beyond her control.

The phantom thralls began to scream, a deafening shard of anguish that pierced the air. She dropped to the floor and held the sides of her head. As a thousand shrieking faces flickered into the air around her, she reached for the door handle with shaking hands. Her senses started and ended with pain. She could feel nothing else. She dragged herself through the door and tumbled down the stone steps. She screamed, but couldn't hear her own voice. Hand over hand, she crawled on her stomach down the cold steps, panting like an animal as she tried to reach her chamber.

She could no longer feel Shub-Nillurath. The warm sensation of an encircling tentacle was gone, dispelled in an instant as her phantom thralls attacked. She tried to reach out with her mind, but the pain refused to let her. 'Isabel!' she murmured, again and again. 'My sweet sister, what has happened to you?'

The Seductress was dead and Saara's world appeared to shrink. She felt vulnerable. She felt mortal. Time stretched as she flailed on the stairs. Minutes feeling like hours elapsed before she clasped the door handle and pulled herself into her study, where she lay panting until she mustered enough energy to look up.

The door was just being closed and a lantern pulsed gently on her desk. She could see no people in the darkness, but a shape lay motionless across the desk. It was Elihas of Du Ban. He was face down across the desk with a steady drip of blood pooling on the wooden floor below his neck. His heavy armour, always so much a part of his being, was now a useless shell, making him look like a turtle turned the wrong way up on a beach. His face was locked in an expression of enraged surprise and his neck was sliced deeply from ear to ear.

A blade whistled from the darkness to rest gently against her neck. It was a thin-bladed sword with a subtle curve, but the wielder was hidden in shadow. Saara panted heavily, but had no strength to turn the blade aside, or even to stand up and face her opponent – someone who could raise a sword to a Seven Sister.

'We're here to kill you,' said a sonorous voice from the door. 'My name is Tyr Nanon.' A short risen man stepped out of the shadows and cleaned Elihas's blood from a longsword. 'I think you know Keisha.'

Saara's former slave stepped into the light, looming over the enchantress. 'Hello, mistress. Do you want a fucking massage, you hateful cunt?'

Keisha looked different. She wore leather armour and no make-up. She showed no expression, just dark eyes and a tightly pouting mouth.

Saara howled in pain as her phantom thralls continued their assault. She wanted to reach out with her mind. She wanted to show them that she was a Tyrant of Shub-Nillurath. But the rage of all those enchanted by the Seven Sisters wouldn't let her. She began to panic. She clamped her hands to the sides of her head and stared up at the dark-blood.

'This world is broken thanks to you and your dead god,' said Tyr Nanon. 'You didn't win every battle, but you won enough. There is much blood on your hands. All I've ever known is this Long War and I know an ending when I see one. This battle ends, another begins.'

She momentarily found her voice. 'You gain *nothing* by killing me,' she wailed, curling up on the floor.

'You misunderstand, my lady,' said the Dokkalfar. 'We're not trying to *gain* anything. Killing you does not reverse the damage you have done. Nor does it give back what you have taken, or bring those you've killed back to life. The battles are done, the beasts are free, the dead fertilize the soil – this is the end.'

The cold katana blade caressed her throat. 'Then why?' cried Saara.

'Vengeance,' replied Keisha.

There will be other tales and other legends, but this battle of the Long War is done. Those who survived will be heroes and myths to future generations, and a few, those blessed with long lives, may enter the battlefield again. . .

For the Long War rumbles on.

AJS

BESTIARY
COMPANION WRITINGS ON BEASTS
BOTH FABULOUS & FEARSOME

The Trolls of Fjorlan,
the Ice Men of Rowanoco

History does not record a time when the Ice Men did not prowl the wastes of Fjorlan. A constant hazard to common folk and warrior alike, the trolls are relentless eating machines; never replete, they consume rocks, trees, flesh and bone. A saying amongst the Order of the Hammer suggests that the only things they don't eat are snow and ice, and that this is out of reverence for their father, the Ice Giant himself.

Stories from my youth speak of great ballistae, mounted on carts, used to fire thick wooden arrows in defence of settlements. The trolls were confused by bells attached to the arrows and would often wander off rather than attack. Worryingly, there are few records of men killing the Ice Men, and those that do exist speak of wily battle-brothers stampeding them off high cliffs.

In quiet moments, with only a man of the Hammer for company, I wonder if the Ice Men have more of a claim on this land than us.
FROM 'MEMORIES FROM A HALL' BY ALGUIN TEARDROP LARSSON,
FIRST THAIN OF FREDERICKSAND

The Gorlan Spiders

Of the beasts that crawl, swim and fly, none are as varied and unpredictable as the great spiders of Nar Gorlan. The northern men of

Tor Funweir speak of hunting spiders, the size of large dogs, which carry virulent poisons and view men as just another kind of prey. Even the icy wastes of Fjorlan have trapdoor Gorlan, called ice spiders, which assail travellers and drain the body fluids from them.

However, none of these northerners know of the true eight-legged terror that exists in the world. These are great spiders, known in Karesia as Gorlan Mothers, which can – and indeed do – speak. Not actually evil, they nonetheless possess a keen intelligence and a loathing for all things with two legs.

Beyond the Gloom Gates is a land of web and poison, a land of fang and silence and a land where man should not venture.

FROM 'FAR KARESIA: A LAND OF TERROR'
BY MARAZON VEKERIAN, LESSER VIZIER OF RIKARA

ITHQAS AND AQAS, THE BLIND AND
MINDLESS KRAKENS OF THE FJORLAN SEA

It troubles me to write of the Kraken straits, for we have not had an attack for some years now and to do so would be like tempting fate. But I am the lore-master of Kalall's Deep and it must fall to me.

There are remnants of the Giant age abroad in our world and, to the eyes of this old man, they should be left alone. Not only for the sake of safety, but to remind us all that old stories are more terrifying when drawn into reality.

But I digress. The Giants of the ocean were formless, if legend is to be believed, and travelled with the endless and chaotic waters wherever tide and wind took them.

As a cough in Deep Time, they rose up against the Ice Giants and were vanquished. The greatest of the number – near-gods themselves – had the honour of being felled by the great ice hammer of the Earth Shaker and were sent down to gnaw on rocks and fish at the bottom of the endless seas. The Blind Idiot Gods they were called when men still thought to name such things. But as ages passed and men forgot, they simply became the

Krakens, very real and more than enough when seen to drive the bravest man to his knees in terror.

FROM 'THE CHRONICLES OF THE SEAS', VOL. IV,
BY FATHER WESSEL ICE FANG, LORE-MASTER OF KALALL'S DEEP

THE DARK YOUNG

And it shall be as a priest when awake and it shall be as an altar when torpid, and it shall consume and terrify, and it shall follow none save its father, the Black God of the Forest with a Thousand Young. The priest and the altar. The priest and the altar.

FROM 'AR KRAL DESH JEK' (AUTHOR UNKNOWN)

THE DOKKALFAR

The forest-dwellers of the lands of men are many things. To the Ro, arrogant in their superiority, they are risen men – painted as undead monsters and hunted by crusaders of the Black church. To the Ranen, fascinated by youthful tales of monsters, they are otherworldly and terrifying, a remnant of the Giant age. To the Karesians, proud and inflexible, they are an enemy to be vanquished – warriors with stealth and blade.

But to the Kirin, to those of us who live alongside them, they are beautiful and ancient, deserving of respect and loyalty.

The song of the Dokkalfar travels a great distance in the wild forests of Oslan and more than one Kirin youth has spent hours sitting against a tree merely listening to the mournful songs of their neighbours.

They were here before us and will remain long after we have destroyed ourselves.

FROM 'SIGHTS AND SOUNDS OF OSLAN' BY VHAM DUSANI,
KIRIN SCHOLAR

The Great Race of Ancient Jekka

To the east, beyond the plains of Leith, is the ruined land. Men have come to call it the Wastes of Jekka or the Cannibal Lands, for those tribes that dwell there are fond of human flesh.

However, those of us who study such things have discovered disturbing knowledge that paints these beings as more than simple beasts.

In the chronicles of Deep Time – in whatever form they yet exist – this cleric has discovered several references to the Great Race, references that do not speak of cannibalism but of chaos and empires to rival man, built on the bones of vanquished enemies and maintained through sacrifice and bizarre sexual rituals. They were proud, arrogant and utterly amoral, believing completely in their most immediate whims and nothing more.

Whatever the Great Race of Jekka might once have been, they are now a shadow and a myth, bearing no resemblance to the fanged hunters infrequently encountered by man.

FROM 'A Treatise on the Unknown', by
YACOB OF LEITH, Blue cleric of the One God

The Jekkan Servitors

The war did not last long. The Great Race of Jekka had no desire for the forests. At length we fought them back to their mountains and threw down their altars.

But their pets had to be defeated. As the masters fled, their servitors covered their retreat. They were terrible, amorphous things of no fixed form, shaping their flesh as their masters ordered.

Fire did not burn them, arrows did not pierce them, blades did not cut them. Only the touch of cold caused them to flee. The mightiest Tyr wielded swords of deep ice and the wisest Vithar conjured snow and freezing winds.

The servitors were defeated, though it cost many lives. In the long ages that followed, whispers remained of the terrifying beasts, that they skulked in Jekkan ruins or guarded long-forgotten lore, but they were never again seen by Dokkalfar.

FROM 'THE EDDA', AUTHOR UNKNOWN BUT ATTRIBUTED TO THE SKY RIDERS OF THE DROW DEEPS

CHARACTER LISTING

The people of Ro – Men of the Stone and followers of the One God

Ro Canarn
Lady Bronwyn – duchess of Canarn
Auker of Canarn – guardsman

Ro Haran
Alexander Tiris – the Red Prince of Haran
Gwendolyn of Hunter's Cross – the Lady of Haran
Ashwyn of Haran – Hawk sergeant
Brennan of the Walls – Hawk major
Lennifer of Triste – serving girl
Symon of Triste – Hawk sergeant

Clerics of the One God
Lanry of Canarn – Brown cleric
Cerro of Darkwald – cardinal of the Brown
Elihas of Du Ban – Black cleric
Daganay of Haran – Blue cleric
Utha the Ghost – former Black cleric and the last Old Blood
Artus of Triste – novitiate of the Blue

Knights of the One God
Ohms of the Bridge – former knight sergeant of the Red
Fallon of Leith – the Grey Knight, exemplar of the One God

Malaki Frith – knight general of the Red
Markos of Rayne – White Knight of the Dawn
Lucius of the Falls of Arnon – former Red Knight
Jaxon of Tiris – former Red Knight
William of Verellian – former Red Knight

Nobles
Vladimir Corkoson – lord of the Darkwald
Hallam Pevain – mercenary knight
Dimitri Savostin – major in the Darkwald yeomanry
Yacob Black Guard of Weir – traitor assassin of Ro Weir
Marius Pevain – mercenary knight
Ronan Montague – lord of Du Ban

Common Folk
Randall of Darkwald – squire to Utha the Ghost
Martyn of Tiris – guardsman
Ronan Stone – guardsman

The People of Ranen – Men of the Ice and followers of Rowanoco

Fjorlan
Tiergarten – the ancient city of Summer Wolf
Halla Summer Wolf Alephsdottir – the Daughter of
    the Wolf
Old Father Brindon Crowe – priest of the Order of the Hammer
Tricken Ice Fang – chain-master
Earem Spider Killer – axe-master
Colm Tide Bound – survivor of the dragon fleet
Lars Bull – survivor of the dragon fleet
Greta Cloud Seer – axe-maiden of Tiergarten.
Arnulph Grief – old man of Tiergarten

Fredericksand – where sits the high thain
Alahan Teardrop Algeson – heir to the high thain's hall

Wulfrick the Enraged – axe-master
Ingrid Teardrop – the Little Wolf of Fredericksand
Rudolf Ten Bears – survivor of the dragon fleet
Wilhelm Speaks in Silence – priest of the Order of the Hammer

Hammerfall – home of the Wolf Wood and the Cloud-men

Rexel Falling Cloud – survivor of the dragon fleet
Anya Cold Bane (Lullaby) – wise woman
Moniac Dawn Cloud – axe-master

Jarvik – formerly the home of the Green-Eyed Lords, now the home of Ursa

Rulag Ursa Bear Tamer – thain of Jarvik
Thran Blood Fist – battle brother of Jarvik
Beirand Rock Heart – battle brother of Jarvik
Harrod – priest of the Order of the Hammer

The Low Kast
Rorg the Defiler – berserker chieftain
Timon the Butcher – berserker of Varorg
Unrahgahr – Exemplar of Varorg

The Freelands
Wraith Company
Freya Cold Eyes – wise woman
Micah Stone Dog – warrior of Wraith

Ranen Gar
Fynius Black Claw – captain of Twilight Company and
    exemplar of Brytag
Vincent Hundred Howl – warrior of Twilight Company

The people of Karesia – Men of the Sun

The Seven Sisters – enchantresses, formerly of Jaa,

now of Shub-Nillurath
Saara the Mistress of Pain
Isabel the Seductress

The faithful of Jaa – Wind Claws and Viziers
Voon of Rikara – high vizier of Karesia, exemplar of Jaa
Kal Varaz – wind claw
Kadri Ramazon – wind claw
Dalian Thief Taker – greatest of the wind claws

Hounds
Kasimir Roux – whip-master
Turve Ramhe – whip-master

Al Hasim

The godless
Kirin
Keisha of Oslan – dark-blood
Raz Mon Vekerian – captain of the *Black Wave*
Jez Ran Rami – first mate of the *Black Wave*
Arjav – bowman of the Creeping Downs
Lylla Vekerian – protector of the Creeping Downs

Dokkalfar
Tyr Nanon the Shape Taker – soldier of the Long War
Tyr Dyus the Daylight Sky – warrior of the Fell
Vithar Loth the Tree Father – shaman of the Fell
Tyr Sigurd – warrior of Canarn
Tyr Kalan – warrior of Canarn
Vithar Joror the Heart's Hand – shaman of the Heart

Mysterious Others
Ryuthula
The Matron Mother

The Shade of Magnus
The Shade of Torian
The Shade of Bromvy
The Shade of Dalian
The Breaking Wave
The Guardian
Corvus

ACKNOWLEDGEMENTS

Finishing a series is at least four times harder than writing any of its constituent parts. I suddenly had to decide things I'd not yet thought to decide, and to seriously consider that writing by zen is not always the best policy.

I really hope you all enjoy this. Thank you for so many things.

Simon Hall, Kathleen Kitsell, Marcus Holland, Benjamin Hesford, Scott Illnicki, Carrie Hall, Martin Cubberley, Tony Carew, Karl Wustrau, Mark Allen, Paolo Trepiccione, Terry and Cathy Smith, Mathilda Imlah, Laura Palmer, Melmo the Sinister Apothecary.